Phantom's Legacy

LUCILLA EPPS

authorHOUSE®

AuthorHouse™
1663 Liberty Drive, Suite 200
Bloomington, IN 47403
www.authorhouse.com
Phone: 1-800-839-8640

First published by AuthorHouse 4/3/2008

ISBN: 978-1-4343-6867-6 (sc)

Printed in the United States of America
Bloomington, Indiana
This book is printed on acid-free paper.

To Gerry Butler, Emmy Rossum,
Jennifer Ellison and Patrick Wilson,
With sincere and heartfelt affection

Author's Note

The terms used in the later part of this story are authentic, and would have been used by soldiers of that era. They are not meant to disparage anyone.

While I have drawn inspiration from Gaston Leroux's work, Andrew Lloyd Webber's music, and Joel Schumacher's film, I would like to believe that the Erik, who emerges from these pages, and the people around him, are their own selves. If their shadows are similar to any within the large body of work now written about them, or to any persons living or dead, it is only meant as a compliment, nothing more. I have tried to write them as they would have wanted me to, with honor and respect. L. E.

Introduction

In February 2006, a friend and I went to see Andrew Lloyd Weber's production of Phantom of the Opera at Proctors Theater in Schenectady, N.Y. In preparation, I read Gaston Leroux's book. Who could have foreseen that a quiet obsession with a character that never existed, that is pure imagination, was beginning?

The musical captivated me, the book stayed with me. What was it about this man in the mask that would not let go? What kept me searching for films and stories based on Leroux's creation? Why did I have that haunting music in my head?

When I saw Joel Schumacher's magnificent film, my fate was sealed. In the film, Erik, as portrayed by Mr. Gerard Butler, is a man of anger, filled with rage, yet he is vulnerable, seeking that which we all want, the love and companionship of another human being. We feel this man's pain at Christine's rejection, his heartbreak when she turns away for the final time, leaving him in his burning lair.

As beautiful as the movie is, there are questions that remain unresolved. When Raoul visits Christine's grave and leaves the barrel organ, he is in a wheelchair, barely able to stand. What happened to him? He looks at Christine's marker, which reads 'Beloved wife and mother', yet Raoul stands very much alone. Where is his family? If he and Christine had children, where are they? He looks and sees the rose with her diamond ring held by a black ribbon. He knows who left this as he lifts his head to scan the monuments of the cemetery. Where is this man? Obviously he would still be alive if he left the rose. Raoul's eyes do not look into the distance with hatred, but with remembrance. What is he thinking about? If Madame Giry is still living, where is Meg, her daughter?

The opening and closing dates of the film struck a chord. If Raoul visits Christine's resting place in 1919, he, Madame Giry, and our mysterious man have lived through World War I. What happened to these people during that time? More importantly, what happened to Erik?

These were questions I wanted answers to. None of the stories I read answered them, or came close to it. Most end a year or two after the Great Disaster, but there are forty eight years to account for between 1871 and 1919!

Then I realized what drew me to the story again and again. All the tales are through the voices of the people around Erik. Where is his side of the saga? Where is his voice?

Several viewings of Phantom later, an idea formed.

Here is a version of events after Erik smashes his mirrors.

With all due respect, this is written with Gerry Butler very much in mind as Erik, Emmy Rossum as Christine (the elder), Jennifer Ellison as Meg, and Patrick Wilson as Raoul. Thank you all for giving life to these people. I hope you would be pleased with how their lives turned out.

January 1871

to

December 1890

Chapter 1

Life can turn on a kiss.

One kiss. One kiss that burned into every fiber of my miserable body. One kiss and she tore me to pieces. That kiss ended everything. It seared my soul. Somewhere in the dungeon of my being feelings long thought buried crashed against years of carefully constructed walls, and tore them down.

I couldn't do it, couldn't force her. I would not break the only person to have ever shown me a measure of trust. So I let her go, let her go with him, her young Vicomte.

It was over, the game we had played; the play that made fools of all of us. It had to end somehow. There was no choice. There was no choice for me.

I had to leave. The police would be hunting me. I could hear the mob's bloodlust in the drumbeat of their boots as it echoed in the tunnels. There would be no sympathy at their hands, and I was loath to become their plaything. Once had been enough for a dozen lifetimes.

I looked around at the grotto where I had dreamed a fantasy, where, for many years, music had been my only companion. Now, like the mirrors around me, that dream lay shattered in a thousand pieces, the music torn, shredded, as was my heart. There was nothing left.

Only one thing remained of her. In the clutched fist of my right hand I felt the weight of the ring, the ring her small fingers had put there. She had gone, but she had given me that, a token of trust, a token of affection.

I closed my eyes and breathed. They were coming. No more time for thoughts that led nowhere. The play was done.

With one last look at what had been home, I walked through the mirror that had brought me to Christine time and time again.

In all my years of living within the bowels of the Opera house I had prepared many routes of escape, in case I ever had to leave in a hurry. Even if the police and the mob searched the tunnels beyond the grotto, they would soon become lost in the labyrinth of darkness.

I walked through the shadows with confidence, broken, shattered, but living. No matter how wretched, lonely, or desperate my life had been, and would be, it was still a life, and I wanted to live. I would not let them find me. My days in a cage were done.

As I walked through the passageways toward the river, I heard the scuttling of rats. A sardonic smile twisted my mouth. All my years of living beneath the theater had not inured me to the dislike of these creatures, yet tonight I joined their ranks. I was a rat leaving his home that was being consumed by fire. Where life would take me from here only God knew, and I never believed in Him.

Chapter 2

It was a cold night in January of 1871, and what had been my home was burning. It was the only home I had ever known, and I had set it ablaze. I had not meant to but rage and anger had driven me to it, rage and anger at Christine, at Raoul, at the beautiful people around me.

Now the police were hunting me, and the fire crews had their hands full taming the blaze of the theater.

I am Erik, had always only been Erik. My mother had not seen fit to grace me with a name. I had chosen it from a book, though to those in their glittering world, I was known as The Phantom, the ghost that haunted the Opera house. There had been other names, names now best forgotten

All that was gone, along with my house. With one gesture Christine had torn my world asunder. With one kiss, she had broken me. Now a new life had to be forged from the ashes of the old one. Decisions needed to be made. I could not consider them here, not in the open. With my home forever gone, there was only one place that beckoned, one place I considered safe, though reaching it carried certain risks.

I had been fortunate in Mme. Giry's goodwill. If not for her quick thinking years before, I would have traded one cage for another. While I had not presumed or assumed her act of kindness anything more than that, over the years we had developed an understanding, perhaps even to a degree, friendship.

It was toward her tiny apartment my legs carried me now. I wandered through the alleys, slinking along the dark and dank streets, keeping to the darkest shadows. At this hour of the night there were few about, and those that were, dared not go near where I prowled. With caution, I made my way toward the one person I trusted with my life, the one person who, long ago, had saved me once before. Would she be willing to do so again? Would she be willing to help a man who had proven himself a murderer? Only she could tell.

Breath steamed from my mouth as I ducked into yet another twisted, back way. Though the main streets would have been faster, I dared not risk exposure there. The police would be everywhere by now, keeping careful watch for their quarry. Through years of prowling the city's alleys, above, as well as below ground, I had learned which routes were best, and which least patrolled by the gendarmes. It also helped to have acquaintances in the not so proper circles of society.

This particular street, with its overhanging balconies and claustrophobic closeness, would have proved a challenge to a brave soul during daylight, much less now, in the dead of night. But it was the route that would take me to Hélène's apartment in relative safety. I walked unafraid through the black shadows of the alley, made even blacker by the dismal, oppressive snow clouds that had been hanging over the city for the last few days. Who would want to accost anyone here? A street filled with garbage, human and otherwise, was not the place for the usual gangs of thieves. This was their home I walked through, their territory, but one in which they allowed me passage. Years before, I had been one of them.

Ducking into a cross street, my foot slipped. Fighting for balance I ingloriously landed on my backside. I dared not even consider what had tripped me. Gathering myself, I became aware of the heavy iron smell around me. Usually, it was better not to even notice the smells in these back alleys, but this was too strong, and too fresh to ignore. Only one thing smelled like that. I lifted my hand to see it covered in blood, fresh blood. Not mine, that was certain. Rising carefully from where I had landed, I glanced around. Everywhere on the cobbled street was blood. My eyes followed the trail of wetness at last alighting on a mound of tissue. I stared at it for a moment in puzzlement, when a feeble cry cut through the silence of the night.

Shock, then horror flooded through me in quick succession. The back streets of any city were privy to nameless horrors, dark passions and lurid crimes. Inured as I was to pain and appalling things done by men to other men, this sight on the street was beyond any name I knew. Only cats or bitches threw their litters on the ground, and even then, they tried to find shelter for their young. This baby had literally been birthed on the street and left for the dogs that roamed in packs, scavenging what they could. If the dogs would not find it, the cold soon would.

I shook my head, trying to clear it from the horror that had come over me. My hands had killed, had wrought death in many ways, but never on an innocent. I had lived in the bowels of the Opera house, had kept company with the rats, but I was still a man, a man of some conscience. No matter what lay ahead, I could not leave this child here, even if its mother had. Mother. The word did not suit the woman who had birthed it.

Time was of the essence. The child could not have been long on the street, yet already its movements were growing weaker. There was nothing I could use as a wrap except my shirt. I had taken nothing from my house. Possessions would only have slowed me in flight, and there was nothing there that I wanted, or desired.

Slipping the shirt from my back, I wrapped the child in it as tightly as I could. The shirt was drenched with sweat and now blood, but it would have to do as a blanket. Holding the bundle close to my chest, hoping that body heat would keep the child alive, I proceeded to the sanctuary that beckoned in Hélène Giry's apartment. If nothing else, the child would find its way to an orphanage. Hélène was sure to know of one.

Chapter 3

Hélène stared at me for a moment in startled surprise, before hurriedly pulling me inside the tiny apartment, firmly closing the door on us.

"Mon Dieu, what_____," she began, but faltered, as her eyes surveyed me. I must have been a sight, shirtless, covered in blood, with the wear of the night plainly visible on my distorted face. Along with everything else, I had left the mask behind, and now confronted my friend with my true face.

I shook my head, indicating the bloody bundle in my arms. "Hers not mine," I breathed by way of explanation.

"Oh my God!" Hélène exclaimed as she finally realized what I held. "Meg, prepare some hot water and linens," Hélène addressed her daughter who had come silently into the room, "and a bath. Our guest is in desperate need of one."

Meg glanced at me. There was no shock in her eyes. She had been there at my 'unveiling', and like her mother, had long known my secret. There was unspoken acceptance of the situation in her eyes as she turned toward the kitchen to gather the needed supplies.

Meanwhile Hélène had grabbed a stack of linens from a cupboard, and taking the baby from my arms, her quick, sure hands began the process of cleaning it. Only a soft whimper now and then indicated that the child lived.

"How long was she out there?" Hélène asked, vigorously rubbing the baby in an attempt to warm it.

"I don't know," I mumbled. I was tired. The ravages of the night were beginning to make themselves felt in the sudden trembling of my limbs. All coherent thought was rapidly fading in the onset of shock from all that had transpired. I craved nothing more than a quiet corner somewhere, anywhere, to rest, and sleep.

Hélène shook her head, busy with her unexpected charge. As her deft hands finished with the toweling and wiping, a lusty wail issued from the tiny thing as if in answer of relief, or gratitude.

Hélène laughed, and so did I. "One thing is certain. She has lungs," I murmured.

Hélène nodded, smiling, her eyes meeting mine. "She will live." She looked beyond me to where Meg waited silently with an arm load of towels. With a light touch on my arm, Hélène looked at me, eyes filled with unexpected warmth. "You surprise me, Erik. You always have. Go take that bath. You and the child need rest."

I looked from her to Meg. There were no masks to hide behind. I had nowhere to run. These two women held my life in their hands. In their eyes, as they looked back at me was only trust.

With a nod to them I withdrew, letting them do their work. I had to regroup, formulate a plan, and somehow continue a life that no longer had meaning.

Chapter 4

"No! It's preposterous!" I cried out, slamming a hand against the table.

"Is it?" Hélène arched a brow at me, her calmness, in the face of my agitation, more irritating than anger would have been.

"I refuse to drag Meg into this!" I threw a nod toward the girl sitting in the chair on the far side of the room, holding the baby in her arms.

Hélène followed my gaze, rose from the table, and approached her daughter, her fingers lightly brushing Meg's gold hair. The two women exchanged a look that was beyond my understanding.

"You don't have a choice," Hélène said quietly, lifting her head to look straight at me. "It's too late for that. Let Meg help you, at least until you settle."

"They're hunting me!"

Hélène met my eyes with a look that never wavered under the torrent of frustration I threw at her.

"Yes, you," she answered calmly, "not a family. Not a man living in the open with nothing to hide."

"You cannot be serious. In case you've forgotten, I cannot very well hide this!" I turned on her, all my fury barely leashed as I indicated my face.

Hélène shrugged her shoulders. "You're an actor and a designer. Put those talents to use. Or did they leave you, along with everything else?" Her eyes flashed a rare hint of annoyance as I sank into the chair beside the table.

In the sudden stillness of the room, only the child's soft gurgle could be heard. Meg held it in her lap, the child now thoroughly washed, cleaned and fed. The women had dressed the girl in a soft, cotton shift, and swathed her in a woolen wrap besides. That one, at least, was content.

Somewhere during the travails of the previous night, they had also found clothes for me, and though they were ill fitting, I was grateful for them.

It was late morning, and we three had shared a tense, silent meal of bread, cheese and coffee. I had been reluctant to broach speech, knowing that I had invaded the Giry women's lives, and that my presence in their apartment had exposed them to danger.

It was not until Hélène had made the suggestion that tempers had flared.

At the soft rustle of fabric behind me, I turned away and nearly flinched as Hélène's hands descended onto my shoulders.

"You have lived through worse than this and survived." Her gentle, quiet tone penetrated through the turmoil in my head. "Don't let your stubbornness and pride stand in the way of a new life." She paused, letting her hands fall to her sides as she came around to sit beside me. "You know that what I propose makes sense. The police will look where you expect them to look, in the sewers, in the alleys, never suspecting their quarry has gone to ground right under their noses." Her hands reached toward mine where they lay on the table, her fingers lightly touching my own. "If anything, that child needs a home, a name. I refuse to take her to an orphanage. I know the horrors of those places only too well. And no, I will not raise her. Two daughters are enough." She rose and came to stand beside me, looking at me with affection. "You saved her life, she's your responsibility. Right now, she is as lost as you. Perhaps together, you'll find what you're looking for." Hélène said gently, walking to where Meg sat with the baby. Her fingers lightly touched the infant's hand.

"This is madness," I nearly growled with leashed anger, for deep inside the pit I called a heart I knew she was right, right in all she said.

"It's the only choice," Hélène looked straight at me.

I rose from where I had been sitting, shaking my head, trying to clear the chaos that clamored within. "I know nothing about....about them," I gestured in the direction of the infant.

Hélène came to me, and this time when her fingers touched my face, the touch was a comfort to the turmoil in my soul. All through what had been left of the previous night I had tossed in nightmares, not all brought on by that night's events. Nightmares from another life had taunted me, and I had nearly given in to the despair I had felt so long ago in that cage in the gypsy camp.

Hélène smiled a little. "Here's your chance to learn. It's not as hard as you think, being a father. It might surprise you." She paused, glancing toward her daughter. "Let Meg help you."

I looked in the girl's direction. She rose, and walked toward us, the infant cradled tenderly in her arms. For a moment, seeing her like that, I thought how right that image was. I shook it off, and brought my eyes to bear on Hélène. "You would trust your daughter with a murderer?"

Hélène's fingers smoothed the rumpled shirt around my shoulders, her eyes meeting mine. "No, but I trust a friend with my child's life."

I threw a helpless look at Meg. Many years before, as a girl of eight, she had discovered my secret, and I had trusted her then. Could we trust one another now? After all that had transpired? She had witnessed my murder of Buquet. What did she think of all this? All evening, even through the morning, Meg had been utterly silent. Only her eyes shared a language with her mother, a language that was beyond me.

As Meg proffered the bundle toward me, she smiled, eyes never flinching from my face. "I'm willing, if you are."

I stared at her for long minutes in amazement. The utter silence in the room was broken only by a light cry of protest from the infant.

With extreme trepidation and nervousness, I accepted the bundle Meg offered. Never in all my life, through all I had done, had I ever held something so helpless, so fragile, as that child at that very moment. The blue eyes looked at me in total trust.

Of their own volition, my arms drew the child against my chest, and I felt a smile rise to my lips.

"What will you name her?" Hélène asked quietly.

There was no hesitation. Looking into the infant's blue eyes, I whispered, "Christine. She will be Christine."

Chapter 5

Having formulated a plan, over the following days, the Giry women and I put it to action.

While they were free to move about, I was not, not until I could devise a way to disguise my face. So while Meg and Hélène acquired vital supplies for my masquerade, I spent time acquainting myself with Christine.

All my life I had cared for nothing and no one, yet I accepted the infant into my heart with ease that surprised me. That first look of trust from her blue eyes melted the hardened core within me, and there was no going back. When my arms held her, the girl's tiny body soothed the demons that warred within me. Christine would be my daughter, a daughter never imagined, but needed. She had come to me on a night filled with despair, as forsaken and alone as I. Hélène was right. Perhaps we two would find something in the new life that beckoned. Christine would have the best I could offer. How that was to be accomplished I had no idea, but she would not live her life abandoned to the mercies of the streets.

I gave the Giry women lists of what was absolutely essential before I dared venture into public. While I was not without means, I could not take the risk of exposure until a proper disguise was in place. For that, I needed their help. The dependence on their goodwill, and my trust in them not to betray me, grated on nerves already stretched to their limits. I chafed with unease within the four walls of the apartment. Each heavy step on the stair, each excited voice within the building sent panic through me in expectation of seeing the police charge through the front door. At times I would catch myself endlessly pacing as if I was a beast in a cage. That thought alone brought aimless steps to an end. Long ago I had been just that.

As items for the masquerade began to appear, I set to work. Masks such as the one I had worn in the theater would not suffice. I needed something finer, something that would pass scrutiny. Meg provided a selection of make-up and wigs, items salvaged from the Opera house. Purchases such as these would have only aroused suspicion on an already precarious situation. Hélène brought items from wardrobe, for I needed clothes, and in this, I was not particular. I accepted the role I was to play, and my taste for fine things had no place in the new life that was being forged. Of necessity I had to blend into the crowd, and fastidious dress would only draw attention.

Along with essentials for me, items for Christine made appearance as well. As unfamiliar as I was to these things, even I detected which woman provided what. Hélène's was always the practical, a shift, a wrap, a stack of cotton sheets. Meg, along with providing clothes for the child, sneaked a toy or two into the basket that was being readied. I smiled at that. Meg was young, no more than seventeen, a year older than her friend and adoptive sister Christine, yet she had accepted to join me in exile, in a charade that held no future for her. She had always been sensible, more so than her friend, yet when it came to this child, even she was proving to lack reason, as were we all. The abandoned infant had gathered the three of us to her tiny heart. Abandoned no longer. She would have a family, or as best as we could come to it.

Chapter 6

Meg stared at her food, picking aimlessly at the pieces. During the time we had sat in the café, she had barely eaten two bites.

I folded the newspaper, arching a brow at her. "The food is not to your liking?"

She shook her head, eyes glancing shyly at me from beneath long lashes. "The food is fine," it was a whispered reply. "It's ..." the girl hesitated, bringing her eyes back to the plate in front of her, and sighed. "This is awkward," Meg confessed, smiling a little.

I looked at her, and seeing the demure smile despite her obvious trepidation, I replied with one of my own. "No more so for you, than me," I admitted, for in truth, the circumstances were awkward for both of us. Events had forced unprecedented closeness, and presented difficulties never foreseen.

I had brought Meg to the café on a two fold purpose. I needed a public place to test my disguise, needed to know that it would pass scrutiny, and I wanted assurance that Meg would be comfortable in the role she was assuming. While she may have willingly agreed to aid me, she did not know me, and I was loath to impose an impossible task on her.

"Where will you ...we ...go?" Meg asked softly, the nervous smile giving way to one that was genuine.

"I have not given it much thought," I answered slowly, meeting her brown eyes squarely, though over the past days, the location and preparation for my self imposed exile had consumed all my thoughts. Through Hélène, I had contacted an acquaintance, setting in motion necessary tasks, but with the addition of a child and female companion, certain of those tasks offered complications.

I smiled at her in an effort to diffuse the strained uneasiness between us. Conversation had to start somewhere if we were to function together and though more and more in recent years, I had chosen to live in isolation under the Opera house, I was not insensitive to the current situation. Meg was as apprehensive of the future as I.

"Perhaps the coast," I answered. "I have always been fond of the sea."

"The sea? I thought____."

I gave Meg a half hearted grin. "I have not spent all my time in Paris," a light chuckle escaped, and I arched a brow at her. "Or under it. I have traveled." That years of that travel had been spent in a gypsy camp as an attraction for a gawking public, only Hélène would ever know.

"I have always wanted to see other places," Meg said with a hint of wistfulness in her tone, bringing her eyes to mine. "Where did you go?"

I glanced over the café's clientele. Despite the feigned ease, I had maintained a watchful vigil. Years of instilled wariness would not be put off by a few minutes of indulgence in a café.

Though it had been several days since the fiasco at the theater, as with any newsworthy event, rumors concerning the fire were flying free and fast. Events at the Opera house were discussed in muted discourse, and even the newspapermen could not help but speculate over the circumstances behind the story. The more lurid of the Paris journals were full of debate over the debacle at the Populaire.

During the time I had worked on perfecting a new disguise, Hélène had supplied me with gossip of the disaster. The inflamed and ever growing fantasies amused me, and perhaps it had been morbid curiosity, or sheer brazenness that had finally prompted my venture into public.

"Russia, Persia, and with the Sultan's army, even the borders of India," I replied quietly, offhandedly, to Meg's inquiry, watching as several people entered the premises to disperse among the seated patrons, one woman joining a group sitting beside the windows facing the street.

"What brought you to Paris?" Meg asked, now thoroughly intrigued, her awkwardness, and lunch, forgotten.

I shook my head, studying her. She looked back at me with undisguised fascination and curiosity, and I could not look away, even if I had wanted to. No one had ever asked me the things Meg had, and the answers had come easily, naturally.

With a deep, indrawn breath, I contemplated what to tell her. I was not about to reveal to this girl that in all those years of travel, in all those exotic places, it had been the sense of utter aloneness and emptiness that had driven me back to the streets of Paris, to the Opera house that had sheltered me, to the one person who had given me kindness.

"It was my home," I admitted truthfully, sipping the coffee a waiter had discreetly set beside the folded newspaper.

If Meg wanted to say anything further, it was lost in a burst of chatter from the group beside the windows, two tables away from us.

"Did you see it?"

"The fire at the theater? How could one miss it. It practically lit up the night."

"They say a disfigured man burned it."

"Oh yes. I heard the story. They say he had no face."

"Oh he had a face, or what was left of it."

"He was the devil himself if you ask me."

"Seven feet tall, at least."

"He was a beast. Imagine, dragging that poor girl to the dungeons."

"She deserved it for her behavior. What a scandal. Perhaps they should make an opera of it."

"It would make for finer entertainment than the production of Meyerbeer ever did." Their collective laughter was soon lost in another round of conversation as the women accosted the harried waiter and began to place orders, their voices drowning each other out.

The comments amused me and I could not stifle the soft chuckle that escaped from my throat. What would the women say if they knew that the man they discussed so casually sat in the very same café as they?

It was the frown on Meg's brow, and the dark look of anger she directed toward the gossiping women that piqued my curiosity.

"What is the matter?" I asked gently, intrigued, as Meg turned her brown eyes to me, the look in them softening, almost pleading.

She shook her head, the gold of her hair glowing in the sun coming through the windows. "They're_____."

I reached a hand towards hers where it lay on the table.

"You can't stop the rumors," I whispered, giving her a wink.

"But___."

I gave Meg a slight shake of my head as I took another sip of coffee. Was the pout on her lips and the frown on her brow directed at me?

"Oh God," Meg breathed, suddenly averting her eyes, snatching at the reticule that lay on the table beside her, finding its contents fascinating.

"What is wrong?"

She shook her head, refusing to look at me, the hands nervously searching through the contents of the reticule. What could possibly have scared her so? She had the look of a creature about to bolt. The nervousness and unease she had displayed when we had first entered the café had returned, and it was evident in all her movements.

When Meg refused to give an answer, refused to even look in my direction, I glanced about the café, eyes finally alighting on the dark blue uniform of the gendarme leaning against the counter, talking to the proprietor of the establishment.

"Calm," I whispered to my companion, hand instinctively reaching for hers. I gave it a gentle squeeze, and when Meg finally brought her eyes to look at me, I gave her a small smile. "Above all, there must be calm." Even as I said the words, I felt far from what I needed her to do. All self recrimination would not undo what I had allowed to happen. A few pleasant words had proved a distraction, and the lapse of vigilance had placed both of us in a precarious position.

It was not what the law would do to me, should the officer choose to pursue matters that concerned me. I could, and would, find my way out of a scrape. I had done so before, and would again, if necessary. The sewers of Paris provided refuge for many, and while not an ideal solution, or the preferred choice, it was one that was available.

However, the increasing pressure of fingers against mine was a reminder that I was not alone in this, and no matter what followed, I had to get Meg safely away from this place, away from me. My own pride and bravura had placed her in danger. Hélène had trusted me with her daughter's safekeeping, and if I could not do that in Paris, how would I manage elsewhere? I would not take the risk. The charade stopped here.

I would send Meg home to her mother, and that would be the end of the matter. I had business elsewhere, and it was time for a discreet exit.

While the policeman continued to sip his coffee, still engaged in conversation, I signaled the waiter and asked for our bill.

"It will be all right," I whispered reassurance to Meg, gathering the coat and hat I had set aside earlier. "You're an actress. Use it."

Meg gave a terse nod, biting her lips to refrain from speaking, though her hands shook as she gathered the reticule and shawl.

Settling the account, I rose, adjusted the hat low over my brow, and extended a hand to Meg. She followed suit, her hand clenching mine, and as we walked toward the door, I saw the gendarme look in our direction for a moment, before turning his attention back to his coffee. We were after all, just another couple out for a stroll on a beautiful, January day.

We lost ourselves amongst the pedestrians on the street, and when I finally stopped, several blocks and turns later, I felt a comforting weight lean against me. It took a moment to realize it was Meg, and my arm slid easily, protectively, around her shaking shoulders. Had she been that frightened in the café and in our subsequent retreat from it? She was young. Had I any right to drag her into a situation that was uncomfortable, at best, for her? Had I any right to drag anyone into a life that had been spent in shadows and darkness?

A sharp indrawn breath and a quick punch to my shoulder startled me. "Don't ever do that to me again! What were you thinking?"

I stared at her, startled to find her looking at me with a mixture of anger and entreaty. With amazement, I realized she was crying.

"I thought I'd_____." She clamped a hand to her mouth, quickly turning away from my eyes, shaking her head.

I don't know what I had expected, but it was not this. Why carry on so? Fright was understandable, and my actions had caused it, but why this?

"I am sorry," I said quietly in an effort to appease her, for Meg's outburst had drawn a few curious glances from passersby. Whatever else there was to say, we could not pursue it here on the street.

I hailed a cab, and when the carriage stopped, reached to hand her in. With a shake of her head, Meg refused assistance, climbing in herself, settling in the farthest corner she could.

Giving the driver an address that would take some time to reach, I seated myself on the seat opposite my companion, studying her.

"You were frightened?"

She nodded, angrily wiping at her face. "Petrified."

"That is understandable. My appearance at best of times is…"

Meg vehemently shook her head. "You don't understand! It's not that way at all." She sniffed, looking out into the streets.

"I should never have put you in that position. I was careless, and I apologize. It will never happen again." No it would not. Meg would go home, and after I concluded my business, no one would ever see me again.

"I wasn't afraid of you. I was afraid for you." Meg's quiet voice broke in on the silence between us. When I made no reply, she continued, bringing her face to look at me. "I was petrified the gendarme would seize you," Meg whispered, shaking her head. "And those imbeciles! Talking about ____." She sighed, glancing at the hands resting on her lap, worrying the cord of her reticule. "I was terrified the police would drag you away." Meg bit her lower lip to still its trembling, and it slowly dawned on me how wrong my assumptions all this time, had been. As I looked at the brown eyes looking at me, in their brightness I perceived something I had not expected to find, in anyone, least of all this young woman. It was something that left me confused and perplexed. Could it be that Meg cared? Cared what happened to me?

"Don't you have feelings for anyone? Doesn't my mother's friendship mean anything to you? Doesn't my silence mean anything at all?" Meg asked quietly.

"In my life, feelings are a luxury I can ill afford," I answered honestly. "I did not mean to place you in such an awkward position, Meg. I had no right."

She smiled a little. "I was never in any danger. You could not have known the policeman would come. It was ____." She shook her head, as if to dismiss a thought.

"No, but I should have been more watchful. My lapse is no excuse, and I should not have caused you fright."

Warm fingers entwined my own. "I may have been scared, but I would never betray you. How many times could my mother and I have betrayed you, and didn't? How many times Erik, could a small child have betrayed the most precious of all secrets? Trust me." Meg smiled, letting go my hands. "You did once, and I trusted you today."

Drawing a heavy breath, I studied her from beneath an arched brow. Though Meg and I had known of each other for several years, only once had we ever encountered one another before, and she had been a child, exploring her new home. Only now was I beginning to realize how different Meg was from her adoptive sister Christine. There was hidden strength and resolve in her, both of which she had displayed to good effect in our retreat from the café.

"Perhaps you mislay that trust," I said looking away, desperately trying to sort the storm of feelings that was sweeping through me. Why did I feel so divided when it came to this girl sitting across the carriage from me? Why did it matter? Why did I care, when life had never given me a reason to?

"Why do you say that?" Meg looked at me in puzzlement.

"Why?! Why choose to come with me?" My curiosity as to her reason for agreeing to come with me into exile would not let the question lie. I had to know. "Why, after the fiasco, after Christine? You cannot possibly be so blind as not know what kind of man I am! Why even consider such a hare-brained idea?" I let some of my frustration free, and my voice had become sharper than I had intended. "I can't even protect you in a damned café!"

Meg did not flinch from my tirade, but met my look with her own, calm one. "Because you were kind to me once," she smiled.

"You are staying in Paris." I said, firmly resolved to hold to my earlier decision.

"No!"

"That is the end of the matter."

The flash from her brown eyes should have been a warning.

"Who will take care of Christine if I stay?" Meg demanded, her tone matching mine earlier. "Or have you thought of that?"

My silence must have given her the answer, for in truth, I had not thought of the child at all.

"I did not think so," Meg replied quietly, with a tinge of disappointment in her tone. "Did you consider what would happen to her if your escapade in the café had failed?" Meg's admonishment brought my eyes to hers, and in them, I saw a reflection of Hélène's resoluteness and firmness.

"I am certain you would have made a fine mother to her," I said after a pause, unable to hide the smile that crept to my lips.

Meg sighed, wearily shaking her head as she directed her eyes toward the slowly passing streets. "It's not about you anymore," she said, this time not bothering to disguise the disaffection in her voice. "There are other people to consider."

Slowly so as not to startle her, I took Meg's hands in mine, squeezing gently. "Perhaps I have been remiss in my understanding of the situation. The circumstances of this current state of affairs," I gave her a faint, sardonic grin, "are awkward at best. It is not by choice you find yourself in this position, and I will not force you. You will stay in Paris. I will not put you in danger again." I was determined to end this debate.

Meg sighed, and I had nearly given up any reply she might make, when she pulled her hands from mine. "I didn't decide to join you on a whim Erik, and my mother had nothing to do with my decision."

"Then why?" I asked gently. It was obvious she would not be dissuaded, and for now, I reluctantly resigned myself to that fact. Meg was right in one thing. If I was to take the child with me, she would need someone to care for her. I would rather it be Meg than a stranger, and if I had to have a companion in exile, it would certainly not be for long. For the duration, we would find an accommodation.

Meg brought her eyes to look into mine, and though they were brimming with tears, she made no effort to wipe them away. She was silent for long minutes, and when she finally spoke, her voice carried infinite tenderness, warmth and affection.

"You're my friend."

Friend. The word was rife with meaning, and subtleties. Of necessity, I had always lived alone. There were few I would dare call such.

"Friend." I savored the word, looking at my pretty companion. Meg smiled, almost shyly this time, the brown eyes lowering from my penetrating gaze. "I think I might like to give the idea a try. I only ever had one, and he was not much of a companion."

At Meg's questioning look, I shrugged and sighed. "It was a toy, nothing but a worn, ragged toy." I finished dismissively, rapping the roof of the cab.

"What...where are you going?" Meg asked as I alighted. I gave her hand a firm but gentle squeeze.

"Fear not. I shall return," I answered, and meant it. All my earlier resolve of leaving her in Paris had dissolved at her words, and my own obstinacy refused to stand under those penetrating, flashing brown eyes. Glancing around the square, taking in the bustle of the pedestrians and street traffic around us, I searched the storefronts for a specific sign. No one paid attention to our exchange. Traffic in Paris was tolerable chaos, best avoided. At last spotting what I sought, I turned back to Meg, giving her a small smile. "There is business I must attend to."

Meg studied me, and I could only wonder what she saw. A man in his mid thirties, dressed casually in charcoal grey, a wide brimmed hat shading his face. It was the face I wondered about. I had done my best to cover up the obvious damage. The rest was hidden with layers of carefully applied make-up and wig. This time, I had chosen one closer to the shade of my natural hair, a brown that blended into a crowd.

"Be careful," she whispered, letting go my hand.

"I shall. I believe a friend has so requested." I tipped the hat to her, and gave the driver an address to take her to, paying him well for his trouble.

As I directed my steps toward the offices, I replayed the entire time with Meg in my mind. Was it possible that this venture we were bound upon would succeed?

I sighed, shaking my head. Stranger things had occurred. No matter what happened now, I was bound on a course from which it was no longer possible to retreat. I had a daughter to consider, as Meg had so instructively pointed out, and her future was locked with mine.

Drawing the hat lower to shade my face, I pushed open the door, and stepped into the bustling offices of Étienne Roulen, architect, mentor, and once a friend to a young, outcast, disfigured boy.

Chapter 7

The small, grey stone house stood alone just beyond the village precinct. It beckoned, as nothing in my life ever had. I had purchased it sight unseen through a trusted solicitor, one who had provided services for me before. Of necessity, the entire transaction had been a quiet one.

The house boasted two floors, rooms enough for a small family, and the privacy I had demanded. A low, stone wall surrounded the front and back gardens, which had an abandoned, forlorn look to them. An intricate, wrought iron gate barred entrance. In the quiet of the morning, the cries of the gulls overhead were loud and clear. The crisp, sea air was a pleasant change to the oppressive smells of the city we had left behind.

We had come to Brittany, Meg, Christine, and I. This particular place was distant enough from Paris to give a sense of security, yet close to other cities to allow me the pursuit of a new venture. Having given up the ghostly profession, there were my skills as a designer and architect to fall back on, skills I had taken care to nurture during the years of solitude. Now they would serve my family in good stead.

Family. Glancing at the young woman standing beside me as she held a baby, I could not help the thought that the three of us, a very young actress and ballerina, an abandoned baby, and a disfigured man made for quite a strange group. For one brief moment as we stood facing the house, I wondered if, after all, I had made the right choice in accepting Meg and the child into my life. Would they not have been better off in Paris under Hélène's vigilant care? What could I possibly offer when I had nothing?

The door of the house opened, and a disparate looking couple hurried down the gravel path toward us.

Meg's light touch on my arm brought my mind to sharp focus. It was time to play our parts. In the brief smile the girl gave me, there was nothing but confidence. I gave her a slight nod in reply. In this, she had more courage than I, for I suddenly found myself totally at a loss, exposed, and facing a situation I could not control.

The man, fairly short and thin, was preceded by an ebullient, matronly woman. Both looked worn from a hard life lived in the country. "Bonjour Monsieur et Madame Marchand. We have been expecting you. Everything is ready, and I hope to your satisfaction. I am Maryanne, and this is my husband, Paul," the lady indicated the quiet man unlocking the gate next to her. As he eased it open, it gave a wail of protest.

"M. Roulen insisted on the utmost discretion in providing a housekeeper and workman," the woman continued, smiling, her eyes flitting between Meg and me, missing nothing. Her bubbly enthusiasm was hard to resist.

"Hmm yes, that was the case," Meg began in all confidence, resettling Christine in her arms. During our travel, we had agreed on a story that would be plausible, uncomplicated, and acceptable. "My husband," she glanced at me as if to reaffirm her words, "is recovering from an accident. Discretion and privacy are priority. That is why we chose to come here." Her tone and manner were at once firm, yet not unkind.

"Of course. We are your neighbors," Maryanne pointed to the nearest house just barely visible in the rising mist of the morning. "I will be your housekeeper, and Paul will manage whatever will be required. Problem solved, non?" She looked from one to the other of us. I made no move, other than to avert my face from Maryanne's inquiring gaze. "We will have good time together, yes? Come," Maryanne wrapped her arm around Meg's in a warm, friendly embrace and started to lead her down the path toward the house, when Christine chose that moment to announce her presence with a cry. Meg tried her best to calm her, but the piercing cries would not be abated.

"Que une belle bébé!" Maryanne exclaimed, gathering the child into her arms. "Paul and I, we raised three. Only one is living now. Oh she must be tired from the journey." The woman gently swung Christine in her arms, and by a miracle, the cries soon diminished.

"And hungry," Meg added.

"Of course," Maryanne smiled. Holding the baby in one arm, she gently steered Meg toward the house. "You both must be as well. Come. I will make you the best meal you have ever had."

As Paul and I bent to gather the few pieces of baggage that had been left by the carriage driver, I glanced at his careworn face, at eyes that exuded kindness toward a complete stranger. He gave me a small smile in return as he lifted Christine's basket, then followed the women down the path.

Whether I wanted to or not, I had no choice but to accept the services of these people. We could not manage without them. Accepting them into our lives was a gamble I had to take, despite the recommendation. M. Roulen had after all provided the solicitor that had found this house, had provided access to my money, and had also secured a position for me with a small, architectural firm. The fact that the firm was a subsidiary of one owned by M. Roulen, and that Étienne Roulen, and a certain, disfigured man had become acquainted on the streets of Paris when they had been boys, was of course, purely a coincidence.

Chapter 8

I settled Meg and Christine into the house, and at first opportunity departed for a meeting with my employers. It had never been my intention to share the house with them, but because Meg and the baby needed a place to stay, I had bought one. It would serve as cover for our thinly veiled illusion of a married couple. The last had been Hélène's suggestion, adding a plausible reason for Meg's and mine co-habitation.

The place was sparsely furnished, with only the immediate necessities of life, a table, some chairs, beds, and a few dishes, but beyond that, there was nothing. I had not really expected much, never having had a home other than a grotto beneath the Opera house. From the look of disillusionment I saw on Meg's face, it was clear she had not been prepared for a nearly empty house.

When I traveled to the office, I settled an account for Meg that she would be free to draw on. Even if I did not intend to share the house, I would not leave the girl and child without means. A semblance of family was needed, if not for ourselves, then for the neighbors. It was after all, the plan we had agreed to in Paris.

The spring breeze freshened as I walked through the gate toward the house. I noted with interest that the gate gave way easily now, without protest, and during my absence had acquired a coat of paint.

It had been weeks since last I had been here. The time had been spent in pursuit of architectural projects, each carefully chosen to make travel to the house impractical. I would not impose on the girl. That she had accompanied me of her free will was one thing. It would be quite another for me to subject her to my presence, despite words exchanged in a Parisian cab. To that end, I sought work that would keep me away from the house, and away from her.

To maintain some veneer of a family for our neighbors' benefit, I made occasional visits, none lasting more than a day or two. These times were difficult, for they necessitated the maintenance of a tenuous illusion, and only aggravated the rising tension between Meg and me. Often during these interludes, Meg refused to speak to me, let alone be near me.

Seeing my furrowed brow one evening Maryanne, in her misplaced concern, said in a comforting way. "She is young. It takes time to adjust to a child and marriage. She will settle down. You will see."

"No doubt," I replied, wondering if perhaps I should send the girl back home to her mother.

On an evening when I arrived unexpectedly, I found Meg reading in the front room. When she saw me, she threw the book down, gave me a cold glance, and without a word, went into the kitchen, from whence proceeded loud banging. When I entered, it was to find her standing by the table, a plate laden with roast chicken and vegetables in her hands. Maryanne and Paul must have left earlier, for everything had been tidied for the night.

"Bon appétit." The words were full of anger as Meg nearly threw the dish down on the table, and disappeared.

Now, as I neared the house, I could only wonder what my reception would be this time. I saw no sign of our neighbors, but then it was Sunday, and like most everyone in the village, they would be at services.

Hesitating at the front door, I noticed a few spring flowers poking through the weeds that were trying to choke them. A groan of frustration and anger from the back of the house drew my attention. Dropping the valise beside the door, I made my way around the house to find Meg struggling with a shovel against stubborn dirt. She must have been at it for some time, for her hair was disheveled, and the skirts bore signs of an enemy that would not give way easily.

"What are you doing?" I asked, curious.

"What does it look like," she snapped, not bothering to stop.

"If you want a garden, ask Paul to dig it for you. You should not be doing such work."

Those words stopped her. Her back stiffened, and the shovel was angrily tossed away. Very slowly, Meg turned to face me, eyes blazing with anger, hurt, and fury. "What would you like me to do? I can't just sit here and do nothing!"

"You take care of Christine."

Meg tossed her head, looking away. "Yes, a job that should be partly yours."

"I have to earn money. I have to have an occupation." I answered levelly, studying her. She was tense, and obviously had been brooding for some time. "At your daughter's expense! She doesn't even know you!" Meg cried eyes boring into me.

"She's a baby."

"She won't be a baby for too much longer! She's growing, and she needs to know her father." She paused, throwing back her hair with a dirty hand. "If you didn't want her, you should have left her in the street!"

The fury those words aroused, surprised even me. Blackness suffused everything, and it was only a miracle of will that kept my hands from grabbing her. I had never intentionally hurt a woman, and I would not start now. "I never_____." I hissed through teeth clenched in rage, unable to even bring the words out.

Meg looked at me, standing her ground in the face of the anger that was clearly stamped on my face. No amount of make up would hide that.

"You don't need to. Your actions speak for themselves." She said quietly and walked to the kitchen.

Stomping after her, I gave full vent to the anger that consumed me. "What would you have me do? Become a farmer? That seems to be the one skill I have yet to master!" I had no idea how loud my voice had become, until a cry from upstairs broke in on the sudden silence between us.

Meg dried her hands that she had been washing, and turned to face me. "No," she sighed, shaking her head.

"Then what!? Speak plainly woman, for you try my patience!"

"I want a companion, someone to talk to." She said slowly.

"You have Maryanne and Paul." I snapped back, throwing off the coat I had been wearing.

"They are not why I'm here!" She cried. "You are! And Christine! She's your daughter. She needs to know you." The crying from upstairs was growing louder.

Taking a deep breath to steady the dissipating anger, I ventured. "What do you propose? That I drop my work?"

She shook her head. "No, but spend time with us, with Christine, with me. I am tired of making up excuses for your absences."

I looked at her, really looked at her. Despite dirt flecked on her cheeks and in her hair, Meg was quite pretty, even with frustration stamped on her face at the moment. She looked tired and worn.

"I am sorry," I began contritely, for it slowly dawned on me how lonely and out of place she must feel. She had left everything she had known in the city to find herself in the middle of nowhere, caring for a child not her own. "I should never have brought you here. If you wish, I will take you to the station. You will be in Paris by evening."

Meg shook her head as she approached the table where I leaned against the sturdy wood. "Have you listened to nothing I said? I don't want to go back to Paris. I want to stay, but only if you are here, occasionally. I want to talk with a friend." She smiled weakly.

I sighed, reaching to touch her gold hair. Its softness amazed me. The gesture had been without thought, and I hesitated once I realized what I was doing. She did not draw away, her eyes never flinching from mine.

"I have lived alone so long that it is difficult to shed habits of a lifetime," I said slowly, quietly. "I have never been around other people, especially under such awkward circumstances." I glanced almost shyly at her. "I have no wish to discomfit you with my presence."

Her hands enfolded mine, their touch warm and comforting. "Christine and I are not other people, Erik. We are your family, and your presence does not discomfort me. Your absence does."

"I will make arrangements," I murmured, looking into pools of deep brown that smiled back at me.

The cries from the bedroom upstairs were too much to ignore now. I smiled sheepishly at my companion. "So, how does one quiet a screamer?"

She laughed, and together, we walked up the stairs to tackle a challenge that promised to be greater than any I had yet encountered.

"Non, non, like this," Meg's voice was filled with amusement, even as she decried my efforts at this, the most puzzling of activities.

I watched, baffled, as her hands folded and refolded the triangles of cotton cloth with the sureness of a master. In a minute, Christine's little bottom was snug and secure. She rewarded Meg with a huge smile, and a gurgle of happiness.

"Now, you try once more," Meg stated, assuming an air of command. With a tug, the cozy envelope around Christine unwound, eliciting a wail of displeasure from the concerned party.

I, who designed buildings, composed operas and constructed intricate mazes, faced a dilemma. Tackle the squirming baby and the mysterious triangles, or lose all dignity in front of my two ladies. No, I could not allow that to happen.

I bent over the now quiet Christine. Her blue eyes widened with curiosity as they focused on the movements of my hands. She suddenly laughed when my fingers brushed across her belly. I chuckled, repeating the gesture, and Christine laughed again.

Meg watched the proceedings from beside the window, an indulgent, warm smile on her lips, eyes intently studying us. As Christine continued to laugh under my tickling, and I puzzled out the folds of cotton, we two laughed as well. At last I swung my daughter triumphantly in my arms, proudly showing Meg an architectural work of art.

With a smile, she nodded approval, and shaking her head, quietly left the room.

Christine and I danced about, she gurgling with contentment, I humming a lullaby as I waited for her to fall asleep. The weight of her small body in my arms was a delight that, with the passing weeks, I had come to cherish. Her innocence had become a healing balm to all the sorrows and wretchedness of the past, quieting the demons that haunted uneasy dreams.

It was six months since our arrival to this place, and three since Meg and I had confronted each other. Christine was no longer solely dependent on mare's milk for sustenance, a fact that made life with her easier to bear, though now it became a matter of discovering foods which would please her palate and not cause paroxysms of tears and denials. In this, Maryanne showed all manner of indulgence, and only waved off my half hearted attempts at putting a stop to her efforts. She and Paul became quiet fixtures in our lives, and perhaps their subtle, warm relationship, began to have en effect on our own.

I made accommodations with the firm, and now spent what time I reasonably could with my family. Bits and pieces of furniture and color began to appear in the house. I accompanied Meg only once on her many shopping trips, leaving it to her to decide what she wanted in the house. I had never had much opportunity for that particular indulgence. Mostly I had borrowed what I had needed to live from the Opera's vast stores. No one ever missed a hanging, or a candlestick. My demand for money from the managers had been more a whim than a necessity. Shirts and suits had not eaten away the account carefully secreted and managed by Étienne's firm.

It surprised me how Meg's delight in even the smallest things gave me pleasure, and with the passing months, our awkwardness with each other slowly transformed into camaraderie. I even began to anticipate the visits home. There were always surprises.

With the onset of warm weather, even the gardens began their transformation. The weeds in the front were pulled back from the flowers that reached for the sun, and a splash of color surrounded the grey house. Meg and Maryanne set out pots beside the kitchen, and a small herb garden blossomed there as well.

I smiled. Who would have imagined that Meg would have the least interest in such activity? There were many things we did not know about each other, and some we never would.

It was close to evening as I entered the house. June was in full bloom, and even here, close to the coast, the heat had begun. I had dispensed with the jacket hours ago, and now laid it, and the valise, in the parlor beside the chair. Twilight doused the room in pale light, diffused by simple, white lace curtains. The room had been painted pale blue weeks ago, and a sofa, low side table, and two chairs now constituted its furnishings. The hearth had been thoroughly scrubbed and cleaned from its winter use, and a frame of needlework, a gift from Maryanne, screened it. A glass of wine waited on the table in anticipation of my home coming.

Christine's cries drifted from upstairs and I smiled, reveling for a while in the ordinariness of the moment as I took a sip of the wine. At nearly six months, Christine had become obstinate regarding certain aspects of her routine. At times she was a handful, even for two of us, let alone just Meg. If the cries were any indication, this evening had proved a trial no less than some others. Hélène's words about being a father echoed in my head, and I chuckled. It had taken Meg and our mutual misunderstandings to make me into one. I was learning, and I suspected, would continue to do so all my life. There was no going back now. The tenuous bond between that child and me which had begun on a street in Paris strengthened with each day. I dared not imagine life without her.

Taking up the valise and wine, I walked upstairs to my bedroom. Following Meg's and mine confrontation, on the very next visit I had found this room furnished with a writing desk, lamps, a chair, and the plain bed made up in quality linens. In the past weeks, this room too had been painted, and curtains added to the window. Meg and our neighbors had been busy.

I set the wine down and lit one of the lamps when the sound of Christine's continued shrieks from the room directly opposite mine startled me. When there was no answer to my diffident knock, I opened the door to find Meg sitting on the bed, her face red and wet from weeping, clutching Christine to her chest. The child's cries were near hysteria.

"What's wrong with her?" I asked gently, not wishing to add to Meg's obvious distress.

"I don't know. She's been crying like this for hours." Meg managed to find her voice through the tears that streaked her cheeks. Her hands clutched the baby tighter.

"Where's Maryanne?" I asked, eyes studying the child and the frantic girl. Anxiety had gripped me when I had first seen the scene, but I dared not let it show before the girl. It would only panic her more.

"They left this morning to visit their son."

"What of the doctor?"

"I didn't want to leave her, and there's no one to send!"

I nodded, gently taking the child from Meg's arms, laying her down on the bed. Her wails and red face were like nothing I had yet seen. "Did she eat?"

"She refused everything. Oh Erik, I'm so scared. I don't know what to do!"

I bent over the squirming child, fingers gently probing for any obvious damage. There was nothing, at least that I had any knowledge of. "There's no injury," I muttered, hands now probing the belly and chest. Meg watched, following my movements with growing fascination.

"How do you know what to do?" She asked in a whisper.

I shook my head, focusing all concentration on my probing fingers. During years of travel I had acquired simple, medical knowledge. "No swelling." Though I could not find anything by touch, did not mean there was nothing to find. There were many diseases that would not make themselves known, until it was too late.

As my fingers neared her face, Christine suddenly grabbed one, and bit it. The unexpected sensation of pain elicited a startled "ouch", and then a low chuckle. Knowledge of what had caused Christine's distress transformed into hearty laughter. I tickled my daughter's stomach for good measure before releasing her.

"What? What's wrong with her?" Meg asked, her face still a mask of concern.

"Teeth," I said. "Our minx is growing teeth. Stay here. I will return." The relief that washed over me at the realization that Christine's suffering had been nothing more than the pain of growing teeth, stunned me. Until then, I had not known how deeply the child affected me. Nothing on earth would pry her from me, not now, not ever.

When I returned to Meg's bedroom, I found her holding a somewhat appeased child. She glanced at what I held, eyes widening in surprise. "Surely you don't intend_____."

"It's the best remedy for her pain," I replied, putting a little of the brandy on my finger. Christine, for one, had no objections to the medicine. After two applications, she settled down, and fell asleep. In her case, it was more exhaustion than anything else.

Meg gave me a speculative glance as she straightened from laying the child down. "You are full of surprises, monsieur Marchand."

I set the brandy bottle on the table beside her bed. "A little on the finger, and rub gently. It dulls the worst of the pain." I moved toward the door.

"Erik?"

I stopped and turned to see Meg looking at me, her brown eyes full of affection. "I'm glad we came here."

I gave her a nod and went to my room. I was exhausted, and yet as I undressed, I feared the nightmares that would come with sleep, as they always did. For the first time in months, that night, they did not come.

Chapter 9

It was the beginning of July, and gentle breezes off the sea dispelled the worst of the heat. None of my current projects required immediate attention, so I took a few days to spend with the family. However, this particular morning Meg hustled Maryanne and Christine quickly out of the house, a look of mystery about her that I dared not question. In a swirl of their best skirts, they were gone, shortly followed by Paul, who went to the village taking tools that needed sharpening with him.

It was a rare thing these days that I was left alone. The constant bustle of activity in the house had become a welcoming distraction, and an unexpected comfort. Though it had taken time to adjust to their cheerful chatter, I now found the utter silence and absence of my family oppressive.

For lack of any other distraction, I unfolded the newspaper that had been left unread from the previous evening. I had made it a habit to leaf through at least two of the many journals available. If I was to be a man of the world, I could not ignore that world altogether, as I had done under the theater.

The theater. The thought brought a chill up my spine. For weeks after the fiasco, there had been rumors and wild stories in all the major newspapers, each more colorful than the next. But as with all things, something new had sparked the interest of the journalists, and the stories faded from the front pages, to a small column on the back, and eventually, receded altogether.

I shook my head. Would the story ever really fade away? The journalists may have let that particular beast lie, but would the police? Were they still hunting me? In the past months, with the peace of this house, and the distraction of a family, it had been easy to forget the reason we were all here. Would I ever escape from it? Could I? What legacy would I give my daughter if she ever discovered my past? Would she look at me with the hurt and disappointment that had been in Christine's eyes? Would she curse me, as her namesake had done? For surely the words Christine had uttered under that house while pleading for her Raoul might as well have been one.

The main stories were for the most part uninteresting, but I scanned them anyway. Wars, inventions, elections, it was all the same. Flipping the paper over, I rose to prepare tea, when my eyes glimpsed the large print on the back page. Leaning closer, I focused on the words, and for a moment, if the world had stopped, I would not have cared.

Young de Chagny fights to preserve family name and fortune amid rumors of scandal surrounding his marriage to Christine Daae, former star of the Opera Populaire.

I collapsed back into the chair, overwhelmed. So. He had married her after all. How very decent of the fellow. And she clinging to her Vicomte, a boy who knew nothing!

"Oh this is rich!" I murmured, feeling laughter rise from deep within my chest. I gave it free reign, laughing as I had not done in months, perhaps even years. "Oh! No vengeance of mine could ever be sweeter! The two of you deserve this!" The laughter broke on a sob as tears streamed from my eyes. A shudder wrenched me. "Oh Christine," I moaned in newly awakened pain, the sobs unstoppable. "Why?" I raised my head to glance about the room, seeing nothing except her eyes as she turned away to walk to him, to her Raoul.

"Why?!" The cry resounded about the kitchen. The sudden crash of crockery against the wall was hollow and empty. As quickly as it had come, the rage and anger that had consumed me drained away, and I stared helplessly at my tightly clenched hands.

Taking a shuddering, steadying breath, I looked around me, at the kitchen where women chatted companionably as they prepared meals, where a baby fussed, and men shared small talk of the day, all parts of a dream.

I forced my eyes once more to the article that had sparked the tumult of feelings. I had wanted vengeance against them, against her for her betrayal. But that had been nearly a lifetime ago. Did I really want that anymore? What purpose would it serve? Had any of us known what we were doing that night? We had all made our choices. Now we had to abide by them.

My fingers brushed against the sketched portrait of Christine that had been included in the paper to spark the public's prurient interest, as if that action alone would atone for what I had done to her, what we had done to each other. "Why?" I whispered. Young de Chagny's plight did not concern me. Christine's portrait did. She looked stunning in her gown, but then, she had always been beautiful. I had been drawn to her and her angelic voice like a moth to a flame, and like a moth, I had not stopped the obsession, until my wings had been scorched in fire.

With a long, heavy sigh, I rose, and went to the back garden. The sun was high, the heat intense, but I could not sit idly in the house, not now. My hands needed activity, or surely I would go mad with the turbulent emotions within me.

Walking out into the garden, I saw the shovel leaning against the garden wall. I grabbed it, and walked to the corner where Meg had begun to dig months ago. She had never progressed very far in that particular endeavor. With a forceful shove, I drove the implement into the earth.

I was so absorbed in the work that it was only the low moan behind me that drew my attention away. When I turned, it was to glimpse Meg's pale face looking at me, eyes sparkling with something I could not fathom, a trembling hand held to her lips. When she saw me look at her, she quickly turned, kicked at her skirts, and ran into the kitchen.

Tossing the shovel away, I started to follow when coherent thought took hold, and I caught myself in mid step. Glancing down, I understood the girl's sudden fright and flight. Sometime during my labors I had stripped to the waist, had even tossed away the small mask that covered the most obvious damage to my face. The bits of make-up that covered the rest had washed away with sweat hours ago. No wonder she had fled. I must have been a sight to her, covered in dirt, my true face revealed, and drenched in perspiration.

Shaking my head in dismay, I recovered the mask and slipped it on. Years past, I had made uneasy peace with the fact that I would forever be alone, that my arms would never know a woman's warmth or softness, never know the feel of one against me. Nature had given me a face that had forced me to live under a theater, hidden away, a ghost, and yet very much a man. As if in a perverse joke, Nature had more than made up for her cruelty to my face with my body. During the years at the theater, I had taken care to keep fit. Climbing stairs and flies had made me strong, and years of other exercise had toned the rest.

Sighing deeply, I closed my eyes against the swell disgust I felt toward myself. Though we had come to friendly terms regarding our cohabitation, and despite the fact that my true face was known to her, I had always been careful to wear at least a small mask or make-up around Meg, and most especially Christine and our neighbors. With them, our explanation of an accident seemed to be enough. But now, all that had been put at risk by my own hand. Would I ever learn to leash that temper, that beast that raged within? Could I even walk into the house without destroying everything that had so tenuously taken root? If it became necessary, arrangements were in place. Meg and her mother would want for nothing.

In order to get into the house, I had to walk through the kitchen, but Meg was there. Would she be able to tolerate the sight of me? The front door was out of the question. There was nothing for it. Steeling myself, I crossed the threshold.

Meg stood by the counter, her back toward me, hands wringing out a cloth. She still wore her fancy dress of pale green, a color that suited her. The gold hair fanned across her shoulders like a veil.

A glance at the table revealed the newspaper and its article gone. I stood in place, watching her in silence. She had to know I was there, and yet she would not face me.

"I sent them away," her voice was a mere whisper as she dropped to her knees and began to scrub at a spot beyond the table.

Only then, did I realize that in my blind rage I had thrown the bowl of rising bread dough against the wall. Flecks of it had landed everywhere.

"Let me help."

"Non!" The cry, combined with a choking sob, was quickly stifled. With a hand, Meg tossed her hair away from her face. "I will manage." There was a tremor to her voice that had not been there before.

"I am sorry Meg," I ventured softly, not wishing to alarm her further. "I did not mean to frighten you." Only iron will kept me in place, because all I wanted was to hold her, mold her to me, feel her body against mine, and feel her human comfort.

Meg stopped scrubbing, her hands laying the cloth aside. With infinite slowness, she turned to look at me. Tears streaked down her cheeks, and her beautiful, brown eyes still held that sparkle I had seen earlier. A weak, trembling smile tried to show itself, but failed.

"You didn't frighten me, Erik." The voice came on a whisper.

"I'll go clean up," I said, at last forcing my feet to move toward the doorway. She nodded, eyes never leaving me.

"You never could." It was a breath, but I heard, and heard the undeniable affection in the voice that had spoken.

Chapter 10

By dawn, I had left the house, and for two weeks, tossed and turned in dreamless sleep, in a bed not my own, in rooms that cried with emptiness. Whatever sparks had flamed that day, I dared not even consider. What could I have been thinking? One moment crying for Christine, the next imagining_____. I dared not finish the thought. Had I been thinking that day at all? I shook my head, and focused attention on the man at my side, and his words. The intricacies of laying stone had not been enough to completely drive away the vision of Meg from my head. With a nod from me, the man rejoined the workmen, and I bent to examine the newest blocks beside the mason.

A small square of blazing white paper appeared before my eyes. "This just came for you." A well known voice said behind me.

I took the note without looking at my companion, and with trembling fingers, opened it. There were only three words inside, written in a light, feminine hand, but three words that elicited a broad smile.

"She must be quite a woman." There was a trace of a chuckle in the voice.

I rose, and finally looked at my companion, still holding a broad grin. "Yes she is, Étienne. She's my daughter."

He smiled. "Go. I'll finish this." He indicated the pile of blocks I had been inspecting. I nodded, and grabbing the jacket I had laid aside earlier that day, made my way to the station, the square of paper with its precious words, clutched in my hand. They were only three words, but three words that gave me the world.

Christine misses papa

Maryanne greeted me with a smile as she opened the door. "They're in the garden," she said quietly, taking the jacket and valise. Her eyes sparkled as I gave her a nod in reply, and walked through the kitchen toward the garden.

Meg stood there, dressed in a light summer frock, her back to me, Christine nestled comfortably against her hip.

For a minute, I stood inside the doorway, watching them. Christine was no longer a helpless infant, but a little person in her own right, with definite likes and dislikes. Her eyes had stayed the brilliant blue I had first seen, and her hair had turned a deep, chocolate brown.

An unbidden smile curved my lips at the thought that someday I would have to approve any potential suitor for my daughter's hand. Would I want to?

At that moment, Christine turned her head and seeing me, a huge smile lit her little face and she began to wriggle out of Meg's grip.

"What?" Meg asked her, as if the child would answer. She had turned slightly, so both she and the child could see me. Little arms strove in the air, reaching for me.

I closed the distance, gathering Christine into my arms. As I did so, my eyes met Meg's over the child's squirming body. A broad smile lit her face, her eyes shining with happiness. Whatever had happened between us that day in the garden lay forgotten, and life settled into a pleasant routine.

Christine grew by leaps and bounds, and we soon found ourselves exhausted simply by escorting an intrepid explorer on our own grounds. To give us a measure of peace, it became Meg's and mine habit to walk to the village, or the beach, if only to have a few minutes of respite. In this, Maryanne was more than happy to accommodate us. I would never have thought a small child could drive one to distraction.

By November of that year, Christine's needs exceeded her accommodations in Meg's bedroom, so we settled her into the small room adjoining mine. When I was home, there was not an evening that I did not sing her to sleep.

With December came preparations for Christmas, a holiday I had never had cause to celebrate. Under the Opera house, it mattered little what day or month it was. For a time, I had stopped caring. One day had been much like the next.

On Christmas Eve, after putting Christine to bed, I found Meg sitting in the kitchen, staring dejectedly at two enormous spiny lobsters squirming in the bucket at her feet.

"What is that?" I asked, though I knew perfectly well what the animals were.

"Our dinner, I think." She glanced at me, her face a grimace of horror. "Paul brought them. He would not take no for an answer."

"Do you know how to cook them?"

"No. You?"

"Not the least idea. I have never liked fish or," I pointed at the bucket, "those."

"What do we do with them?"

"Give them a stay of execution, for now." I smiled at her, and moved the bucket to the farthest, coolest corner of the kitchen. "Paul and Maryanne deserve a good dinner." I chuckled.

"Ugh." Meg shook her head.

A determined hunt through the pantry produced a meal to rival the best hotel in Paris. It was a meal spent in quiet companionship, small talk, and laughter. Perhaps it was the first time we truly felt at ease with one another.

When Meg presented the package carefully wrapped in fancy paper and fastened with ribbon, I stared at her in astonishment.

"Go on, don't just stare at it. It's for you." She teased with a smile. My fingers actually trembled as they tore at the paper. It was an old book, a copy of the Meditations of Marcus Aurelius. Its worn state looked frighteningly familiar.

"I found it, after the mob was done. It was the only one they left whole." She said quietly.

I nodded, unable to speak for fear of what to say. The book was a reminder of the life I had left behind, yet this girl had cared enough to pull it from the dust of ruin. When her soft hand clasped mine, I looked into eyes that looked back at me with affection. "I thought you would want to have it." She hesitated then added. "Was I wrong?"

"No," I whispered, brushing fingers over the book's faded binding. I had no words for her gesture. No one had ever cared what happened to an outcast, let alone a faded book. I tried to smile, failing miserably in the effort. "Thank you," I mumbled, too overcome to make any other answer. Making a feeble excuse, I went to the garden. She had been there, had seen how I had lived, had seen the hell that had been my life and yet did not run, did not turn away.

"Good night Erik," Meg murmured some time later. Turning to look at her as she stood silhouetted in the light of the lamp she carried, the yellow hair a gold veil over her shoulders, I could not help thinking how beautiful she was. In the year we had been here she had blossomed. She was no longer a girl but a woman, and somehow, she had ever so slowly begun to tame the beast within me.

"Good night, Meg," I answered, feeling a strange lightness in my heart. As I watched her disappear into the house, I wondered if something had begun to grow here beside Christine, something tenuous and precious.

When I came to the kitchen the following morning, it was to find Meg already seated at table, cradling Christine on her lap. They were sharing a light breakfast. There was no sign of the bucket with its curious residents. Of course there wouldn't be. After Meg had doused her light, I had taken the bucket, and borrowing Paul's horse, had ridden to the river, and given the two lobsters their freedom. Someone long ago, had given me mine. It was a favor I could never repay.

"Merry Christmas," I said, laying an oblong package on the table. Meg's eyes widened with surprise, and setting Christine down, she carefully peeled back the plain, paper wrapping from the frame and its contents. Her hands lifted to her mouth, and for a moment, I thought she would cry. "I don't know what to say," she whispered.

"Then say nothing." I smiled at her.

She rose, closed the distance between us, and lightly, ever so lightly, touched my face. "Thank you."

"You are welcome," I said, smiling back at her.

It was the first picture to grace our home, the first of many. That first portrait of Meg holding Christine as they had appeared that day in the garden, nearly six months previous, became a catharsis, and I could not stop drawing them.

The months flowed by, and what had been warm camaraderie developed into solid friendship. We laughed easily together over Christine's exploits, and it was easy to forget that our life here was just a charade. But was it? Was what had gone before a dream and this the exquisite reality?

I had fully expected Meg to leave soon after that first Christmas, but she stayed, only occasionally making short visits to her mother in Paris. She always returned, and her presence, her smile, gladdened my heart.

Whatever magic had sparked in this house, I was glad for it. After the fire, there had been little to hope for, much less believe in. Here, in this house on the Channel coast, something was growing, something I dared not put a name to. It was a fragile thing, at once impossible and yet comforting and necessary.

When the days grew longer, I resumed efforts in the garden so haltingly begun by the two of us the previous year. I constructed brick planters for Meg's herbs, and when she left for yet another visit to Paris, I installed the stone bench I had asked the mason to carve, the trellis to shelter it, and planted climbing roses on either side. With years, they would shade the bench and provide a peaceful place to rest from day's labors.

"Happy Birthday," I said, leading her into the garden. Meg had just returned from Paris, and for some reason, my heart sang with quiet joy. The feel of her hand in mine was a sensation I had thought never to experience. It sent quiet quivers of exaltation through me.

She was utterly silent. Not a movement, not a flutter. Her hand slipped from mine.

"You don't like it?"

When she turned to face me, the expression on her face was one of disbelief, astonishment, with a shade of something else. Her brown eyes looked at me in wonder. It was her nineteenth birthday.

Without a word, her hands framed my face, eyes boring into mine, and slowly, lightly, she kissed me.

With that kiss, something changed between us and though the camaraderie remained, something hovered on the edge, elusive and tension filled. Though I tried to pretend everything remained as it had been, a smoldering fire had been sparked by that innocent touch of lips. Nightmares that had lain dormant returned with full force and often

I woke shaking, drenched in sweat. Voices clamored within my head, voices from a tortured past, among them all a voice whose words had burned into the very fibers of my bones.

This time I would not run away and hide as I had previously. I could not do it to Meg or Christine again, but the looks that passed between us bordered on dangerous ground. Somewhere in that kiss a boundary had been crossed and what had been a charade, could be thought of as such no longer.

I devoted myself to Christine, now a precocious toddler who had come to rule the household. I drowned time with her for Meg's nearness frightened me. Not the woman, but the potential, explosive emotions that simmered in the air whenever we were in a room together.

In the heat of obsession I had made advances to Meg's sister Christine, with disastrous results. I would not destroy Meg that way. Hélène had entrusted her daughter to my hands and I would not destroy or betray that trust in me, not for anything. So I turned my attention to my daughter. There, my heart was safe, and the turbulent chaos within my soul could find rest.

With the approach of cooler weather, so too, the turbulent sparks between Meg and me seemed to cool. They were just under the surface, in a touch, in a look, but we made pretense of their nonexistence, and our lives settled once more toward winter routine.

Chapter 11

It was winter of 1873, and I was uneasy, restless. Watching Meg and the child, their laughter and games, I could only wonder where all this would lead, for surely the road we were bound upon had to have an end. We could not live in this house forever, not like this. The tensions of the summer were only bound to resurface, and this time, I was not certain either Meg or I could deny their existence. I would not give in to heedless passion, could not, not this time. I had done so once before, the results of which had been flight from Paris, and a burning Opera house. A friend had placed trust in me, a trust I would not betray. Then too, I was nearly thirty eight years old, and Meg just nineteen. Even if I did acknowledge feelings for the girl, what future would there be for her? What could I possibly offer other than a distorted face?

When I saw Meg working alongside Maryanne in the kitchen, Christine clinging to her skirts, I found it hard to believe that two years had passed since we had come to this place. Life had taken a very different path from what I had expected the night I slinked away from the burning theater. In the peace of this house, in the comfort of a family, it had been easy to forget that it had been my hands that had brought us here. In tormented dreams, I still saw Christine, could hear the echo of those words she had cast. Did they still hold true? I did not know anymore. Meg, the child, even Maryanne and Paul, were parts of a life never imagined, a life that soothed the raging monster within. Would I ever have the strength to leave it if I had to?

I shook off the thought, turning my attention to the beautiful woman at my side. What would come would come. For now, I savored the quiet exhilaration that sang in my bones from Meg's delight.

"Oh it's beautiful!" She exclaimed, turning full circle to better view the surroundings. Even though the January day was grey, the stained glass windows showed off their splendor.

I had brought her to the chapel, for it had occurred to me that while I was familiar with her work, saw the results of it every day, she had never seen mine, except for the sketches which filled the walls of our home. This had been something I had taken on outside of other projects.

Buckets of paint, ladders, and stacks of tiles stood about in various places, protective tarps thrown over them. Near the west wall, the workbench overflowed with sketches and diagrams. I smiled with secret pleasure as I watched Meg explore the place.

While Meg leafed through the sketches, she lifted her eyes to glance at me.

"You're doing all this?" She gestured to include the entire structure, brows rising in wonder.

I nodded, enjoying the delight of her company.

"Alone?" Her eyes followed me as I stepped closer toward her.

"I find the peace and quiet help settle troubled thoughts." My fingers reached to touch the gold hair straying from beneath her hat.

"When will you finish?"

"Other projects allowing, perhaps two, or three weeks." I looked at her smile, and sensed myself teetering on a precipice.

Meg raised her eyes to mine. "I'd like to come and see it then."

"Of course," I replied. I could barely breathe. We were but a step from each other. Her dark eyes shone with inner fire.

"Why this place Erik? I thought you did not believe in Him." Meg said softly.

My fingers brushed against her face, against the smoothness of her skin, and before I knew what I was doing, my lips touched hers. The heat of contact seared through me, but what astonished me more than the impulsive gesture, was her response to it. She melded into the kiss, and instead of pulling away, as reason screamed for me to do, I let it deepen, let the sensation of her sing through me.

When we finally broke away, and I could pull air into my lungs, I caressed her face, at length answering her question. "I will never believe in Him. In my life, there was never much cause to do so, but something about this place drew me here, and I could not allow it to fall to ruin." It was as close as I was willing to admit to anything of my previous life.

She cast a smile in my direction. "You rescue babies, now chapels. What will you do for an encore, Monsieur Marchand?"

I sighed and chuckled. "That we will leave for the Fates to decide. Come," I held out my hand. "It's time to leave." She held my fingers firmly, and if she had been surprised by our kiss, she did not show it.

As we walked out of the building, I knew I had broken a trust and my own vow to myself. I had damned myself with that kiss.

Sleep, when it finally came, was a tortured affair. I tossed and turned in the bed, and every lash of the whip that had ever struck me, I felt now, felt the rage, even as a child in that cage, and I turned it on him, on the keeper who would take away even the rag I dared call a toy. The straw chafed at my bare feet, and I choked in the closeness of the dark tent, but I would not give in to the tears that stung my eyes. They were not tears of pain but fury, fury at the ones who paid money to see me, paid the gypsy to torture me. I refused to give him the satisfaction, no matter that he would lay bare my back.

From the wilderness and chaos of rage and hurt, a voice called, a soft voice, a girl's dulcet tones, calling, but I couldn't hear over the laughter and jeering. Turning, I saw a girl in a white gown, long brown hair fanned over her shoulders, tears staining her cheeks. Slowly, she turned and disappeared into the darkness of the grotto. "No!! You can't leave me here!" It was my own voice echoing against the walls.

"*I'm here. I'll always be here.*" That soft voice came from far away, but I would not listen. In helpless rage I stormed and screamed, but the girl was gone and the leering face of the keeper above me only drove me to frenzy. My hands seized his throat and began to squeeze.

"Erik! It's me! Oh God! Erik!" I felt a sharp sting against my cheek. Pain brought reality, and when my eyes snapped open, time stood still with horror and realization. My hands were firmly around Meg's throat.

In an instant, I released her, mind scrambling to sort through the nightmare scene. Meg wore only a thin shift, sat on my bed, hair loose. What was she doing in my bedroom? I stared at her, numbed with shock at what I had nearly done. Dreams, even fevered ones, were no excuse for what had occurred.

She sat unmoving, tears flowing down her cheeks. "You were screaming." She said in a shaky voice, and I was surprised she spoke to me at all.

"Oh Meg," I sighed, closing eyes against the misery and remorse I felt. How could I even begin to apologize for nearly choking her?

She rose, not looking at me. "I think I better leave." She moved slowly, as if she too, tried to comprehend and sort through the shock of what had transpired.

This time, there was no debating the matter. I packed and left the house, unable to even bring myself to say farewell to Christine. Taking a last look at the house before heading toward the village, I glimpsed Meg standing beside the roses. I was uncertain whether I would ever see this place again.

I asked Étienne to find me work, anywhere, as long as it was well away from the house. I wanted not the least temptation of going near it, or Meg, again.

"How about London? They've lost their chief draughtsman."

"Fine. Anything. I'll even mix the mortar if I have to. I can't go near her again."

"What did you do this time? Forget her birthday?"

I shook my head and gave him a pathetic grin. "If only it was that simple. I nearly killed her."

Étienne pursed his lips. "London is best then. I will arrange it."

I nodded assent, too ashamed of my own behavior. My friend, and sometime mentor, had to protect my own family from me.

"Sir?" The clerk's voice was hesitant.

"What is it?" I answered, only mildly interested, for I was busy finishing the current designs.

The man cleared his throat. "A package has arrived for you, sir."

I lifted my head from the table and gave the man a cursory glance. "Leave it in the front office."

"Yes sir, but_____."

I straightened, laying the pen down with a deliberately slow movement. "Leave it there. I will attend to it."

The man hesitated.

"Did you not hear me?"

"Ah sir, it's not that kind of parcel."

"What do you mean? Speak plainly."

"He means me," Meg's voice filled the silence. I could only stare at her as she stood inside the doorway of the office, dressed in travel clothes, a stylish summer hat shading her face. The door closed silently behind her as the man withdrew, leaving us very much alone.

"Will you forever make me ask you to come home?" She said, the voice catching on a cry she could not contain.

"I thought it best ....I could not bear....I don't know what to say." I sounded stupid, even to my own ears.

Meg's eyes fixed on me, and in three steps, she was beside the draught table, grasping my hand. "Then say nothing, only come home." At those words, reluctance dissolved. My arms twined around her and drew her close, holding her in a comforting embrace. I had never held a woman like that, and I was never more frightened than at that moment. She was precious, she was goodness, and I had nearly destroyed her. Despite that, she had found me. It was her twentieth birthday.

Having made arrangements with the firm, and securing another draughtsman to replace me, Meg and I returned to France, and the place I had begun to call home. It was late summer, and I had been away for six months. Though I was glad to see the house and our neighbors once more, something had changed. An invisible door had closed, and I sensed a withdrawal within myself, a distance between me and everything else. From now, it was the way it had to be. The beast that resided within me had only proven the truth of Christine's words. My hands would destroy that which I most cared for.

My daughter sensed the change in me, and her demands for attention grew ever more fervent. She refused to let go when I held her, and I could put her to bed only when she had fallen fast asleep. When I sang to her, she would cling to me ever more tightly, as if her small body could soothe the turmoil within. She would never know my anger. We had made an unstated vow to each other the night I had picked her up, and no matter what, that was one vow I would not break. I would protect this child with my life.

With the approach of Christine's third birthday, the uneasiness that had arisen between Meg and me only grew worse.

I had returned at Meg's behest, but I was not the same. I spoke to her for politeness' sake, but the easy friendship we had known was gone. In its place was something bordering on formal. I avoided being alone in a room with her. If she attempted contact, I moved away. Though I was always courteous, I did not allow anything more to show than that.

We moved through the days like automatons. After a time, Meg gave up efforts to elicit a laugh or a smile from me, even gave up efforts to touch me, though occasionally I saw her hands clench against the desire to do so. An uneasy silence descended between us, and in its midst that January of 1874, we celebrated a child's third birthday.

In her excitement, I doubted that Christine noticed the tension between maman and papa. She tore the wrappings off her present in barely contained glee, exclaiming "Oh Papa! Merci! Maman!" as her eager hands freed the doll and its extensive wardrobe from layers of tissue. She embraced and kissed each of us in turn, then ran to show Maryanne and Paul her prize.

The matronly lady and her husband had become steady companions in our lives since my return from London. I dared not be alone with Meg, and the couple had assumed the roles of chaperones and grandparents all at once. If they questioned the sudden change within the household, they did not speak of it.

Meg and I exchanged glances as Christine's exclamations of delight drifted to us from the kitchen. Maryanne had baked a cake for her, and I could only assume the child had discovered it. We were in the parlor, where sketches of the house, garden, Meg and Christine festooned the walls. After the first portrait, I had never stopped drawing them, the two women that had guided me here, to this new life. Meg had framed many. Now her eyes looked at me with sadness. There was nothing I could ever do or say, to undue what my hands had wrought.

With a sigh, she turned and walked away, and in that movement I recognized Hélène, the dignity, the poise, and I shook my head in sadness. I had failed even her, the one who had trusted and believed in me. With ponderous steps, I followed Meg into the kitchen, and for this night, for our daughter, we made pretense of laughter and delight. The child would have a family, especially on this night, no matter the cost.

"I can't live like this." Meg's exasperated voice exploded in the tense silence of the parlor. We sat on opposite sides of the room, the lamps casting deep shadows over our surroundings. The fire in the hearth crackled and sparks flew as Maryanne stirred the logs.

"You refuse to look at me, let alone speak to me!" The young woman's cry echoed in the room. I saw Maryanne's shadow disappear around the doorway, and heard the front door close. We were alone in a silent house.

It was late February, a month since Christine's birthday, and we had not spoken to each other in days.

"What would you have me say? That it will never happen again? That I will not kill you the next time? What were you doing in my room?"

"You were screaming." Meg rose from her chair, hands held tightly clenched at her sides. "You were shouting a name, to not leave you." She added quietly. "I tried to wake you." She sighed, turning away.

I hung my head in misery, running fingers through tousled hair. "There is no excuse for what I did."

"You were dreaming." Meg fixed her eyes on me, the brown deepening with some emotion I could not comprehend.

"Dangerous dreams," I muttered.

"Are they always so bad?" She asked.

I raised my head to glance at her, rose and turned my back on her. "Sometimes they're worse."

There was heavy silence broken only by the crackle of the fire.

"Why …why won't you touch me? Surely you have feelings for me? That kiss in the chapel, that was not imagination!" Her voice shook as the words poured out. "Did Christine hurt you that much? Did you love her? It was her name you were shouting! My God, what did she do to you to hurt you so?" The flood gate had opened, and her questions tumbled one over the other. I heard the plaintive tone in her voice, the plea for understanding, but one I was not prepared to ease. How could I ever bring myself to explain an obsession I barely understood myself, let alone the hell that had been my life before Hélène found me? So I remained silent to her pleas, to her questions.

"Please talk to me. Don't turn away." Meg's voice bordered on desperation. I faced her, staying well away on the other side of the room. Tears fell from her eyes, but she made no move to wipe them away.

"Go home Meg," I said quietly, not looking at her, could not. The hurt in her eyes was too much to bear and I dared not comfort it in any way.

"What?"

"Go home, back to Paris. You should have gone there a long time ago."

"My home is here, with you, with Christine!"

"There is nothing for you here!" I shouted at her, my insides screaming with the hurt of the words, the pain I had to give her, for I no longer trusted myself around her.

She stared at me for long minutes, then drew her brows together. "You call all this," she swept her arm in a circle to include the house and gardens, "nothing? It's our home!"

"Yours is in Paris, where you should have been all along. I should never have brought you here. How could I have been such an idiot!"

"I came because I wanted to." Meg said quietly.

"Now you will leave, because I wish you to." I said darkly, not daring to give voice to that which cried for me to hold her in my arms and stop this verbal duel.

She was brave under the latest assault, the tightening of her lower lip the only sign of the anguish she no doubt felt. It was evident in her eyes. Those she could not mask.

"It's because of what happened isn't it? You're afraid you'll hurt me."

"Meg, I almost killed you. I made a promise to your mother. I broke it once already. Next time might be too late."

"You stopped."

"Only because you had strength to bring me out of the nightmare. What if next time you cannot? What then?" I studied the way her hands worried at her skirts. "Go to Paris, Meg. Find a good man to be a husband to you. Have a family of your own."

"You and Christine are my family." She returned, glancing at me. "Can you let me go so easily?" She asked. Tears stained her cheeks, though she was no longer crying.

"No," I sighed and knew the truth of the word even before it was uttered. "It has to be this way." I said slowly. "My hands would destroy you."

"You don't know that!" She cried.

I sighed and shook my head. "I am not willing to take the chance."

"Erik, don't send me away!"

I could not face her, or the anguish that poured out of her voice. I closed my eyes and ears against the choked sob that came from across the room and the sound of her steps on the stairs. I stared out the window at the falling snow, sensing the world fall apart around me.

When sometime later I heard the sharp click of heels against wood, I turned to see Meg standing in the doorway of the parlor, dressed in heavy woolens, a shawl thrown carelessly over her hair, a packed valise at her feet.

"Please, ask me to stay," her voice begged me.

"I cannot. I have nothing to give you."

Her eyes bored into mine. "You're wrong, so very wrong." She picked up the case. "If you ever come to Paris, you'll know where to find me."

The door closed quietly after her.

Chapter 12

Meg's absence left an unfathomable void in our lives. When Christine questioned where and why maman had gone, I could not, with an honest heart, find a satisfactory answer.

I endured through the days because I had to, because there was a child to care for. Her cries for maman only twisted the invisible knife I had thrust into my chest. Not even Maryanne's gentleness could soothe Christine's torrent of tears, and I would never admit to mine.

When duties with the firm demanded attention, Christine's hysterics when she saw me gathering the coat and hat, were unendurable. No amount of reassurance, from me or Maryanne, would quiet her.

After that, I made temporary arrangements for Maryanne and Christine to stay near where I was overseeing a project. I would not have my daughter's tears and accusing looks on my conscience. Maryanne walked with the child by the construction site every day so Christine could see papa working. Once reassured of my presence, my daughter's fear of losing me lessened, and our goodbyes in the morning became fairly civilized affairs.

However endless Maryanne's patience and kindness during the weeks following Meg's departure, I knew I could not depend on her services forever. I could not very well drag her from place to place. That she was willing to aid us during this difficult transition was enough.

I could no longer abide the house. There were too many memories, too many questions lacking answers.

With the aid of a solicitor, I entrusted the house to Meg and her mother, settled an account for them to draw on, and left the shores of Brittany, and eventually, France.

Christine and I traveled. We saw the capitols of Europe, and sifted the sands of Egypt through our fingers, never staying in one place for long. We gazed upon the masters in museums, heard heavenly music in concert halls, yet there was always restlessness in my heart, a yawning emptiness that even Christine could not fill.

In each house we stayed, I demanded there be a piano available for use. I could no longer live without music. It consumed me, and often I would compose late into the night, surrounded by candlelight, shadows, and ghosts.

Days flowed into months, the months into years.

The world was changing at breakneck speed. Buildings were going up everywhere. There was demand for everything, from the mundane, to the exotic. It was at once exhilarating and frightening, a strange place to be for one who had lived most of his life in a dungeon. The more time I spent surrounded by people and the heartbeat of everyday living, the more I wondered how I had ever lived in that hell under the Opera house. How had I managed to retain sanity?

With demand for new construction high, the small firm I had started many years before flourished, and soon I found myself in a position of acquiring others, expanding my holdings to satisfy demand. After years of Étienne holding the company in trust, and as a subsidiary of his own firm, I had assumed rightful ownership, and like the business, I thrived in architecture's domain. I kept the name Marchand, a name not my own, but one that had served well in the past. For what was I, but a merchant in buildings?

The firm prospered, and its reputation spread. Contracts for work came from as far away as Prague, Vienna, even Budapest. I accepted most of them as they would give Christine an experience of other lands, and for now, I had no wish to be near France.

It was while we were in Prague that an offer from the French government arrived. It had been forwarded from Étienne's office. The request gave me pause, and then I laughed bitterly at the irony. They wanted Marchard to restore the Populaire! I, who had burned it down, to restore that prison that had held me. It was a sick joke! A polite, if somewhat terse and tidy rejection was sent.

I was finalizing figures for the latest in a series of proposals, when a tentative knock on the door of the office roused me from melancholy musings. "Come," and though I had not intended it, my tone sounded imperative, even to my own ears. The clerk who shuffled in bobbed his head.

"Pardon sir," he said nervously, proffering a note. "This came from your housekeeper."

I snatched it, mind preoccupied with numbers and engineering details. The clerk nearly bolted out of the room. What did Suzanna need now? The woman was hopeless.

The minute I read the note, I silently apologized to the kindly, old lady. Grabbing my coat and stick, I hurried from the office to hail a cab.

Minutes later I was running up the stairs of the house, tossing the coat and cane aside.

"Christine! Christine!"

"Monsieur Erik!" Suzanna appeared at the top of the stairs, wringing her hands. "Oh, sir!"

"What is it, Suzanna? What's wrong with Christine?" My tone demanded an answer.

More hand wringing, more sighing. "Oh sir, she's in a mood."

"Suzanna, if you don't tell me now, I will toss you over the banister." The hardness in my look gave no doubt that I would do it.

"But sir, it is not proper for me to talk about."

Patience nearly at an end, I ascended the last few steps to tower over the housekeeper.

"Out with it woman!" I roared.

"Monsieur Erik, you are a man!" She moaned under my volcanic stare.

"Astute power of observation, Suzanna. Yes, I am a man and I'm Christine's father. Now tell me, what's wrong with my daughter." My voice had gone deathly quiet.

"It's... it's her courses, sir!" She moaned, hurrying past me to the safety of the kitchen.

So, the years had caught up with us. I leaned against the balustrade a moment, allowing the news to sink in. Years spent traveling, playing duets, chasing birds in the park, all now bittersweet memories. Christine had changed before my eyes, and I had not even realized. I shrugged out of the jacket, folding it over the banister, taking time to adjust to the news that my daughter was no longer a little girl, but on her way to becoming a young woman.

With a sigh, I slowly approached Christine's room, the plaintive sobbing coming from within melting my heart with tenderness.

I opened the door to find her curled up on the bed, crying, hands wrapped around a doll. I smiled gently as I recognized it. It was the one Meg and I had given her on her third birthday. Christine's hands now clutched it as if holding onto her fleeting childhood.

"Christine," I ventured gently, sitting down on the bed, fingers brushing her hair from her face. "My dear, sweet child."

"Oh papa," she moaned, and pressed herself into my chest. My arms folded around her, holding her as tightly as she wanted me to.

"I'm so miserable," she sobbed into my shoulder. "I just want to die."

I caressed her hair, lightly kissing the top of her head. "Oh no, my dear. There is no reason for dying."

"It hurts," she wailed, "and I have no friends! We are always going somewhere! And always you want more lessons!" She cried out, curling into a ball, the river of tears unending.

I looked at her, unable to reconcile the memory of the tiny bundle I had found on the street, and the young girl now finding herself on the edge of womanhood.

"Am I as bad as that, little one?"

"You want me to do all these things and I try. I don't want to disappoint you, but sometimes it is too much." Her sobs had quieted, and now she lay on her side, hands once more clutching the doll.

"It is only that I want you to be accomplished in many things and have a choice about what you will want to study, that I give you lessons. We may discontinue any you wish, for as long as you wish."

"Truly Papa?" The question was tinged with doubt.

I smiled a little, though she couldn't see it. "Truly." It was an easy concession to make. At twelve, Christine had mastered more than some grown men in a lifetime. She spoke five languages, played well enough to accompany her father, and sang to melt iron hearts. She knew her figures well enough to help me sort accounts, but her true talent lay in design. I had already incorporated some of her ideas into my work.

Christine turned onto her back, her striking blue eyes looking at me, the tears at last at an end. "What about friends?"

"What about them?"

"Will we stay anywhere long enough for me to have them?"

"Have we moved that much?"

"Yes, Papa. Just as I get acquainted with someone at school, we go somewhere else."

I studied her face. Unbidden flashes of memory came from the depths, of faces looking to me in trust, pleading, two faces that melded into one. I shut my eyes against the vision, against the swell of desolation. "Where would you like to be Christine? Where would you like it best?" I asked gently, caressing her cheek.

She frowned in thought, then a wide smile split her face. "Italy. I liked Italy best, Papa."

I smiled too, and tousled her hair, making her giggle. "Italy it is then. My project here is nearly done. We might as well begin preparations." I started straightening the bed covers. "I will place you in charge of making our travel arrangements."

"Oh yes! It will be our best trip!" She flew into my arms, showering me with kisses.

I held onto her, drinking in that moment. I had left a baby girl somewhere, and now found myself holding a young, tender, girl-woman in my arms.

Chapter 13

Italy proved a good choice for both of us. Our new home was sizeable, though not ostentatious. It boasted a vineyard, an olive grove, and acres and acres of open land. I purchased a pair of horses, a black stallion for me, and a gentle mare for Christine. She took to her new companion with such zeal that it was hard to separate the two. While I enjoyed the freedom and peace of riding, and reveled in Christine's company, still, there was a sense of comfortless emptiness deep within my bones.

The staff accepted us warmly, never questioning the particular stipulations regarding our privacy. Those requirements were never breached. It was the first time in many years I felt at ease. Over the years I had begun to relax the ingrained vigilance borne from long experience, and came to thoroughly enjoy life in the country.

Christine chose to attend a school in Rome, one that would challenge her skills, and one that was not so distant from home that she could not make an occasional visit. I refused to have my daughter see me but once a year, as was the norm with such establishments. We had come to rely on each other's company far too much to allow ourselves to be separated for long.

Spring came in all its glory to the country, and with it, a thirteen year old Christine, home for a few days' break. Her excitement, as she ran about the estate exploring and acquainting herself with friends old and new, was infectious. I laughed and smiled with her as she cuddled the new kittens in the barn, and fed her pregnant mare a carrot. She was still a child, but occasionally, a glimpse of an emerging woman flashed through, and I had to shake my head in wonder.

We had an easy rapport, my daughter and I. She never hesitated to state an opinion, and I never forbade her a thing. There was no need to. She accepted my wishes regarding most things, and I respected her choices if she decided not to follow my advice. However of late, there had been questions, questions I had no idea how to answer, for my life had not encompassed such experiences.

The sun had set, and I was enjoying a few, brief minutes of relaxation on the portico, winding down from a busy day. I had ridden the perimeter of the estate, checking progress, savoring the rejuvenation of everything after winter's hold, perhaps even to a degree, my own. Christine made me laugh and relish life as I had thought I never would. Surrounded by her unfailing love and cheerfulness, it was easy to dismiss dreams that haunted restless nights.

The enormous crash and cry that followed shattered the peace and quiet of the evening. It had come from my study, a place that even Christine understood was not to be disturbed.

The noise did not alarm me as much as the cry. It had been Christine's, and it set me in motion. In three bounds, I was staring at the carnage my study had become. Even as the heat of anger surged through me, I forced it down. I had made a promise to this child, and I would not break it, not that one.

Shock, dismay, guilt, they there were all leveled at me through her blue eyes. "I'm sorry!" She cried, tears running down her face.

"Mom Dieu! What did you do?" I wondered out loud, stunned at the destruction facing me. Books, music sheets and sketches lay everywhere in a wild tangle. Two of the candlesticks from the piano had been dislodged, along with their contents. I was glad that this time, I had not left them burning.

"I didn't mean to! I'm sorry!" She choked back a sob.

"My dearest, even a tornado would not have accomplished what you have done." I said gently, now thoroughly bemused at the massacre.

"My foot caught against the carpet." Christine confessed, tears subsiding, now that she knew I would not vent anger at her.

"I see." I did indeed. As I stepped into the room, glass crunched underfoot. "What?" I stopped, and glanced down, to see my shoes reflected several dozen times.

"Your mirror. It broke when the candlesticks fell. Sorry."

"Anything else I should know about?" I asked, stepping carefully over the shards.

She shook her head. "No. I think that's everything."

Then I saw the blood running through her fingers, and whatever I had been about to say, died on my lips. My heart suddenly broke with tenderness and guilt that I had not seen her distress earlier.

"Oh Christine," I said softly, slipping an arm around her shoulders. "Come, we need to clean that cut." We walked toward the bath where I proceeded to wash and bandage her hand. A slow smile lifted the corners of my mouth.

"You prying little vixen," I said gently, studying her. "Did you find what you were looking for?" I tied the bandage with a knot.

"I don't know what I was looking for." She glanced sidelong at me with guilty eyes.

"Why Christine? Why not ask me?"

Christine sighed and leaned her head onto my shoulder. "I miss maman. I miss her so much. Why did she go, Papa? Why did she leave us?"

So there it was; the crux of the matter, the reason for all her tears, the source behind the destruction in the study. She had been looking for something, anything to give her a connection to a woman she would barely remember. Suddenly the recent questions, the furtive footsteps in the dead of night, all made sense. Christine was searching for her mother. It had never occurred to me that eventually this might happen, that I would need to confront my conscience regarding decisions made under circumstances wrought by my hands.

I held her close, leaning a cheek against her hair. How to even begin to try to explain a tangled situation such as Meg's and mine? How to confess feelings I barely understood, even now? That there had been feelings for Meg was an undeniable fact. That the demons that pursued my nights had nearly driven me to kill the woman Christine knew as maman, was a shame I would take to my grave. No amount of forgiveness would ever erase that.

"She had to go Christine." Was all I could say. It was truth, if not the entire truth.

"But why? Was it because of me?" She cried against my shoulder.

I continued to hold her, realizing how fragile she was, how vulnerable. Whatever I said, my words would have to be carefully chosen.

"Did she not want me?"

The question wrenched my heart. For a moment, a flash of memory came out of nowhere, of a small child crying "Why don't you want me?" Involuntarily, my arms around Christine tightened, and I kissed her hair. "Christine, if anything, maman would have stayed for you." I had never told my daughter how she had come into my life. Perhaps that question would always remain unanswered.

"Then why didn't she? Didn't she care?"

I closed my eyes, reliving the pain of Meg's departure and my cruel words to her. Even now, ten years later, the sting of them remained. Feelings neither of us had dared to name or acknowledge had grown, but there had been too many demons and shadows in the way. So I had done the only thing I could. I sent Meg away before I would destroy her. I suppose I never took Christine into account then, or how Meg's absence would affect her.

"She left for me, my heart." I said quietly.

"For you? I don't understand. Papa surely you didn't____." My daughter turned suddenly wondering eyes on me.

With horror I realized the implication of her statement. "Oh Mon Dieu, child," I whispered, hands framing her face, holding her eyes with mine. "I cared for maman too much." Even as I said it, I knew it for the truth it was, knew it in the depths of my heart. "I would never intentionally hurt either of you." I smoothed her hair. "No, maman left because something happened between us. It had nothing to do with you, my heart, but everything with me." I kissed her cheek. That was the closest to the matter I would get. It would have to satisfy Christine's yearning for the mystery of her being, of just having papa.

"I love you, Papa, and I'm sorry about the mess."

"So you should be, you little Pandora," I teased her, and gently drew her to her feet. "Your punishment will be to clean it up."

"Yes, Papa," she flashed me a smile. "Will you stay with me, talk to me?"

"If you wish." We walked companionably back to the scene of mayhem.

"Oh it does look terrible," Christine whispered, now that she was confronted with the field of battle.

"No doubt it will be restored to order."

She tiptoed to kiss my cheek. "Sit and I'll take care of everything." She dashed down the stairs in a flurry of skirts. I shook my head in wonder at this child who had brought solace to my life when I had most needed it. She was fast becoming a young woman, but still had a child's need for comfort and approval as our conversation had proved. I had not thought Christine's memories of Meg would be so strong. She had only been three years old when her settled world came to an end. Her questions about a mother, about herself, would only deepen if I did nothing and let the situation lie.

While she busied downstairs, I took advantage of the time alone, and walked to my bedroom. A firm press on the lock of the dresser released the hidden compartment. Three items lay within, but only one interested me now. With a sigh, I reached for it, and closed the compartment.

The photograph had yellowed, but it was still discernible. It was the only thing Meg had left behind, other than a house full of memories. I had thought she had forgotten it in her hurry to pack, but with time, realized she had left it on purpose. It was a photograph of her holding Christine on her lap. On the back, written in Meg's elegant hand, was a date. It was the day she had hurried out of the house in her green dress, the day she had seen me in the garden, the day something had begun to flourish between us. I slipped the picture into the pocket of my jacket, and went into the study.

Christine was already hard at work straightening the field of battle. On a tray beside the winged chair a sumptuous meal of bread, cheese, fruit and wine awaited me. In all the commotion that had followed the crash, I had forgotten all about dinner. As I ate, and she cleaned, we talked companionably of school, her friends, and plans for summer. While I watched her, I had no doubt that questions regarding her mother were far from over. If anything, our conversation had only been the beginning.

Long after she fell asleep, I walked into Christine's room, a small smile twisting my lips as I saw her sleeping. I found it incredible that she shared my life, that this child had allowed for a new existence. She was my life, and my heart filled to overflowing tenderness for her.

Taking the photograph from my pocket, I set it on the table next to her bed, and ever so lightly, brushed a hand against her hair, murmuring, "Sweet dreams, my dear one." Closing the door, I returned to the study, now put back to order. I poured a glass of wine and turned toward the neatly arranged desk, and chuckled. Christine, having thoroughly disarrayed her father's room, had put it back together so that I could not find anything.

A few minutes' search produced the pens and paper I needed. Sleep tonight would be elusive at best. Christine's questions had stirred embers of an emotional fire that had never really been doused. Had I done the right thing in sending Meg away? Was not Christine her daughter as well as mine? Of necessity, she had spent more time with the child than I, had endured my sudden disappearances and fits of anger, yet despite what had happened, she had found me, and brought me home.

With a sigh I turned to the sheets scattered on the desk. Sometime during my musings, I had allowed my fingers free rein and what they had produced stared back at me. A young woman holding a child against her hip, both smiling at each other, the woman's long hair streaming in the breeze off the sea.

I closed my eyes against the swell of wistfulness. What had been done was done. I barely remembered my mother, and most times wished I didn't. I could not let Christine be without hers, not after this evening. Taking the sketch, I wrote an address on the bottom. It would have to do.

Walking downstairs, I slid the drawing between sheets of Christine's favorite music which lay propped against the rack on the piano. What she would make of it would be her choice. I only provided the means.

Chapter 14

It was January 1886, and my fifty first birthday. Christine and I had spent it strolling through the streets of Rome. She had come to the office early, and no amount of pretext would dissuade her from her intentions. She wanted her father on her arm and so I accompanied her, relishing her company.

At fifteen, Christine was rapidly blossoming into a beautiful, young woman. Where girls her age were already seeking potential suitors, my daughter's interests lay in the study of ancient buildings, her school and music, and to a degree, her father. Over the past months I had noticed a certain protectiveness develop in her manner toward me. It was subtle, a glance now and then, a firmer touch of the hand, more evenings spent in each other's company when I was in the city, but it was there none the less, and I was grateful for it. With the years, melancholy had begun to gnaw at me, and in this, I was thankful for Christine's nearness. She drew me out, never letting me brood overlong, as of late I had been wont to do.

Now in the late evening as I sat at the piano in our apartment, letting fingers bring forth music, I smiled with tenderness and affection as I recalled our day together. We did not have too many. Her school kept her in the city, and business prevented me from staying in any one place for long.

"I don't think I've ever heard you play it like that before," Christine's voice broke in over the music.

I glanced up from the keys to see her leaning against the doorway of the salon, watching me, smiling gently. She had tossed a light gown over her shift, and her dark, glorious hair fell over her shoulders.

"I am sorry my playing woke you," I said, lifting fingers from the keys. "You have school tomorrow. I should_____." For some reason I let the statement hang, avoiding her scrutiny.

"You didn't, and I was only reading." Christine shook her head and came toward the bench where I was sitting. "You know how much I love it when you play." She leaned down, kissed my cheek, and slid beside me onto the bench. "I don't have too many chances these days to listen, but this," her fingers began to pluck out the melody I had played earlier. "It's beautiful," Christine paused, letting the music hang in the air between us. "Like her," she glanced toward the framed portrait atop the piano.

I followed her gaze to the eyes looking back at me from the frame. I had drawn the other Christine in a fit of wistfulness and never could bring myself to discard it. She had gone with her Vicomte, had cast words that had burned me to the core, and yet, I still held feelings for her in my heart.

I made no answer and began to play softly, avoiding my daughter's penetrating look.

"You always play this when we're here, when you're with her." Christine's voice was gentle, yet it demanded response.

"It was written for her," I replied, lost in music, in memory, consumed with a flood of feelings that I feared to acknowledge.

"Did you love her?" That question, an echo of one I had heard not so long ago from another, would not be put off with silence, not this time.

"There were some feelings," I acceded. I would not lie to my child, or to myself, not any longer.

Christine leveled her blue eyes on me. "Did she hurt you?"

What a question! "No more than I hurt her," I answered quietly.

There was a long, drawn out silence between us as Christine studied the drawing, then me. "Was she my mother? My real mother?" Her voice was gentle, so gentle that at last it stirred me to look into her face, to confront the yearning for understanding, for answers that were elusive.

I stopped playing and lightly caressed my daughter's cheek. "No," I breathed. "Your maman," I stopped, not quite knowing how or where to begin. As I looked into my daughter's questioning eyes, I was certain of only one thing. When my fingers lightly touched Christine's hair, I told her the truth, the absolute truth that lay in my heart. "I loved your mother."

I sat there, facing the young woman, shocked by what I had been reluctant to acknowledge all this time. Was it possible that a man like me had been allowed that one thing in life that made the striving, the struggle worthwhile? Was it possible that love had grown between Meg and me?

When I looked into Christine's eyes, memory teased me with Meg's sidelong looks, the secretive smiles she had occasionally cast in my direction, the blush that had suffused her cheeks when I had been near, the diffident touches of her hand, the warmth of her lips when we had kissed in that chapel. It all made sense. The feelings both of us had been reluctant to acknowledge, had been there all along.

I sighed and dropped my hand from Christine's hair. Too late for turning back. I had made my own choice in that matter, and I had to abide by the consequences. I had after all, sent Meg away, given her away, but the knowledge did nothing to stop the heavy sigh, or the tears that welled and spilled down my cheeks.

Christine's fingers lightly brushed the tears away. "I am sorry, Papa. I did not mean to hurt you." She wrapped her arms around me in a brief embrace.

"Oh, my dear, you never could. I did that a long time ago, when I sent your mother away."

Christine pulled back, eyes looking into mine. Her hand caressed my right cheek. "I don't think Maman ever let go. She's still in here, isn't she?" Feather light fingers touched my heart. She studied me with such tenderness that I almost fell to weeping once more.

"Your mother will be with me to the day I die." I answered honestly.

Christine's hand brushed along the mask. I stayed her wrist, eyes silently pleading. A lifetime ago another Christine had ripped it off, plunging us both into a fire of misery. I did not want to lose my daughter that way.

She kissed me. "Please, Papa. Let me see."

I was helpless in my daughter's spell. I could only pray that our years together would overcome any revulsion.

With gentle fingers, Christine let the mask slip away. I knew the years had not been kind to that side of my face. I confronted it every day as I shaved. I felt my daughter's lips against the ravaged cheek, felt her arms twine around me in a tight, loving, embrace. I drew her closer, and the only sound in the room was the combined beat of our hearts.

Chapter 15

"What a splendid day, Papa! Everyone had a wonderful time! The meal was superb, the wine exquisite and the conversations entertaining." Christine exclaimed in sheer joy. A wide smile lit her face all the way to her eyes.

"And the musicians?" I asked, teasing.

"Fair," she laughed, mussing my hair, kissing my brow.

"We must see to it that next year they do better." I said, unable to keep the stern tone I had wanted to.

"Oh most certainly. Otherwise, we won't hire them, ever again." This time, she wrapped her arms around me, and pressed her cheek against mine.

With a contented sigh, I closed the book I had been reading, and patted the arm she had wrapped around me, savoring the moment. There would not be too many more.

At sixteen, Christine was a glowing beauty, on the verge of starting her own life. Soon she would be gone, and once again I would be plunged into solitude. I suppressed a pang of melancholy. This time, there would be no miraculous rescue, no one with whom to share laughter, no one with whom to share ideas, no one to listen.

Christine had come home for Christmas, immediately taking charge of the household. Fresh greens and red ribbons brightened every room, and baskets of pine cones refreshed the air. Adopting a tradition from Germany, we set up a pine tree in the main room of the house, and festooned it with ribbons, cones and paper decorations of our own making.

With our staff we had sung songs and shared a feast earlier in the day. As each member of the household departed for celebrations with their families, Christine had given each a small gift.

Evening had come, and we were alone in our house. I sat in the winged chair beside the fire, legs extended to soak in the warmth. Sometime back, the slow creep of years had made itself evident in occasionally pained joints and slower movement. Though I still kept a regular regimen of exercise, I could not deny that I was no longer a young man. If nothing else, the encroaching grey in my hair told me so. I let the momentary silence in the room beat against the sudden swell of bittersweet feelings.

"What are you reading, on this night of all nights?" Christine asked, peering over my shoulder at the faded volume in my lap. "Hmmm. Marcus Aurelius. That does not seem like you." She said, propping her chin on my shoulder.

I set the book aside, glancing at her. "Your mother found it for me. She thought it had value."

Christine pursed her lips in thought. "I can't imagine you and the emperor in philosophical discussion."

I chuckled. "My dear, there are always surprises."

She kissed the top of my head. "Yes, I suppose there are." She smiled at me, and held out her hand. "Come, Papa. Let me show you something." Her tone had turned serious, but was filled with love and tenderness.

I grasped her slender fingers, allowing her to lead me through the candle lit hall toward my bedroom. The door was sealed with ribbon. Raising a brow in a silent question, I looked at her. She smiled, and from somewhere, produced scissors, handing them to me.

"Merry Christmas, Papa," Christine said, kissing me on the cheek. "I love you."

She was a vision of an angel, with her dark hair pinned up, setting off her long, slender neck. Red silk and white lace swathed her in flattering layers. At her throat, on a thin gold chain, the ruby pendant I had given her that morning sparkled warmly in the candlelight. My daughter's eyes looked at me with all abiding love.

Intrigued, I cut through the sash, and opened the door. There were candles burning everywhere, casting a golden glow over the few furnishings. Everything was the same as that morning when I had left it, except for a large package standing propped against the dresser.

With tremulous fingers, I worked the paper and ribbon loose. The paper fell away, and I had to shut my eyes against the threatening tide of tears.

Within the hand carved frame was a collage, but far from an ordinary one. Christine had collected bits and pieces from all our travels, and here, among the pictures of buildings, boats, and pyramids, she had placed bits of sand, shells, and pieces of her old dresses. Ribbons from her hair, a broken pin I had made into a pendant, they were there too, scattered among the memories. Dominating the whole was a portrait of a man. He had a wistful smile on his lips, and his eyes looked out into the distance, as if seeking someone.

For a moment, I wondered why Christine would give me a picture of a strange man. Then I understood, and the tears began to flow freely. This was how Christine saw me, whole, no masks, no disfigurement.

I felt her hand entwine around mine as she laid her head on my shoulder.

"You are beautiful, Papa."

Chapter 16

Rome was at its best in spring. The gardens came into bloom, calm breezes blew through the streets, and everyone busied themselves cleansing the dankness of winter away. The oppressive heat of summer had not yet set in, and life in the streets was merry.

We had come to the city on a two fold purpose. I, to finalize a reconstruction project, and Christine to continue her studies at the Academia di Bella Arti. She had finished with her formal schooling but had decided to pursue the talent for design that was her all-consuming passion. Early on, while she had still been a child, I had given her full support in the choice of study, surprised and proud that she had continued with the rigorous discipline architecture required. But then, she had lived and breathed it all her life, it was what she knew, and my pride in her had only grown. Her work and ideas had won high acclaim, though already she had encountered difficulty, simply for the fact that she was female. I thought to aid her by having arranged for a tutor outside of her classes, and outside of her father's influence.

Now I sat at one of the outdoor cafés around the school, enjoying the ambience and the warmth of the sun. Negotiations for my work had been successful, and I only waited for my daughter to join me.

"Ah, Papa. You are wonderful, and I love you!" Christine exclaimed, giving me a quick kiss on the cheek before seating herself opposite me. She was eighteen, and a stunning, young woman.

"What, my dear, have I done to deserve such high praise?" I asked, sipping the coffee a waiter had brought earlier.

"You have shown and taught me many things." She worked loose her hat, setting it aside. Her hair was pulled up, with just light curls softening the frame of her face. The blue eyes sparkled with inner fire. "You have been a most patient teacher. Thank you." She smiled as the waiter set a cup of tea before her.

Quite at a loss at what to say, I drank my coffee. "Did Signore Rossati approve your work?" I asked.

"Oh yes, he accepted me as a student, though reluctantly." Christine gave me a speculative, sidelong glance. "He was most surprised. I suppose he never had a girl as a pupil before. The poor man was nearly beside himself with nervousness." She laughed, casting me a look from beneath her lashes. "He's asked me to help with the set designs at the theater. I told him I would speak to you first."

I studied her, the eagerness in her eyes, but also wariness. "My dear child, why would you need my approval if it is something you wish to do?"

She sighed and drank a bit of her tea. "Because every time a theater is mentioned, a look comes into your eyes."

"A look?" I raised a brow.

She shook her head. "I can't explain it any better than that. Just a look that becomes a wall. You'll go to concert halls, but you have never entered a theater, not that I can remember. Why?"

Why indeed. I looked to Christine's eyes, and to my surprise, found no softness there. "I was not always an architect, my dear, and theaters bring memories," was all I would say.

She drew her brows together. "For now, I'll accept that as an answer, but we are not finished on that subject." Christine's tone had grown firm and I knew from long experience she meant what she said. Of late, she had grown impatient with my evasive answers, and my reluctance to broach certain subjects only spurred her curiosity. I knew that I could not stave off the truth from her forever, but I could not bring myself to confront the deep, murky ugliness that had brought me to this point. I loved her too much to have her walk away in fear, in disgust of the man who had become her father.

"You will come and see the new production?" She asked, her tone softening a shade.

I sighed and gave her a nod. "If you wish."

"Papa," there was warning in that voice.

"Very well child. I will come," I relented. Christine arched a lovely brow, and in that one gesture, in the tilt of her head, I was reminded of Meg and how she would question with just that one subtle gesture. A sudden pang of guilt and loneliness twisted my heart. The time for should have been and could have been was over.

Perhaps my daughter saw something in my expression, for she reached out a hand to clasp mine. "You promise?"

I smiled at her, wrapping her hands in my own. "Yes, I promise. Now, surely you did not ask me here so we could argue over a theater. What is it?"

"You will not be angry?"

"My dearest, have I ever been cross with you?"

"No, but then there has never been a situation like this." She was earnest, if somewhat hesitant. Suddenly the ribbons of her dress proved very interesting.

"What is it, my dear?"

After a few moments of hesitation, she blurted. "I met someone, at the Academia."

"Why would that make me angry?" I asked my tone softening as I saw her awkwardness in broaching the subject. Some time ago, I had come to terms with the fact that Christine would one day meet and marry a young man of her choice. It was not something I accepted lightly, or easily. That particular pleasure had been denied me. I would not deny it to Christine.

"I.... I asked him to join us for lunch, Papa." She finally let it out, glancing shyly at me from beneath her lashes.

A smile tweaked my lips. "I see," I said quietly.

"I didn't think you'd mind. He's sweet," she lifted her eyes, her fingers once again grasping mine in sudden enthusiasm. "And he's handsome."

"Humph."

"Oh, not so handsome as you!" She smiled assuaging her father's hurt pride.

"This boy of yours, does he have talent?" I asked, teasing her.

"He sings, Papa. Like an angel." The last she breathed with a lost look in her eyes.

I smiled, my heart overflowing with tenderness. It was the awakening of her first blush of womanhood, and I could not be so cruel and unkind and forbid her the first romance. My hand patted hers, eyes softening.

"If you'd like your young man to join us, he will be most welcome." A huge smile lit her face. She rose, gave me a quick kiss, and ran off.

If I had had the chance, would I have been so besotted by the first blush of love?

You fool, a voice somewhere inside me growled. _You were besotted, and you were not so young._

All that was long ago and yesterday.

Chapter 17

Christine had been right. The young man who approached our table was indeed a striking figure. Tall, lean, he carried himself with an easy grace that was natural, that bordered on regal, without any pretense. His dark brown hair fell around his face in unruly waves to just brush his shoulders, and a warm laugh seemed to come easily. Everything about him was immaculate. If this was Christine's heart's desire, I would not object too strongly.

Christine's face lit up as she saw him approach. She rose, ran to his side to lead him forward. I noted how easily her arm slid through his. He smiled warmly at her, his light blue eyes sparkling.

"Papa, this is Phillippe Antoine. Phillippe, my father, Erik Marchand." Christine made the introductions, almost breathless with enthusiasm.

I rose, waiting for the inevitable, startled reaction. Over the years, I had developed finer methods of disguising my face, but there were times when I still donned a mask. While theatrical make-up had improved, I had aged, and most times my face could not bear the irritation. The old explanation still worked. It allowed me to live in the world of men.

There was no reaction on his face except for an open smile. His blue eyes looked directly at me as he proffered his hand. "A great honor to meet you, sir. Christine had mentioned her father was an architect, but

I was unaware that it would be you. The Marchand firm is well known for brilliant innovations."

I extended a hand, which he grasped warmly, firmly. "I did not realize my reputation extended beyond the realm of architecture." I said, intrigued that a youth of no more than eighteen would have the least interest in that subject.

He smiled. "I'm afraid my parents instilled an appreciation of the arts, and not just for the theater. It's become somewhat of an obsession."

"Indeed," I murmured, and despite an earlier presumption of doubt, found myself charmed by him, and not because of flattery. Whatever his background, this fellow had breeding. It showed in every gesture, though without the arrogance of the usual sort of aristocrat.

I gestured, and we seated ourselves. While the waiter took our orders, I studied the young people at the table. It was obvious they were comfortable in each other's company and that their friendship must have developed over time, though Christine had never mentioned it. Perhaps she had been afraid to hurt my feelings. Where our easy rapport had continued, there were times when I found my daughter studying me with a puzzled expression in her eyes. It was during those rare times that I could almost see Meg in those blue eyes, as if it was she watching me, and not Christine.

To cover up the sudden swell of melancholy, I sipped the glass of wine.

"Christine told me you sing," I began, curious to draw the young man out and reluctant at the same time. However, conversation was called for and Christine had been studying me with those penetrating eyes of hers.

"Yes," he said, setting down his own glass, "a little."

"Oh that is not true, Phillippe! You sing beautifully!" Christine exclaimed, the adoration evident in her face.

Phillippe smiled at her. "Despite what Christine may say, sir, I am still training."

"Singing requires utmost discipline," I said in carefully measured tones, probing the strength of his resolve for the craft.

"Indeed it does, but it has been a passion as long as I can remember. My mother taught me, and arranged for a teacher at the Academia during my stay in Rome."

"Your mother is a singer also?"

"At one time, she sang at the Paris Opera. She no longer sings, though I believe she longs for it. My father tried to persuade her to become a voice teacher. She has refused to do so."

"And your father?"

"He is with the French diplomatic corps."

"And you? What do you wish to accomplish?"

"Oh Papa, enough, please." Christine groaned. Phillippe winked at her, as if to say it was all right.

"That depends on a set of circumstances. I will be required to fulfill my obligations with the army. It is a promise I made my father. After that, perhaps the stage. Who knows?" He said with a definite twinkle in his eyes. "However, there is an informal performance at the Academia this evening. It would be my honor to invite you, sir, and Christine, as my guests. I will be singing a few selections."

I glanced at my daughter and saw the 'please, papa' written all over her. I smiled and gave a slight nod. "Expect us this evening."

"With pleasure. Now, if you will excuse me, I must attend rehearsal. Until this evening." Phillippe rose, lightly kissed Christine's hand, executed a bow to me, and left.

Christine's eyes followed his figure until it disappeared in the crowd on the street. I could not fault her for her infatuation. Everything about that young man had been impressive.

As I watched him leave, I could not help a pang of sadness. Something in his movements reminded me of a much younger self.

Chapter 18

I escorted Christine to the Academia that evening, my resolve to attend the performance faltering when I saw the crowd. It was not the press of people that made me hesitate, but something else, something elusive. It certainly was not for the mask which hid my face. One face among many made little difference, and over the years I had grown accustomed to moving and living amidst people without the fear that had driven me to live under a theater.

"Papa, you promised Phillippe you would attend." Christine said, disappointment at my breach of a promise evident in her tone, when she noticed my reluctance to walk further.

We stood to the side of the main entrance, people jostling around us. I looked at her, and through the veil of years, saw a flash of dark brown hair and another set of eyes looking at me. I shook the memory away. Would that ghost never leave me? Would she forever haunt my dreams?

"I have no wish to spoil your evening, my dear," I said softly, my fingers gently pressing hers. "Go, and enjoy the company of your young man." Why did my heart want to melt when I looked at her?

"You will wait for me? So we can sing tonight?" Christine asked, her eyes searching my face.

"Yes, I will wait. Now off you go." I kissed her lightly on the cheek, and shook my head as I watched her disappear into the throng of young people streaming through the door. There had been a time early on, when I had had to use firm but gentle persuasion on her to practice her singing and playing. Now it was my daughter who had to persuade me. While my voice was still good, the passion it had once felt had left with the years. If not for our occasional duets, I would have left off singing years ago.

I chose to walk back to the apartment, finding the vibrant night life strangely consoling. Soon, Christine would be gone. If the looks she had given Phillippe were any indication, she would not be mine for very much longer. I would have to let her go, as I had had to let go Meg, and the other Christine.

Sighing with weariness, I ascended the stairs of the building. It was not physical weariness that slowed my movements, but melancholy. Years had flown by, and the baby I had found had blossomed into a young woman. All too soon, solitude would hold me in its grasp once more.

The rooms were utterly silent. Lighting a few candles to dispel the night, I shrugged out of the constraining coat and jacket, poured a glass of wine, and stared at the piano, and the framed picture atop it. Letting fingers trace the outlines of the face in the portrait, I allowed memories to overtake me. She had been a brief light in my darkness. I had drawn her as she had looked that last night, the rose in her hair somehow appropriate. She had been a rose, and like a rose, had shown her thorns. With one gesture Christine had plunged me back into hell, and yet, even after all that, after words that seemed a curse, a part of me still kept her close, still held onto her memory. Why? So many years past, and the memories remained as fresh as if it had all happened yesterday. Would she ever let me go? Would I let her?

Drawing a long breath, and a draught of wine, I sat on the bench and began to play, though the music felt empty and without heart. Giving the keys a strident bang, I rose, grabbed the glass of wine, and went to the study. I pulled an old, worn folio from the locked drawer of my desk, and as I laid it down, stared at the leather binding for long minutes, suddenly unable to open it, much less destroy it.

Lost in thought and memories, I went to sit on the balcony, letting the cool night envelop me in its darkness.

"Papa? Papa? Where are...?" Christine's voice finally reached me and I glanced at her as she stood in the doorway of the study, radiant and smiling. "I expected to find you playing, not sitting out here and brooding." She kissed me affectionately, her arms wrapping around me.

"I am not brooding, my dear, only thinking."

"With you, it is sometimes the same thing." She extricated herself from my embrace and disappeared into the study.

I rose, watching her with interest as she began to straighten the mess on the desk. "When will you ever realize you need a manager? How can you possibly find anything?" Her hands busied with papers and forms, and I only smiled.

"Did you enjoy your evening?"

"Yes, papa. Everyone had a marvelous time. Even Signore Rossati was there though I suppose_____." Her enthusiastic chatter was interrupted by a loud plop. The leather folio had been knocked down by her quick movements. It had landed on the floor, the sketches within scattering in all directions.

"Oh these are beautiful!" Christine exclaimed, bending down to gather the scattered sheets. "Are they from a play?" She raised her eyes to look at me.

"A production that failed." I heard myself say as my eyes glimpsed the sketches Christine held.

She knelt on the floor, now thoroughly engrossed by what she saw. I had never shown her these particular sketches, though she had seen many of my other drawings. She was the light in my life, and I wanted none of the ugliness from the past to touch her.

"This man in the mask," Christine's voice was tinged with puzzlement as she studied a drawing, then me. "It's you!"

"As I have said before, my heart, I was not always an architect." How did I even manage to speak!

"You were an actor?" There was a trace of disbelief and amusement in her tone.

I gave her a sardonic grin. "A player in a bad play." Somehow I managed to cover the pang of the heartache the memories had awakened with a pitiful joke. It had all been a terribly bad joke.

Christine studied another drawing, lifting her face to look at me. "This woman," she held out the sketch of Christine, "it's her, the one you loved isn't it?" Her voice was soft and gentle, penetrating through the fog of misery. "Is that why you don't like theaters? Because something happened between you and her?" My daughter's penetrating eyes did not waver from mine.

"It was all a long time ago," was all I could say.

Christine rose, and holding the drawings against her chest, came toward me.

Her fingers lightly brushed against the right side of my face. "You never let her go. Did you really care for her that much?"

"Please, Christine, let it be." Anymore gentle probing from my daughter and I would break.

"All right," she acquiesced, turning her back to me, and began to place the sketches back into the folder. At last straightening from her work, Christine turned to face me. She twined her arms around me, and laid her head against my shoulder. "I wish you could have been as happy as Phillippe makes me." She sighed, holding me close.

I caressed her hair, savoring the comforting embrace. "You like him that much?"

"Yes, papa."

"Then, my dear, you have all my blessing to pursue your dream." I held her for a long time, stroking her hair. After all these years, she was still the balm that healed me, that chased away the demons of the night.

Only after Christine left, did I note the drawing that stared back at me from atop the binding of the folio. It was not mine, but my daughter's. Seeing it, my heart squeezed with a mixture of love and regret. In the picture, Meg looked back at me, smiling, as if she held some secret she would not share, and in my mind I heard the faint echo of her voice calling, *"I will always be here."*

Chapter 19

Over the following weeks, our relationship with Phillippe developed into a convivial fellowship. He became a fixture in our lives, and Christine glowed whenever her young man was around. Always respectful of her, Phillippe treated her kindly and my doubts and hesitation toward him dissipated. He was what she wanted. It was evident from the way she held his hand, the way her eyes lit up when he was near. When I heard him sing, I had to concede that he indeed had talent. He had a strong, tenor voice that even now, at his young age, would make a powerful presence on stage.

I gave them what privacy I was able, and still maintain a watchful eye. Most times the two of them were either at the Academia, or exploring some corner of the city. Occasionally, they would stop by the offices and invite me to an impromptu lunch. There was nothing about this young man and his conduct toward my daughter I could object to.

It was not a surprise then, when late one afternoon, I came home to hear their voices coming from the salon in counterpoint to the strains of the piano. They were laughing. Having no desire to interfere, I made my way to the study, letting their music and voices float to me. I smiled. They were certainly good together.

I threw the coat and hat on a chair, poured a glass of wine, and eased from the day's labors, when I heard Phillippe's voice.

"Non, non, ma chèrie. That one will not do. Let's try this. It's something my mother taught me." A few stray bars of music accompanied his voice before he plunged into the melody.

With the first words, the world crashed around me. It could not be! The Fates could not be so cruel! Would they never let me be?

The song continued, though in the rising blackness of fury and anger that swept through me, I could not hear or see. Christine's voice had joined his in the duet, but all I knew was the rage that consumed me. Two others had sung this, two, who years ago, had earned my scorn and vengeance. I had been there, overheard them, as they declared love for one another, as she had betrayed me.

Gasping for breath, I clenched a chair for support. The pieces fell into place. The mother an opera singer, the father a French diplomat. All had been before me, and I had not seen!

So, they had made a son, Christine and Raoul, and he was here, in my house, another de Chagny stealing my Christine. No. He would not steal her, not this time! Never. Never!

The music had finished, and their easy laughter floated to my ears. Blind, black fury seized me.

"Never!" I shrieked, slamming open the door to the salon. The glass panels shattered with the force of impact as they slammed against the wall.

"You will never have her! Get out! Get out of my sight!" I screamed at the boy sitting behind the piano, slamming the cover down. Its crash echoed in the sudden stillness.

Two sets of eyes stared at me in stupefied wonder. The boy clutched his hands to his chest, not daring to breathe. He had barely pulled his fingers from the keys before the cover slammed down. In my fury, I wished I had broken every one of them.

"Out! Out of my house! You will not steal her from me! Not this time!" I cried in rage, reaching for the nearest object to hand. It made a satisfying crash against the wall. Others followed. Even consumed by all encompassing pain and anger, I noted Christine hustle a bewildered Phillippe out the door.

My wanton destruction ceased as quickly as it had begun. I stared at the ruins of statuary and mirrors, stared at my daughter as she stood in the doorway, watching me, impassive.

"You will never see that whelp again." I looked away from her, breaking to pieces inside.

"Why Papa? What has he done?" She was perfectly calm, her voice never betraying the confusion she must have felt. Her eyes never left me.

"I forbid it! It is enough!"

"No. All this time you've..."

"No questions! You will obey me in this matter!" My anger was far from over, but her calmness seemed to quiet the turmoil of my heart.

My daughter came to me, unafraid, standing her ground. "If you ask me to do this, father, please explain why."

How could I? How could I tell her I did not want another Christine stolen from me? "In this one thing child, please, obey me."

"That is something I will not do!" She cried back at me. "Not without an explanation!"

"You will not see him, and that is final." I grabbed a chair for support. Suddenly the weight of the years was too much.

"Father," Christine's voice was ice behind me. "If you do this, and won't tell me why, I will hate you for the rest of my life."

So there it was, a choice. Bare all the ugliness, or lose my daughter by my own hand.

Choking on a rising sob, I sank into the nearest chair. The silence in the room was absolute. I had lost Meg and the other Christine to my hands. I would not lose my child that way.

I looked at my daughter, at her expectant face looking at me with love and affection despite the destruction surrounding us. There was no doubt in her eyes, only an appeal for understanding. So I told her, the whole sordid mess we had made, Christine, that insolent boy, and I. I did not leave anything out.

The sun was rising by the time she kneeled beside me, and took my face in her hands.

"Look at me, Papa. Papa. Look. At. Me." Each word was distinct, finally penetrating the fog in my head. Eyes reluctantly focused on my daughter's face, on eyes that looked back at me with all abiding tenderness.

"I will never leave you, Papa. You will never lose this Christine." She kissed my forehead, gathering me to her breast. For a long time we sat together, Christine holding me, as fifty four years of bridled despair, torment and pain dissolved in anguished, shattering sobs.

Chapter 20

I don't know what she told the boy, or anyone else. I found myself at our villa with Christine at my side. She was daughter, nurse, and companion. She allowed no one outside the staff to see me, and only her gentle insistence occasionally probed the malaise I wandered through.

We walked in the olive grove, or sat quietly in the herb garden, her companionship comforting in the quicksand of emotional turmoil. During evenings filled with Christine's music, I found hazy memories filling my head, yet I could not find focus or purpose, and my frustration only grew. Something vital to my life was missing yet I could not recall what, or why it should be important. Often I found my hands reaching toward the piano keys, only to hover just above without touching them. I remembered what they were for, but I could not recall what to do. I would turn away in disheartened defeat, Christine watching from a distance, concern furrowing deep lines in her brow.

It was early one evening and I was reading in the library when voices drifted to me through the open door leading to the portico. One I recognized as Christine's, the other was a man's.

"How long can you possibly stay here like this? It's been nearly two months. Rossati is furious and worried, and everyone else is in an uproar. I can't hold them off for too much longer, not with vague excuses. You have to come to Rome, sooner or later. I would rather it'd be now."

"I can't leave him."

"He's a grown man. You have a staff."

"You don't understand. I can't leave him."

"Hire a nurse then, but you have to come to Rome. At least put in an appearance."

"He's my father. I will never abandon him. I promised."

There was a long pause. "Promises. They have a way of getting back at you." A long, drawn out sigh accompanied the words.

"You don't want to join the army, do you?"

"Never thought about it much, and never cared, until I met you. Now, it's the last thing on my mind, but it is what my father expects."

"I wonder if they all have expectations."

"I don't know about all of them, just mine. All he's ever asked of me was that I serve my country. The rest was up to me. My mother went along with his wishes, more I think, because it was the one thing my father really wanted then any love of country or duty. I think somewhere the two of them made an agreement about me and I find myself in the middle."

"It must be hard to be torn like that."

"Sometimes. I think my father was shocked when he realized I could sing. That I actually wanted to. I remember him staring at me almost as if he didn't know me. It was the only time I recall my mother arguing with him. He acquiesced to her wishes to train me, but I think it broke his heart. That's why I agreed to the army business when he asked me."

"I don't think my father ever expected me to have an interest in his business. I think it was quite a shock when he realized I had talent for it."

"It is unusual." Their light laughter was followed by a drawn out pause. "You need to go to Rome, at least for a little while, at least to appease Rossati."

"How can I? My father's ill, and if I meet with his staff, they'll crucify me."

"Your father didn't teach you all this time to be strong for you to back out now. I don't think he'd want to leave his business in the hands of those vultures, do you?"

"They're good men."

"They may well be, but they still need direction."

"I'm terrified. I wouldn't know where to begin."

"Surely in your experience, you know some of these men, and they know you. At least make an appearance so they know the firm, their position, is secure."

"It still does not solve the problem. I can't leave my father."

"Christine, your father's business is at stake."

"I don't know that I can do this. Wouldn't a letter suffice? A letter that Signore Rossati could give them?"

"Rossati doesn't have the influence you do. Go down there, let them see you, tell them your father's recovering, and come back. That's all."

"That's all." She sighed. "What about him? How can I possibly leave him?"

"You two have a relationship I don't understand. What is so difficult about leaving for a few days? You have a houseful of staff that can look after him. You need to go to Rome."

"It's not the same. I promised my mother I wouldn't leave his side."

"Your mother?"

"I can't explain. Not now. Help me. What do I do?"

"I can't give you an answer. You have to decide what you need to do, what is best for both of you. Parents never make it easy, do they?" A good hearted chuckle followed the statement. "Come, I need to stretch my legs. We won't solve the problem here."

"No, you go ahead. I'll sit here a while."

"All right. Think about it Christine. You have to make a choice."

I rose and walked toward the open door, watching the shadowy figure of a tall youth disappear into the shadows between the buildings.

"Who was that?" I asked Christine, glancing at her, noting the worry etched on her brow.

"A friend," she said, eyes fixed on the spot of shadow where the youth had blended into the night.

"Your mother," I ventured slowly, "she is well?" I did not know who this person Christine had mentioned should be, or why the very mention of the word 'mother' stirred a pang of undeniable yearning for someone lost to me.

Christine looked at me, eyes softening, a small smile on her lips. "Yes, Papa, she is fine. She worries about you."

I nodded, trying to remember a face but it was lost in hazy memory, and all I could feel was emptiness. I sat down next to my daughter on the bench, the warmth of her hand entwining mine a succor of comfort.

"This business in Rome, is it that important?"

"Yes, Papa, it is." Her reluctance in admitting it was evident in the tightening of her fingers against my own.

"Then you need to do as your friend suggests." I returned the reassuring pressure of her fingers, glancing out into the darkness. The youth was no longer there, though I knew he would not be too far away. Something about his walk, about the way he had carried himself was familiar, though I could not remember why.

"What about you? I don't want to leave you here by yourself." Christine turned her eyes on me.

I smiled a little for her. "I'm hardly alone." As I looked into her eyes, I vaguely remembered an echo of a voice calling to me once in the wilderness of a nightmare, a voice that had tried to chase away the demons of nightmares. Now the voice seemed to speak through the eyes of my daughter, and its resonance, for a moment, filled my heart with warmth.

"Do what you need to do, Christine. I am not going anywhere."

She sighed, leaning against me. I wrapped my arms around her, and we sat on the portico, listening to the music of the night.

Chapter 21

"Are you out of your mind!? He tried to kill me!" The boy's voice had an undercurrent of genuine disbelief.

I glanced at the two young people standing together in the farthest corner of the salon, trying to ignore their hushed whispers. Instead, I concentrated on the newspaper spread over my knees, but their subdued tones had risen, and the boy's exclamation made me raise my head and watch their by play with curiosity.

"Of course not," Christine tried to soothe him. "It was a misunderstanding."

"Misunderstanding!"

"He thought you were someone else." She said quietly.

"I thought you were my friend, not_____."

"Please!" Her voice cracked inside the room like a pistol shot. The young man shot me a glance then quickly averted his eyes.

"Christine, don't ask this," his tone begged for leniency.

"I am asking. It is the only way I will go to Rome." She caressed his cheek and smiled. "You're the one who urged me, remember? So you get your wish, and I'll know my father is safe."

"Christine," his shoulders slumped in obvious distress.

She tiptoed, kissed his cheek, and whispered something in his ear. He nodded once, his hands dropping from her shoulders. He looked in my direction, and for a heartbeat, our eyes met in a glance of speculation.

That was how, for the next several days, I found myself in the reluctant company of a young man while Christine journeyed to Rome.

It became a carefully choreographed dance of circumvention between us, though even in that large house, total evasion was impossible. Both of us were uncomfortable with the situation, let alone each other, but we tolerated the circumstances because of Christine. Often I found him sitting at the piano, playing Mozart or Chopin, even music that stirred echoes of familiarity, though why that should be, I could not fathom. On other occasions I would find him on the portico, strumming a guitar, still with that one, haunting, tune. When he would see me, he never left off his playing, choosing instead to continue, with perhaps a little more emphasis, and I left him to it, spending time in the library, his music strangely soothing and healing in the malaise that possessed me.

Gradually, as Christine's absence wore on us both, I stopped avoiding his presence and would sit in the salon, listening to him play. He had talent. That much was evident in the music that poured forth from his fingers. Whoever had been his teacher had done well in not murdering the swell of passion that flowed from his notes. For his part, the young fellow no longer gave me looks like a scarred rabbit when I came into a room, or did he pretend to not notice my existence.

At week's end, we began to share meals, though we limited our conversation to the mundane, ordinary things. Our fellowship had not progressed that far.

By Sunday evening, I began to wonder if this had been Christine's idea of retribution for whatever slight I might have caused her in the past. I sensed that the youth too, was uneasy and that he chafed at the duty my daughter had apparently charged him with.

He gave me a demure grin as he rose from the table and headed toward the piano. I shook my head, hiding a small smile. It seemed my child had exacted punishment on both of us.

His music swelled through the room, and his voice joined in with a low, humming accompaniment. It was not music from the old masters. Over the course of the past days he had played the tune many times, though I never paid much attention. Now something about the music, about the way he played, spoke to me. Rising from the table, I walked to the piano, and standing behind and to the side of him, watched his hands as they moved over the keys. Deep within, memories stirred as if from slumber, and when I looked at him, doors that had been closed, creaked open.

"No, no, no," I broke in over the melody, slipping beside him onto the bench. "It should be this way." I played the bars, humming the tune. "It is not music for a funeral. Try again."

He stared at me for long minutes, as if realizing my existence for the first time, then played the tune once more.

"Better, but you need to put more passion into the notes. He is not singing of just the night, but what he does not have, will never have." My fingers ran through the notes one more time.

Blue eyes looked at me in astounded curiosity. "How do you know this piece?" His voice was a hushed whisper as his eyes continued to study me. "It's my mother's favorite."

Somewhere in the house, a door opened and closed, and footsteps echoed against the tiled floor of the foyer.

I smiled a little. "Is it?" I questioned, my fingers finishing off the last bar of music.

"Yes," he continued to study me, eyes unwavering. "She insisted on me learning it, but somehow it always made her sad. She never said, but I could sense it had something to do with her teacher. Whenever she mentioned her mentor, it was always with affection."

"Affection?" I breathed, unable to bring myself to look at him. The music, his words, her presence in this room in him, had unblocked the fog that had been in my head for the past days. Once, I had given a young girl music, letting her voice soar with angels. Now her son returned it to me.

In the silence that followed, only the click of heels against the wood floor of the salon could be heard.

The boy dropped his eyes and shook his head, the unruly waves of dark, brown hair falling across his brow. "She never elaborated of course, and my father never speaks of it, but yes, I think my mother holds great affection for her teacher."

I sighed and brought my eyes to bear on him. In truth, he was a handsome young man, with barely any trace of Raoul to him at all. He had inherited only his father's eyes. The rest was her.

"He must have been a good teacher to deserve such remembrance," I whispered.

He chuckled. "From the way Mother tells it, he was strict, but never unjust."

I nodded, raising my eyes to look at Christine who was standing across the room, intently watching us, hands clasped tightly at her sides, her entire body tense. I threw her a small smile before turning to the boy.

"It is a teacher's duty to bring out the best in a pupil," I paused, rising from the bench. "If you have a desire for music, I suggest you follow your mother's advice. She sounds like a good woman." I gave his shoulder an affectionate squeeze, then crossed the room and firmly pressed Christine's hand, giving her a light kiss on the cheek.

"He's a good man. Hold on to him," I whispered and went outside to the portico to breathe in the night.

That evening I accepted Phillippe Antoine de Chagny under my roof, and into my house. He had not stolen my child, but given me back my music, my daughter, and Christine. That night, through his music, Phillippe's mother released me from her chains, as once, long ago, I had released her from mine. What remained between us would always be affection.

Chapter 22

Fall found Christine and me in Rome once more, in our apartment, where all trace of my destruction had been effaced.

Work continued to find me and pile on the desk, but I was no longer alone in dealing with it. My daughter was beside me, her level head alleviating the administrative part that for years, I had detested. We worked beside each other in the study, her presence a steady comfort as it had been throughout the years, except now, I found her a necessary partner.

While she continued her studies with Rossati, more and more Christine accompanied me on inspections of the various ongoing projects. While her presence was usually greeted with curiosity by the workmen, the foremen, to a man, exalted the virtues of their "Bella Signorina". I never dared ask what magic she had used to influence these men while I had been afflicted with malaise, but whatever it had been, I was glad for it, and grateful that she had been courageous enough to step in when her father could not.

Glancing at her as we sifted through stacks of correspondence, I could not hide the smile of pride that stole to my lips. What would Meg say if she knew that the child she had helped raise worked alongside her father? Did she know Christine had talent for it? With a shake of my head, I answered my own questions. Of course she would. I had not given Christine Étienne's address for nothing. I knew she and Meg corresponded, though I never inquired into the nature of those letters. I did not dare pursue a matter I myself had closed the door on.

Recovery from the affliction that had possessed me was swift, and soon I resumed obligations to the firm in full. Knowing Christine was there as support made the assumption of duties easier to bear than when I had had to leave a screaming child in a lonely house, with only a housekeeper for company.

Phillippe became an integral part of our lives, joining us for dinner or a musical evening, for it was clear that he was indeed what Christine wanted. I would not begrudge him kindness. He was not at fault for what had gone before. We had all made a muddle of things that fiery night, his parents and I. It did not mean the children had to pay for our mistakes.

I accepted him, and through him, accepted her, his mother, and the fact that a part of me still cared for her. I had wanted her voice to give life to my music. Instead she had given me music of a different kind, freeing me from a prison worse than the cage had ever been. The kiss Christine had given in that grotto had allowed for a new life, for a daughter, and now, as I looked at Phillippe sitting at the piano, his elegant hands unerringly picking out a Chopin mazurka, a son. Through her son, Christine had given me what so many years past I had wanted.

Watching him and my daughter as they sang together, I shook my head in bemusement. Their affection was evident in the way they looked at one another, the blending of their voices. It had developed beyond friendship and though love sparked in their eyes, neither had broached the subject. I suspected Phillippe was afraid to and Christine probably did not wish to hurt me.

I left them to their playing and went for a walk through the streets of the city.

When I finally cared to stop and look where my wanderings had brought me, the ruins of the Forum lay scattered about, its once glorious magnificence nothing more than shadow and dust.

A low chuckle worked its way from deep inside my chest, and soon I was quietly laughing, the sound lost in the din of traffic. What was all that we had done in that house but dust and ruin itself? Yet something had risen from those ashes, something none of us would have expected.

She had done it. With that one kiss, Christine had given life to something more than a shattered man. We were done with each other, Christine and I, but a thread would always connect us. I could now accept it for the gift it was, had always been. Whatever Fates had bound us together under the Opera house, it seemed our children would continue it, for there was only one solution to the matter that I could see.

Chapter 23

"Does he know?" I asked Christine as she came into the salon, carrying my coat, hat and walking stick. She was all bundled up in a thick coat that did nothing for her.

"No, Papa, I don't think so." She shook her head. Her dark hair was immaculately styled, with a few crystal pins sparkling here and there. "He's curious, but I haven't told him anything. It's not my place."

I nodded acceptance of that statement, and took the coat she held out to me. What the boy would make of the situation, I could only guess, but it was not my place to reveal his parents' secrets. If he chose to pursue the matter, he would puzzle out the tangled web soon enough.

"Time to go, Papa," Christine commanded, thrusting the hat and stick at me.

"You are a cruel task mistress," I murmured.

She smiled. "When it concerns you, yes, Papa, I am. You would not want me to be any other way. Now, no more hesitating. We will be late."

I smiled at her and put on the hat. Her hold on my arm as we left the apartment was firmer than usual, as if she was afraid I might bolt and run. In part, she would have been right, but months before I had given my daughter a promise, and now I had to fulfill the bargain. Even so, when I saw where we had come, I understood why she held on so tightly. I stood still, staring at the opulence of the theater, at all the people streaming in, and for long moments, just stood there, unable to move. In nearly nineteen years, this was the first time I approached an opera house. A cold shiver of dread ran up my spine as my eyes took in the crowd, the lights, and the excitement. In my previous life, I had accepted the world of the theater, had made it a refuge and a home where I could hide from the world. It had been a carefully constructed illusion, as had been the life spent in the labyrinthine tunnels of another grandiose house. Now, standing on the street, surrounded by the glitter of society, I suddenly felt uneasy, exposed, and out of my element. The grand house on the opposite side of the street seemed to mock me with its decadence and I stared back at it in defiance.

Christine's hold on my arm tightened. "This time, Father, I am not letting you go." Her penetrating eyes studied me, softening a little when I sighed.

Drawing a deep breath, I fell in step with Christine as she led us into the grand foyer. In another life, I had stalked through the foyer of another theater, reveling in my mastery of it. I had loved it and cursed it. It had been home, and a prison. In a fit of anger and desperation, I had broken the chains that had bound me to the place, broke it, and had not looked back, until now.

We made our way through the press of people toward the cloak room, occasionally exchanging small pleasantries with acquaintances along the way. I could not help the remembrance of my once former home, now reduced to a mere shadow of its once glorious self.

From Étienne's correspondence, I knew that the Populaire had not been restored. No architectural firm wanted to touch it for the sheer volume of work involved, let alone the expense. Stories of ghosts haunting the premises had begun to circulate once again, though this time I knew I wasn't responsible for their creation. Probably someone hearing rats or cats scurrying about the place had given rise to the new rumors. According to Étienne, a new theater had been built not too far from the Populaire, but it was nowhere near the capacity or status that the former had achieved. Several members of the French government had begun a renewed effort to have the Populaire restored, the loudest among them a certain Comte de Chagny. Inwardly I chuckled at that. He would have that place restored? If so, he was a bigger fool than I thought.

"Papa, you haven't heard a word I said." Christine's voice at last penetrated through my thoughts.

"I am sorry, my dear. I was only thinking." I covered my lapse with a smile, thinking my eyes deceived me. The elegant beauty standing beside me could not possibly be my daughter.

She arched a delicate brow at me. Her elegant white gown sparkled, setting off the ruby pendant at her throat to good effect. She smiled, and laying a hand on my arm, Christine kissed my cheek. "You will not brood tonight. I forbid it." With that, she led the way up the grand staircase. A hazy memory clawed its way to my mind as we walked the steps. I shook it off, preferring to smile at my daughter instead. This was what I wanted to remember, the love of my child, her smile, her companionship.

We were seated in a private box, and a few minutes later, the curtain rose. If I had thought the surprises were over, I was greatly mistaken. Christine's designs for the sets were impressive, and for this once, I was glad that she had persuaded me to abandon an evening at home. It was, after all, the opening night of this particular piece, and I could not have backed out on my promise to her any more than I could have abandoned that baby in the street nearly nineteen years before.

Philippe's performance was greeted with thunderous applause, and while pandemonium reigned in the loggia, Christine navigated our way to the dressing rooms. For a horrified moment I stopped, thinking I'd come face to face with them. Understanding my unspoken dilemma, Christine touched my cheek. "It's all right, Father. They're not here."

I gave her a brief nod of acknowledgement as she opened the door and we entered Phillippe's dressing room. He was wiping off the heavy makeup. Christine left my side to go to him, and they quietly started talking. I felt awkward, and an intruder on their moments together.

To cover my unease, I moved toward the small table that held his personal things. "It was a fine performance, Phillippe," I began, studiously avoiding looking at the two young people at the other end of the room. Among the trinkets scattered on the table, I spied a small, framed photograph of a beautiful woman with dark curls framing delicate features. It was a face I would have known anywhere. After all, I had taught her to sing. I allowed a half smile to form and chanced a glance in Phillippe's direction. He had finished combing his hair back in place and reached for the jacket Christine held out to him.

"Your parents would be proud of you," I said, eyes studying him with a hint of amusement. Was it possible that over the past months I had developed a genuine liking for this scion of Raoul's?

"I think my father would prefer his son to be anything but an actor," he answered, slipping on the jacket. "He considers it beneath the de Chagny dignity."

"That may well be, Phillippe," I said, eyes once more drawn to the photograph on the table. "He may not always agree with your chosen profession, but I would like to think he at least respects your choice."

"He disapproves, mostly. I never could get him to explain why."

I shook my head, eyes firmly focused on the photograph before me. *My dear boy, how could he? How could she?*

"Is this your mother?" The raw pain I had expected at the first sight of Christine's portrait had never come. Affection remained in its place, affection for a friend, and perhaps, someone even dearer than that.

"Yes sir. Shortly after I was born, I believe," Phillippe answered, looking at me with curiosity.

"She's quite beautiful." My eyes met his. "You look like her." I brought my eyes to Christine and saw her carefully watching me. "I will see you both later. Now, I wish to walk." I moved toward the door, but before my hand could open it, Christine's fingers closed over mine.

"Where are you going?"

I looked into my daughter's blue eyes, and for a heartbeat, I saw other eyes looking at me. I shook off the vision and touched Christine's cheek. "I just wish to walk, nothing more."

Her hand on mine would not release me, nor would her eyes.

"Christine, my heart," I said softly, gently pressing her hand. "I will not leave you." I kissed her, and walked out into the silent halls of the theater. No, I would never leave my daughter. That much was certain.

As my steps echoed in the silence of the theater, a low chuckle rose from my throat and an unexpected lightness spread to my feet.

"I will never leave you." Was that what Christine had meant by giving me back the ring? Was that her token? Whatever her silent message, the fiery night under an opera house had broken the chains we had both been too blind to see. Now it seemed, new ones were forming, but I could live with those.

Chapter 24

I did not lie when I told Christine I would not leave her. It was a promise I could keep now, without hesitation. That one festering wound of the past had been healed by my children, for in truth, in a few short months, Phillippe had become like a son to me.

While memories remained, they no longer ate away at me with bitterness and sorrow. I could remember her, his mother, with fondness and love. It was far from the all-consuming, self-destroying obsession it once had been. No. Only affection now reigned where once jealousy had held sway. I could accept that a part of me would always love her, that she had awakened something in me I thought never to find in the darkness that had been my life. She had brought light into that world, and given me something I had never dared hope for. If it had taken the children to help me understand this, then I was more fortunate in them than I had a right to be.

When I returned to the apartment, I found Christine and Phillippe sitting beside the hearth and a warm fire, holding hands.

"Papa, you're back!" Christine exclaimed, running up to give me a kiss. I extricated myself from her eager embrace, smiling at her. "Did I not say I would not leave you?"

"Yes, but I was concerned. Sometimes your walks tend to last all night." Her eyes looked away toward the fire, and Phillippe.

"Christine, look at me," I gently turned her head to face me. Her brilliant, blue eyes were bright with tears. "I made you a promise. I will not break that trust." I said softly, carefully stepping out of reach of her hands. "Now," I at last shrugged out of the overcoat, "there is something that needs doing. Immediately. This very evening." I walked into the salon, keeping a stiff, formal air. "There has been far too much clandestine activity for my liking." My voice was as stern as I could make it.

Christine and Phillippe looked at me with stricken faces. "Sir, we have done nothing wrong." Phillippe rose from beside the fire, speaking in their defense.

"Papa, you know...." Christine began, assuming her most reasonable tone.

I held up a hand, throwing both of them a cold glance. "It is not about right or wrong. It is about what is proper. Enough of these hushed conversations and stolen moments." I reached for my daughter's hand, drawing her closer, and looked into her eyes. "No more secret glances. It's over."

"No," she breathed, eyes growing dark. "You can't." Her hand in mine squeezed with force. "Why? What reason did we give that you would do this?" Her eyes implored me, tears welling, but refusing to fall.

I brushed a hand against her hair, drawing her away from her young man's side, stealing a glance at him. Phillippe stood beside the hearth, watching us, reluctance to interfere warring with the need to fight for her playing across his face.

"Christine," I began quietly, only to have her turn away, effectively pulling her hand from mine.

"Not this time, Papa. You can break all the furniture you want, I will not give up the man I love!" She turned back to face me, this time the tears unabashedly falling down her cheeks.

"My dear," I said, arching a brow, gathering her hands in mine. "Who said anything about giving anyone up?"

"You said it was over! I heard you!" Christine stood defiant and beautiful. Looking at her, I could not help a smile as recollection of another defiant, young woman came to mind.

"Christine," Phillippe tried to soothe her, his eyes fleetingly catching mine, but she shrugged off his attempt as she moved beyond his reach.

"Yes, those were my words," I agreed, stealing a glance at Phillippe as he once more stood silent, giving a shrug to his shoulders, and a shake to his head. I gave him the briefest of smiles as I drew Christine closer, caressing her cheek. "But did you let me finish?" I paused, taking a heavy breath. Looking at her, so lovely, so in love, brought to the fore the realization that the moment I had dreaded had come. I had to acknowledge and accept that she would be mine no longer. With a sigh I forced down the pang, and smiled for her.

"My dear child, would you think me so cruel as to take away your happiness?"

Christine looked at me, understanding slowly filling the pools of blue of her eyes. Her lips trembled as she tried not to cry. Her arm slipped around my waist, and she rested her head against my shoulder. "I didn't want to....I was afraid...." She whispered.

"I know," I whispered back, kissing her hair. For a moment, for eternity, we held each other. I closed my eyes against the swell of desolation and love for her that swept through me as I released her from the embrace.

Smiling gently, I lifted her face to look at me. "No more sneaking around, no more stolen kisses. I will not tolerate it in my house." I glanced over at Phillippe. "If there are to be romantic rendezvous, then I want them to be between husband and wife." The words did not come easily, but the look of happiness and joy in their eyes was reward enough. The ache in my heart was assuaged by Christine's smile and kiss to my cheek. Holding her hands in mine, I led her to Phillippe's side, and taking her hand, I placed it in his. "I give you my child. Make her happy."

Chapter 25

It was over. Mercifully, it had been brief, and quiet. While the singing and dancing in the house continued, I stole a few quiet moments in my study.

There had been no question about where to hold the wedding. Since I would not venture near Paris, let alone the de Chagny estate, Christine had proposed an elegantly simple solution. A small, private wedding at the villa, and the big affair at Phillippe's home. He agreed to the plan, not overly questioning the reasons behind it. No doubt his curiosity was piqued by my refusal to travel to France, much less his parents' estate. My own excuses in that matter did not make the situation clearer, but he accepted them, more out of politeness than real understanding. I suspect he was too busy with rehearsals for a new opera to pay much attention to details. The intense schedule of preparation did not leave the young man time for anything. When I was able, I took Phillippe in hand myself, and I was relentless. Never mind that he was family. I showed no favor, no mercy. He would either succeed or not. The choice was his. At one point, Christine had to use her gentle persuasion to allow us a respite.

"Please, papa, my ears are ringing," she said softly one evening, kissing my cheek. "And you two have been at it for hours. You need to eat." Phillippe and I left off, exchanging a smile, only to pick up later. Christine had shut herself in her room when we picked up again, only to join us a few minutes later, her voice lifting above ours, eyes flashing. It was midnight when we finally ended, and the three of us enjoyed a small meal. We laughed over tidbits of gossip, united in music, in spirit, in heart.

My eyes now glanced at the framed picture on the desk, fingers tracing the lines of the so well remembered face. With my discovery of Phillippe's identity months before, I had been careful to keep any sketches remotely connected to the past well away from his sight. Even the portrait of Meg holding a six month old Christine on her lap had made its way into the crammed study at the villa, for I could not be too far from the warmth of those eyes, and the softness of that smile.

As I looked at the sketch of Phillippe's mother, my heart swelled with affection and gratitude for the woman who had given me so much more than I had ever had any right to ask. A stray tear made its way down my cheek, and I accepted it, even savored it.

A soft knock on the door broke my reverie.

"Father? I thought I'd find you here. Are you all right?" Christine floated toward me, a vision in white satin and lace, her own creation. Diamond studs sparkled in her ears, a gift from her husband. Around her throat she wore the ruby I had given her years before. She was a stunning young woman, cultured, poised, educated. I was proud that she was my daughter, that she had accepted all those lessons. Most of all, I was grateful to her for the love she had given me, the life she had allowed me to live.

"Yes, my dear, I am quite all right," I said, reaching for her hand, smiling lightly. "I was just saying 'Thank you' to a friend."

She frowned slightly, her eyes darting to the portrait behind me. "Christine? Why? I thought she hurt you."

I gently squeezed her hand. "Without Christine, without the heartbreak, I would never have had you, never would have found a family." I paused, looking at her, filling my eyes with her. "It's your wedding day. You need to be with your young man, not your maudlin father."

She smiled at me, kissing me on the cheek. "I love my father, and I want him to dance with me." She drew me after her into the main hall, where the celebrants cleared the floor.

To the strains of a waltz, Christine and I danced through nineteen years of memories.

Chapter 26

Before they left on their extensive trip to France, I presented my gift to the young couple.

Phillippe was intrigued by the leather folio while Christine raised a brow in my direction when I passed the leather binding into her hands. She had lived and breathed architecture for too long not to know what the folder contained. They opened it, eyes widening in wonder.

"Yours, wherever you wish," I said, watching them leaf through the plans.

"Oh, it's beautiful!" Christine breathed, scanning the layouts. It was a house for the two of them, and their children. I would build it wherever, and whenever they wanted.

"It is quite impressive, and we are grateful," Phillippe spoke softly, eyes drifting to Christine. "However, it seems my wife has something else in mind." He smiled wickedly.

It was my turn to be curious. My eyes too, turned to Christine. Under the weight of our combined gazes, Christine shook her head, closed the folio, and turned on us.

"Do you want the practical or sentimental reasons?" Her eyes flashed, daring us to respond. By mutual agreement, Phillippe and I remained silent. Her tone softened when she spoke.

"Phillippe is a singer. He will travel considerably, and often. He will also have to fulfill his duties with the army. I do not want to live in an empty house, and I do not wish to be alone. You, Father," she gave me a pointed glance, "will need assistance with the new business you've taken on. You will require someone who is close to you, who is familiar with you to scrutinize the work of your managers. I have been around your work long enough to know what needs to be done, and how. The foremen know me." She smiled dangerously. "They know not to trick me. Besides," she took a few steps closer to me, her blue eyes fixing me to the spot. "I made a promise once. I mean to keep it. Phillippe?"

He handed her another folio which Christine thrust into my hands. "We will accept this, Papa, if you build it." She finally smiled.

I opened the binder, glancing through the sketches. They were hers, with all the fine detail included. They were designs for an addition to the villa, accommodations for a small family.

"Very well," I said, closing the folio. "The terms are agreed on. When you return, it will be waiting for you." I did not even attempt to argue my daughter's logic. Long experience had taught me that I would lose, regardless. What she had said regarding my businesses was true, and whether I admitted it or not, I could no longer work alone. If assistance was required, I rather it would be someone I trusted implicitly and I could not think of anyone better suited for the position than Christine. For selfish reasons, it would be a continued joy to have her around me.

"It seems, Monsieur, that you and I have been caught in the same web." Phillippe murmured conspiratorially, glancing with affection at his bride. Her back was to us as she straightened piles of documents on my desk.

"Indeed."

"Oh yes," he winked at me, "her name is Christine, and she used a similar argument on me." Phillippe chuckled. "And no, I couldn't find anything to fault her logic there either."

We laughed together, our voices ringing through the peacefulness of the villa.

Chapter 27

It was May of 1890 when I met Christine at the dock in Naples. She had returned from her trip, ebullient and alone. For tortured minutes as I watched her descend the gangway, I thought the worst. Seeing the devastated look on my face, Christine dashed the worries away with an enthusiastic embrace, a smile and a kiss.

"No, Papa, nothing like that." She chuckled, pressing her lips firmly against my cheek. "Phillippe had to stay for a while longer. Some family business. He'll be here in a few days." She wrapped her arm firmly about my waist.

Our journey to the villa was quick, during which Christine regaled me with stories of Phillippe's triumph at the theater, the various sights they had seen, and gossip from the streets. One item remained strictly off our agenda, the grand affair at Phillippe's home. While I could accept his parents as distant shadows and tenuous family links, neither would I actively seek them out. It was enough that our children united us in a way none of us would ever have expected.

We arrived at the house to be greeted at the door by nearly everyone who worked at the estate. Once more, as on that day when we had first come to this place, I felt awkward that such affection be bestowed on us by all these people. One by one, the women enthusiastically embraced Christine, while the men gave her respectful nods and bows. The warmth and love these people had for her was genuine, as over the years, Christine had become a part of all their families.

An unexpected swell of love I had only for my child filled my heart as I watched her laughing over a joke with the farm hands. The four months of her absence had been long ones, but business and work had kept me occupied. There had been letters of course, a whole profusion of them. Almost every day there had been a note. Each had been read and saved. Even though she was mine no longer, and was another man's wife, a part of me longed to keep my daughter close. I had let her go, yet she had returned to me, and I was glad that my days would not be filled with solitude.

"Papa?" Her voice broke into my thoughts. We were standing on the portico. The welcoming party had dispersed, and we were alone in the warmth of the early afternoon.

"Yes, my dear?"

Christine's eyes studied me, as if weighing the next words. "I met her." Christine's voice was quiet, subdued. I watched as she struggled to find her way.

Of course once I had become aware of Phillippe's identity, I had known that such a meeting would be inevitable. My two Christines, face to face. Life presented interesting ironies.

"I wanted to hate her for what she did to you, Papa, but I couldn't. I just couldn't." Christine embraced me, putting her head on my shoulder.

I held her tightly. "I never did my heart. How could I? She gave me a daughter and a son." I kissed her, still holding onto her.

"She is beautiful, and quite charming, for a Comtesse."

We stood on the portico for long minutes before moving into the house. We did not mention Christine or events in France again.

After a leisurely meal, I led my daughter into her new residence. I had followed her designs, with a few embellishments of my own added on.

"Oh Papa, it's wonderful!" She exclaimed as we walked into the main bedroom. I had had it completely furnished. Fresh bouquets of flowers and herbs stood in vases placed around the room, lending the surroundings a delicate, welcoming scent. "You remembered Madalena!" Christine picked up the well worn doll from the bed.

"How could I not? We have been through quite a few adventures, she and I." The poor thing was nearly in shreds, but I had never had the heart to part with it. In my mind I could clearly see and feel Christine's delight as she had freed the doll from its wrappings that one birthday. Something else too had held me back from consigning Madalena to permanent exile. When I looked at the threadbare clothing of the doll, I saw Meg and Maryanne, and how lovingly the women had sewn each stitch. For that alone, Madalena stayed.

"Come. There's more."

Christine replaced Madalena on the pillow, and I led her toward another room. This one was barred by a door wrapped with white ribbon. At Christine's curious look, with a flourish I produced scissors, and in an echo of a few years past, she cut it, entering the room. Her eyes went wide and only an indrawn, startled 'Oh' revealed her surprise.

A hand carved cradle stood beside the window, and the rocking chair next to it overflowed with knitted and hand sewn blankets. A large basket filled with clothes and toys stood on a low table. There was even a wooden horse, patiently awaiting a future rider.

Everyone from the estate had made something for her, and her future children. It was all here, all their love, all their goodwill. On a shelf beside the door stood the toys I had made for her when she had been small.

"Oh I don't know what to say!" She cried, the tears from her eyes falling unchecked. I wrapped an arm around her and led her back toward the main hall.

"They all love you, my heart. They are all glad you will stay." I hugged her closer, chucking her under the chin. "None is happier than I, my dear. The work over the past months has been strenuous for your old father. I need assistance promptly."

She smiled through the tears, knowing I was drawing her attention away from the room above. She nodded. "Fine," she sniffed. There was something in her eyes when she looked at me that gave me pause.

"What is it?"

Silence

"Christine?"

Suddenly she hugged me fiercely and smiled. "There will be a baby here soon, Papa."

Chapter 28

As massive transformations swept the world, so too, did they overtake the estate. I purchased a motorcar. It allowed for faster and more comfortable travel. In the intervening years, being bounced around in a carriage had lost its appeal. I now preferred the comfort of trains and the new motorcar. I also had a second telephone installed at the villa, as one was no longer sufficient. Since Christine worked alongside me, we both required quick and ready access to contactors and worksites to carry on our business.

The most significant differences were, of course, with Christine. They intrigued and bemused me. I marveled at the changes brought by her growing baby. While most days she would be fine, there were bouts of sickness and moods and oddest cravings for the strangest combination of foods. The women of the estate clucked around her like mother hens until one day, not wishing to hurt their feelings, Christine begged my interference in the matter.

She accompanied me to the worksites as much as her condition would allow. Acting in the capacity of my chief manager, Christine took careful note of materiel, contractors, and men working particular jobs, while I consulted with the foremen and engineers. Later we would confer and decide if anything needed to be remedied at a particular site. I found her quick and sharp mind an invaluable asset, not only because she was my daughter, but because somewhere, in all the years, she had become an indispensable partner in the business, and my life.

As the months wore on, and Christine grew bigger, she stayed closer to home, electing to work from the office at the villa. It was safer for her, easier for me. I had never cared for the administrative part of the business. I was most content mixing mortar and laying stone, even after all these years. Sometimes it was the only way to show the youngsters how it was done.

When Christmas came, Phillippe arrived, taking a much deserved break until the baby came. The new opera had been a success, and his popularity with the audiences had only grown. Even the reviewers, who made or broke careers with one stroke of their pens, did not seem inclined to find fault with the young man. After my first, reluctant attendance at the opera the previous year, I had now seen him on stage several times, and with each performance, he only improved. He would have a most interesting career.

With Phillippe's arrival, we now waited for a signal, none more eagerly than Christine. Poor thing waddled and could barely stand up once she sat down. The doctor had been alerted, and everything was in readiness.

I finally could stand the gloomy silence that had fallen over the salon no longer. The young couple had not spoken to each other in hours. Phillippe was reading, Christine flashed him murderous looks, and I was tired. I sat down at the piano and played a few bars of something light before plunging into a Mozart sonata. Anything was better than the tension filled silence.

"Enough you two, you would bore a brick to tears. Come," I waved them toward the piano. "Sing for me." I played softly, trying to entice them out of their reverie. "Sing!" I cried, banging the keys.

The sudden noise had the desired effect. Phillippe dropped his book and Christine flashed her eyes at me. "That's better. At least I have your attention. Now," I smiled at her. "Stop accusing your husband with your eyes for your condition. If I understand correctly, there must be two involved to achieve your present state. You are just as guilty as he." All the while, my fingers teased the keys, bringing out light, airy notes. "Phillippe, pay heed to your wife." I brought forth a waltz.

With a penitent smile, Phillippe offered Christine his arm. She took it, and soon smiles and laughter replaced gloom. After a couple more dances, Christine tapped me on the shoulder, extending a hand. "You owe me a dance, Father."

Exchanging duties with Phillippe, I escorted my daughter to the floor. As the notes filled the air, and we turned to follow the melody, Christine's eyes fixed on me.

"I'm scared, Papa. So terribly scared," she whispered.

"It will be all right, my heart," I replied, trying to reassure her, having absolutely no idea what was ahead for her, except pain.

"Please stay with me," she pleaded, tears welling in her eyes.

"Christine, it's not my place."

"Please! You must. I'll feel safe with you. You've always been there."

I remained silent, not quite certain what to do. I could sense her fright but this was totally out of my depth.

"Don't leave me with a stranger!" She cried, clinging to me, tears falling down her cheeks.

Torn, I held her, signaling to Philippe. He left off playing, and came to us.

"Papa, please!"

I couldn't do it to her. I couldn't bear her fear, her pleas. I held her as closely as possible. "All right, we will both be with you." My eyes silently spoke to Phillippe. He nodded, gathering Christine into his embrace.

January 1891

to

November 1892

Chapter 29

"Why don't you want me?" The plaintive, small voice cried from behind the curtain where the slight, pitiful form huddled, shaking in fear.

"Satan's spawn! I'll show you why!" Cruel hands seized the one wrist they could reach, and without the merest hint of compassion, dragged the crying child toward the one mirror in the house.

Despite the child's protests and tears, the cloth covering his face was yanked away, and his head held in place so he could not avert his eyes from the sight that greeted him. It was more his startled surprise as the protective cloth was pulled from his face that elicited the loud cry rather than seeing his own face. His hands had felt it often enough when washing to know that there was something not right about the way he looked. Why else would his mother keep the doors and windows barred?

"Think on that, you child of the Devil. While you're at it, pray to God for forgiveness for your vile existence!" The door slammed and locks turned.

A moment later, the mirror lay shattered, yet the child's fascination had not been broken by the act itself. He bent to pick up one of the shards, turning it this way and that, examining with chilly curiosity the face that Nature had bestowed upon him. The right side of his face had a half melted, puckered look to it, as if it had been burned in a fire, with the skin never healing properly. It had never acquired a natural skin tone, remaining an angry red, as if in echo of the growing pain and anger within the boy. There was no hair to mark his brow, or any that covered that side of his scalp. Only a few tufts of light, brown hair grew there, and they were not enough to cover the damage that extended beyond his ear.

He dropped the piece of mirror. Little hands scrambled for the cloth that had been so rudely tossed aside. Tears ran in rivers down his cheeks, but he would not give voice to them. It would only bring more harangues, and another night locked in the cellar.

"Oh never mind that child, come with me. She doesn't know what she's doing half the time," the kindly, feminine voice muttered as hands gathered up the boy and carried him from the room. "You'll always have a friend in old Mary. I'll always be here."

"*I'll always be here.*"

"…..here."

"Humph?" I groaned as none too gentle hands shook me awake.

"The baby. It's coming."

"Baby?" I asked, turning onto my back, prying eyes open to see Phillippe bending over me. For a moment I stared at him, mind unable to sort through the fog of uneasy dreams.

He chuckled. "Yes, baby. Christine's baby. It will be here today."

"Baby! Oh Mon Dieu!" I sat bolt upright and realized that I had slept on the sofa in the library, in all my clothes.

"That must have been some dream," Phillippe said dryly, watching me.

"More like a nightmare," I said, running a hand through disheveled hair. It had been a long time since I had dreamed that particular dream. Old Mary. She had been Mother's companion until _____. I shook the thought aside. That path led nowhere.

"The doctor?" I inquired, still recovering from a restless night. It was useless to even straighten the clothes.

"Already here, along with the nurse," Phillippe laughed lightly. "Christine refuses to let him near her until you have a talk with him." He handed me a steaming cup of coffee. "It should be a most interesting day."

I nodded thanks, drained the cup, and stretched. My body felt as if it had been run over by a dozen horses. A glimpse out the window told me daylight was still a long way away.

As if reading my thoughts, Phillippe announced, "It's four in the morning."

I shook off the lethargy, and gave him a half hearted grin. "Tell your wife to please not strangle the doctor. We may have need of him later." I made for the stairs, Phillippe following close behind.

"For the baby?" He asked, concern drawing his brows together.

"No. For us," I threw over my shoulder, running up the steps to the study to change into clean clothes.

If I knew my daughter at all, it would be a most interesting day indeed.

"Signore, this is most irregular. The husband perhaps, but you?" The doctor gave me a quizzical look as if to underscore the fact that I had gone totally mad. He was a good man, qualified, and well known to all the members of the household. He had taken care of fevers, babies, and broken bones for years. It was my respect for him which made me swallow the sudden swell of anger.

I signaled him to join me in the corner of the room. "It is my daughter's wish that we stay." I said in an undertone so Christine would not hear.

Phillippe sat beside her, holding her hand, softly singing a folk song from the South of France.

My voice softened when I looked back at the man who would bring her baby into this world. "She is frightened of what is to come."

"Understandable. Most first-time mothers are," he agreed.

"It will be easier for her if we stay." I was not backing down.

Reluctantly, he nodded assent. "Very well. In the end, it might make my task easier as well. However, you must do exactly what I say, when I say."

"Fair enough," I nodded agreement.

We repaired to our respective posts of vigilance.

During the interminable hours that followed, and Christine's labor intensified, Phillippe and I took turns singing to her in an effort to ease her mind, to distract her from her pain. Other than the tisane I had given her earlier, there was nothing else that we could do for her. This was her struggle, and we could only support her in it.

By late afternoon, when I began to think Christine's torture would never end, she found reserves of strength somewhere to follow the doctor's instruction to push. The stream of colorful curses which she let loose would have made gutter rats blush.

Phillippe and I exchanged glances as she fell back against the pillows for a minute's respite.

"Now. Again." The doctor instructed, and as we lifted her, new curses reigned down on us. This time, we were unable to hide the slight smiles that united us. I would never have believed my daughter capable of such language.

Christine grunted and struggled, her hands gripping ours in a death grip. Through clenched teeth, a muffled groan escaped her, followed by a child's lusty cry.

We eased her back to let her rest. Phillippe sat beside her, and taking her hand in his, he wiped Christine's face, lightly kissing her. She was exhausted from the ordeal, but still managed a weak smile in return.

On the other side of the room, the flurry of activity continued as the nurse cleaned and wrapped the baby in a warm blanket. The doctor came to Christine's side, smiling, and patted her hand.

"You did well, signora. You have a healthy girl. I'll come and check on you in a little while." He left the room, headed, I suspected, for the kitchen. We were all tired, hungry, and in need of respite, none more so than Christine. It had been a long day, but one that would be remembered.

Relieved that her pain was over, relieved that her child lived, all I could do was smile at my daughter, and lightly squeeze her hand. She smiled back, eyes brimming with tears.

I nodded to her and walked to look out the window. It was a few days shy of Christine's 20th birthday. As I looked out at the gathering twilight, my mind recalled scenes and memories in a kaleidoscope of color and voices. A newborn cradled in a bloody shirt, Brittany, and a family on the beach, a flash of golden hair, a young girl learning to dance, a young woman on her wedding day. Now, that same woman had become a mother.

I turned to look back into the room, eyes falling on Phillippe. He still sat with her, his wife, their heads bent over the bundle in their arms.

United after all, his mother and I, united in a most unexpected way. I sighed and shook my head. It would perhaps never be over between us. How could it? A family had grown. A family I thought never to have.

Just then Phillippe rose and approached me, his arms gingerly cradling his daughter. He grinned, holding her toward me. "We'd like you to meet someone," he said, handing the child into my arms. With a glance toward his wife, he turned back to me, his blue eyes shining. "This is Erica."

Chapter 30

Erica. Tiny, precious Erica. There was not a child more welcomed into the world than that charming, little lady.

Her arrival was heralded with unmitigated joy by everyone. The women from the estate were all eager to help settle the new arrival into her home, and the competition between the ladies grew so fierce that Christine's frustration exploded one sunny afternoon.

"You are all a bunch of clucking hens! This is my baby! Let me take care of her! And you," she flashed stern eyes at me. "You are the worst of the lot, Papa." Despite her words, she kissed me affectionately on the cheek.

Chastened by my daughter's gentle, yet firm reprimand, I left her alone with her daughter and went to the stables. I needed to do something, anything, to distract my mind from the direction it had been taking lately.

Too many visions and dreams had once again begun to haunt my sleep, though this time they were not dreams of a nightmarish past, but visions of another baby, and of a woman with golden hair, laughing, teaching me what I had to know to be a father. In those dreams I could hear the whisper of Meg's skirts, feel the warmth of her against me, and feel the exquisite taste of her lips when she had returned my kiss.

I pushed the thoughts deep into the locked recesses of my heart. What use in wishful thinking? I had let her go to make her own life. It was too late for dreams. I was fifty six and the occasional pains in my joints told me I was fast becoming an old man.

I swung into the saddle and rode out. I had everything that long past in my dungeon I had never even considered dreaming of, and yet, restlessness and hollow emptiness filled the space where joy should have been.

Erica's birth had been an occasion beyond happiness, and completed my family, yet something intangible was missing.

Even the work I had devoted years to, no longer proved satisfying. When projects drew me away from the house and family, restlessness and longing for something ephemeral and unattainable seized me, and I went through the motions, never finding the work absorbing or gratifying as I once had.

Phillippe proved to be a doting father, spending what time he could with us. His career on stage was assured, though as the weeks slowly turned to months, a guarded look suffused his eyes, and I knew his time with his family grew ever shorter. His commitment to join the French army loomed with the approach of his 20th birthday. He had made an agreement with his father and though I bore no love for Raoul, I respected his son for holding on to a promise made many years before.

Christine took up her work beside me once again, though we made certain accommodations in the villa's office for Erica's cradle and toys. Neither of us was willing to be too far from the baby, even in a houseful of staff.

Christine sensed my unease and restlessness, for after I had sung Erica to sleep one evening, she slipped an arm around my waist, and held me close. "You always loved me well, Papa. You were always what I needed."

I kissed her forehead, sighing deeply. What could I say? How could I explain to her what she had always meant to me?

Christine dropped her arm, turning to look at me, her blue eyes studying me carefully. Her fingers entwined closely around mine. "What you want, it's not here, is it?"

I squeezed her hand, my eyes probably giving her the answer, for she gave a nod and we quietly walked out of the child's room.

No, what I wanted was not here, not in Italy, not in this house. It had been left on the coast of Brittany, in a little house surrounded by a struggling garden, a place I had called home.

Chapter 31

Gold. A sea of gold, and I was drowning in it, willingly, joyfully. Soft, silken gold tickling my nose and chest as I buried my face in it and breathed in the fresh scent of her, breathed in the ecstasy of holding her against me, her arms wrapped tightly around my neck. Gold cascaded down her back and my hands could not get enough of it as they buried themselves in it. Her light laughter rang in my ears and I just held her tighter, laughing with her.

"I'm never far away. I'm always here, always with you."

"….with you." The words resonated in the silence as my hands sought once more to bury themselves in the gold, only to encounter the harshness of tangled bedding.

Eliciting a half strangled groan of frustration, I threw the blankets off of me and stared at the beamed ceiling, allowing the cauldron of feelings that the dream had stirred to subside. After all, it had only been a dream. It was always only a dream. The gold sea was gone. I had sent Meg away, back to Paris, back to a life that had been familiar to her. Had it been the right thing? Who knew? At the time, it had been the only choice.

With hands that shook with barely leashed control, I pulled on the dressing gown. My fingers could still feel the touch of that silken, golden hair. No amount of distraction would ever erase that memory. It had burned itself into me the very first time I had ever touched Meg's hair.

I wandered to the office, relinquishing any idea of more sleep. I poured a tall glass of wine, thinking to at least complete pending sketches. Architecture's discipline had always served to calm me in the past, but tonight, the ordered, measured lines of the plans made no sense at all. With a cry borne of frustration and anger, I threw wine and drawings against the wall. The sound of shattering crystal echoed my own shattered heart. Why!? Why had I let that one go when she had begged me to stay? I sighed, gathering unraveled nerves under control.

I had what I had never even dreamed. Why was it not enough? I had a daughter, a son. They had named their child for me! Why then this emptiness that consumed me?

Running fingers through my hair in an effort to quiet the demons that the dream had awakened, I glanced at the documents that had once again accumulated on my desk. With Christine and Erica in France for an extended visit to the de Chagny's, I once more had to cope with work my daughter had made so easy. She was right. I needed a manager, to not only oversee the office here at the villa, but the one in Rome as well. A rueful smile rose to my lips. Perhaps I needed a manager in my life, regardless.

On top of the usual assortment of reports and correspondence lay Étienne's letter from Paris, along with a listing of buildings available for auction. Earlier that day, we had conferred regarding our selections for possible investment. Now the addresses stared back at me, and for a reason I could not define, I circled another on the list. I dropped the pen, rose, and walked toward the window. It was only an address, a meaningless number in the tangle of Parisian streets, yet it stirred memory and feelings long buried.

The clang and clamor of the camp rang in my head, and I could smell the horses, the closeness of the tent, the oppressive, pungent smell of the crowds, their cackling laughter still hurtful in memory as it had been then, in that cage.

Involuntarily, my shoulders twitched in anticipation of the sting of a lash that would never come, not any more. How many times had I felt that lash, not only from him, the keeper, but from my own mother? She never could bear the sight of me, even with a cloth over my head.

I sighed. Her rages had been unpredictable, and I had learned early to keep well hidden from her sight. If it had not been for her companion, she would have killed me. I smiled at the bitter irony. Perhaps that might have been preferable to what came after.

I shook my head in sadness for the remembrance. She sold me, like a piece of furniture, into a life that became worse than Hell could ever be. The scars on my back bore testimony to some of it. When Hélène Antoinette Giry found me, I had been like a dog that had been beaten one too many times. Under her unflinching gaze, I turned on my keeper, and with his own lash, strangled the breath from him. The gypsy's cry had summoned the police, and in one fateful instant, a girl reached out her hand and pulled me from a cage, to safety, to shelter under a theater, sealing both our fates.

A cynical chuckle rose from my chest. I had been freed from the life of a slave to assume the life of a ghost. For even then, I knew I could not let anyone in that theater see me. So I became a shadow, haunting the halls, haunting the streets, for I had been only a twelve year old boy, with a boy's endless curiosity.

I had roamed the streets around the Opera house, knew every inch of them, above and below, especially that one particular square. Paris became my domain, my kingdom, one that in my anger my hands had destroyed.

When I left Paris, it was not with any intention of return, ever. I was finished with it, as it was with me. There would be no going back to the city that had been home for so many years.

Yet Étienne's proposal and fleeting memory had once again stirred the seething restlessness and yawning emptiness inside I had barely managed to keep at bay. The siren voice I heard in restless dreams called me across the distance, pulled at me, called me to what once had been home.

With a sigh, I turned from the window and sat behind the desk once more. No, I could not go back there. Even if events of the past lay forgotten in memory and dusty police records, there was nothing for me in Paris, nothing but shadows, and my heart.

Chapter 32

"My dear boy, if one makes a pretense of reading, one should at least bother to turn a page or two," I said, handing Phillippe a tall glass of wine.

We were in the library at the villa. Early summer had come and oppressive heat had settled in. Even during the evenings there seemed no respite from the inferno, despite open windows.

Phillippe had returned from France that very morning, alone, exhausted, with a look to him that bespoke deep concern. I had found him sleeping on the sofa in the salon in the wee hours, still in his travel clothes, his valise carelessly tossed aside. I had left him there, his state of tiredness only too familiar. Many a consultation on projects had left little time for restful sleep.

Now in the early evening, when he had cleaned and dressed, agitation and gloominess hung over his head like a cloud.

"What weighs so heavily on your mind that you worry that one page?" I asked, arching a brow.

He tossed the book aside, accepting the wine I offered with a curt nod of thanks.

"Home," he shook his head and drained the glass in one gulp. "I don't know what to make of it." He rose from the sofa where he had been sitting and walked toward the open window leading to the portico. He leaned against the wall, his tall, lean frame sagging as if in silent defeat.

"All is well, I trust?" I questioned, turning my back on him, not trusting myself to not reveal the sudden anxiety that gripped me. Christine's letters from France had been evasive, not her usual, effusive style, and Phillippe's vague explanation of his wife's extended stay with his parents had left me only with questions.

"I wish I knew," Phillippe answered. "No one is talking. My parents walk around the estate like two shadows, neither speaking to the other. Mother locks herself in her room, refusing to come out, her cries pitiful to hear. My father rages at her, though I know he does not mean to. He loves her, but her refusal to do anything, to see anyone, drives him to frenzy. He spends hours in his office, just staring out the windows, silent tears in his eyes. It's as if they are both holding some secret neither will divulge, and it's ripping them to pieces." He paused, and I had to draw a deep, steadying breath.

His words aroused cold fingers of dread that spread up my spine to seize my heart in a merciless grip. I continued to stand facing away from him, not trusting myself to move, to react. I had not thought to ever concern myself with Phillippe's parents, least of all his father, not beyond the casual, polite inquiry. However his words, and Christine's vague references in her letters, brought stark realization to the fore. Despite efforts to forget, to bury the past, the connections I had sought to sever would not let go. I chanced a glance at him. Phillippe looked out into the night, their union here in my house, under my roof, in pain, as they seemed to be. Was it possible that I could care for them, for Christine, for Raoul?

"I fear for them, Erik," he whispered. "This time, Mother was at best uneasy with Christine, and Erica's presence only elicited distress and tears. Not even Meg could calm her when she saw the baby."

At the mention of that name, I looked sharply at him. "Meg?"

He nodded. "Mother's friend, Meg Giry. She and her mother came to stay at the château to help father through this crisis." He shook his head and poured another glass of wine. "Not even she would say what had happened between my parents. Everyone walks and talks in hushed whispers to the point that I felt as if a ghost was stalking through the halls of my home." He ran a hand through his unruly hair, throwing me a small smile. "In any case, Meg was genuinely intrigued by Erica." He looked at me for long minutes, his blue eyes riveted on my face.

I dared not even breathe. If he had not yet discovered the tangled connections of his household, I would not help him.

"She said the name was an interesting choice for a girl."

I turned away from his scrutiny to refill my own empty glass, allowing a small sigh to escape as I did so. Meg was there. Good. A blessing for her friends. I drew a deep breath and closed my eyes against the momentary heaviness that had descended over me. I knew Meg would never leave a friend in pain, never be too far away from her sister.

Phillippe apparently was not finished. He left his place beside the window and walked toward the bookcases, seeming to study the volumes packed on the shelves. I turned carefully away and crossed the room toward the window. We were replaying our old game of avoidance.

"Madame Giry made an interesting remark when she held Erica. Something that at the time I thought most curious," he paused, and I wondered if he would continue when the silence had stretched beyond the limits of endurance. When he would not speak, with reluctance I took the opening he offered.

"What would that be?"

"Her exact words were 'even he is here.' A curious comment, given that it was a family matter that had drawn us to the château."

I stood still, eyes riveted on the darkness beyond the window. Hélène and her cryptic pronouncements! A woman of few words, Hélène never said or did anything without reason. Would she forever be my conscience? Was she purposefully trying to give this boy hints where his parents maintained silence? Why?

"During my stay, Mother seemed to break her silence and sadness only when I played for her." Phillippe resumed the narrative, walking past the bookcases, only occasionally glancing in my direction. "The first time my father heard the music, his face turned livid, and I'm convinced he would have torn me apart had it not been for her. I had never seen such fury in him before, but when he saw Mother's face and the tiny spark of light in her eyes that the music gave her, he only kissed her, and walked away. After that, all she wanted was the music. She hummed it incessantly, as if holding onto it for dear life, as if holding onto someone."

Oh dear, dear Christine! Still singing my music? Am I still singing songs in your head after all these years?

"What does your father say to all this?" I asked, making an effort to keep my voice steady.

Phillippe sighed. "Father fears for her. He thinks the music a good distraction to what afflicts her. He tried to persuade her to teach, to use her talent, but she refused to listen to him, preferring the silence of her room. All this seems to have unleashed a ghost that seems to hover over both of them."

A ghost! You have no idea how right you are Phillippe!

He came to stand beside me, and I dared not look at him for fear I would see her, and give way to the tears that were barely held in check. My Christine was in pain, and there was nothing I could do to help her.

"I think by the time I left, my father grew resigned to the fact that it was not his comfort Mother sought in her anguish, but that of someone else, someone who had given her music." Phillippe's voice had grown quiet and his eyes darkened with thought as he studied me. "The hurt I saw in him when he understood and accepted it made me hurt for both of them. What do I do, Erik? Neither is talking, both are in pain, and Mother cries for her angel of music. What is to be done? Where do I find an angel of music?"

Chapter 33

Long after Phillippe had gone to bed, I remained in the library, thoughts and emotions tumbling in a wild, erratic tangle.

His words had left me shaken and drained.

What had happened in his home to cause such grief and distress? Why was it I should concern myself with them, the two who had once betrayed me? Why would his mother cry for an angel of music when she knew there was no angel? That only a man had existed behind the illusion? Why hold onto music that had been designed for one purpose and one alone? Why hold onto memories when I had told her to forget?

I sighed, and walked to the piano in the salon, carelessly running fingers over the ebony wood. The crack of thunder overhead and the flash of lightning echoed the turbulent thoughts that milled through my head.

I slid onto the bench, letting fingers give voice to the unease that gripped me. Like my thoughts, the music had no reason. It was music for music's sake, something to distract me from the seething cauldron of emotions Phillippe's words had awakened.

Thunder boomed, giving voice to the turbulence churning within.

That something dramatic had occurred at the de Chagny estate and that they were in pain was obvious from Phillippe's description. Even

Christine's letters had hinted at some of this. That it should matter, that I should care, and that somewhere in my heart I found sympathy for their plight, surprised me. After all, had it not been because of them that events in Paris had spiraled the way they had?

And Meg. That name alone had sent a tremor of delight and anxiety through me. Phillippe had mentioned her last name still as Giry. Had she not married? Had I condemned her as I had sentenced myself? Would she be another ghost to haunt my memory?

Thunder cracked overhead, its anger rattling the windows, and in its wake the music swelled through the house.

Whatever had occurred, Phillippe's mother's family was around her. They would help, especially her mother. Hélène was, for all intents and purposes, Christine's mother. Hélène had cared for her as her own when the girl had come to live at the Opera house. She had continued to be a mother to Christine even as the latter had grown into a young woman. What would have drawn her to the de Chagny's in that capacity? What would have drawn all the women together to help one of their own? What would make Raoul angry? He was not one to have anger in him.

Lightning lit up the night sky with a brilliant flare of violet followed by another violent crash of thunder, as if to underscore the tumultuous chaos of the thoughts bouncing in my head.

I let the music soar, losing myself in its melody. Regardless of what had transpired in France, my rose was in pain, and there was nothing I could do to ease her from it, nothing.

The thunder and lightning faded, and rain beat against the stone of the portico in a staccato rhythm. In the house, the thunder of the piano echoed pain, hurt, and anguish. "Oh Christine," I sighed, lost in the notes that filled the space. "My rose."

"It's you," it was a whisper behind me. "You are her angel of music. You haunt her dreams." Phillippe spoke softly, slipping beside me onto the bench.

I continued to play the music that I had played for Christine when I had brought her into my world, aware of him but unwilling to let go the music. "If I could, I would not," I murmured.

"I wondered," he shook his head, quietly chuckling. "The night Christine came back from Rome I began to suspect. You played just a few bars of this but you played it with negligence, as if you knew it by heart and didn't need the notes to guide you." He paused and glanced at me from beneath his dark brows. "You never did answer my question that night, about how you knew the music when it had been something my mother's teacher had taught her." His penetrating eyes came to rest on my face. "She never spoke much of her life at the Opera, and when she did, it was only in reference to the teacher who had taught her to sing, the one she remembers as her angel of music." Phillippe shook his head, glancing away. "She never spoke of him in front of my father, but when she would tell me stories, a look of sadness always shaded her eyes, and I could tell she held special affection for this one person. It was always a mystery and I wondered what would make her so sad. What happened, Erik? What happened between you?"

The question was gently said and I no longer had the right to hide the answers from him. The young man would get no answers from his parents, of that I was certain. If I did not tell him, he would continue to probe on his own and perhaps come to unpleasant conclusions.

I rose from the bench, and poured wine, though I had no taste for it, and I would not drown the emotional turmoil in an alcoholic stupor.

"An age old story Phillippe. Boy loves girl, she loves another, boy loses girl. You know the end."

"You were in love with her?" His surprise was genuine.

I smiled bitterly, though he could not see it. I stared out the tall windows at the beating rain, the events replaying themselves in memory. Had it really been nearly twenty years since that night? "Love? I don't know. I never knew the meaning of the word, the feeling until____." With a heavy sigh I turned to face him. He was still sitting at the piano, his eyes watching me. A small, mirthless chuckle escaped me. "I believe 'obsessed' would be a better word for it. I fell under her spell and I could not let go. To me, at the time, that was 'love.'"

He lowered his eyes, as if my admission was too much for him to bear.

"Then what happened if you loved her?"

I laughed unpleasantly at his innocence. "Beyond some unsavory events, your father happened."

"Did she...did she love you?" He asked tentatively.

"There might have been some feeling," I answered slowly, shaking my head, not wishing to acknowledge the twinge of hurt that remained in remembering just what that feeling had been. "But it was not what I had hoped for," I answered, running hands through my hair, closing my eyes, resisting with sheer willpower the rising sadness the words elicited. I had thought the feelings buried. "She was young, very young, and I _____." I sighed, recalling Christine's reaction when she had seen my true face. With irony twisting my voice, I finished the thought. "What could she have possibly felt for me?"

"And my father?"

"They had known each other when they were children. He was a safe choice." Strange how easily the words came out.

He shook his head, trying to comprehend it all. "How sad, for all of you."

I clapped him on the shoulder, and shook my head. "It is long past us." I moved away, eyes roaming over the paintings on the walls. "I would like to think I have become a better man for it. It is what you make of life's experiences that count."

"Did you?" He asked.

"Did I what?"

"Make it count."

"In some small way, perhaps," I gave him a small smile, remembering a newborn cradled in a bloody shirt, and with a sigh, at long last, sipped the wine I had poured earlier.

Phillippe rose from the bench, eyes bright with sudden eagerness. "Make it count some more. Help me help my mother."

I looked into his eyes, and despite their color, saw her, pleading for me to say yes.

"You still care for her that much I know." He said slowly, studying me carefully. "It's obvious, from the way you speak of her, the way you have treated me. Help her."

"I will not deny it. A part of her will always be in my heart." I glanced sharply at him. "I will not interfere in her life again."

"You won't need to," he said as he began to pace about the room, his brows drawn together in thought, his voice becoming more firm as he went on. "Whatever happened to her, I know she will continue to be uneasy until she has something of you, something more than the music, something she can hold onto, something to let her know you live." He glanced at me, and I could almost see the thoughts race through his head. "It can't be anything obvious, nothing that would upset my father.

Something small then, something hidden in plain sight." He paused in his pacing to stand beside me, eyes locked on the portrait of his wife, as she had been at sixteen.

"What do you have in mind?" I asked intrigued that he would conspire behind his father's back, with his father's antagonist.

"It will be her birthday soon," he began, eyes narrowing as the plan in his mind came to fruition. "I believe it would be acceptable for a mother to receive a locket from her son, with his portrait in it." The conspiratorial smile he flashed in my direction was not lost on me. I raised my good brow. "A most interesting idea."

He nodded, a wide grin spreading across his lips. While he proceeded to describe what he wanted, I sketched it out.

"That should do I think," I leaned back from the table letting him see.

"Nice touch that," he indicated the drawing in question.

"You wanted her to know it's me."

"Yes, yes I did."

"I used to spend a fortune on them for her."

"You sent them?"

"Every opportunity I could. You have no idea how hard roses are to find in the middle of winter."

He chuckled. "I can imagine." His eyes grew serious. "I am sorry, Erik."

I shrugged, gathered up the drawings, and slid them into an envelope. "Take these to the address on top. It should take no more than a few days."

He nodded, his demeanor suddenly growing serious. His hand came to rest on my arm. "I am sorry, but they are fortunate to have a friend in you." He disappeared down the hall, leaving me alone with my thoughts and memories.

Friend! The irony twisted inside like a knife. I would just as soon have killed Raoul in that cemetery than do anything for his benefit. But she was hurting, my rose, and I could not leave her in anguish, not like this. Because of her, I had a family. No matter the years between us, there was still feeling where I had thought only hurt and disillusion to be. So I helped him, her son, my son, to bring Christine what comfort I could. I could do no more.

Chapter 34

"Oh Papa, it was awful," Christine's voice carried the weight and sorrow of whatever she had been a reluctant witness to. Her face, once full of laughter, was drawn and pinched with anxiety and concern. She had pulled her lustrous, dark hair into a loose chignon and moved about the small kitchen with purposeful movements. I had given the housekeeper the evening off, sensing Christine needed time alone with me.

She had arrived earlier that day, the ebullient, young woman I had known replaced by one of serious demeanor. Even Erica's boisterous antics produced a smile with difficulty on her mother's face. If anything, I noted that Christine held onto her daughter more tightly, as if reluctant to let her go. All day, we skirted around the subject of events in France, both of us reluctant to broach it, both of us too busy for a conversation. Christine and Erica had gone to see Phillippe immediately on their arrival to Rome, while I had had to finalize details at a worksite.

As evening settled, we finally found time for conversation. Erica had been put to bed with difficulty, and now, as Christine prepared a light supper for us, I poured the wine, giving her time to sort her thoughts. If anything, Phillippe's vague descriptions of events had at least given me warning. I said nothing, only watched her with interest and curiosity as she gathered the plates and silver and set them on the table.

"There was no stopping the tears," my daughter sighed, shaking her head. "Even Meg was helpless against the flood." Christine's eyes briefly met mine in a look that bespoke mutual knowledge of the woman behind that name.

"For weeks, the Comtesse walked like a ghost in the halls of her own home, pale, thin, and broken. Poor Raoul, he was at wit's end what to do for her. She refused to eat, only taking the bare minimum that maintained her function, and we had to force that." Christine said her voice filled with sorrow. She had set our supper on the table, but in truth, neither of us had much desire to eat it. I handed her the glass of wine, and side by side, we walked out onto the balcony of the study, looking out into the brightly lit, evening streets of Rome.

"After a while, he left us to deal with her," the resumption of the tale continued as we stood beside each other. For a heartbeat, I thought how, in the span of a few months, my daughter had matured. Where had my little girl gone?

"I suppose his helplessness in the face of the situation, and her withdrawal from him, angered him, and for a few days, he raged at her to get herself together. She shut him out, in her anguish crying that he had dragged her from her home to a life of whispers and scandal." Christine paused, drawing a deep breath, bringing her eyes to look at me, her hand fiercely taking hold of mine.

"Oh Papa, the look of hurt that came over his face when he heard those words, I hope to never see on anyone again. She didn't mean to say it, I am sure of that, but her words cut him to pieces." She sighed and laid her head against my shoulder. I held her lightly against my chest, giving her time to compose herself. Her words, on top of those that Phillippe and I had shared a few weeks prior, only served to confuse the already unquiet pot of feelings and suspicions stirring within me. Patience nearly at an end with the careful dance around the issue, I withdrew from Christine's embrace and looked into her tear filled eyes. "What happened, exactly?"

"You don't know?" She asked, her surprise catching me off guard. I drew my brows together in consternation. "Should I? You and Phillippe have not exactly been forthcoming with details."

"He did not tell you?"

"Tell me what? He seems as confused by matters as I am."

"Then they did not tell him. Poor Phillippe." She hung her head and looked away. "It's not something I could write about, not there, and not," she turned back to look into my eyes, "hurt you, knowing____." Unable to hold my gaze, Christine once more turned away to look out into the street below.

"What is it? What is hurting them so badly that they hurt each other?" Was that me asking that question?

"They lost their baby girl." Christine's quiet words fell like hammer blows against my heart. "She lived only a few hours. Oh God!" Her cry ended in a muffled sob as I gathered her against my chest, holding her tightly to me, the enormity of the event settling over me like a dark shadow. All my suppositions had not even come close to this. I held my daughter within the warm circle of my arms, letting her wash away the pain she felt with the tears that soaked into my shirt.

Once, I had wanted to punish them for loving each other, for hurting me. It seemed that time and circumstances had exacted a vengeance of their own. I sighed, and my arms around Christine tightened. We had all been younger then, and fools in the game life played with us. Even so, would I have wished this on them, the loss of a child? Closing my eyes against the swell of remorse, guilt, sorrow, and affection that waged a war within me, I wondered which part of me would win the silent battle, the man I had been, or the man I strove to be?

"She was so small, so fragile," Christine resumed, the tears at an end, though her voice still trembled with sadness. "They named her Antoinette." She disengaged from my arms and moved to stand on the opposite side of the balcony, eyes looking into the distance. "What do you do, Papa, what do you do when those you love hurt so much?"

I came to her side, lightly caressing her cheek. "You love them, and you help, however you can," I said slowly, looking into her tear filled eyes, and knew just which part of me had won.

She nodded and leaned against the balustrade. "After a while, even Hélène and Meg were at a loss what to do. Christine refused to let go, her tears endless. Oh, Papa it was pitiful to hear those cries."

I remained silent, allowing her to sort through the emotions that were sweeping through her. My own, I held in check. All the years would not undue the events that had led to this, nor would I necessarily want them to. They had given me a child and perhaps in a way, had allowed me to make peace with that Erik who had only wanted to lash out with the anger and hurt that had been heaped on him.

"When Phillippe came, and played for her one day, it was as if he threw the Comtesse a lifeline." Christine turned to face me, a faint smile tweaking at the corners of her mouth. "When Raoul heard the music, he stormed into the music room, fully prepared to tear Phillippe in two. Only Hélène's touch on his arm and the look in Christine's eyes when she saw him stopped him. His shoulders sagged, and with a choked sob, he bent to kiss her and walked away. We didn't see him at the château for several days after that. I suppose he needed to be away, to overcome his own pain, and to accept the fact that what she wanted, what she needed, was not his comfort, but that of her angel.

"When Phillippe played your music, it was as if for the briefest of moments, she was transported elsewhere, away from her anguish. Your songs seemed to give her a measure of solace. She wrapped herself in them as if they were blankets of comfort and none of us, not even Raoul, had the heart to take that away." Christine paused and looked out into the night, at long last taking a sip of the wine that had stood untouched on the small table beside the doorway.

"One morning, Meg came to the house carrying a small satchel, exchanging looks with her mother even I couldn't understand. She hustled Christine into the Comtesse's bedroom, and locked the door. They did not come out for the rest of the day, and what transpired, I don't know. When Christine came to dinner that evening, she appeared calmer, a little more at peace, if such a thing is possible in grief. A few days later, the courier came." Christine glanced at me, her blue eyes holding a knowing sparkle, as her lips lifted in a gentle smile. "Hélène accepted the package. I think she knew what it would contain, for she sought out Raoul, giving it to him. On opening it, his face blanched as if in recognition of something. Hélène held his shaking shoulders, whispering in his ear. He nodded, his cries of misery eased, I think, by whatever Hélène said. He gathered himself with difficulty, his hand clutching whatever had been in that packet. With heavy steps, Raoul walked to the music room where Christine sat at the piano, picking listlessly at the keys. He looked at her, nearly sagging with the weight of the sorrow, anguish and hurt he no doubt felt. Hesitantly, he presented to her what he held. She stared at it, then at him, and whatever hurt they had inflicted on one another in the previous weeks, disappeared in their embrace. He held her, and she cried in his arms."

Christine shook her head. "I don't know if Raoul was aware of the locket's contents, or if he'll ever want to know. I believe the etched rose with its ribbon was enough to let him know who sent it. With reluctance he accepted it and gave it to her, clasping it around her neck, knowing that it would ease her pain." Christine raised her eyes to mine, her hand lightly brushing against my cheek. "With that one small thing, you helped them find a way to heal themselves." She leaned in close and kissed me. "There is love there for them I think. Good night, Papa."

Christine slowly walked into the darkness of the apartment, leaving me alone on the balcony in a chaos of emotion I dared not examine too closely, and a swirl of visions that sought to overwhelm me. Only one kept battling its way to the surface, only one that eased the tumult within, only one that brought fleeting comfort in the emptiness I had carried so long.

As I turned to follow my daughter into the apartment's darkened rooms, I knew that despite my earlier claim of never going near Paris again, I would have to go there, if for no other purpose than to claim my heart. Long ago, a girl with golden hair had taken that heart when she had left a small house in Brittany. Now it was time to take that heart back again. But would she accept me after all these years?

Chapter 35

"Then we are in agreement?" I asked, as Étienne shuffled the papers back into their folder.

He rewarded me with one of his jovial guffaws, his blue eyes crinkling with mirth. "Total and absolute. I have grown a bit tired of running the business myself. It will be only for the better if we combine the companies." He shook his head. "It will be like when we started, only with more money!" Étienne laughed and I joined with him. "Was there any doubt that I would agree?" He slid the folder into the leather case beside his chair, raised his brows, and gave me a quizzical glance as he asked. "How many years have we known each other?"

"Probably longer than both of us care to remember," I answered quietly, a small smile breaking the seriousness that had come over me.

"Hmm. In all that time, have we ever had cause for mistrust?" He closed the case and finished off his coffee.

Étienne had come to Rome to finalize our negotiations for the investments in Paris, and we had taken advantage of the time to discuss the merger of our businesses as well. We sat in one of the cafés near the Forum, and having concluded the business at hand, were enjoying a little relaxation.

"If truth be told Erik, in many ways, you remain a man of mystery." He raised a brow at me, giving me one of his irresistible smiles.

"It is the magician in me. I like to keep in practice," I answered, sipping my coffee.

He laughed. "I should remember that! You led me on more than one merry chase with your mazes."

"They kept you from the galleys," I glanced at him, "and the butchers of the army."

He flashed me a smile. "I didn't know you'd be that efficient at it," he paused for effect, "or that deadly."

I shrugged, looking out into the street. "I protect my own," I said quietly, remembering just how efficient that protection had been. He and Hélène had been what constituted a family to me, and there had been nothing that I would not have done for them. Their acceptance had allowed me to live, if in a strange and distorted way. They had never judged me, though in some unspoken, intangible way, I had allowed Hélène to become my conscience. She had never questioned my activities, but did not necessarily approve of them either.

"There is one thing more," I began, not certain in my own mind whether the idea had merit, or whether it was a fool's errand built on an ephemeral dream and a hopeless wish.

"As I said, a man of mystery," Étienne raised a brow, signaling the waiter to bring another round of coffees. "What is it?"

"This," I proffered a piece of paper with an address on it. "Has it been sold yet?"

He glanced at the sheet. "It was on the list I sent?" I nodded.

He stared at the address once more. "Yes, it's near the Bois de Boulogne. I know the place. Dilapidated and very expensive. Used to be nothing but fairgrounds there before they built it up." He glanced sharply at me, his blue eyes narrowing with thought, his bushy brows drawing together in an uncharacteristic frown. "What's your interest in it?"

"Has it been sold yet?" I ignored his question.

"Not that I know of. I can call to make sure. What's going on? Or is it to be yet another mystery?"

I shrugged and tucked the note back into my pocket. "I don't know, Étienne," I admitted. "Perhaps nothing, perhaps everything," I looked away from his scrutiny, allowing my eyes to roam over the buildings surrounding us. "Perhaps it can be our first, combined interest." I gave him a weak, ironic, smile.

He studied me but I would not give him the satisfaction of discovering my secrets. I did not know myself why I asked what I did. Ever since Christine's revelations of several weeks prior, I had wrestled with uneasy dreams, chaotic, swirling emotions, and nights spent over drawings that would perhaps come to naught.

Christine had stayed on in Rome, close to Phillippe, close to me, running my offices smoothly and efficiently, while Erica managed to sow chaos everywhere. At nine months, she was an adorable terror, never too far from her mother's watchful gaze, or her father's presence. Phillippe was finishing his season with the theater and making preparations for his departure for the army in October. He and his family spent what time they had together.

If Christine noted my broody demeanor of late, she did not question it. In fact, she seemed to understand it and left me to sort the dived road that lay before me. Events in France had been sobering, for all of us. She had eventually told Phillippe as well, and after the initial burst of anger and anguish, he had come to an accommodation with his father regarding his military service and professional career.

"If it is still available, will you tell me why we'll be buying a small piece of land when, for the same amount, we could have double the property?" Étienne's crisp, clear, businesslike manner startled me from abstract thought.

I shook my head. "When I know the answer, you'll be the first to know." I rose from the chair, bringing our meeting to a close.

"Erik! I need something more than that. Investors like to know__ ____."

I cut him off with an impatient gesture. "No, just you and me."

"Erik, that's an awful lot of money." His tone had become serious with the turn the conversation had taken. He too, had given up his seat. We stood beside each other under the warm Roman sun, with the bustle of the street around us.

"I know," I answered quietly, snatches of conversations replaying themselves in my head, visions of faces tossing about as if in a kaleidoscope. Then tossing him a twisted, half smile, I amended. "Think of it as an investment." I glanced away toward the pedestrian traffic, eyes drawn to a couple surrounded by children. The youngsters jostled one another, vying with each other for a better vantage point near the railing of the archeological pit where men were busy digging up what Imperial Rome had left behind.

"A school after all, is an investment, an investment in the future." I said quietly, clapping Étienne on the shoulder, the smile widening even as the thoughts that had milled around for weeks finalized themselves in words.

"A school," he said slowly, eyes studying me as if he didn't know me.

"Yes, my friend, a school." I tapped his shoulder again. "Come to the office. We will buy our building and start planning."

"You have a thought as to what this school is to be?" His steps joined with mine as we headed away from the café.

"Not exactly, but I do have a director in mind. She will decide what she wants."

"She?" Étienne shook his head. "You are a man of mystery."

Chapter 36

Under Étienne's dogged persistence and scrupulous attention, our project progressed with speed and efficiency. The land was purchased the very day we discussed the matter, the existing building razed soon after, and within days of that, a new one began to take its place.

As per our agreement, Étienne hired men who were skilled and who needed to feed their families. With the days growing shorter, we added extra crews, giving them incentive in higher wages if they were willing to work longer than usual. Most of them agreed, and the building I had envisioned, soon began to take shape.

While the building itself presented little difficulty, it was the second part of the scheme that prayed upon my already frazzled nerves. How was I going to persuade Christine to accept, let alone run a school? What had I been thinking? What made me think she would want it, or be willing to do it? Did I even know her?

Nearly twenty years had passed since the events of that fateful night, and while the world and we had changed, still, the basic character of us remained.

Patience had never been Christine's strength, or mine for that matter, yet to be a teacher, one required loads of it. Certainly she had trained her son, and trained him well, but teaching others was something else entirely. Why did I think she would have the patience for some wild street urchins, or even be willing to find herself in their company? And if not the street urchins, even the progeny of the titled gentry could prove to be a challenge, perhaps even more so. What possessed me to believe Christine could, or would, accept the challenge? She had never been one for giving, her head always filled with dreams and visions of her 'angel'.

I had dashed those dreams and romantic stirrings thoroughly with my blind and bitter jealousy, but then I had been twenty years older than she, and no longer satisfied to play the invisible, ephemeral 'angel'. I had wanted, needed, a lover of substance and by the time things began to spiral out of control, I was no longer content to be only a dream, an illusion. So I had gambled all on Christine's acceptance, only to burn in a fire of bitter rejection and hurt, as much as the theater had burned that night.

Yet unbeknownst to us, something grew from those ashes of bitterness, fear, and jealousy. Through her son, Christine and I had found each other again. Twenty years on, life found us at similar crossroads, much as that night had been, only this time, it was she who had to decide the outcome of the gamble. I could only present her with the option to choose. The rest was up to her.

However all this was to be accomplished, I had to be careful. It would no longer be only the two of us who would bear the consequences of our actions. I had interfered in her life once, only to have the world crash quite literally at my feet. I could not do so again, and however *indirect* Phillippe's scheme of the locket had been, I dared not show my face at the Comtesse's door! Not now, and perhaps not ever. How was I to convince her to become the director of a school she would not want? Would I have to call on the services of the ghost once more?

Erica's soft gurgle drew my attention to her sleeping form, and away from the chaos in my head. The child slept peacefully, undisturbed by the world around her. Drawing a long, deep breath, I smiled down at her, pulled the covers gently around her and turned to look out the window. Would that all of us could lose ourselves in such peaceful slumber.

A weak smile worked its way to my face. Would anyone have ever believed that I would become someone's grandfather? Would I?

I looked down at Erica's small body once more, and could not help the pang of sorrow and sympathy for distant friends that stabbed through me.

Perhaps in the end, the reason behind the building and all the uncertainty was nothing more than a desire to help a friend in pain.

The loss of her daughter and the departure of her son for the army would leave Christine in solitude. If anyone knew the pitfalls and dangers of that, it was me. Music and architecture had sustained me, had given me purpose when I had despaired of ever having one. Christine would be alone, and even though she would have Raoul, Meg and her mother near by, their presence would not be enough to support her. She had always been sensitive and fragile, prone to a dependence on others for strength. She needed a purpose, something to sustain her through her recovery.

I sighed, shook my head, and glanced out the open window into the darkened street with its glittering gas lights. The cheerful strains of dance music from somewhere beyond carried even over the din of night time traffic. A light, almost cheerful chuckle escaped me as the tumultuous thoughts of the past weeks finally took shape.

Music. It had bound us once. It seemed destined to do so again. Music. Her angel could give her that. This time, he didn't need mirrors or illusions to present it to her. There were two angels beside the rose, two, who of necessity, could be extremely persuasive. Even so, I had to tread carefully. This was not a game to be dismissed lightly. A life was at stake, the life of someone who, long ago, had brought light into my world of darkness. Perhaps now, I could bring that light into hers.

Chapter 37

With Phillippe's departure for the army at the end of October 1891, Christine, Erica and I drew closer together, and spent our time at the villa, breaking our idyllic existence only when a project required urgent and immediate attention. Even so, it was I who traveled to oversee details of construction, and discuss matters with engineers. Christine remained near her daughter, managing the offices in Rome, and Brest as well.

Throughout the years, I had maintained the firm where a much younger me had come in quest of something better than a life in a dungeon. Étienne had held the small company as a subsidiary of his own until such a time as I deemed appropriate to assume rightful ownership. The scheme had worked for us, until the fire. Up until then, I had been content to remain a silent partner. After circumstances forced me into a new life, I had no choice but to assume control of the company that, in effect, was my own. I had never told Meg. There had never been a need to. A part of my new life had begun within the walls of the small offices in that port city of Brittany, and I never could bring myself to sever all ties to that coast, especially those to a small, grey house that had cast its magic over a once forlorn man. I may have given it to Meg and her mother, but in wistful, wishful dreams, that place tugged at me. It, more than anywhere else, was home. It was where love had grown, where I would be once again, with Meg beside me, if she would have me.

Trepidation and uncertainty aside, I had to go to her. I had let her go, not considering her feelings in the matter, only my own, and the fear that had consumed me then that my mere presence endangered her life. For that, I had sent her away. Now I would have to ask her forgiveness and her acceptance, the consequences be damned. I was not getting younger, and life lived alone was no life at all. I would see that woman with golden hair, if only to settle the unresolved question between us.

True, I had my child and grand -daughter to keep me company, but their companionship, no matter how loving, could no longer fill the yawning emptiness inside me. My soul cried for a partner, cried out for the one that had filled it, even if for the briefest of times.

The scrape of steel against steel brought a clashing end to my thoughts and harsh reality to my daydreams. The point of the rapier was mere centimeters from my face. If I was not careful, a new scar would join the damage that was already there and that was certainly one thing I did not need.

Bringing my mind to focus on the business at hand, I lunged into a counter attack, driving my opponent across the yard. This was not a mere practice session. We had agreed to play dirty. If I was to travel to Paris, I needed to know that I could still hold my own in combat. I had not lived all this time to become victim to thief looking for a wallet to steal. Though swords were no longer de rigueur, still, the exercise was good, and it had kept me in shape for these many years.

Dust churned under our feet as my opponent and I struggled for advantage in our battle. Neither of us wore protective gear, having chosen to take, and accept, chances with the weapons we wielded. We were too well matched, neither of us willing to give ground. We stared at each other over crossed blades, and a wolfish grin appeared on my partner's face.

"Yield," he demanded, catching his breath.

"Not today," I returned, eyes on the sharp blade pointing in my direction, but also catching sight of Christine as she approached the yard. It was time to end this. The morning was nearly done, and there was business that needed attention. "And certainly not to you," I allowed a sinister chuckle. In a series of thrusts and parries, I drove him toward the fence.

Despite the discipline of this sport learned long ago, I had allowed Christine's approaching figure to distract me. In a move I should have anticipated, my opponent disarmed me, his blade fixing firmly to my throat. "Yield."

"Not this morning," I breathed, and summoning an old, dirty trick, kicked his shin. A grunt of pain followed, with the blade lowering for an instant. I needed no more than that to turn, bring my arm up, and let the slim blade slide from its hidden sheath beneath the sleeve of the shirt. The sun glinted off its honed edge as I held it toward his eye.

"Yield to me," I demanded, chest heaving, eyes glinting with near sinister pleasure.

He smiled, nodding approval. "You have me. Well done."

I stepped away, retracting the weapon, noting Christine standing by the fence. My partner noticed her presence as well, and the serious demeanor in her stance. Glancing from one to the other of us, he gathered his weapon and gear. "With maneuvers like that, you will hardly be prey to pickpockets. There is nothing more I can do for a student such as you, signore." He gave me a slight bow. "It has been a privilege."

I returned the bow, watching him disappear around the corner of the barn, before turning full attention to my daughter. She held a towel out to me, and as I wiped the dripping sweat off me, the blue of her eyes deepened, and a thoughtful frown creased her brow.

"What is it?"

"A courier arrived," she said softly, "from Paris. He's waiting for you in the office."

I gave one brief nod, picked up the sword that lay in the dust and joined her on the way back to the house.

"So, an unexpected ally in the field," I murmured, handing Christine the letter the courier had brought.

Having discharged his mission, she had taken the man to the kitchen where he had been given food and drink.

Now we exchanged glances as she read the document. I walked out onto the portico, looking out over the expanse of the estate, and beyond, but I was not glancing at the olive grove, the vineyard, or the rolling fields. I only saw a girl with golden hair, a shovel in her hands, standing defiant and lovely in the spring sun.

"You will go there? To Paris?" Christine asked, coming up beside me.

"Yes," I whispered, turning to look at her. "I should have done so many years ago." I caressed her cheek.

"You will find maman?"

I sighed, looked into my daughter's eyes, and knew that in all the years she had been in contact with Meg, she had to have known it would all come to this.

"Yes, I will bring her here," I assented, smiling at her. "Providing she's willing. She may decide a Tuscan estate is not to her liking."

Christine chuckled and smiled gently at me. "I think maman will like it anywhere you are."

"Do you really think so? She's used to Paris after all, to all the finest things___." Christine's fingers on my lips stopped the flood of babble. Her eyes looked directly into mine.

"Maman loves you, not the things you can give her." She smiled, and rising on tiptoes, lightly kissed my brow, whispering. "She has always loved you. All this time she has waited for you to come to her. She would never say it of course, but I could see it in her eyes, in the way she moved. She loves you, and only you."

I returned her smile and wrapping an arm around her waist, led her back into the office. "I should never have let her go."

Christine gave me a light kiss on the cheek, disengaging from my embrace. "If you had not, you would not have been doing this." She indicated the letter lying on the desk.

"Perhaps," I said, as wistful memory rose to the fore. I shook it off, pulled a leather folder from my desk, and placed it in Christine's hands.

"What's this?" She glanced at the plain binding, then at me, her sharp, blue eyes narrowing.

"All the documents you will need, should anything happen to me while I'm in Paris."

"Why should anything happen?"

I sighed and turned away from her. "I may still be, very much, a wanted man. Burning the theater was only one of many things my hands have done." I admitted with reluctance.

"It was a long time ago, Papa. Surely by now the police would have forgotten about it."

"I doubt they ever forget anything, my dear. I am certain it is all written down somewhere, and is collecting dust, waiting for the appropriate moment to be resurrected. No, I must proceed with caution. That includes providing for my family," I brushed fingertips against her cheek, "and securing my manager's position. She has been an invaluable asset to me." I kissed her brow, and went to pour a glass of water from the pitcher standing on the low table beside the windows.

"This thing you have embarked on, are you certain the Comtesse will accept it?" Christine's soft voice was hesitant as she asked the question I myself had asked a hundred times.

I looked at the woman standing in the office beside my desk, hardly able to reconcile the boisterous girl who had chased birds in distant parks with the young lady who so ably ran my offices and household. The years had certainly played with us.

"I am not certain of anything, Christine, least of all this. But it is something I have to do, need to do. I will not force her decision, not this time. It is in her hands. All I can do is give her this one thing because it is all I have. It is all I can give."

Christine gave a slight nod. "I hope you are right. Even with your unexpected ally, she will be difficult to persuade. She has shunned public life for some time."

I gave my daughter a near wolfish grin. "Then we are fortunate to have two Graces on our side. Perhaps our ally's discreet support of this venture will help sway her. Come, I'm famished, and I smell Anna's fabulous cooking, even in here." I steered Christine through the doorway, the letter from Paris abandoned, but not forgotten.

Chapter 38

"What magic did you use? She is a different woman. Still my mother of course, but she smiles now, and the shadows in her eyes have begun to disappear. How did you do it?" Phillippe asked, stabbing into his lamb with gusto.

It was late October of 1892. Phillippe had come to Rome on army business. Christine was seven months pregnant with their second child, and Erica had decided that evening to create havoc. In no uncertain terms, her mother had chased us out of the apartment, making it clear we were not welcome for some time. We took advantage of the hours afforded us to have a leisurely dinner, away from two grumpy ladies.

We had come here, a small restaurant beside the Tiber where no one knew us, where we were afforded privacy.

"She is happy then?" I covered the sense of relief and reprieve I felt within by sipping the wine that had, up until then, remained untouched.

"I don't know about happy," he answered around a mouthful. "More at peace, I would say, certainly that. She no longer frets, trying to seek her 'angel.'" His eyes, when they met mine, glinted with shared, conspiratorial understanding. He chuckled as he set his wine glass down. "It's not as if she could get away from him, even if she wanted to. He's around her, in the very walls of the building she walks through every day. Recently, she even braved one of father's functions."

"And he?" I asked, looking out over the river.

"Oh he is happy to have her back, and more than a little relieved that she has found something to occupy her mind." He paused, setting aside his knife and fork. When he resumed, his tone sobered. "I think he had nearly given up on ever hearing her sing again. When he heard her practice for the first time, he cried. It was as if some burden had been lifted from him, and whatever gulf there might have been between them appears to have vanished. They seem to have reached contentment."

I made no reply but continued to stare at the darkened river, at the flickering lights of the city reflected off its murky waters. A sense of quietude settled over me, and I gave myself over to it, drawing comfort from it.

"What happened between them, with Antoinette, has changed them." Phillippe said, his penetrating eyes studying me. "Oh, they're still the parents I remember, perhaps more so. But this whole business with the school has done something for them. It's drawn them closer together, if that's possible. What did you do?"

"Nothing. Only constructed a building, one of many," I finished off my wine, thus averting his scrutiny.

His brows drew together in thought, then he shook his head. "Yes, but not everyone gives away the building they construct to a philanthropic cause, and then provide money for its upkeep." He threw me a conspiratorial glance, then turned his attention to the coffee the waiter had brought. "In any case, whether you choose to tell me or not, that is your affair, beau-père. However it was accomplished, I'm happy to see my mother laugh again, or at least make an effort at it." His tone once more acquired a serious overtone, even though a smile tweaked at the corners of his mouth. "I hope some day she'll know who it was that made her smile again. I wish to be there to see her face."

"I did not do it for that, Phillippe." My eyes flashed with a hint of danger that he would think I had had some shallow purpose in mind with the entire scheme.

He flashed a grin. "I know you didn't. It's interesting that the three of you should dance so carefully around each other without them realizing _____." He trailed off, his eyes narrowing in thought as he studied me carefully. "She never knew your name, did she?"

"No," I answered, looking away. "She only knew me as her teacher, and a shadow at that." I added quietly.

His laughter brightened the suddenly somber mood that had come over us. "Never fear. Your secret is safe with me. Even so, I would be a poor liar if I said I did not want to know what finally convinced my mother to break through the despair she had plunged into."

I turned my eyes on him and not for the first time wondered at the fortune that had brought him to me as a son. "Perhaps it is not what, but who convinced her, you should question." I said quietly. The last letter from Étienne had hinted at a heated exchange between the Comtesse and Meg when he had visited the de Chagny premises to negotiate terms with Raoul. He, of course, could not, or would not, give specifics. Such gossip was not in his character, but knowing the sisters as I did, and having been on the receiving end of one's scolding, my imagination could fill in the rest. "Perhaps next time you meet your aunt, you should ask her."

"Meg?" Phillippe laughed. "Yes, I suppose if anyone could convince my mother to do anything, it would be her. She has not been one to take 'no' for an answer. A few times as a boy I found myself on the receiving end of her scolding." He winced dramatically.

"Just so," I agreed, fondly remembering Meg's scorn at me during an aimless cab ride.

"Do you know what happened between them?"

"No, and it would not be for me to say, even to you. Whatever was said between your aunt and your mother, none the less, seemed to have the desired effect, for everyone. Let us give them their peace." I rose and gathered the coat and hat. "It is time to go home. Your general will be looking for you." I slipped the fedora low over my brow.

Phillippe laughed brightly. "My general seemed happy to be rid of me earlier."

I laughed with him. "Now, she will want you back, and I for one, do not wish her ire to fall on me."

We settled our bill and walked toward the welcoming glow of the apartment. A light, almost carefree spring came to my steps as we walked toward home.

I would go to Paris, I would face Meg, and I would do so as Erik Marchand, architect, businessman, father, grand-father, as a man, not a phantom, or the shattered ghost I had been.

Chapter 39

When silence and darkness finally ruled throughout the rooms of the apartment, I sat before the hearth in the salon, staring into the embers of the dying fire, unable to quiet the trepidation that surged in my veins. Despite my daughter's words, doubt consumed me. After all these years, would Meg accept me?

Étienne's recent letters and documents lay scattered about on the sofa, forgotten and neglected. I had done my best the past few hours to concentrate on the dry facts of figures and reports, but memories intruded with sharp focus, and voices echoed where I desired only silence. They had once again come to the fore, to haunt yet another sleepless night. Of late, more than once, I had awakened to recurrent nightmares of flames and cries of agony.

A soft sniffle drew my attention to the doorway to see Erica standing there, one tiny fist pressed to her mouth, a rag doll hanging from the other. The blue eyes were huge with fright.

"What is it, ma chéri?" I asked gently, scooping her up, looking into her tear stained face. Smiling, I wiped the tears away and kissed her hair.

"Scarries," she whispered, snuggling against me, wrapping tiny arms tightly about my neck. I held her to me, her small body a comforting weight against the resurging heaviness of my soul.

"Let's see if we can chase them away, shall we?" I said, kissing her once more, a lullaby I had sung to her mother rising from my chest. I carried her to the sofa, and as we sat together before the fading fire, we wrapped ourselves in gentle songs, banishing the ghosts that had disturbed our sleep.

Scarries. Yes, we all had ghosts that followed us, imagined or not, Raoul and Christine no more than I. A time came when we all had to confront them, when we had to lay them to rest, or allow them to rule us. Whatever had haunted the de Chagny's, they had buried their monsters.

The time had come to bury mine. I would go to Paris and confront that last ghost that haunted me. I had to heal the gaping wound that had been left behind. Perhaps in the healing, I would heal something within me, heal the man that had cried out his rage and hurt so many years ago.

Chapter 40

It was nearly midnight, yet I still stared at the building across the street, shadowed in the glow of the gas lights surrounding it. I stood on the street, heedless of the lightly falling snow, of the chill that even the new cloak would not ward off, eyes invariably drawn to the feeble light coming from the window of the small house just beyond the screen of shrubs bordering the street.

There was still scaffolding shrouding the main structure, but the heart of the building had been completed. Étienne and the crews had done a supreme effort in bringing my once uncertain vision to fruition. The building, while large enough to accommodate several dozen students with facilities to support them, was not overbearing or ostentatious. Its appearance blended into the surroundings, making it appear ordinary. Yet within its walls something extraordinary would take shape. Music would flow from here, music she would give to others, as once I had given it to her.

"Will you forever make me ask you to come home?" Meg's voice came from beside me as her arm twined around the crook of my elbow.

"No," I sighed, giving that arm a light squeeze with my fingers. "I have run away for the last time," I returned softly, freeing my arm as I slowly turned to look at her. "I have been away long enough." My fingers reached to touch the golden hair spilling from beneath a loose scarf thrown negligently over her head. Meg's brown eyes looked at me with the same impassioned pleading as they had that night I had sent her away, eighteen years previous. Here, on a street in Paris, on a chill November night, the feelings of that night returned, and it was as if time had not passed at all. She was beautiful. If anything, she had grown only more so. I was fifty seven years old, and she would be thirty eight. We were no longer young, and I was no longer tormented by demons from a painful past. Only one ghost remained, but that one would wait. It was not going anywhere, and for the present, I only wanted to bask in the warmth of Meg's eyes.

"I have come home to stay, if you will have me." I took her gloved hand and held it to my heart, eyes looking into hers, wanting to do so much more than just hold that hand, but not finding the courage to do so. I trembled like a schoolboy about to kiss a girl for the first time.

Meg only smiled in reply, her free hand caressing my masked right cheek. A light, flexible mask covered that side of my face, not the cumbersome thing I had worn under the Opera. Often it was no longer even that. Constant improvements in theatrical make-up had allowed me to experiment and devise several solutions to the matter of my disfigurement. After all, I had played in the theater long enough to be able to walk away with some of its secrets.

But for this night, I had chosen a mask. It was how she had last seen me.

"I have tea waiting," Meg answered, once more sliding her arm through mine. "Come. It will get cold."

I fell into step beside her, only too relieved to feel her near me to question the lack of an answer to my question.

Our steps crunched softly in the new fallen snow as Meg steered the way through the narrow gate, leading us to the small house within the enclosed garden of the larger building. The light I had seen earlier still burned, now a welcoming beacon of warmth.

We shook snow from our shoulders in the tiled foyer, and as Meg hung her shawl on a hook, I glanced about, taking in the sparse furnishings and the smell of newness all around.

"Will the owner not mind the mud we seem to have tracked in?" I asked, dismayed at the mess we had left behind on our way to the kitchen. It was a nervous effort at breaking the moment of silence that had fallen.

Meg's back was turned to me as she fixed our tea, but I heard her chuckle. "No, I don't think she'll mind. She's hardly ever here, although I think she looks forward to taking up residence," Meg turned, setting our cups on the table.

I froze, sudden dread seizing me.

"What is the matter?"

"I cannot be here." I began to weave my way back to the front door. "Not in this house."

"Why not?" Meg followed close behind.

"I cannot be where SHE will be, not now, not ever." My hand touched the knob of the door.

"She?" Meg questioned, her bafflement at my sudden flight growing. Admittedly, I was not at all certain of my actions either. At her words, I had flown like a frightened bird. What was the matter with me? I was acting like a schoolboy!

"Yes, she," I closed my eyes trying to hide the dismay I felt in even mentioning the name in this woman's presence. It did not matter that I knew they were sisters. It did not matter that I had found a measure of understanding of events deep in my heart. I found it difficult to admit to this woman my weakness, for I loved her beyond anything I could ever have imagined, and I did not wish her to think less of me for allowing the whole affair at the Opera to spiral beyond my control.

"Who Erik? Whom do you mean?"

"Christine," I whispered, hanging my head in defeat. I would not hold anything back from her, not now, not ever.

"Oh," Meg's voice was a sigh, followed by rising, warm laughter. "You thought that she _____?" Her sentence drifted off as she shook her head, her yellow hair glinting in the light from the lamp. "Oh my dearest, not Christine." She glanced at me, raising a brow. "It took nearly a war to convince that one to at least teach. No. This place is my mother's." She came to stand within inches of me, eyes searching mine.

"Hélène?" I murmured, mesmerized by those brown pools.

She nodded, smiling. "At least for now."

An unimaginable flood of relief brought an almost bashful smile to my face. Meg's fingers brushed imaginary dust from the shoulders of my jacket. "Besides, where would you have gone in the snow in just this?" She gestured toward the hooks on the wall where her shawl, and my cloak, hung side by side.

Her hands framed my face. "At least stay for tea."

My fingers brushed against her hair. "Considering the time, breakfast might be more appropriate."

Her palm rested against the masked side of my face. "A very late dinner."

"A lifetime," I bent to lightly touch my lips against hers. "Or what is left to me."

"A lifetime," Meg returned the kiss. "I like the sound of that." Her hands found mine and our fingers twined fiercely together as Meg slowly led the way toward the darkened interior of the house.

I stopped her before the open door leading to the small room beyond. A lamp burned low on a stand beside the bed.

With a deep sigh I turned to face her, once again seized with nervousness and uncertainty. "Be certain Meg, absolutely certain of what you accept," I whispered, only too well aware of the diminishing will power to keep my arms from pulling her close.

She smiled, her fingers smoothing back the few loose strands of hair that had dislodged from the wig. "I know what I want, what I have always wanted." Her eyes met mine in a silent question.

Rising on tiptoe, she kissed me, and with slow, deliberately tender movements, removed wig and mask, laying them on a table beside the door. "I have always wanted this," her fingertips brushed my lips. "Only this." Her lips followed where her fingers had touched.

I pulled her close, arms wrapping tightly against her back, holding her as closely as possible. I drowned in the ecstasy of her, weak with the sudden flood of relief and fulfillment at once. I gave myself over to the sensations, only savored the moments, for under Meg's lips, and the warmth of her hands, I could not think, did not want to.

I had come home, to my golden sea, and I clung to it much like a shipwrecked sailor clings to shore after being tossed about in relentless storms.

I lost myself in her, with her, for she filled the emptiness, the hollowness I had carried so long. Where hands touched, lips followed, leaving trails of blazing passion behind. Her whispered sigh against my ear spoke of mutual longings and desires fulfilled, and somewhere in the hours we were no longer Meg or Erik, but US. She was mine, completely, utterly, as I was hers, and would be, until sunset came to claim us. Even then I would dare the Fates to hold her from me.

Chapter 41

My eyes snapped open and for a heartbeat, I thought I had had an extraordinary dream, but the soft sigh next to me confirmed exquisite reality. I glanced at the beautiful woman sleeping beside me, her golden hair a fan on the pillow. I smiled, with difficulty refraining from gathering her into my arms. I had no wish to wake her, and for a few quiet moments, savored watching her. Strange, but after years of being alone, waking in her bed, waking with her beside me, felt extremely right. A slow smile of unbridled happiness and humor spread to my lips. Watching Meg while she slept felt more intimate than our vigorous exercise of only a short while before. This time I could not resist, and with a feather light touch of lips, kissed her shoulder.

I had found my way back to her, and she had accepted me. Each of us would no longer be alone, adrift, apart, joined only loosely by the child we had raised. We had made a tentative effort at family in the years in Brittany, but we had been young, inexperienced, haunted by demons from a murky, painful past. Too much had stood in our way. Now we would be a family in earnest. All my life, all those years, had inexorably drawn me here, to this woman's side, and woe befall those who tried to tear us asunder. She was mine to protect, and I would do so, fiercely, beyond question, in this life, or the next.

A low groan of self-recrimination escaped from my throat. How could I have been so stupid! Of all the things I had planned and prepared for, protecting Meg had not been one of them! I had dared not even think in that direction. I had not thought beyond the point of showing up at her door! Would I bring her grief even as we began a new life?

With a frustrated and whispered "merde", I eased out of bed, careful not to wake her. Tossing the discarded shirt over my shoulders, I padded toward the washroom, heedless of the creeping cold. How could I possibly have been so thoughtless! With morning's light, I would take steps to rectify matters. For Meg, I had to do it. I could not take the chance. All my experience and years of travel had not left me without knowledge and resources, and I would not give her sorrow.

Absorbed in thought, I completely disregarded the unfamiliar furnishings around me until a twanging, dull pain shot through my foot. "Merde," I sucked air to still the agony in my toe. So now I was walking into furniture! It had not been enough that I had acted like a fool earlier. Now I was proving to be one! Hopping on one foot, and cursing myself for an idiot, I backed into the table, and the crash of porcelain against the floor followed. Why was it that when one tried to be quiet, the most noise followed?

"What are you doing?" Meg asked sleepily from the doorway, the peignoir barely held on one shoulder. "What's all the noise?"

I smiled sheepishly at her. "I'm sorry if I woke you. I tried being quiet. Seems the table won this round," I rubbed the still throbbing toe.

She shook her head, smiling. "The noise didn't bother me, your absence did. You are nervous and skittish like a child. What is the matter?" Her eyes studied me carefully.

I reached for her and enfolded her against my chest, arms holding her fiercely, hands brushing through her hair. "I'm sorry Meg," I whispered. "Please forgive me."

"Forgive you? For what?" She pulled away, looking at me, at the distress on my face.

"For not protecting you, as I should have," I said miserably, caressing her face.

She grasped my hands, kissing them. "You didn't do anything I did not want you to."

"Meg, what if there is a child?"

"Then I will consider myself extremely fortunate."

"What if it has my face!" I cried, grasping her shoulders. A part of me wanted her to see sense, but all of me wanted, needed her to stay.

She smiled and kissed me. "Then, my dear Erik, we will have to love it more, won't we? Now, no more talk. I'm cold, and our bed is still warm."

She drew me after her, and I had no desire to resist.

Chapter 42

Morning found us in a pleasant tangle of arms and legs, tired, sated, complete. With a satisfied sigh, I drew Meg closer, kissing her hair. "I suppose I should make an honest woman of you."

"Hmmm. Yes, as soon as possible please," she murmured, snuggling even closer.

"Meg," I had to try once more for reason. There was still time, but it was quickly running out. "Please. I can make a tea. There won't be any danger to you."

She raised her head from my shoulder to look into my eyes, her hand reaching out to caress my ravaged face. "It frightens you, the possibility of a child?"

"Yes. Passing on this," I pointed to my cheek, "terrifies me."

"Erik, I love you, all of you." She sat up, took my hand in hers, and placed both on her belly. "If a miracle happens, I expect you to be there to raise our son." Her eyes suddenly turned serious and her fingers lightly caressed my right cheek. "I don't think we will be selling our child to gypsies." The tenderness in the eyes looking at me spoke of love and understanding beyond what words could say.

I looked at her, fingers brushing through the gold that cascaded over her shoulders. "She told you."

Meg nodded, her hands resting against my chest. "Everything," she paused, took a deep breath, and continued. "The night you sent me away, I thought I would die. I could not stop crying. Poor Maryanne must have thought I had lost all reason. Even when she took me to the station in the morning, I still could not stop the tears. She tried to console me, saying fights between husbands and wives were a healthy thing, now and then." Meg chuckled and raised a brow. "I couldn't dash the poor soul's illusion, so I listened to her words, but on the inside, I was inconsolable." She bent down to kiss me, her hair brushing deliciously against my bare chest. "You were cruel that night, my dearest."

"I am sorry Meg," I whispered, caressing her shoulders. "I had to do it, and I knew no other way. I was terrified that if I stayed near you, I would kill you."

She nodded, giving me a lingering kiss on the brow. "I didn't understand, not then. I couldn't understand why you wouldn't touch me after you kissed me in that chapel. You had feelings for me, I knew you did. You couldn't hide it any more than I could hide mine."

"I made a promise to your mother," I said slowly, looking into the brown eyes that looked back at me with tenderness and unbridled passion. "I dared not betray that trust. Your mother and I were like brother and sister to each other, perhaps more so. She entrusted me with you, and I would keep my promise to the only one who ever showed me kindness. Except I broke that trust when I nearly killed you. I was afraid Meg, afraid of losing you, of losing Hélène, all because of the nightmares that ruled me. So I did what, at the time, I thought was right for you."

Meg nodded in understanding, rose from the bed and drew her peignoir over her shoulders. "When I showed up at mother's door, I think in a way, she had been expecting it." She gave me one of her charming smiles, tossing discarded shirt and pants in my direction. "We had a very long talk that evening, my dear, a very long talk."

I shrugged into the clothes, and followed Meg into the kitchen. She was already starting preparations for breakfast. A telltale rumble from my stomach brought a smile of delight to my face. Yes, a bit of exercise would make one hungry. I watched her gorgeous figure with unmitigated interest as she moved about the small room, thoughts of further delights to come painting wonderful visions before my eyes.

"Here, make yourself useful." Meg thrust a small bucket of coal into my hands. With a lingering kiss to her neck, I laid a fire in the stove. Its heat would soon warm up not only the kitchen, but some of the house as well.

The next thing I knew, a wet cloth and a small broom were being offered me.

"What?"

Meg arched her brow, indicating the broken cups still lying on the floor. "You made the mess, you clean it up."

I smiled. So, this was how it was going to be, and I would not have it any other way. I accepted the instruments of my punishment, scraping up the broken china and wiping up the tea spill without complaint.

Tossing the bits and pieces away, I glanced out the window. Workmen were already busy on the scaffolding, their chatter punctuating the comfortable, momentary silence in the kitchen.

"It's quite a building. Why did you do it?" Meg asked, as she stood beside me, following my gaze toward the activity around the structure outside.

I shrugged, and turned my attention back to her, back to the woman I cherished above all. "I don't know," I answered honestly, taking up the teapot from the counter and setting it on the table.

Meg's eyes narrowed with thought. "You still love her."

"Meg, please," it was a half strangled groan of misery. I certainly did not wish reminders of a past I'd rather forget.

The comfortable weight of her arm fell about my waist as she hugged and kissed me, her fingers brushing through my hair. "Of course you do. You would not be the man I fell in love with if you didn't, and you would not have done that." She gestured to indicate the building outside.

"It was all a long time ago," I answered, drawing slightly away so I could look into her eyes. There was no recrimination in those eyes, only abiding love and affection. "And we were all fools." I added quietly. "I have come home to my heart, to the only place where I ever wanted to be."

She kissed me, drawing me to a chair, her insistence more than anything making me sit down. "Yes, we were all younger then, and all of us were fools," Meg agreed, taking the seat beside me. She poured the tea, while I divided the bread and cheese.

"I don't think Christine realizes how fortunate she is to have a friend in you," Meg began, taking a bite of the cheese. "But then, she never paid much attention to anything, her head always filled with her 'angel.'" She rolled her eyes, winking at me.

I chuckled a little, remembering. "No, she never was a patient pupil."

"How did you manage to teach her anything?"

I shook my head, smiling broadly. "It wasn't easy."

She chuckled, her eyes holding a twinkle of shared amusement. "No, I suppose it could not have been." Our mutual laughter filled the house with warmth.

"You should see her now. Quite the disciplinarian with the youngsters, though they all love her. I think it's because she tells them stories about the old Opera," Meg flashed me a mischievous smile, "and her teacher."

"She's teaching?" I asked, curious.

Meg laughed a little. "Oh yes. I know you intended for her to head the school, but she would not hear of it, and it would not have suited her temperament. You know that as well as I. She refused to even listen to me on that subject, shutting herself in her rooms like a child."

"Then how did you persuade her to teach? From what I understand, she has shunned public life, and after her loss, I would not think she would want to be among children."

Meg pursed her lips in thought, glancing at me from beneath her long lashes. "It took only a reminder of who taught her, who gave her the music she clung to, and that he would not be pleased to know his talent, his efforts, had been wasted."

"Ah." I leaned back in the chair, unable to quite hide the broad grin.

"Besides, with Raoul as a patron of the school, she could not have very well refused to help in the cause." Meg shook her head, smiling a little. "All of us in Paris once more, gathered here because of a building." Her hand reached to caress my cheek, her eyes fixing on mine. "Oh, my dearest, it was all worth something. Perhaps we all walked away that night with something more than the sum of all of us." She leaned forward and brushed her lips against mine.

I grasped her hand, kissing it. Too many conflicting emotions had begun to swirl through me at her words, and I didn't want to delve into that pit, not with her beside me.

Meg rose, trailing fingers over my shoulders as she rose to stand beside me. When next she spoke, her words were tinged with light amusement. "Yes, indeed. We all walked away with something that night, Christine perhaps more than any of us." She patted my shoulder and gave my neck a delicious, ticklish kiss. "That young fool and Raoul ran for the North country that very night. Lord only knows what they were thinking." Meg sighed, wrapping her arms about me. "Obviously they weren't. They disappeared, blissfully unaware of the ruckus their flight caused, and I imagine they would have been happy to stay up there, in their dreams, had not harsh reality knocked sense into their heads." She paused, sighed, and resumed her seat, and breakfast.

"What happened to bring them to their senses?" Curiosity won over the reluctance to discuss this particular subject.

Meg shook her head, finishing off her cheese. "Raoul's brother, Phillippe, was killed in a hunting accident. That left Raoul the only surviving heir of the de Chagny estate. It took his father devil of a time to find him and send him the news. Those two fools were secreted in their hideaway, and it took almost four weeks to find them."

"The police are slipping," I said dryly, finishing off my own breakfast.

Meg threw me a grin. "No, not the police, but the Count's own men. Raoul's carefree ways were well known. The Count wanted to keep things quiet. When his men eventually found the couple, and brought them to the château, the Count was already in a rage that Raoul had not presented himself at his brother's funeral. When the old man discovered that Raoul had not gone with just any actress or singer but the one at the center of all the rumors and whispers about the Great Disaster, he was fit to be tied. Worse still when Raoul stood his ground and told his father that he and Christine were married." Meg shook her head, looking off into the distance. "I'll give him credit. He stood by her in the face of the storm, giving not one inch of ground, despite his father's threat of disinheritance."

Meg rose and took the dishes away. "Oh no doubt he would have done it, had it not been for Raoul's mother. She interceded on Raoul's behalf, if only for the fact that Raoul was their only remaining heir, and money and prestige in the family meant more than anything else. Christine's existence was ignored, her tie to the family not discussed, and preferably for everyone, she was not to be seen."

"Not a happy situation," I murmured, watching Meg as she moved about, thoughts drifting to long ago when an article in a newspaper had sparked a flare of temper and anger.

"No, least of all her. The poor girl could not go anywhere without whispers exchanged behind her back. Yes, partially she and Raoul brought it on themselves, but the treatment they received was harsher than it needed to be. As if it was not hard enough on them already, it became harder still when Christine discovered she was with child."

I snapped my head up to look at her. "Phillippe?"

Meg acknowledged with a nod. "An elopement was one thing, but now there was a child on the way. How much worse could it possibly be?"

I let out a long, slow breath, only now becoming fully aware of the monsters that Phillippe's parents had had to overcome, and somewhere in my heart, I felt only sympathy for them.

Meg's arms around my shoulders brought immeasurable comfort in all the heaviness that floated about in the kitchen.

"Just so," she whispered, kissing my ear. "Raoul once more faced his parents with the news. There would be no hiding it in another month. Whether they approved or not, they would have a grandchild, and another, potential heir. A small, formal wedding was held, more to save family honor than preserve their standing. At this point, I think, the Count seemed resigned to covering his son's supposed indiscretions. Phillippe was born six months later." Meg looked pointedly at me. "He and our Christine are nine months apart, almost to the day." She smiled at me, drawing her fingers against my cheek. "Something of poetic justice in that, and in their love. All of us close, and yet worlds apart."

"Did his family ever accept her?"

"No, not even after the child was born. On the Count's insistence, they named him Phillippe, for Raoul's brother. So even that, the pleasure of naming their son, was taken from them. For four years, they lived under a pall of near tyranny from his parents, and if it had not been for Christine, the parents would have made another sycophant out of that child." Meg sighed and shook her head in sadness. "I would never have believed that girl could grow a spine, not in a situation like that, but apparently she did."

"Where was Raoul? I would think he would have been by her side." I questioned, more and more intrigued by Meg's narration of events.

"He wanted to, no doubt of that, but after all that had happened, he bowed to family pressure and duty. Partially to make up for his mistakes of the past, and to appease his father, he took a commission in the army. His service left Christine alone most of the time. His absence made her a virtual prisoner at the château. She dared not venture anywhere without him. When they did manage to go out, even Raoul's presence could not stave off the whispers. Eventually she gave up trying to break through the barriers of society. She realized she would never be accepted among the gentry as one of their own, so she chose to stay at the château, devoting herself to Phillippe. She discovered he had true talent for music, and began to teach him."

"What about Raoul's parents? Did they not object to this particular activity on Christine's part?"

Meg chuckled. "That was about the only thing they seemed to approve of. They were, after all, discreet patrons of the new theater and its school. They could not object to a musical education. They did object to their son mixing with someone below his status." Meg threw a small bucket of coal onto the fire in the stove, closed the door, and wiped her hands on a towel. "The Count died soon after Raoul finished his service, and the mother left soon after that, to live out her days in the South. Raoul saw her only once after that, on her death bed."

"Probably better for everyone that way," I murmured, vague recollections of my own mother flooding my mind.

"In their case, it was a blessing. With her death, they were free, but they had changed. Christine put her foot down and insisted their son be able to pursue his heart's desire. Raoul caved in only after she agreed that Phillippe would serve his term in the army. I think Raoul still felt the sting of what their actions had caused, and he thought that if their son served the country, some of that stain might wash away from the family name. Christine agreed, more I believe, because she loved Raoul, and would not stand against him in the one thing he asked."

She sighed, eyes leveled on me, her hand wrapping around mine. With a sigh, I drew Meg into my arms and held her close, nestling her head against my shoulder. Why had I waited so long to have this? Why had I made her wait so long in uncertainty? I kissed her hair, arms tightening about her. I would never let her go, not again.

With a light kiss to my neck, Meg disengaged from the embrace, her fingers tracing the line of my jaw. "When Antoinette happened, I thought that finally those two would find some peace, but it was not to be." Her eyes glistened with tears. "Their heartbreak nearly tore them apart."

"Christine told me," I said gently.

Meg nodded, her hand squeezing mine a little harder. "I knew she would," she began to lead the way back to the bedroom. "Oh my dearest, I truly believe it was your music alone that kept Christine from plunging over the edge. It was the only thing that took her mind off her misery. If it had not been for that, I believe she would have been lost to us."

I nodded in understanding. "But why was Raoul so angry? Surely, it was no one's fault the child died."

"No, of course not. He was angry at himself for causing the situation in the first place, angry at himself because he did not know how to help her, and he was furious with you, for her lingering memories of you, and because your comfort was what she wanted, not his." Meg's deft fingers slipped the shirt off my shoulders with ease. "It was not easy for him to accept the fact that his wife still had feelings for another man, especially a man he had thought long forgotten in a grotto under the Opera house." Meg smiled, her lips trailing delicious kisses along my shoulders. "Jealousy is not an easy thing to bury. He eventually made uneasy peace with the fact that you would always be a part of her life." Her hands brushed lightly over my back and chest, the smile on her lips full of promised delights. "As you have always been a part of mine, ever since you found me in that passageway."

I bent to kiss her, lips lingering over hers, tracing the lines of her cheeks, jaw, and the long, slender neck. She laughed beneath the kisses.

"I cared not for a prying vixen in my lair," I mumbled against her ear, teasing it with my tongue and teeth. "Most especially a vixen whose absence would bring her mother's ire on my head." My fingers slipped the peignoir off her shoulders. She stood in her glory before me, and my eyes could not get enough of her.

Meg tossed her head, looking askance at me, lips pursed in speculation. "And you accept her in your lair now?"

I smiled, fingers trailing over her shoulders, down her arms and back again. "Without hesitation, ma chère, for she is my heart and I can no longer live without her." My hands buried themselves in the gold hair cascading over her shoulders. "And because for the last eighteen years, the thought of doing this alone," I lifted a lock of her hair to my nose to take in its heady, jasmine scent, "drove me nearly mad with desire."

Meg twined her arms around my neck, her curves delightfully pressing against me. "I still have a mother."

"Hmmm. I have a feeling she will be not be looking for her errant daughter this time, or any other time, here, or anywhere." I lifted her and gently laid her on the bed. The promise and desire in her eyes mirrored my own, but we had time. There would no longer be unfulfilled longings, no more cold and empty dreams. We were both home, where we had longed to be.

Chapter 43

"Hold still, I can't do this if you fidget."

"I am at your mercy," I said with a mischievous grin. It took all my will power not to gather the lovely woman into my arms.

We were in the vestry of a tiny chapel outside Paris proper. Meg finished combing the hair of the wig into place, giving me a long look of appraisal.

"There. You are now presentable, Monsieur Marchand." She smiled, tugging at the silk cravat at my throat. "Hmmm. Quite charming."

"As you are ravishing," I whispered, kissing her hand. She was dressed in a cream satin creation that set off her figure to best advantage. Tiny, white silk flowers had been twined in her hair, and a light, lace veil cascaded down her shoulders. The three strand pearl necklace I had given her the previous evening was her only jewelry. Within the next few minutes I planned to remedy that situation.

I felt awkward in the silver gray suit, silk shirt, and cravat, despite the fact that they were the latest fashion. However this occasion had called for something special, and I would have been the last to disappoint my future wife. The cloak lay folded over a chair.

I looked at Meg smiling up at me, and realized I trembled with nervousness.

The oak door creaked open, and the curé, a thin, affable and balding man, peered at us over his spectacles. "Are you ready?" He asked.

Meg grasped my hand and squeezed. "Yes, I believe we are," she answered with a smile. "We'll be right out."

"Very well." He left.

"Your last chance, Meg Giry," I whispered.

"Not on your life Erik Marchand. I've waited much too long for this."

"Well then, let us to it." I offered my arm. She laid her hand lightly atop it, and we walked into the chapel, toward the altar.

It was the first day in many that the winter sun had chosen to cooperate. Its rays through the stained glass windows filled the space with brilliant color.

The curé opened the bible, looked at us, and squared his shoulders. "Are the witnesses assembled? Who stands for you, mademoiselle?"

"I do," a voice answered from the shadows. I had had eyes only for Meg and had failed to notice the figure beside one of the columns. It now came forward and in the patchwork of light from the windows, I recognized the striking, elegant form of Hélène Giry. She smiled at me, her eyes warm, radiating genuine affection as she inclined her head slightly in greeting. I returned the gesture in a small bow, at a total loss. I had never expected to see her again, certainly not in circumstances like this. A warm surge of affection flowed through my veins as I returned her greeting.

Nearly twenty two long years had passed since she had helped spirit me out of Paris. Now she was here to bear witness to my union with her daughter. What did she think of all this? Had she expected events to take the turn they had? Had she known something from the very beginning? I dimly recalled the looks that had passed between mother and daughter as we had formulated a plan for my then uncertain future. Did Meg have feelings for me even then? Our conversation of a few days before had only confirmed it. Had Hélène suspected? It had been her insistence that Meg accompany me into exile. Nature and time had taken their course, and if Meg's mother had seen something between us that we had not, I could never resent her for it. She had allowed me to find a new existence, had allowed me to find my true heart in Meg, for she was my life, the part that had always been missing.

I glanced at my bride to be, only to be rewarded with a smile of mystery and a promise in those gorgeous eyes looking back at me.

"And you monsieur? Who stands for you?"

I looked around, wondering if there were any more surprises. I shook my head. "No one. I have no one."

"Perhaps I will do?" Étienne's unmistakable deep, rich tones rang out in the silence. "This is one morning I did not care to shut myself in a stuffy office." He came forward from the back of the chapel, nonchalantly flicking imaginary dust from his coat. As he took his place beside Hélène, a broad smile lit his face, and his eyes twinkled with mirth. "Your young lady," he inclined his head slightly in Meg's direction, "sent a very urgent message, begging my immediate assistance on this particular morning. Of course, being a gentleman, and your friend, I could hardly refuse such a plea." He smoothed his full mustache with one, broad hand.

"You have saved me from folly, but not embarrassment." I laughed lightly, abashed that in all the time we had spent poring over documents the past few days, I had never once thought to ask him to stand as witness at my wedding.

"Such is the duty of friends," he dipped his head in a bow.

"Well now, are we ready?" The curé asked, glancing over our varied group. Even he could not hide the smile that tweaked the corners of his mouth.

Meg looked to me, and I could scarce believe that in the next few minutes, she would be my wife.

"Dearly beloved_____."

"No!" Meg's sudden exclamation froze the blood in my veins. Had she changed her mind? What was going on? I was not the only one baffled by the sudden outcry. Étienne and Hélène exchanged glances, and this time, even Hélène seemed puzzled.

"Wait!" Meg's hand squeezed mine tightly, her eyes pleading for patience. "There's someone _____ ." The rest was lost as the door of the chapel slammed open.

"I am sorry to be late," a voice echoed in the silence, a voice I had taught to sing with angels. "There was an accident...blocking...the...road..."

At the sound of that voice, my back stiffened, and my eyes closed tightly against the threatening tide of remembrance. What was SHE doing here? Now, of all times? Had not everything been buried in the ashes of the Opera house? What would have made her come here? Who would have asked her?

A gentle touch on my clenched hand brought me back to why I was here, and I understood. Of course. Meg would have asked her sister to attend. I sighed, bowed my head in reluctant acceptance, and slowly exhaled the breath I had been holding. Meg was right. It was time to confront this particular ghost and put it to rest.

"Any more surprises?" The curé asked, peering over the spectacles, as if searching for more phantoms.

Meg smiled, shook her head, and briefly touched my hand. "That's everyone. I promise."

"Are you sure, mademoiselle?"

"Yes, I'm sure."

"Without further ado, let us proceed." The ceremony was brief, but by no means diminished in its meaning. When I took Meg's fingers in mine and slipped the ring where it belonged, I at last felt complete, whole, no more a ghost or phantom, but a man, and now husband. As she slipped the twin of her ring on my finger I nearly cried for the joy of it. The kiss to seal our vows was light, yet it burned through me, to the very core with deep and abiding love only for her. I looked into her eyes, willing her to know I was hers, and hers alone. She smiled in reply, and with the faintest inclination of her head, turned to accept congratulations from the curé.

I closed my eyes, drawing in a deep breath. There was no more reason to put it off any longer. Slowly, I turned to face Christine. She wore a veil, but it wasn't heavy enough to obscure her features. She was still beautiful, despite the sorrow etched around her eyes. A gold locket with an etched rose on its cover hung suspended from a gold chain around her neck. It was the only adornment she wore over the dark blue dress. Gloved, trembling fingers touched the locket.

"You sent this?" She asked, the voice tremulous.

I inclined my head. "And your son. He worries about you."

"Christine? Who is she, really?"

"My daughter."

At her startled surprise, I elaborated. "I found her that night. She needed a home."

"You named her for me?" There was wonder in the tone.

I smiled a little. "It was the only name I could come up with at the time."

A half choked sob escaped her, and she pressed her hands to her mouth, trying in vain to stifle the racking sobs that threatened to tear her apart.

I took a few steps toward her, gently, lightly, putting my hands over hers.

"It's all right. Everything is quite all right, Christine," I said quietly.

She looked at me then, eyes studying me with burning intensity.

I smiled at her. "It really is all right."

"I am sorry, Erik. I treated you badly when you showed me kindness. I was so frightened, so divided in my feelings. I didn't know. Didn't want to know. I was afraid of what you stirred in me. I am sorry for the way it all came out."

I drew one of her hands into mine and raised it to my lips. "We all made mistakes that night, but I have you to thank for giving me a new life, for teaching me to love, to live. Without you, I would not have a daughter," I glanced toward Meg and her mother, "I would not have Meg. So you see, it all came out all right."

Christine bit her lower lip and nodded. I could see tears falling down her cheeks, and I did the only thing I could. I offered a handkerchief.

"You have a fine son, Christine. You taught him well." I paused, unsure how she would react to the next words. "You are a credit to your teacher."

She looked at me, and it was as if my words had taken away the weight of years. I understood then that she had come to ask forgiveness, and perhaps, to bury her own ghost. I took her gloved hands in mine and brought them to my lips.

For long moments we stood there, her eyes fixed intently on me, as if she tried to burn me into her soul. "I tried so hard to forget, but I can't." Her voice cracked with new tears.

"Then remember me as a friend, nothing more."

She nodded, and slowly, slipped her hands from mine. "Friend."

"Friend," I replied. "And friends of the heart have nothing to forgive each other for."

She smiled then, a faint, tremulous smile.

"Good bye then, friend of the heart."

"Farewell, Christine." I answered with sincere affection.

She looked at me one last time, turned, and with regal dignity, walked out of the chapel.

With a strange mixture of melancholy, regret, and affection, I watched the Comtesse de Chagny leave. She was troubled, and I fervently hoped that my words had brought a measure of comfort. I had meant every one of them.

A comforting weight slipped around my waist, and I drew Meg close. "She needed to see you."

"Perhaps I needed to as well." I kissed her hand, eyes still riveted on the open door of the chapel.

"She'll be all right. She needed your forgiveness, and to forgive herself."

In reply, I drew my bride tightly against me, kissing her lightly. "I needed to give her thanks for you."

Meg smiled at me, took my hand, and drew me toward the waiting group at the altar.

December 1892

to

February 1894

Chapter 44

We stayed in Paris long enough to formally settle Hélène into her new domain, and for me to settle outstanding business with Étienne. Hélène was quite willing to take up the post of director of the new music school in full, not the temporary position she had occupied for the past few months. I strongly suspected that it was one daughter's long awaited marriage and the proximity of the other within the school's premises that was responsible for Hélène's ready acceptance of her new profession.

While Meg busied herself sorting through piles of wardrobe at her mother's former residence, Hélène came to me, one of her secret smiles brightening her face. "I never thought to see a day when the two of you would be so happy. You surprise me, Erik. You always have, and perhaps always will. I am glad I went to that carnival and helped pull a boy out of his cage." She lightly touched my hand. I took it, kissing it with affection.

"You gave me kindness when none would. It is a debt I can never repay."

Hélène looked in Meg's direction and slightly shook her head, her fingers caressing my face. "Whatever debt you think you owe me, you've repaid. You gave each other happiness." With that she turned away and went to help her daughter.

The following morning I showed up at Étienne's office even before his staff. I found him nearly buried under reams of drawings, plans, and sketches.

"Ah, my friend. You have come. Good. Perhaps you will be kind enough and lend your opinion." He thrust papers aside to grasp my hand with his own, callused one.

"What is it?" I asked, slipping off the cloak and hat, tossing both on a chair.

"These came yesterday." He hunted through the deluge of documents that overflowed his desk, finally drawing out a stack of papers, thrusting them in my direction. "It's another proposal for restoration. I don't know why they bother. They have been turned down by all the firms, even the ones in Vienna and Prague."

While I studied the documents, he continued his bluster. "It's been the same request for the past few years. They circle around, hoping they will find a fool to do it. Apparently the government does not understand that no means no. I had hoped that they'd give up on the idea by now."

As my eyes scanned the words, a slow cold hand of ice squeezed around my heart. So many years later and the memories of that one night and all it had wrought slammed to the fore with all its haunting reverberations. All the years, all the nightmares, the voices, and the one pervasive cry that would not go away, that would no longer be stilled, had brought me to this office, to this city, to confront the specter that had once again begun to haunt my dreams. This was the ghost I had come to confront, the one ghost that remained.

With shaking hands, I lay the papers down on the only uncluttered surface of the draught table. "They've gone to everyone?" I looked out at the busy street below, not daring to face my friend. "To all the houses?"

"Like I said Erik, it would be a ruinous undertaking. They were lucky to have built the thing in the first place. Even if the government was to guarantee funds for the project, and I have my doubts on that score, what fool would want to touch it? It would be ruinous, and it would take years."

I continued to stare out the window at the brisk traffic, at the people going about their lives.

When I made no reply to his statement, he glanced at me from the mass of paper he sorted through. "Erik, are you all right? You look as if you'd seen a ghost."

I looked at him then, with the full weight of the past years behind my eyes. "Curious you should put it that way, my friend. Perhaps I have. Me."

"You? I don't understand. Why should it bother you? I know you used its basements_____."

"No Étienne. I lived there. It was my home, and I burned it." I said quietly, and moved away from the window to study the drawings spread out on the table, almost afraid to meet his eyes. What would he think of his friend now, when secrets could no longer be kept?

"You what?" He whispered in disbelief.

"I burned it," I said at last facing him, running a hand through my hair.

He stared at me, a question in his eyes. "The Great Disaster? That was you?"

I gave him a lopsided grin. "Yes Étienne that was Erik, a poor, devastated wretch of humanity." I paused and shook my head, glancing back at the drawings. "Now I can't even recall why. To make them pay for years of cruelty and degradation?" I shook my head. "Maybe for a kiss," I added quietly, remembering the grotto and Christine.

I felt his hand grip my shoulder. "We all do crazy things for love, my friend. Yours might have been a little extreme."

"An act of a desperate man, Étienne. I had nothing to lose then."

"And now?"

I tapped the documents on the table and faced him. "I must bring it to account. I must let the ghosts rest or they will destroy me." I paused, glancing at him. "Tell them I will do the work." I sighed, closing my eyes against memory, against the kaleidoscope of faces dancing in a dizzying vision before me, faces of those I loved. In low, almost whispered words, I added. "I burned it. I have to restore it."

"Do you realize if we take this on, how much it will cost?"

I gave him a nod and a faint smile. "I know what it will cost if I do not do this. Years ago I turned them down. Now they've given me a second chance. Perhaps my old ghost is not as dead as I'd like him to be," I chuckled without any mirth in it. "I have not struggled these twenty two years to attain something decent within myself only to leave a gaping wound from the past behind. No. If my life now is worth living because of my wife and daughter, then at least, I must do this for them."

His blue eyes crinkled with a hint of amusement. "Your young lady, she is quite special, no?"

I gave a nod in assent, touching the gold band around my finger. His firm hand clamped onto my shoulder. "From the beginning, I could sense she held your elusive heart."

I chuckled. "At least she has made an honest man of me."

"Oh not so, my friend!" He twirled the ends of his mustache. "That is an impossible challenge! For anyone!"

I cocked my good brow at him and the office rang with good humored laughter. Long ago, Étienne and I had become bound together under extreme circumstances. We had both seen the world from the gutter, as refuse of humanity. We had become acquainted at a construction site. He had been sixteen, I thirteen, and we had both been learning the trade. In the beginning, he had taken me under his protection from the work gangs. With him, my masked face had never been in question. He had taught me to mix mortar. I had stolen food for him. We had become partners through adversity. We had started an architectural firm together, and time had brought us together once again, to the city where we had started.

When our laughter died down, I looked at my friend, fleeting memories of our beginnings on the streets of this city flashing through my mind. "If I am to live as a man and not a ghost, I have to do this."

He nodded in acceptance. "Very well my friend. I will do as you wish. I will tell them."

Perhaps an hour or so later, as we discussed the initial proposal to the government, Étienne's staff began to drift in. His assistant dropped a copy of the day's newspaper on the desk.

"That should get everyone talking again," he said, indicating the headline.

"Oh get that trash out of here!" Étienne threw the paper back at him. "And close the door!"

"But monsieur, it's the third time this month it's been seen!"

"That's what I mean. Now it has you in a buzz. Take yourself and that trash out of my office so I can discuss some true business."

Étienne's man visibly wilted. "Yes, monsieur," he said meekly, picking up the newspaper.

"What is all this about, Étienne? Let me see that." I indicated the paper. The man passed it to me with hesitation.

"Oh Erik, please, not you." Étienne shook his head and studied the drawings spread out before him.

For the moment I ignored him, studying the article that seemed to hold so much interest and derision at the same time. It was mostly speculation and inflated supposition, but it was the headline which really drew my attention.

SPECTER HAUNTS ABANDONED OPERA HOUSE

"I did not realize that newspapermen had so little to write about these days. Ghosts do not seem the usual fodder for the men with the poison pen," I tried to disguise encroaching unease with a glib remark. Even the mere thought of a ghost brought tension to my frame, let alone a ghost at the Opera house.

"It is as I said Erik, trash. They write about a ghost, and all of Paris is a buzz."

"But messieurs, it is true! Le Fantôme has been seen." The hapless assistant insisted.

With a slow, deliberate movement, I turned to the man, eyes staring at him as if seeing him for the first time. "What did you say?"

"Le Fantôme de l'Opéra. It's been haunting the abandoned theater for some time now. Or so people say."

"The Phantom of the Opera." My voice was deathly quiet.

The man shrugged. "That's what people call the ghost. Some even say they have heard it sing. Always the same song, over and over again."

"Eugène, if you know what is good for you, leave this office at once." Étienne said from behind his desk. The man glanced at him and made a hasty retreat, closing the door behind him.

"It is all just talk Erik. Nonsense that feeds on itself. Pay it no heed."

I heard his words as if from a distance. "Le Fantôme. That's what they used to call me."

"Erik, my friend, you should know they are all stories made up to amuse the public and keep the gossips busy. Besides, it's tradition to have ghosts in the theater." He chuckled.

"Étienne," I turned to him. "The Phantom of the Opera was me. I haunted that house for eighteen years. This," I held out the paper, "is real. Someone is out there because of me, someone who doesn't deserve to be."

He came to me and placed a hand on my shoulder. "You and I have pulled each other from more scrapes and fights than I care to remember. You saved me and mine from starving in the street. You have built a school for your Christine, and you made an abandoned child your daughter. How much more debt do you need to repay?"

I looked him squarely in the eyes. "How many died that night because the police locked the doors?"

His silence was my answer. "I thought as much. They never could account for everyone. If they could not, then I must."

He looked at me, meeting my eyes with his. "It will break you, and I would not wish to see you hurt again."

"It might break me, but it will also heal me." I said clasping his hand. He nodded, and we turned our attention back to our interrupted discussion.

Chapter 45

After a quick meal at one of the small restaurants dotting the city, I walked Meg back to the rented rooms we called home for now.

When I held the door open for her, she looked at me, her brown eyes filled with a question. "You're not coming in, are you?"

I shook my head and kissed her hand. "No. There is something I have to do."

She kissed me then, lightly laying her hand against my cheek. "All evening you have been distant. What is it?"

I caressed her face, eyes looking into hers with all the love I held for her. "I need to asses the damage to the Opera house if I am to restore it." I spoke quietly, though there was no one about but us.

For one brief moment, Meg closed her eyes, wrapping her arms tightly about me as if taking on my long buried pain.

My arms twined around her, the cloak for a moment hiding her within its folds. "I have to." I murmured.

She nodded, her arms squeezing a little tighter. "Tonight?"

I sighed, pulling away, looking down into the wondrous pools of brown that held my heart. "Especially tonight."

Reluctantly, she released me. "Be careful. I've waited too long for you to lose you to an errant piece of masonry."

I smiled, kissing her. "For you, I will take precautions."

"Don't be long."

"Not from you." I said and descended the stairs. I don't know why I did not tell Meg the true reason for my nocturnal visit to that house. I had never had cause for self reproach over any of my previous transgressions, not even over Buquet, but burning the Opera house was a crime even my hardened heart could no longer forgive. Perhaps too, it was the growing contrition over the fiasco which now drove me to that house, and the guilt of causing the unintended deaths of so many. I had only wanted a distraction with the chandelier. It had been a spectacle that had backfired in that the police had locked everyone in, and it had taken time to open all the doors. By then, the fires had spread, and many had died who had not needed to. It was something only I could expiate.

It was here at a crossroads of my conscience that I fought for an answer, one I was almost afraid to find, let alone share with my wife.

As my steps carried me toward the colonnaded giant that for years had been sanctuary and home, I wondered which part of me would win the struggle for an answer, the man or the architect. Even I dared not explore that road too closely.

In my exile, the colonnaded monstrosity had haunted my dreams. Now that scarred remnant of opulence would either redeem, or destroy me.

The Opera house had been built in a large open space which had eventually become the centerpiece for the transformation of Paris. To a young boy roaming its monumental size, the theater had been an infinite playground. To an outcast young man, it became inspiration. I gave up terrorizing the ballet girls and began to study architecture in earnest.

Étienne's tutelage had given me the basics. I began to drift to various construction sites, learning what I could before too much suspicion or curiosity drove me on. These wanderings had an unexpected benefit other than knowledge, money. It allowed me to acquire books, education, and a bit of comfort. For the rest, I stole what I could, where I could, without too much notice. Through Étienne, I obtained access to the University, and if everything else in my life had to be a lie, the architectural certificate was not. It, at least, had been earned honestly, and it was the one thing that much later in life, I could cling to without regret. If I had to live in isolation, at least I had not totally wasted the chance Hélène had given me.

Even early on, while I created havoc in the kitchens or anywhere else my fancy took me within the theater, I knew I owed Hélène a debt that had to be repaid, that would be worthy of her. So I began to study in earnest. Not only architecture, but music as well. The theater was a wondrous world, all its secrets, all its schools laid out before me. Where Nature had given me talent, I now put it to use. No one ever noticed a shadow hovering just within the deeper shadows of scenery, or perhaps the extra hand at the ropes. No one noticed, and their world was mine.

But there was always one who knew, one who kept her secret, one who became my conscience, for no matter what I did, whether within the theater walls or outside in the world, Hélène was ever present. To her, I would not lie, could not, even if I had wanted to. Her actions long ago had sealed an invisible bargain between us, and her unwavering, silent friendship was all that stood between me and madness. For no matter that I lived surrounded by people, I was ever alone, would always be alone. Only the knowledge of Hélène's quiet presence somewhere in the theater above, was my consolation. When she married and left, I closed my heart to everything. My actions began to stir the mystique of the ghost in earnest, and there were times I wished they would catch me and put an end to the wretched solitude. Eventually Hélène's absence became a wound I could not assuage with music alone. I packed what I needed, left the theater, and France. Restlessness took me to one place or another, even for a time, to Persia, but loneliness brought me back to the house that I called home. On my return, I even went so far as to demand a salary from the manager in return for set designs and scores, a sum which was paid on a regular basis, and which kept me in comfort.

When Hélène returned to the theater and assumed the post of ballet mistress, the years of solitude had taken their toll. Even she barely recognized her charge in the man I had become. We parted, distant, though she never betrayed me, and with my unspoken promise to guard her two daughters. She had returned with two young girls in tow, one a quiet, shy brunette, the other a boisterous blonde who bore an uncanny resemblance to Hélène. Even though she never said so, I understood the latter to be Hélène's daughter. The other was an orphaned child, the daughter of a Swedish violinist. Hélène had brought her to the Opera so the girl would not starve on the streets. It soon became evident that the child had untapped talent she was afraid to use.

I would never know what possessed me, but something about the girl's fragility obsessed me, and I began to teach her, appearing to her as an 'angel' that she believed existed, that had been sent by her father. The poor child had no idea, and by the time my conscience began to whisper that it was wrong to use her, I was powerless to stop the deception. So we both spiraled down into a fire, a fire that consumed both of us.

That fire had consumed the theater as well. As my eyes studied the structure across the street, I tried to reconcile the Erik that had roamed within those walls, and the man that now stood facing those same walls, and found I could not. The one had been driven by despair and desolation. The other rose from the scorching flames to become a father, husband, and a man of standing within society. The one had to atone for the actions of the other so both could find peace.

A sudden chill breeze picked up. Drawing the cloak closer, I ducked into the heavy pedestrian traffic on the square, losing myself in the sea of humanity.

It was December 1892, and the beginning of Christmas festivities. Despite the chill and snow, vendors had set up stalls and carts of goods around the square, taking advantage of the public's generous mood. Even at this late hour, the vendors were doing brisk business.

I prowled the entire perimeter of the theater, eyes scanning the structure that once had been home with detached interest. If I was to restore this place, I needed to see for myself the extent of the damage that had been incurred during the fire, and later, by sheer neglect. A much more thorough evaluation would be done by the engineers, but for now, I had to rely on my own knowledge of this house. Then too, I needed to discover this new phantom. I had to know who had fallen into such an unhappy state as to have resorted to haunting this place.

Stopping here and there around the square, my eyes scanned the structure carefully, from the ground to the cupola. It was obvious that over the years attempts had been made to clean and repair the major damage, each effort abandoned with mixed results. These attempts had been half hearted at best, but at least the windows of the cupola had been boarded up, keeping the interior fairly protected. Or so I hoped.

I would have to slip inside and see for myself what had been wrought on the interior. The thought brought a grin to my lips. Me, sneaking into my own house! The irony was too much.

Stopping at one of the vendors, I made a purchase of a lantern, candles, and some oil, and as the shopkeeper counted out the change, I checked to make certain the well hidden, slim blades were in their places. The lasso was no longer practical, though I had never been without a weapon close to hand. Though I was fit, I was now at an age where I would not trust myself to come out the winner in a scrape, not without serious damage.

Giving a satisfied nod to no one in particular, I made my way through the crowds toward the doors of the theater. Working quickly and efficiently within the deep shadows cast by the columns and gas lights, I could not help a self-satisfied smile as the rusted lock gave way under gentle probing from one of the blades. My not so proper education still had its uses.

Slipping inside, I pushed the door to, finding myself in the blackness and utter silence of my former domain.

This seat of music had been my playground, my inspiration, my prison, my purgatory. Like the prodigal son, I had returned to confront the demon that still haunted me.

Chapter 46

Wandering the labyrinthine depths of my former house, I worked quickly, efficiently. Over the years, through neglect, the once shimmering grandeur of this place had become a dusty, shabby remnant of opulence. While some care had been expended on cleaning the outside, the scars of the disaster were still very much in evidence here. Mirrors had cracked, masonry had fallen, shattering the marble beneath, and an all pervasive smell of decay cloyed at the nose.

Closing my mind to all except the work, I walked through tunnels and passages known only to me, checking and springing the traps and mazes I had constructed during the years I had dwelled here. It would not do for any of my engineers to be caught in snares of my own making. Surprisingly, many of the mechanisms were still intact despite the neglect of years. One by one, I disabled them all, briefly amused by thoughts of what rumors these improvements would spark once they were discovered. But that was for another day. Time grew short, and I had yet to survey the upper portions of the theater.

I walked unerringly through the passage that once had led to the dressing rooms, my steps echoing forlornly in the dismal silence. Eventually they brought me to the tiers of boxes. I stopped at an all too familiar place, for a moment pausing to touch the wall of the yawning gap of what had been box five. It had been here that I had become so hopelessly ensnared by the incredible voice of a young girl.

I shook off the memory and continued the survey. I had to finish. It would not do to be caught by an intrepid gendarme. I had made a promise to my bride, a promise I was determined to keep.

The thought of Meg filled me with comforting warmth. Never in all my life had I dreamed love for me would be possible, not even with Christine. That had been raw, uncontrolled awakening of Erik as a man. I had had not the least idea what to do with the feelings the girl stirred, only that I wanted her voice, needed her to give life to my music. So I had decided to claim her, oblivious to her fear, insensitive to anything or anyone that would stand in the way of conquest, uncaring beyond any reason to whatever consequences befell. Even Hélène's eyes, with their silent reproach could not persuade me to leave off. From my first glimpse of Christine I was bound on a spiral of tragedy. The end could not have come about any other way.

Once again, it had been a young dancer who had held out her hand to me, pulling me from a fire of my own making. Meg had chosen to come with me as I struggled to find life as a man. It had been she who had laid firm foundations for Christine and me. I had had no choice but to build on them. It had been Meg who, through her steadfastness, had slowly begun to open my eyes to what life and living was all about. In the quiet resoluteness and determination that had marked the years in Brittany, feelings had developed between us that years later still surprised me with their intensity. I would finish here, go to my wife, and show her what she meant to me.

The sudden, piercing yowl of a cat drew my attention from pleasant thoughts to the large, empty square of darkness below. The stage. I had almost forgotten its existence. Now, as my eyes focused into the blackness, I perceived something moving there, a darker shadow than the rest. In the silence, my ears finally caught the trembling voice as it struggled to find a melody.

So, was this the Phantom that now wandered these forgotten halls?

Melting into the shadows, I made my way toward what remained of the orchestra pit. From there, I would have a good vantage point, and see just who haunted my old domain.

The shape upon the stage staggered in a poor parody of a dance, the layers of rags swathing the figure swaying with its erratic movements. Veils covered the head, themselves topped by a tattered hat. The hands that ceaselessly rubbed against each other were covered with nothing more than torn rags. When the reedy voice took up the melody once more, I closed my eyes in pity. A woman then was the new ghost of the Opera. A woman in deep distress, if not altogether far gone to reason. From the look of it, she had lived on the streets for some time. Would anyone be able to help her? Would I? Even if I could, how would I? What would I do with her? No matter. I had to try. That is why I had come.

Forcing down a sense of unease, I climbed onto the stage, my movements silent. Years of prowling in this theater had not been lost to the intervening years.

As the woman continued her unsteady dance, my ears at last caught her mumblings, and I recognized the Italian. There were many who aspired to the theater or the opera in Paris. Many found themselves used up after the first glimpse of glory. Had she been one of these? Had she foundered after a small triumph?

With a sudden sob the woman collapsed into a heap on center stage, her cries frightful in their utter pathos. So absorbed was she in whatever obsessed her mind that she did not notice my approach, or the creak my shoes made on the stage. I kneeled at her side, drawn to her more for her obvious misery than the original intent of my visit here.

As her sobs continued, my hands reached out to her almost of their own volition. She raised her veiled head, seizing my hands in a death grip. With a heart wrenching wail she pillowed her head against my shoulder and whispered. "Mi caro Piangi."

If it can be said that the blood runs cold and the heart stops beating on occasion, it was for me at that very moment.

I was glad of the blackness around us. It masked the horror that stole across my face at the discovery of her identity.

In her glory, I had relished terrorizing her. I had done everything I could to make her life on stage miserable, to humiliate her, to make her give way to Christine.

Now she was a sorry heap of rags, reduced to beggary and misery. Apparently my hands had wrought more that night than a fire. That she took me for her lost lover bore witness to her deep distress.

"Merde," was all I could whisper to the shadows surrounding us. I closed my eyes against the onslaught of remorse and blame. For even though I had not hurt Piangi that night, only knocked him out, this is what my hands had done. They had reduced this woman to a life in the street.

As I struggled to make sense of the chaos in my head, she continued to cling to my frame as if that alone would save her, her cries more wretched than some animal's in pain, and still her voice whispered her lost lover's name.

Rocking back on my heels, I allowed her the fantasy as I held her, perhaps a little more closely.

What was I to do with her? Allowing her to return from whence she had come was out of the question. Leaving her to the mercies of any institution did not bear thinking of. I could not take her home, and I could not foist her off on an unsuspecting friend.

As the shock of my discovery began to slowly fade, and coherent thought returned, I realized that once more Erik had been called to save an innocent. In an echo of the past, I knew just where Erik would find help.

How in the world was I ever going to explain this to my wife?

Chapter 47

"Mon Dieu! What happened?" Meg exclaimed in astonishment when I finally came to the hotel and our rooms, disheveled, without the cloak, shaking uncontrollably.

I moved past her to fill a large glass with wine, though more spilled on the floor than into the glass. My hands would not stop trembling.

"Erik, please, talk to me," Meg came up beside me just as the glass and wine crashed to the floor.

"Cagare!" I swore, clenching hands into fists against the mantel.

"What is it?" My wife's gentle yet firm voice finally penetrated the chaos in my head. I turned to look at her and a faint smile lifted my lips. Steadfast as she always was, Meg calmed the occasional storms within my soul. Now her eyes pleaded for an answer to my turmoil.

"Oh Meg," I began but the words died even before they had a chance to form. How could I even begin to tell her?

"I'm here."

"Meg," I started, once more searching for words, when I finally noticed the state of her undress. The peignoir was barely there. Any other time, the invitation would have been welcome. Now, all my fingers could do was gently lift the flimsy material and cover her shoulders.

"Get dressed," I said slowly, "and I will try to explain."

"Carlotta!" Meg's cry of shocked surprise mirrored my own at the discovery of the Opera's new phantom. "Mon Dieu!"

"Indeed."

"How? Where is she?" Meg's questions were punctuated by the fastening of clasps and buttons as she dressed.

"The how I am not certain." I shook my head, closing my eyes against the visions of the pitiful sight I had witnessed that night. "I suspect Piangi's death unraveled her."

Meg said nothing as she pulled on gloves. "The where is she's in a carriage below. Meg, what do I do with her? She is lost to reason." I looked imploringly into my wife's eyes, grasping her hands, as if holding onto them would end this nightmare that had opened up before me. "She thinks me Piangi returned to her." The uncontrollable shakes had begun once more.

Then Meg did something totally unexpected. She giggled. "You Piangi? Oh my dear, sweet Erik! You are in trouble indeed if she thinks you Piangi." She touched the flat of my stomach as she lightly kissed me.

"Meg, please. What do we do with her? I can't return her to the street!"

"No my dearest, you cannot do that." She tossed a wrap over the dress she wore.

"Then what is to be done? We cannot keep her here."

"No, we cannot." Meg closed the distance between us and looked into my agonized face. She took my hands in hers and held fast.

"Have you never wondered what I did after I left? Have you never wondered what I did with your money?"

At the silent answer in my eyes, she smiled a little and caressed the masked side of my face. "Let me show you something, my heart. Let me show you something that might lighten your conscience."

Chapter 48

"The hospital of Saint Hubert, please," Meg quietly instructed the driver before entering the carriage. I followed, dreading the journey. Mercifully, Carlotta's pitiful form lay sleeping, bundled into the warmth of the cloak.

All through the drive I could not meet my wife's eyes. Remorse over the fate of the woman I had disliked so much in my earlier life hung around me like an invisible shadow. Not even the scars that ravaged my former home had shaken me so deeply as the lamentable heap of rags now lying on the seat of the carriage. Had I spent all these years in a vain attempt to surmount the past, only to have it resurface, to have it throw me back into the pit from whence I had come? Was I still, after all, the demon that the gypsies had thought me to be? Would my hands continue to wreak chaos on all that they touched?

"We're here," Meg said gently as the carriage came to a stop. Her hands seized mine, her eyes forcing me to look at her. "Whether you believe it or not Erik, you are a good man. You could have left her," she nodded toward our unexpected guest, "in the street, but you didn't. You could have left a child to its fate, but you didn't." She pressed her hand to my heart. "It's in here, that which I love. Come with me, dear, sweet husband, and let me show you what Erik Marchand has done."

We exited the carriage, Carlotta's minimal weight cradled in my arms. She barely stirred as Meg led the way through an iron gate toward an old building surrounded by cypress trees. It was late, but lights could still be seen within a few of the many windows. The snow crunched softly underneath our shoes.

Almost instantly after Meg rang the bell, the door was opened by a young woman dressed in a white nurse's uniform. Her face was partially hidden in the shadows cast by the lanterns on either side of the door.

"Bon soir, Julie. Is Gilbert here?" Meg asked.

"Oui, Mademoiselle. Come in. I'll fetch him." As she stepped aside to let us pass, the light struck her face, and even though I was burdened, I started at the face that looked back at me. Inured as I had been from earliest memory to pain and the grotesqueness of my own visage, this young woman bore silent witness to horrors even I could not contemplate. Though she was perhaps no more than eighteen, the scars crisscrossing her face made her seem a woman of twice that age.

I followed Meg to a small sitting room, while Julie disappeared down the hall, as silent as a shadow. Meg indicated the sofa where I lay my burden down as gently as I could.

"Meg, you have changed your mind?" A young man entered the room minutes later, his white coat rumpled, his hair disheveled.

"Oh no, Gilbert. I am leaving. I only came to bring you another charge I'm afraid." Meg indicated the sleeping form on the sofa then took my hand and pulled me forward. "C'est mon mari."

The young man thrust out his hand. It was only now, as my eyes fully fell on him that I noticed the left half of his face was barely there. The scars that had healed the wounds must have been a daily reminder of whatever trauma had caused them. Yet he smiled as he continued to hold out his hand.

Slowly, I returned his grip, mesmerized by the apparent ease with which he accepted his fate. I, who had thought my own face too repulsive to bear, had hid it behind a mask. This man did not. I was looking into a near echo of my own face, a face that had somehow found acceptance in the world, or at least, this part of it.

He pressed my hand, laughing. "Meg had warned us she was leaving to get married. For once, I am glad it is not another tall tale for her children."

I threw Meg a sharp glance, a look she chose not to see.

"We brought you a patient, Gilbert. She's had a few shocks. She will not know who or where she is. I'll explain in the morning. Are there rooms we can use?"

" Mine," he answered with a smile. "Julie and I have duty tonight. Don't worry. We'll take care of her," he said, indicating the woman on the sofa with a slight inclination of his head.

"Thank you, Gilbert. Bon soir." Meg slid her arm beneath mine, and before I had time to form any questions, began to lead me through silent halls, past many closed doors, her warmth holding me fast.

"I found this place a year after I left," my wife's soft voice began to weave around me. "It was in a sorry state, and they couldn't keep a staff for more than a few months. My mother and I, we started working here, doing what we could to help. With the money you left, I hired workmen to repair what needed to be done, and doctors who were willing to face a challenge. The abandoned fields behind, we turned into gardens where we grow herbs for the balms and tinctures." Meg paused, giving me a small smile as she shook her head. "I remember Christine's surprise when she discovered what I did. Keeping it from her would have been useless, though she never realized the reasons why I took this on, not I think, until a few days ago. There was only one secret I needed to keep from her, and that was you." She smiled as she caressed my face, continuing her tale. "This is a hospital where those like Julie and Gilbert have a chance. He was my first orphan, the first child to come through these doors. He was no more than twelve when they brought him here, badly burned from a fire. He wanted to study medicine. I used your money for his schooling."

I remained silent, too stunned at her disclosure to speak, uncertain of what to do, or what I was feeling. Meg once more grasped my arm, and we continued our walk.

"I've worked here these past years, caring for the Eriks and Gilberts no one wants to see. Most of them are orphans. We do what we can. Some heal and leave, others decide to stay and help, like Gilbert."

"And Julie?" I finally found my voice, eyes studying the woman before me. The obvious love she bore her charges suffused her very essence.

For one brief moment, Meg turned her eyes away, and I understood that whatever other tragedies were hidden within these walls, this one would not be easy to hear, or tell, by the way Meg looked at me.

"She was left here, by her own mother. The woman apparently did not wish a daily reminder of her husband's 'indiscretion.'" Meg's voice, though level and collected, began to paint images in my head far worse than a painter could ever have produced. "The scars were her father's gift after he was done with her. She was no more than eleven years old. It was a mercy she did not carry her child to term."

I reeled with the impact of those last words, and thought I would be ill right then and there. Whatever horrors I had endured in that cage in the gypsy camp, had been nothing to what I was hearing.

Meg's gentle hands grasped mine as she looked at me, full of understanding, full of compassion.

"This is why I stayed. These children had no one to show them kindness, no one to extend a shred of understanding." She brought our entwined hands to rest over her heart. "As you had no one. In these last years, you were always here, giving them what you never had." She smiled a little, the smile softening the solemn mask her face had become during the tale. "Your hands did this," she gestured at our surroundings, "not mine." Whereupon my wife tenderly kissed me. I could only embrace and hold her within the circle of my arms. There was nothing I could say in answer to the revelations that had been made.

After a time, we made our silent way to Gilbert's tiny, administrator's rooms.

It was morning the following day, and I still reeled from the discoveries and revelations of the night before. Meg had left early to discuss matters with Gilbert, while I tried to find composure and rest.

That Meg had a kind and generous heart was something I had known since first encountering her in my dark domain. That she would lavish love on children not her own was not in itself a surprise, considering the love and care she had given Christine, and how much she wanted some of her own. That she had used the money I had given her was expected. It had been hers to do with as she pleased. That she had used it all for this one purpose left me astounded.

Finding myself at a loss as what to do until she returned, I wandered into the sitting room, hoping to find distraction to the chaos of thoughts and feelings I dared not sort out.

I found myself the object of curious eyes as the children gathered in that room looked up from their books, their nurse and teacher giving me an inquisitive, if somewhat shy glance.

"My apologies," I murmured, making ready to withdraw, but the young woman smiled and answered. "It's all right. Stay. We'll be finishing the lesson soon."

I accepted with a nod, and as she called her students back to order, my eyes swept over the disparate group sitting in a circle around her. They ranged in age, from perhaps sixteen, to the little one of no more than three, huddled by herself and playing with a tattered doll.

Seeing her, a small smile escaped me as I recalled my own daughter at that age, now a grown woman with a child of her own. Perhaps it was the girl's innocence, her utter dependence on others that drew me to her, or just the wistful memory of Christine. For whatever reason, I gathered the child to me, allowing her fingers to explore the face I would not let others see. From the first, it was evident that this child was blind, and for the duration of that day, we became fast companions, for she refused to leave my arms.

When my eyes finally caught a glimpse of Meg's gold hair over the gathered heads, I smiled to myself, adding a bit more verve to the tale I had been weaving. If Meg had spun stories for these children, I would not disappoint them. I had begun to tell tales of caravanserai, and nomads, and somewhere along the way, my hands had begun to spin simple magic. The gamins and even some of the nurses and doctors began to appear in the tiny room, listening to tales of faraway lands.

Finishing a particularly lurid tale of bandits, I signaled the show was over. The children protested, reluctantly accompanying the nurses back to their rooms, all except one. Céline still clung to me, refusing to let go.

I was exhausted. Not all of what I had told had been fanciful make believe. Six years of travel through Eastern lands had imparted interesting experiences.

Meg approached, smiling, smoothing Céline's hair. "Now do you see? Now do you understand? You are a good man, Erik Marchand, even when you don't want to be." She kissed me, twining her arm around mine.

When I lay the child in her bed, I raised my eyes to Meg's, eyes that perhaps had been opened to more than what had been beyond my own past and pain. I was not alone, had never been alone, in misery, despair and suffering.

"Let's go home Meg, truly home this time."

Chapter 49

The highly anticipated and celebratory homecoming was finally over. Greetings and congratulations had been dully exchanged, then one by one, everyone discreetly left. At long last, Meg and I had some peace, had time alone.

I was overjoyed to be at the estate once more, startled to realize that until Meg stepped through the door of the villa, it had just been a house, nothing more. With her beside me, it had become a home.

She and Christine fell into each other's arms, laughing and crying at the same time. While Meg reacquainted herself with little Erica, Christine came to me, holding me tightly for a long time. I kissed the top of her head, returning the embrace, holding her as closely as her swelled condition would allow.

"Merci, ma chérie fille," I murmured to her.

She gave me a final squeeze before disengaging her hold. "I'm glad you found what you were looking for, Papa."

I smiled at her, brushing a hand against her cheek, giving her a lopsided grin. "That and more besides."

She kissed my cheek, hustling her family away, giving me a final smile over her shoulder as they disappeared into the house.

Now, it was just my bride and me. Our journey home had been uneventful and though Carlotta's fate still troubled me, I was assured of one thing. Her care would be the best. If she could not regain her sanity, at least she would be safe and protected, not exposed to ridicule.

"Come," I took Meg's hand, slowly leading her up the stairs to the study. The connecting door to the bedroom was ajar. Lamps had been left burning, giving the rooms a welcoming, warm, glow. There was time, lots of time. I wanted her to know me, wanted her to know the man who had been away from her for so long. I wanted no secrets between us, not on this part of our journey. There would be no more ghosts between us, no more demons to drive us apart.

I watched in contemplative silence as Meg explored the cramped room, her fingers trailing over books, sketches, and the overflowing music sheets scattered atop the upright piano, the pictures in their frames crowding the desk.

I relished each smile, each glance she directed my way. Most of all, I cherished her. Only once did she pause in her exploration, only once did her hands hesitate over a framed picture.

"I will not lie to you. There will always be a part of her in my heart, but it is you I love Meg. You alone."

Meg turned and came to me, her dark eyes filled with inner fire. Her hands reached toward my face and tenderly unmasked me.

"I love you, Erik Marchand. You, as you are. No masks, no pretense." She walked past me toward the bedroom, loosening her golden hair as she did so. I followed, mesmerized by her.

Meg walked toward the wall where Christine's collage hung, now surrounded by pictures of the family. Meg studied the various portraits, but only one seemed to hold her interest. When at last she turned to face me, there was a small smile curving her lips.

"That is how I have always seen you, even when you were being not so good." She lightly kissed me, then continued the investigation of her new domain.

I eased out of the jacket, laying it over a chair. "I'm sorry Meg. This will have to do for a while."

She stopped a bare hand's breadth from me, lifting her eyes to mine. The smoldering look I saw there sent delicious quivers through me.

"It's fine. It has everything I need right here."

Her fingers lightly brushed the outline of my face, trailing down toward my chest where she began to loosen the buttons of the shirt, one at a time. Each touch of her fingers, each feather light kiss set fire to my soul. I savored the sensations she awakened, rejoiced in the spell she held me under. I relished the sudden and utter weakness that overtook me as her fingers slowly worked their way down.

If I had thought I had known passion before, I was wrong, so terribly wrong. Passion was being in my wife's arms, being loved by her eyes alone. I breathed deeply, calming the impulse to gather her into my arms. I would not distract her from what she so obviously enjoyed doing. So I stayed unmoving, savoring my agony.

With slow, deliberate movements, Meg peeled back the shirt, running fingers lightly over my chest.

"Do you like what you see?" I asked in a barely audible whisper.

She kissed what she had revealed, raised her head, and smiled as her hands pushed the shirt off my shoulders. "Allow me to see the rest and I will let you know."

I could hold back no longer. My hands buried themselves in her glorious, gold hair, drew her forward, and I bent down to kiss her.

"What about now?" I breathed, coming up for air, looking into her eyes.

"Hmm. Once more, so I can be sure."

I complied, this time lifting her and depositing her on the bed.

"Ah mon chèr mari. Tu es tres charmant," she sighed, twining her arms around my neck.

"I'll be something else soon enough," I whispered, teasing her lobes with gentle kisses while my fingers loosened the buttons of her dress.

"I have always loved you," Meg breathed into my ear as I turned to kiss her once more.

Chapter 50

Christine and Phillippe's son was born a week after our arrival. He was a most welcome addition to the growing family, and this time, I was grateful that Christine had her mother beside her to help through the ordeal.

Despite Christine's pain, the women exchanged looks and smiles that I could only wonder at. At one time, I caught Meg stealing a glance in my direction, a look that was at once full of mystery, secrets, and unspoken possibilities.

Christine named him Gérard Phillippe. When everything quieted down and the new mother finally rested, Meg and I walked out into the gardens.

Twilight painted everything in gentle, pastel colors. This had become my favorite time of day, the quiet settling after a day's incessant bustling. With Meg beside me, I felt the twilight had finally found me. Perhaps here, with family around me, I could at last find rest and respite from a struggle to overcome a murky past.

With my arm nestled against her waist, I walked down the path with Meg, who was my wife, who now filled that part of me that for years had been hollow, that had cried out to her even before I knew it.

Long ago we had become partners in a tangled endeavor. We had become integral parts of each other even then, and over the years, the bonds had strengthened, not grown less, despite our separation.

Though my daughter knew what lay beneath the mask I wore, it was only with my wife I discarded my prison, only with her, because with Meg, I felt whole, complete.

We walked through the olive grove to my favorite place, the hill overlooking the valley below. From here, in the peacefulness of the coming evening, we watched the stars appear above us.

Meg leaned her head against my shoulder, and I held her a little tighter, fervently giving silent thanks to all the Fates for her, for her heart, for her love.

I kissed her hair, murmuring softly. "I am glad you are here."

She nestled even deeper into the embrace. "There is no other place I would ever want to be. Your arms are my home."

I held her for long, quiet minutes, relishing the wonder of holding her.

"Christine is a beautiful, young woman, Erik. You did well."

I laughed softly, teasing a stray curl of gold hair against my fingers. "A reliable source tells me I had help, lots of help."

She laughed. "How else, my dear, would you have lived to tell the tale?"

"How indeed."

"Oh Erik, I did not wish to be away," Meg broke the embrace, turning to look into my eyes.

I sighed, reaching to lightly caress her face. "I know." It had taken time and the affection of a distant friend, before I could release the chains and demons that had stood in our way the first time. I would never have been able to give Meg then what I could now, which was my soul.

"Christine started asking questions I had no answers to," I began, "and housekeepers, well…" I let the statement hang. "I let her find you. You were the only mother she's ever known. I could not be so cruel and rip you from her heart for ever or her from yours. I gave her Étienne's address, to give her a connection to you." It had after all been so easy. All of those years apart, and I had known exactly where Meg had been, where I would find her, but I had sent her away for a reason, and until the dark demons left me, there would have been nothing for her.

Meg chuckled. "I did wonder how she found me." My wife gave me a sidelong look. "But then, I knew her father, and understood that under his tutelage, she would become a resourceful, young woman."

"My dear wife, do you mean to imply that I would have given our daughter an untoward education?"

She laughed and pressed her hands against my chest. "Consider the source of that education, my dear."

"Hmmm." I pursed my lips in thought. "True. She has learned a few tricks," I admitted, and deep down inside, could not hide a shade of pride at how well Christine had learned those lessons. They would hold her in good stead someday. "As perhaps have I," I murmured, and pulling Meg close, slipped the diamond ring on her finger. I finally had had time to find one that suited her.

"Merry Christmas, Madame Marchand," I whispered, this time kissing her with all the love in my heart.

Chapter 51

Paris in January was a dismal place. It was made even more so for lack of Meg's company. I had had to leave my bride in Italy and join Étienne, so we could begin the restoration of the Opera house.

From the outset, it was clear that this would not be a simple project, nor had I expected it to be. The damage from the fires had been thorough. It would take years to put to order.

Étienne's negotiations with the government proved long and arduous, and as they dragged on, our frustration only grew. With our agreement to do the work, came an inordinate amount of foot dragging. It was nothing less than what I had expected.

Not content to idly wait while the powers that be made up their minds, I purchased apartments not too far from Étienne's offices, and while he presented our proposals to the officials, I began the task of assembling crews. Only the best and most trusted men would work here. I would not allow any unskilled hands near the Populaire. The men would come from Rome, Vienna, even Prague, and all the places that I had once called 'home' at one time or another.

Contracts for various portions of the work were already in place. It remained to only receive government approval, and funds.

As the weeks wore on with no end to the negotiations in sight, I chafed at the bureaucratic nonsense. I spent many a long evening studying the survey reports from engineers, familiarizing myself with the details of their findings. Most I already knew, from my own assessments weeks before. While there was considerable damage, most of it had been confined to surface areas. The structure itself, the heart, had been left unscathed. This alone would make the work easier.

Meg's absence was an aching gap in my heart. I had had to leave her behind as there would not have been time to devote to each other, not as I wanted to, and she had needed time with her family, time with our daughter. So I had come to Paris alone, but now her absence, and the inactivity ate away what little patience I had left.

Surprising perhaps even myself one evening, I summoned a cab, giving the man an address before I could change my mind.

Julie gave a start when she saw me at the door, but with a slight nod, ushered me in. Once over the threshold, my resolve and reason for coming, faltered. I did not belong here, and I began to wonder why I had come at all. Yet I stayed, for there was nowhere else to go. Cold, empty rooms were very unappealing. This was where Meg had been, where she had given her heart, and right then, I needed to be as close to her as I possibly could be.

The thought of my wife elicited a smile. Strange how after so many years alone, the mere thought of Meg brought a comforting sensation where, for so long, there had only been emptiness. It was strange but pleasant to belong with someone so completely that the mere thought of her filled me with warmth. It was something I had never dared hope for.

During the three years Meg and I had spent together, shades of these feelings had developed though neither of us could have put a name to them had we even tried. Both of us had been inexperienced, and perhaps not ready to face the challenges that faced us. So we had gone our separate ways, each to sort a path, but time and our hearts had brought us together once more.

Those years had given each of us a foundation, a foundation not only for our separate lives but for the US that came later. It had come late, but it had come. It had been there all along, from the moment Meg had handed me a bundled newborn. It had been an US, whether unacknowledged, or as now, an all pervasive love, and I rejoiced in it.

Julie brought a tray with tea, and as I drank the steaming liquid, Gilbert joined me, taking a much needed break from his rounds. Polite, ineffectual conversation broke when the one question I needed an answer to slipped past my lips.

"She's gained weight, and some of her voice." Gilbert smiled. "For some reason she will not give up the cloak."

"Let her keep it." It was time to leave. Gilbert accompanied me to the door.

"Please extend our regards to Madame."

I nodded, and this time did not bother with a cab. A long, brisk walk would settle the pot of agitation the visit had stirred.

Chapter 52

It was February 1893, and as the days wore on and the government continued to vacillate on a decision, more often than not, the long winter evenings found me at St. Hubert's.

Purposefully, I avoided going or being anywhere near Christine's school. That part of my life was over. Though on my wedding day Christine and I had come to an accommodation, there was no need to reopen old wounds, for either of us. It was done.

At first, my visits to the hospital were short. I told myself that I came only to ask after Carlotta's progress, yet each time I walked through the doors, I seemed to find a reason to stay.

Even before I became aware of it, these excursions grew to be a regular part of my evening and welcome distractions from reading mind numbing reports or listening to Étienne's justified grumblings. He seethed with frustration at the bureaucrats holding us back. Like me, he was eager to begin the work. Each day of delay would make the work that much harder.

Julie became accustomed to seeing me on the doorstep of the hospital and she would have tea ready and waiting even as I walked up the path to the house. A faint smile began to replace the coldness I had seen on her face. Knowing her history, I could not begrudge her the dislike of men, or the near open hostility that on occasion, flashed in her eyes. At times, I wondered that she could function at all.

As my visits grew longer and more frequent, Gilbert and I developed camaraderie of our own. We would share the tea in his office while exchanging small pleasantries. Perhaps it was the common bond of our faces that drew us together.

One evening Julie greeted me with barely contained excitement. Putting a finger to her lips, she led me toward the sitting room. From the hall I could hear a voice that for years, in an earlier life, I had tried to silence.

Carefully, so as not to disturb the scene, I looked around the doorway to be greeted by a sight I would not have thought possible. A thin, but no longer frail, woman stood in the center of the room, singing an Italian folk song for a gathering of Meg's gamins. While her voice was shaky, it was fair. It would never be operatic again, but from the rapt attention in the room, it was sufficient to hold interest for an audience. Given time, it could be trained again.

I turned away and began to walk toward Gilbert's office. I could not help a light chuckle as I recalled the many times the char women at the Opera house had covered their ears so they would not have to endure Carlotta's screeching. Yet now, for an unknown reason, hearing the sound of that voice gladdened my heart. The years had indeed played with us if the sound of Carlotta's shrill tones elicited fond memories. Perhaps she was not as lost as I had thought.

"I never thought I would be glad to hear that voice again." A soft, gentle, and familiar voice said beside me.

Deep in my thoughts, I had not seen Hélène approach. Her appearance here was not a total surprise. Like Meg, she had devoted years to this place and would not have abandoned it lightly, even after assuming her new profession.

I looked into her eyes, smiling. "If truth be told, nor I," I admitted. No matter how I had treated her before, Carlotta did not deserve the merciless coldness of the streets.

"She is not so far gone that a good teacher would not know how to bring the best out of her." Hélène said, laying a hand on my arm.

"It would take more than a teacher to tame that one." I replied, recalling all the times Carlotta had stormed in her tantrums.

Hélène chuckled, her fingers on my arm squeezing a little harder. "Then perhaps in this case, fire should fight fire. Good night, Erik." She gave my arm a final squeeze before slowly walking away.

I sighed, watching Hélène's elegant figure disappear down the hall. I had never assumed or presumed our association more than it was, yet our invisible bonds had strengthened with the fact that her daughter had become my wife. Even now, after all these years, she was still my conscience, still my friend, and perhaps for the first time, I realized that she was more, had always been. Hélène, despite being only three years my senior, was the mother I had never had.

Chapter 53

Finally in late March of 1893, Étienne at long last received agreement from the authorities to begin the restoration. Like eager boys of sixteen, we dove into the work, glad to put an end to aimless waiting.

With work on the Opera house begun in earnest, I decided to send for Meg. I could no longer be without her. While I awaited her arrival, my visits to St. Hubert's continued.

With each day, Carlotta's voice improved slightly. She lost the tremor in it, and often she could be found in the sitting room, entertaining the children with songs from her native country. While I knew her repertoire was not limited, she preferred the songs of her homeland to those of her operatic career. The children loved no matter what she sang. They gathered around her and listened, none making a sound until the performance was over. For her turn, the woman seemed to almost blossom under their attention, as if that was what she had needed to break her from the prison of her misery.

I shook my head as I walked toward Gilbert's office. Never would I have believed that Carlotta would ever be one to tolerate a group of street urchins around her. Perhaps time spent on the streets had mellowed her fiery nature.

After a brief exchange with Gilbert and his staff, I arranged for a piano to be sent to the hospital, along with one of those small, hateful dogs Carlotta had once adored.

I was assured a few days later that the small creature had become everyone's pet. It had managed to throw one and all into an uproar at least twice when it had disappeared, only to be found later, nibbling sweets in Carlotta's lap. I laughed. At least that had not changed!

With a piano now installed in the sitting room, I was free to play, and often did, late into the evening, or until politeness chased me back to my own, cold, and empty rooms.

As with Carlotta's singing, my playing developed an audience as well. Soon, music filled the evenings at St. Hubert's. Those that could not attend the impromptu gatherings could at least hear music through the halls.

When Julie tentatively asked me to teach her to play, I agreed, with one stipulation. That she in turn teach Céline. More than once, I had seen the child clamber onto the piano bench, her little fingers unerringly plucking out a melody. Despite her young age and blindness, there was talent in that child, and I would not see it wasted. It was a bargain Julie consented to easily. Despite her previous coldness, I sensed that she harbored special affection for this one child. So at fifty eight, I became a teacher once more.

Chapter 54

It was mid May when Meg telephoned to announce her arrival to our house. Leaving the work in Étienne's capable hands, I repaired to Brittany to be with my wife. I had no desire to be anywhere near the Opera once the engineers commenced their work in the labyrinthine tunnels. There would no doubt be awkward questions once they came upon my various improvements. I had made them to prevent intrusion into what had been my home, whether by purpose or unintended blunder. I had no desire to relive that life, and certainly not through someone's curiosity. That life had been full of hopeless despair and longing that surely madness would have followed had it not all burned that one night.

I had barely stepped from the carriage when Meg's arms seized me in a tight embrace, her lips warm on my cheek as she kissed me. Returning her greeting in equal measure, I was once again overwhelmed and delighted that she had consented to be my wife and partner.

Taking up the valise, I let her lead me into the house, the house we had shared so many years before. When the door closed, I held her close, relishing her nearness. Never again would I be alone. She filled my days and nights, and never again would solitude hold me in its prison.

Meg gave my shoulders a squeeze before drawing back a little and smiling, ordered, "Close your eyes."

"My dear heart," my meek protest ended under her fingers as they pressed against my lips.

"You heard me." She commanded.

Giving her a speculative glance, I complied, allowing her to guide me. With a light kiss and a whisper of "You may look now", she released me.

The parlor was as I remembered it, with one major exception. A small piano had been wedged beside the window. It was placed so there would be maximum light for composing. Blank music sheets lay atop the gleaming, ebony wood. Overwhelmed by Meg's gift, I grazed fingers over the keys, letting the swell of sound drift around the small room. The instrument had been expertly tuned.

Meg's arm slipped around my waist, and I drew her close, kissing the softness of her hair.

When she spoke, her soft voice wrapped around me with its love. "I knew how much you missed your music when we lived here. This time, I did not wish you to be without it. I did not wish to be without it. If we are to live here again Erik, I want your music to fill the days."

I smiled, kissing her. "It will, and we will, at least for a time." Meg did not question the answer. She smiled, took my hand, and led me through the short hall to the back garden.

Where before it had been a bare patch of earth, it was now a lush, blooming sanctuary. The path and the planters I had made remained, as well as the stone bench beneath the trellis, now overgrown with the climbing roses. We had begun this garden awkwardly, with halting efforts, but like us, it had flourished.

Like the garden, the once lost man and an abandoned child that had become our daughter, had thrived here. As with the flowers, Christine and I had set healthy roots under Meg's vigilant care.

"It's beautiful," I sighed, drawing her close. She leaned into the embrace, and for a few minutes we remained silent, each of us lost in thought.

At last Meg broke the stillness, turning to look at me. Not for the first time was I astounded by the burning passion I saw in those lovely eyes. Her hands reached to caress my face.

"The day I saw you here, in so much pain, you have no idea how close I came to breaking the rules. I had to run, had to hide, or I would have come to you right then."

I sighed, the memory of that afternoon as fresh as if it had been yesterday. The bare glimpse of her face as she had hurried into the kitchen, the swirl of her skirts as she had jerked them to keep from tripping, the stiff back as she strove to contain her cries, all the fleeting memories bringing the emotions of that day to the fore.

I may have been distressed then, and my mind in chaos, but I had seen something in Meg's eyes before she had quickly turned away, something that twenty two years later still seared through me with surprising force. It had been raw desire. Only now I understood how close to the brink we both had been. It had taken the last shred of tattered will to keep from touching her in the kitchen that afternoon long ago.

I pulled my wife close, kissing her lightly, brushing a hand through her magnificent, golden hair. "I was so afraid you would. I don't know if I would have had the strength to say no," I whispered, finally acknowledging the nerve-racking tension that had been between us that day so many years past. Looking into her eyes, I at last admitted the truth even to myself. "I would never have wanted to hurt you, not like that. You deserved better than a broken man."

Meg smiled, nestling her head against my shoulder. "I did better. I have you."

I held her tightly to me, breathing in the wonder of her. For several minutes we stood like that, neither daring to move and break the moment.

When at last Meg raised her head to look at me, her eyes seared me with fire. When her lips closed over mine, they ignited a fire of a different kind.

Twenty two years of long buried passions found release. We loved as if tomorrow would never come, as so long ago we had not dared to.

Chapter 55

Our three weeks of absolute contentment eventually gave way to practical matters when I had to return to work. Reluctant to be apart again, Meg and I agreed to divide our time between Brittany and Paris, as practicable.

I was most anxious for Meg to see the progress that had been made at St. Hubert's during her absence, as I knew she was eager to see her gamins.

We walked into the hospital one evening to be over run by anxious children, all grabbing onto Meg, all bursting with questions.

Giving her a light kiss, I walked to Gilbert's office. The chaos behind me, my wife would have to sort out on her own.

By the time Meg joined us, most everyone had gone to sleep. A peaceful silence had descended upon the halls, broken only by the soft tones of a simple melody teased from the piano in the sitting room. The gentle music drifted through the open door of the office. Gilbert and I exchanged a glance.

At Meg's questioning look, Gilbert nonchalantly shrugged his shoulders. "She has been most diligent in her lessons during your absence, monsieur." He said, giving me a mischievous wink.

"Good," I nodded approval. We were both enjoying Meg's growing bewilderment far too much. "And the other?"

"Lessons also practiced, as you directed. In fact, they do it together now."

I raised the good brow in silent query. Gilbert smiled. "After a heated debate, of course."

"Of course," I agreed with a chuckle. Before departure for Brittany, I had left specific instructions with Gilbert regarding Carlotta's singing, as well as a stack of songs for her to practice. They had been carefully chosen, each more demanding of the voice and its range.

"What are you two hiding?" Meg inquired, her curiosity piqued.

"Nothing, love. Come, it's late," I said, leading her out of the office. With a glance back at Gilbert, I forbade him to give anything away.

As if she noticed the comforting music for the first time, Meg stopped our progress, studying me with her dark, knowing eyes. "You sent the piano, didn't you?"

I remained silent. What could I say?

She smiled. "It could only have been you." We resumed our walk toward the main door of the hospital. "You have a good heart, my dearest, and it shows in the most unexpected ways." Meg added in a voice that was a caress, squeezing my arm tighter.

I held her close on the ride back to our apartment. Somehow in all the years, this woman had gentled the raging beast that had dwelled within me. I kissed the top of her head, closing my eyes, savoring the pleasure of holding my wife to my heart.

As summer wore on, routine once again re-established itself in our lives. We fell into it easily, as if twenty years had not gone in between.

I spent the days at the Opera house, where work had advanced well, despite my absence. The underground surveys had been concluded, and while I reviewed the reports one day, Étienne came into the office carrying an oblong package. Ironically, it was the same office where Firmin and Andre had held court during their brief tenure as managers of this once elegant house. With time and patience, it would be so again.

Étienne set the parcel atop the clutter on the desk, giving me a knowing look. "I thought perhaps you would know what to do with this," he said, smoothing his thick mustache. "They found it by the underground lake," he sighed, as his fingers tapped the wrappings. "In any case, I thought it would be safer with you than at an auction house." He said quietly and left, closing the door softly behind him.

I placed a hand over the worn, dusty, material. The brilliant scarlet and gold was faded now, but my fingers knew the fabric intimately. It had covered the mirror that had brought me to Christine time and time again.

It did not matter how I tried to escape the life that had been. Somehow, pieces of it continued to find me.

I shook my head, partly in bemused wonder, partly in sadness for the man who had existed in this place, who had cried for understanding, for a shred of compassion, for the love that was granted even to the lowest of the low. That man had had nothing but loneliness and emptiness as consolation. Only music had been his salvation, music and then her, an angel that had brought him a ray of hope, a ray of sunshine to the pit of hell he called home. As with all dreams, that one had shattered. She had left, her last words as near a curse as his former appellation had been.

Closing eyes against the onslaught of memory, I brushed my fingers over the object on the desk. By its length, it could only be one thing.

The man who had haunted these halls, who had toyed with the managers, had been another Erik, not me, and yet that man had given me life. He had brought about the father, the architect, and now the husband. I could not deny him forever.

When my fingers closed over the sword, years of struggle against the shadow of my former self melted away. In that one moment, I accepted the shadow of the man that occasionally visited my dreams. There really was no choice. Perhaps in healing this house, that shadow too, would find peace.

Drawing a deep breath, I placed the sword beside the chair and returned to the reports.

Meg spent her days either in her mother's company, or with Christine at the school. The two women remained friends, and always would be. After all, they had grown up together. While their husbands maintained hostile distance, these two women never would. They were sisters, despite being opposites in nature. Even early on, during their years at the Opera, their differing personalities had been striking. Where Meg had been boisterous, unafraid and ready to face challenges, Christine had been shy, timid, and impressionable.

Perhaps that had been the why of the whole affair to begin with. In Christine, I had found someone I could mold into anything I had wanted because of her vulnerability. I had been snared by her pure voice, then by her beauty. I had used whatever means necessary to bind her to me, to hold her under my spell. If being an angel to her was what it took, then I became one to her. It had taken so little effort. The price exacted for that deception had been high. I had used her, and used her badly.

While I carefully avoided being anywhere near Christine, Meg was overjoyed to be in her friend's company once more. I did not ask what transpired between them. What Meg related was her choice, but her pleasure in Christine's friendship was obvious.

Two evenings each week, we would visit St. Hubert's. Meg refused to totally abandon her former work, and I had my own reasons for these expeditions. Meg had guessed at these, but never voiced her suspicions. Her smile was enough as we would part in the hall, and I took my place beside my student.

Julie had indeed been most studious during my absence. Though she never volunteered any information about her past, it was clear that at least part of her education had included music lessons. Her playing came naturally, and she did not struggle with the basics, unlike most people.

It was the other student, the one I trained by day during the noon breaks at the Opera house, the one Meg rarely inquired about, that surprised me.

During the three weeks of my absence, she too had made astonishing progress. Her voice had achieved confidence, clarity and strength. Though at times our sessions were no more than shouting matches, still, Carlotta was nowhere near her former, contentious self. Life among the destitute had apparently mellowed some of her fiery nature. Still, the emerging woman retained her passion. For no reason that I could define, that pleased me. I hid a smile as I recalled Hélène's words of fighting fire with fire.

Despite heated arguments, Carlotta proved willing enough to cooperate in her instruction. She did not overly question the sudden appearance of a masked teacher within the hospital walls, and I tolerated the presence of her dog. We found concord through music.

Carlotta's improvement gratified me. Despite our history of animosity toward each other, I was genuinely pleased that she found solace in her singing. I too, had gone through an upheaval when my children had saved me through music. Now, it seemed, it was up to me to pull Carlotta from hers. The irony did not escape me.

If music had been a healing balm for me, I let it be for Carlotta.

Chapter 56

I leaned against the door jamb, totally hypnotized by the sight before me. Meg sat on the bed, her back toward me, brushing her gold hair. The lace of her robe spilled around her like a cloud, and for a moment, I had to remind myself that this vision was real, that the angel sitting before me was my wife.

I smiled, walked to her side, and taking the brush from her hands, I continued what she had started.

Sometime before, I had divested myself of mask, wig, restraining jacket and vest. In my wife's presence, I had ceased to hide behind a disguise. She desired the real Erik, not the affectation.

Meg smiled as I began to brush her hair, though she remained sitting with her back against me, leaning into the firm strokes with obvious pleasure.

My surprise for her earlier that evening had been a pleasant revelation for both of us.

We had gone to St. Hubert's as usual, only to be greeted by the most unexpected of gatherings.

Erica had run up to us, and as I gathered her into my arms, her mother stood haloed inside the doorway, holding baby Gérard.

"Hello, Papa," Christine greeted me, smiling over Gérard's squirming body. Meg reached for him, and as his mother passed him into Meg's arms, the two women exchanged a look that was quickly broken by more excited greetings from inside the house when Meg entered.

Still holding onto Erica, I shared a quiet moment with my daughter.

"You'll have us here for quite some time, Father," she said, finally unclenching Erica's grip on me. "Phillippe received new orders that will keep him in France for quite a while." Between us, we set Erica down and watched her run into the bustling hall of the hospital.

At last I could draw Christine into a tight embrace. "It will be good to have you here, child," I murmured, kissing her lightly. "All of you." Despite Meg's presence, I had missed Christine's company.

She smiled, returning my kiss. "We'll be staying with Phillippe's parents at the château. We'll never be far away." She paused, holding my hand. "His mother, she is very different now."

"Indeed," I breathed, looking away into the darkness beyond the trees.

Christine looked around as if searching for the right words. "She's more affectionate, more at ease with me." She chuckled. "She hardly lets Erica out of her sight. She dotes on that child as if her very life depended on it. She is even worse with Gérard."

I gave her a half hearted smile, brushing back a few stray strands of hair from her eyes. The knot of anxiety that had gripped me dissolved at those words. I looked into Christine's eyes and found shared thoughts behind them. We had not mentioned the past or my connection to Phillippe's mother, yet the Comtesse's loss, and our struggle to fight for her, had strengthened the bond between the Comtesse and myself, strengthened the connection I had once sought to sever completely.

"In her way, the Comtesse loves and cares for you." I kissed Christine's forehead, pleased that my two Christines had come to an understanding.

"I have grown rather fond of Phillippe's mother." Christine said with a wide smile.

"I know," I murmured, and taking her hand, led her inside. I was startled to find that a small gathering had turned into a sizeable audience. Not only were Christine and her family present, but over the milling heads, I caught sight of Étienne and Hélène.

Those of the hospital staff not on duty had assembled as well for this one special evening, and as everyone jostled for space, children ran among the adults, grabbing the spaces right around the piano.

I had planned only for Meg to be present that evening, not the full house this had become. I wondered how the two students would react to all the curious faces trained on them.

The two women did not seem fazed by the audience in the least. In fact, it was as if Carlotta had needed a crowd to surround her. Her voice was firm, without any hesitancy in it. Julie's accompaniment was clear and assured. I could not help but notice the brief glances she cast in Gilbert's direction, or the smiles he directed at her. Perhaps music had not been the only thing that had begun to flourish at St. Hubert's.

When everyone said their goodbyes and goodnights, and only Meg and I remained, my wife took my face in her hands and kissed me. We did not need words. They had been said before. I wrapped her shoulders in the voluminous shawl, and walked with her back to the apartment.

Now, brushing her hair, I was falling in love with Meg all over again, and I never wanted to stop.

She reached to touch my hand, and leaned back against my chest. Setting the brush down, I circled my arms around her and buried my face in her neck, kissing the smooth, wonderful length of it.

"Je t'aime," I whispered, teasing her earlobe with gentle kisses. She laughed and finally turned to face me. There was a glow in her eyes I had not seen before, a glow that radiated from deep within, to shine around and through her. Holding my hands within her own, Meg drew them down and placed them over the slight swell of her stomach. Her eyes never left my face.

Realization dawned with a thunderclap. The hints had been there. I had just been too distracted to pay much heed. Meg's gradual refusal of wine, her opting for looser clothing, her preference for some of my herbal concoctions to settle her stomach, all clear indications of her condition.

"My dear, dear wife." I drew her into a fierce embrace, holding fiercely onto her, emotions tumbling in an erratic dance between ecstasy and fear. I was enthralled and terrified at the prospect of bringing a child into this world. I dearly wanted her to have the baby, yet I dreaded the thought of what its inheritance might be. I broke the embrace, kissed her, all the while looking into her deep, brown eyes. "How long?"

She continued holding our hands over the slight bulge. "The day we came back to our house. Four months."

"Why did you not tell me?"

Meg dropped her eyes, still holding onto my hands. "I knew you feared it, and I needed to be sure." At length she raised her eyes to meet mine. "I did not want to lose this miracle. I did not want to lose you." She held our hands firmly over her abdomen.

"Meg you will never lose me." I drew her to me, holding her tightly.

"You are still afraid."

"I won't lie. The idea of my face on our child terrifies me."

She lifted her head from my shoulder, seizing my face between her hands. "It will be all right Erik. He'll be all right. Just please, tell me you want him."

I looked into the brown eyes I loved, my heart crying out with all my passion for her. I folded her to my chest, stroking her hair. "I love you Meg, and whatever happens, I will love our child." I kissed her forehead, looking into her eyes. "Never doubt my love for you. It is unexpected news. We are not young."

She chuckled, and pressed a hand against mine which still rested against the swell under the frothy, lace gown.

"Young enough it seems."

"Meg, I never expected to find love, let alone a wife. Now there's a child. I---." My words died under her lips.

"Be with me." She leaned back against the pillows, drawing me down beside her. Hands and lips traced blazing trails of sensation over my chest and back, and I drowned in an ocean of exquisite joy.

I remember only vaguely pulling away from her for a moment to mumble something incoherent.

Hands pulled me down, and she sighed contentedly. "Yes, we should. He needs to know how much he is loved, and that he's wanted."

Chapter 57

If I had thought the changes in Christine during her first pregnancy had been puzzling, the changes in my wife were mystifying, joyful, remarkable, and frightening.

Despite my bemused delight in Meg's condition, there was a shadow of dread within me. No matter how I tried to fight it, it dogged my waking hours. I did not speak of it, but Meg knew, for she would often find me either walking in our garden in Brittany, or designing nonsense at the apartment. Each time she would find me, she would kiss me, and hold me fast. It was the only balm that soothed the doubt, the fear that the child would have my face.

Meg's changes were the more amazing because they were the result of our love. The child growing within her was a part of each of us, and I was startled again and again with the knowledge that within her, Meg carried a part of me, that she had wanted me that much.

One day, as we enjoyed a respite in our house, Meg gave out a startled cry. I leaped from the piano bench, and in three strides, was at her side. She clutched her side, her face a grimace of discomfort.

"What's wrong? What can I do?"

She pulled my hand to her belly. "Tell your son to stop kicking his mother," she hissed, and I felt a powerful kick from within. She sucked in a deep breath to still another cry.

"He's a fighter," I said with a soft smile, brushing a hand against her face. "Like his mother."

"Humph. You don't have to carry him."

"No, I just love his mother," I kissed her, with passion this time, and as if in desire for attention, there was another kick from inside her. "I love you too," I laughed, holding my hand over the spot where he had kicked.

It was curious how easily I accepted the child as a 'he'. Not for any selfish desire to have a son, but perhaps because Meg wished it so, and I would not contradict her on the matter.

As her time neared, there was only one thing we disagreed on. It took much gentle persuading, chocolate, and evenings filled with music to dissuade her from her heart's desire to have the child in our house, and accept my less romantic, but more practical solution to the matter. On this one subject I was adamant. I would not risk her life over the child's. I wanted her near capable doctors if it was required. She protested at first, eventually acceding to my wishes. Rooms at St. Hubert's were prepared, and we settled into a routine of anxious waiting.

He was born at dawn, on a mild, February day, in 1894.

With a supreme, last will effort, Meg was freed of her burden, and as the lusty cry filled the room, I looked into her exhausted face, and knew he would be our first and last. Even though I had given her a tisane to dull her pains, watching Meg's agony as she struggled to give birth to our creation tore me apart. There had been little I could do but hold her hand, wipe her brow, and tell her how much I needed her beside me.

I bent down to kiss her, wiped her face, and whispered, "Je t'adore." Purposefully, I dismissed the activity behind us. I had eyes only for her. She met my look, giving me a weak smile. I took her hand in mine, and with the other, smoothed the hair from her face.

I had given her what she had wanted. She would have to be content with her one. It would have to be enough. Any future children would kill her, and I would never live through another nine months of uncertainty. Neither of us was young, and I dearly wanted Meg beside me in the coming years.

When I bent to kiss her once more, I saw the nurse approach with a bundle in her arms. I refused to acknowledge the sudden dread that rose within. I had given Meg a promise, and I would abide by it.

As Meg reached to gather the bundle from the nurse, the latter whispered in her ear, then quietly left. It was only then that I noticed we were completely alone. Everyone had gone, and the only sound in the room was the hammering of my heart.

"Our son Erik," Meg broke the silence, her touch on my arm bringing awareness of where I was, and who I was to meet.

I looked at my wife, then at the bundle in her arms, and the perfect, little red face looking back at me. All the years, all the dread, found release. I let the tears flow and wash away the pain of the past. It had all been for this, this moment as I took our son into my arms.

"I was so afraid," I whispered at last, eyes never straying from the miracle cradled within my embrace.

"I know," Meg leaned her head against my shoulder.

"Despite my promise Meg, I had not wished for a child."

She eased herself back against the pillows, flashing me a stern look. "You can't put him back."

I laughed, kissing her. "I would not want to. I'm very glad he's here."

Meg squeezed my hand, and closed her eyes. I sat beside her, cradling our son, watching her sleep, only too well aware that these would be our last, peaceful moments together for quite some time to come.

I looked at the miracle in my arms, and smiled. "Welcome to the world, my son."

February 1894

to

January 1916

Chapter 58

We named him Erik of course. Meg would hear nothing else and I would not gainsay her. While she recovered, our daughter became her constant companion, and the apartment filled with joyous laughter and visitors. There was never a lack of arms to hold Erik *fils*. He accepted all with good grace, and his father with bemused wonder.

Watching Christine as she held him, I could not help but compare their contrasting entries into the world. While they were sister and brother in everything that mattered, their beginnings were as night and day.

With her arrival, Christine had formed a tenuous family around her. Meg and I had done the best we knew how. Meg had been very young and I unprepared for life with a child. We had muddled through, but with Meg's departure I had been forced to hire housekeepers to maintain order in our lives. While these women had always been kind to Christine, they could never replace her maman. It had been a wound that not even I could fill or lessen. The times a project had kept me away from my daughter had been devastating for both of us. There had been too many times when she had refused to let go my coat. I had had to force myself to walk through the door, seemingly oblivious to her cries. Yet each of her tears, each of her cries of 'papa' had been raw wounds in my heart. When Christine had grown older, I took her with me to construction sites whenever, and wherever I could. While her formal schooling may have been somewhat haphazard, we had made up for it with lessons of our own. We became inseparable, and over the years, my love and admiration for her had only grown.

Now, watching as Christine helped her mother with the baby, I could only shake my head in stupefied wonder at it all. The family that had formed around an abandoned child now welcomed its own into their eager embrace. Erik was born into loving arms, and unlike Christine, who had spent most of her childhood alone, Erik was assured of playmates in his niece and nephew. Even now, Erica was demanding time with 'her' baby.

To preserve order in the chaos our apartment had become, I reluctantly acknowledged the need for a permanent housekeeper. Meg could not handle everything on her own, nor would I allow her. She needed rest and peace. The birth of our son had been exhausting, and she did not need the additional strain of running our household.

As I prepared to leave for work one morning, it was to find a well dressed lady standing on our doorstep. Her silver hair was pulled away from her face, and her simple dress was immaculate. There was no startled reaction in her plain, but kindly features when she beheld my masked face. Perhaps the surprise was on mine, for she smiled and slightly bobbed her head in greeting. "Bonjour, Monsieur Marchand."

"Ah Jeanne, you are here. Come in," Christine said from behind me. "Come in, and please, wait for me in the kitchen. It's straight ahead, and on the right." Christine ushered the woman inside, seemingly oblivious to the dark look in my eyes.

"Who is that?" I demanded, startled that my child would allow a stranger into my house. Perhaps a shade of anger colored my voice for Christine raised a brow at me, standing defiant, despite the fact that she held a baby in her arms, and her two children pulled at her skirts.

"Your new housekeeper," Christine answered. "A gift, Papa, from someone you knew once. Jeanne helped raise Phillippe. She will help you, at least until you two can manage it on your own."

I closed my eyes, clenching my teeth against the retort that threatened to storm from my chest, fighting the sudden swell of exasperation. "I want nothing from…..her." I managed to choke out.

"Whether you want it or not, Jeanne will stay. Your days are spent at the Opera, and maman needs time to recover." Christine paused, looking first at the sleeping child in her arms, then at me, the stern look in her eyes softening. "Will you and Christine go on forever avoiding each other? That does not sound like the love you once spoke of, Father. Allow her this one thing. Despite the years, despite the past, I believe the Comtesse cares for you. She is most eager to meet Erik _fils_." Christine swung Erik in her arms, gathered her children around her, and headed for the kitchen.

I pulled on the coat, pretending perhaps even to myself that Christine's words were just that, words. Yet even as I reached for the fedora, I knew it to be a lie. My daughter, as always, knew where, and how, to find her mark.

A soft touch and a kiss brought me around to look into Meg's shining eyes. She smiled at me, and caressed my face. "Our daughter is right. You can't avoid the de Chagnys forever."

"Meg, you of all people, should know why," I said slowly, unwilling to open the door on feelings best kept hidden.

Meg's fingers smoothed the lapels of the coat. "It's been a long time Erik, too long to carry that last demon in your heart."

"Christine and I have said what needed to be said."

"Yes, you and she. What about him? What about Raoul?" Her eyes searched mine.

I avoided her look by placing the hat on my head. "Do not ask the impossible."

Meg threw up her hands, eyes flashing with rare anger. "You are hopeless! Both of you! The two of you are worse than those children in the kitchen!" Meg stared at me for a minute, then shook her head in dismay. "Go play swords again in the cemetery if that will put an end to your stubbornness, Erik Marchand. How long will you and Raoul go on hating each other? How long will you two persist in this foolishness?" She turned on her heel to leave, but my hand caught hers, drawing her back. I would not let her walk away angry.

Drawing a deep breath, I made an effort to calm the cauldron of feelings this conversation was stirring. "Meg, please understand. When last I saw him, I wanted to kill him. I drew his blood." I paused, the image of Raoul's bleeding shoulder suddenly too vivid a vision. "It is unlikely he would wish to see me," I added softly, brushing the hair away from her face. "I wanted to exact a terrible price for his life. It is not something they would forget."

Meg's hands framed my face, her eyes holding mine. "No, not forget, but forgive. There is forgiveness, Erik. I'm not asking you to be Raoul's friend. I only ask you to consider forgiveness for him, for you. It was all so long ago. You three have children between you. For their sake Erik, don't let this last shadow fester."

I took her hands in mine, kissing them. "You may ask, and I will consider."

In the end, Jeanne stayed. Her help was invaluable as Christine was busy with her own family and work, much less our own. Because of Phillippe's protracted absences as a result of his service, Christine had insisted on maintaining her position as manager of at least a part of my businesses. She refused to confine herself in a house with screaming children, and refused to relinquish my offices to the impersonal care of clerks. She stood her ground, despite mine and Phillippe's combined efforts to dissuade her. In the end, we relented. Secretly, I was glad for it, and proud of her, of the woman she had become. Occasionally she would catch me watching her, and I had to hide a smile. How had it come to be that Fate had given me such a remarkable child?

Meg recovered quickly, and soon our life settled around the new, demanding, but so loved person we two had made.

Like Christine when she had been small, our son had his moments of rage, but for the most part, Erik was a good child to his mother.

After six months, it became clear he had inherited Meg's gold hair and my green eyes. Each night as I sang him to sleep, I marveled at the union of us peacefully slumbering under the covers.

"You are besotted by your own creation, my love," Meg's tone was a gentle caress as she took my hand in hers.

I looked at her, smiling tenderly. "Allow me this indulgence, wife. There will not be another like him." I lightly brushed my lips against hers.

Meg caressed my face, eyes brimming with tenderness. "No, not like him. He has a father who loves him, who protects him."

I drew her into the circle of my arms, holding her fast, comforted by her. I had never known a father, though I suppose I must have had one once. Only memories of a screaming woman remained, and pain. Always fear and pain.

I shook my head in denial of those memories. That was not the legacy I wanted for my son. He would know love. He would know family.

I drew Meg out of the room, and into our own. Time for us alone had become nearly nonexistent. I had expected that, if raising Christine had been any indication. We used every opportunity afforded us. Now, Meg's eyes mirrored what mine asked, and it was gratifying to know that with a son between us, the passion had only grown deeper.

Chapter 59

It was early 1897, and Erik's third birthday when we finally installed the new chandelier. It was the final, major piece of delicate renovation left. We had taken the carcass of the old one and dumped it in one of the many old, forgotten vaults. After all, even before its construction had been completed, the Opera house had served as a prison and storage dump for the various armies and revolutionaries that had stormed through Paris. One more piece of debris added to the rusting pile of refuse in its bowels would hardly matter. If by chance someone were to find it later, at least they would have a mystery to solve.

A few stuffed shirts from the government came to oversee the installation. While Étienne's son, Eduard, played nice with those particular gentlemen, Étienne and I exchanged a pained look. They had not cared about this building for twenty years. It was only now, as renovations were nearing completion that the powers that be appeared more attentive.

While we directed the crews in handling the fragile monster, Étienne clasped my shoulder, giving it a squeeze. I acknowledged his camaraderie with a nod. In the years we had worked alongside each other, countless bottles of wine had been shared during long evenings spent consulting reports. There was little that remained hidden between us.

He, a grandfather several times over, had welcomed my son's arrival with armloads of toys, and entertained Christine's children with tall tales of magicians and wizards. I had cast him a warning look which he shook off, continuing his tales. The children's eyes widened in wonder at the seeming miracles Étienne described. Seeing that he would have his way, I gave up directing the stories to another theme, and stood back, watching the spellbound children.

He took the family to see the steel tower that had been erected years before. The structure had been cause of derision and division among the architects all over France. Even I had had reservations concerning the strange design. However it had turned out to be a success, and the structure would always bear its creator's name. It had quickly become the new attraction in the city, for residents and tourists alike.

Paris and the world were changing. Étienne and I were relics of a life that was rapidly fading into memory, giving way to a churning, seething cauldron of oil, steel and gas. It was a world that frightened me for I no longer had much reference to it. I had changed and adapted to life as I had had to, but this new world was quickly outgrowing my understanding. Only Meg and our son held me grounded, helped me make any sense of it at all.

While our children would move easily enough in this new world, Étienne and I would not. It had been why we had taken on Eduard and several young men during the course of the renovation. The new flock of architects could still learn from the old men, and we would pass our business into their skilled, capable hands. The renovation of this building in particular provided an appropriate backdrop to this change of guard.

While I had always drawn pleasure from architecture's discipline, I was tired. I wanted to spend time with my family, something I had not been able to do when Christine had been small. I did not want my son growing up not knowing his father. So I looked on this as my last project. This place was where it had all begun. It might as well end here.

Étienne and I lifted a glass to each other that evening in our favorite café. I stared at the burgundy liquid, unable to drink it.

"We have finished it. The young will take care of the rest. Paris will have its grand house back, and I'm sure there will be a smashing spectacle for its re-opening as well. Perhaps like its architect, we will have to buy our own tickets!" Étienne laughed and downed his wine.

I did not join in his merriment, but continued to stare at the untouched wine. For years, I had lost myself among the Opera's vaults, labyrinthine tunnels, had even made the grotto my home. I had roamed its dark passages, ostracized from humanity for the face I had been born with. One night I had left my house in fire, a fire that had mirrored my own rage. Years later, I had returned to heal the damage.

For nearly four years, the Opera house had once more been home. Almost like a forlorn lover reluctant to leave his amour, I found it difficult to pass my house to someone else's hands. Yet turn it over I had to. It was not mine, nor ever would be again.

I downed the wine in one gulp, rose, and gathered the coat and hat. "Good night, my friend. Perhaps like the Opera, we are finished. There is hardly a place for fossils such as you and me in this new world of steel." I said, slipping the fedora on my head.

Étienne rose, leaving five francs on the table. During the years, we had taken turns paying for our inebriation. It had been his turn to pay.

"Allow me to walk with you, Erik. Let me walk you to your Meg, before you do anything drastic."

I chuckled. "I have done that once already. Not tonight. She would never forgive me a second time."

He laughed, and we walked beside each other through the evening streets of Paris.

Chapter 60

With Erik's safe arrival into the world, Meg once more took up her work at St. Hubert's, though only on a partial basis. She refused to leave our son to the care of a housekeeper anymore than necessary, and by the same token, refused to leave her gamins at the hospital. That place had become as much a part of her as the Opera house was a part of me.

During the renovation years, I had continued my visits there as well. Soon, it was not just the piano that was the only instrument for the children to play. A violin appeared, followed by a cello, even a flute came our way. I dared not question the source of the bounty. The look in Hélène's eyes, and her small smile when she occasionally sat in on our practice sessions, was answer enough. Though she did not come often, her visits were always welcome.

Despite additional lessons that had been wheedled out of me by the children, it was Carlotta who truly astonished me. It was not her progress as a singer but the woman herself that surprised me.

In the months of her residency, she had slowly shaken off the distress that haunted her. Now she shined with new vitality and purpose. She smiled, and when the children saw her walking her dog in the gardens, she allowed them to play with it, even appeared to tolerate their company. It was a new, almost frightening Carlotta that was emerging before my eyes. Whatever had happened to her would always remain a mystery, for

I would certainly never ask, and no one would dare remind her of a past she would not wish to remember.

When I broached the subject to Meg, my wife only smiled and kissed me. "You not only gave her a life back, you gave her a new one."

I never considered the reasons behind Carlotta's re-training, other than it was something I had to do, needed to do for her. Singing and its discipline would keep her occupied. It would give her a reason to recover from whatever had tormented her, but beyond that, I had no idea what to do. What purpose would there be for her to sing again if she would not use it?

As for the latter, that question resolved itself one evening. While walking past the sitting room toward Gilbert's office, I heard her with two of the younger girls practicing scales. The voices would make a pleasant blend, once harmonized and trained. Carlotta's thick Italian suddenly blasted through the doorway in a torrent that left even my ears numb. I hated to think what the girls endured under that scathing tongue and those piercing eyes.

"I believe our lost lady has found an occupation," Gilbert said over my shoulder. He was smiling. Anyone within a few yards of the sitting room would have heard Carlotta's scolding.

"So it would appear," I answered, following him to his office for our usual tea break.

In the months that followed, Meg and I witnessed Gilbert and Julie marry and welcome a son of their own. Their happiness was evident in the looks they gave each other. It was a happiness that Meg and I could easily share, as we two had found our own. They named the boy Alain, and within a year, he and Erik became playmates.

With a family, Gilbert's tiny supervisor's rooms at the hospital were overrun. Indeed the entire facility was. It was old, and the influx of new patients strained the available resources to the limits and beyond.

Several days after work on the Opera house concluded, I found myself in Étienne's office, in conference with Eduard and his team.

When Étienne came in and saw me, one of his hearty laughs ensued. "Looking for another project? I thought we were finished."

I smiled at his blustery greeting. "Perhaps there is a little more left in this particular fossil."

"Ha! You, my friend, have years left. I count mine in days now. Show me." He pushed his way to the table where the plans lay spread out. He glanced at them, then at me.

"A noble idea. Who is paying for this marvel?" He crossed his arms over his chest and raised a brow. I stared at him, saying nothing.

"I see," he muttered, glancing at the curious faces gathered around the table. Then drawing close to me, Étienne ventured in a low tone. "While you are at it Erik, will you place the entire world on your shoulders?"

"You saw the place."

"Yes I did, but it does not mean_____." My arm clasping his cut him off in mid sentence. "Yes it does," I said quietly, firmly, eyes locking onto his.

He sighed and shook his head. I let go of him as he stepped back. "Hopeless. You are hopeless."

I chuckled. "Funny you should say that. I seem to recall Meg saying those very words."

"Humph. A wise woman, your Meg. She agrees with me. Now, show me what we will do."

That night, after we had put Erik to bed, and sat beside each other in the salon, I outlined the plans to Meg.

"Then we will not be leaving Paris?" She asked, nestling closer into my embrace.

I kissed the top of her head, caressing her cheek. "No, my dearest one, not for at least another two years," I murmured, drawing her closer.

"Good. I'm not ready to leave it, not yet."

I sighed, smiling a little. Even as the city was changing around us, it was still home, and many memories remained. It had brought Meg and me together in the most unexpected way. "Nor am I," I whispered into the shadowed quietude of the room.

While we sat there, surrounded by the silence, enveloped in peacefulness, I could not help the sense of melancholy that was slowly sweeping me away. Like the fading light at dusk, I felt the years closing in and a new, unnamable restlessness stirred within my bones.

The world was hurtling forward and I was fast losing ground. It would soon be a world I would no longer have a place in. It would never remember us, all of us, our loves, our triumphs. Meg was right. Only the one thing remained, and then perhaps, we would all be done.

Drawing a heavy breath, I bent to kiss my wife. She murmured softly but did not stir. She had fallen asleep within my arms. I smiled, kissed her hair, and gently extricated myself from her comfortable weight. She never woke as I stretched her on the sofa and covered her with a wrap.

Sleep would not come for me this night, that I could feel. There was only one thing to do.

Taking up my coat and hat, I silently walked to Erik's room and looked at him. He was sleeping soundly in his bed, a hand curled around a favorite toy, the yellow hair spread on the pillow like a halo around his head.

I brushed his cheek as I bent to kiss him. "Good night, my son," I whispered, and quietly left the apartment.

I did not know where the night's wanderings would take me but I could not sit beside Meg with dark, brooding thoughts running through my head. She deserved the best I could offer, not the fearful and haunting speculations that tumbled through my mind.

As I walked, I felt the agitated stirrings of something deep inside, something I had sought to leave behind in the bowels of the Opera house. Walking the gas lit streets of Paris, I feared this coiled beast as I had feared nothing else in life.

Chapter 61

I cannot remember when the numbness in the left arm began but I ignored it as I continued my aimless wanderings. The rising dread within me would not be abated with drawings or wine. Only exercise would keep the beast from rising. To that end, I quickened my pace, despite the sudden spasm in my chest.

Over the past few months there had been similar episodes of numbness in my arm and hand. Always I dismissed them, for they passed within a few hours. So would this. Meg knew nothing of these episodes, nor would I tell her. I wanted her to have a husband for a few more years, not an invalid.

As my pace increased and I shrugged deeper into the bulk of the great coat, the lights around me suddenly wavered, and my lungs strove for air.

Some deep instinct of self preservation directed my legs toward the steps so that when the crushing fist of agony squeezed my chest, I had not far to fall. As the air rushed from screaming lungs, and the merciless fist of unendurable pain threatened to tear me apart, I remember turning my eyes heavenward. A glint of gold above stared back at me.

"Not like this. Oh not like this," I barely whispered as darkness overtook me.

Voices. The rumbling of wheels. Cacophony of noise, lights and pain. Weightlessness, then a soft, yielding something beneath me. Darkness. A soft, soothing sense of coolness against my skin, then merciful oblivion.

Light. A horrific pain in my chest, but at least I could breathe, if only in shallow, agonized breaths.

Something soft touched my face, and soothing, dulcet tones came to me as if from far away. I turned my head to follow the sound, regretting it the moment it happened. A moan of agony escaped. The soft touch was back, this time holding my head more firmly to the pillow.

On opening my eyes, I thought I dreamed. An angel was bending over me, dark brown, wavy hair falling around her pale face. The brown eyes that looked at me were filled with sadness, compassion, and something else that in my befuddled state I could not name.

I must have passed into oblivion once more, for when next I woke the angel that smiled at me was Meg. Her smile of relief and joy spoke volumes. "Bonjour, mon coeur," she grasped my hand, pressing it against her wet cheek.

I gave her a weak smile in return, surprised that I could manage one at all. "Ma chéri." Somehow I found a voice too.

When the door opened, Meg turned from me, giving my hand a squeeze, and rose from the bed to meet the woman who had entered. Though their voices were low, I was not so overwhelmed with pain that I could not catch some of what they said.

"I don't know how to thank you." It was Meg.

"De rien. You know I would never let you do this alone."

Even through the fog of slowly dissipating pain, I knew that voice. I had taught it to sing.

"Should you need anything, anything at all, you know where to find me." A pause followed, and if the women said anything more, it was too faint for me to hear. The door closed, and my wife once again looked down at me with love filled eyes.

Before anything could be said, Gilbert, Maurice and a nurse walked into the room.

"You are awake. That is good. You gave everyone a scare, monsieur," Maurice looked at me over the rim of his glasses. He had been a recent addition to the hospital staff, and had quickly become a favorite amongst the patients. "This was not your first crise cardiaque I suspect?" He asked, arching a brow at me.

My eyes drifted to Meg, to her suddenly pale face. The truth would have to come out. I could not hold it from her any longer, not in front of these doctors, who would tell her in any case. "No," I whispered.

Meg suppressed a cry by pressing a hand against her mouth. She turned away from the men, from me. Gilbert came to her side, his voice low, seeking to comfort her.

Maurice nodded. "I thought as much. You were extremely fortunate that your son-in-law and his compatriots found you in time. I will not lie to you, monsieur. It was a very serious episode. For now, it would appear that you are out of danger, but in a most delicate state. We will make an examination to be certain."

Whereupon the two physicians began their work while Meg sat beside the window, watching the process in strained silence.

The proceedings ended with Maurice giving me pills to swallow. "From now on monsieur, you are under orders of your wife. No work, no strain, and if I hear otherwise, I personally will tie you down to this bed." His eyes flashed with serious intent. He turned to Meg, handing her a bottle.

"One of these every day, until they are gone. I will come and see him, depend on it." He grasped her shoulder and looked into her face, his features losing their sternness. "Get him away from here, from Paris. If he stays, it'll kill him." With Meg's silent nod of acknowledgement, Maurice left the room.

Gilbert had remained by the bedside through all this, his eyes missing nothing. He glanced toward Meg, then me. "If you know what's good for you Erik, do as she says." Then in a much lower voice, added. "Or at least make it appear so." He gave my shoulder a pat before leaving.

As the fog of the medication began to overtake me, I saw Meg bend over me, her eyes brimming with tears and something else. With surprise, I realized it was anger. "If I didn't love you so, I'd kill you for what you did to me." Her lips burned on mine as sleep claimed me.

Chapter 62

Recovery was slow and I chafed under the constant scrutiny of not only Meg, but Maurice as well.

As soon as I was able to walk on my own, Meg took the family to Brittany. During my recuperation, Maurice made several visits. For the duration of his stay, his eyes would never leave me and invariably, he would find an opportunity to make an examination. He would nod, pack up his bag, and spend a pleasant afternoon in our garden.

In the end, I grew resigned to his poking and prodding, not because of his desire for me to do so, or even for Meg, but for my son.

It was on one of those occasions of Maurice's pestering examinations that I saw Erik's eyes carefully watching us. The look in his green eyes would not have been out of place on a twenty year old but in his three year old face, the concern for his father was shocking. It suddenly dawned on me that he understood more than I had thought. In that moment when our eyes locked over Maurice's probing hands, I wanted nothing more than to live for him, to teach him to play the piano, to see him grow and change into a young man. I wanted to be there for him, as no one had been there for me.

From that day, I accepted the visits and pills with resignation. I could not turn back time no matter how hard I fought against it. I was no longer a young man. My wife and son were miracles granted in a life that had been mostly filled with darkness and pain.

I looked at Meg as she held Erik in her arms, at their laughing faces and I wondered why such gifts had been bestowed on a man like me. Whatever the reason, I was ecstatic to have them both beside me. If for nothing else than that reason alone, I stayed away from Paris and the work at St. Hubert's, trusting the young men under Étienne's charge to complete the work I had started.

While the months wore on and I became stronger, it was not unusual for Meg to see her two men bent over the piano keys, or sitting beside the window, reading adventure stories. Erik was a voracious reader, always hungry for more. It did not take long before he was drawing books from the shelf and reading on his own. It mattered little what the subject was, as long as it was something new. One day I even saw him poring over a volume of architectural designs.

With the passage of time however, I noticed that at times my vision failed me and things that had been clear, became blurry. Reading became more a strain than pleasure, and soon, even my excuses failed to satisfy me.

Noting my distress, Meg urged me to see a specialist, something I refused to do. She shrugged her shoulders against my stubbornness, busying herself in the kitchen baking treats for Erik.

Struggling to shave one morning, I gave voice to a colorful curse as the razor bit into my cheek for the second time, and blood welled between trembling fingers.

"Here, give me that. I refuse to pick pieces of you off the floor." Meg took the instrument of self inflicted pain from my fingers, and after wiping off the blood, finished the job of scraping my chin. Her hands moved with practiced confidence. Though I held perfectly still, I could not help a smile deep inside.

Through all our years, together and apart, we had first and foremost ever been friends. Through the years of raising Christine our friendship in many ways had surpassed the bonds of marriage. There was little, if anything at all, that Meg did not know about me. My chin had, of necessity, become well acquainted with her touch, and she with the razor she now wielded so expertly.

When Meg finished and wiped my face with a towel, my wife smiled at the reflection of us in the mirror. "You are still my gentle and kind wizard," she said, kissing my cheek.

The faces looking back at us were not bad, if a bit older. It had ceased to bother me to be without a mask around Meg, or our children years ago, but I still wore one in public. Men in their prejudice had not progressed that far. Now as I looked at us in the mirror, I became aware, perhaps for the first time, just what a good combination Meg and I made. I drew her hands around my shoulders and held them there, drowning in her comfort. Her hair was still gold where mine, what remained of it, had gone grey. A few lines were just starting to set around her mouth. Age was not being too kind or gentle to me. Deep lines had furrowed the brow, crinkled the eyes, and set themselves firmly from nose to mouth.

I sighed, letting go Meg's hands. In a few years, it would no longer matter what I looked like. The left side of my face would match the right and no one would ever know there had ever been a man with a mask.

Two weeks later, I wore glasses for reading at home. Arrangements were made to make a pair that would fit with a mask. While it was something I needed to grow accustomed to, the glasses proved a considerable improvement to my life.

Of course Erik thought they were a new toy, until papa convinced him otherwise. He tried them on, gave a disgusted shake to his head, and handed them back. That was the end of that.

Chapter 63

By the time he was nearly five, it was evident Erik had inherited some of his father's musical talents. The rest were completely his own. While most children played games, my son could be found at the piano, without any urging from us. Scraps of his compositions could be found everywhere and we had to be careful what was thrown away. Once, Meg tossed a piece of wrapping into the fire only to be confronted with a shrieking tantrum. Erik had written a song on the back of it for the 'Italian lady' as he called Carlotta. His heartbreak however was temporary, as he went to the piano and composed another.

Even at this young age he grew impatient with most of the classical compositions I presented to him. I thought the masters would present a challenge. However he tossed them off, preferring the challenges of List, the Hungarian who had taken Paris by storm a few years before, and those of the up and coming Russians, such as Rachmaninoff. In his search for new material, Erik even discovered a pile of my half finished and forgotten scores that had been tossed aside during the years. He latched onto those, and for the next few days, nothing could tear him away from those scraps of paper, or the piano.

One day as we sat at the piano together, he began to play the piece he had fashioned from all the bits and pieces he had found. They had been just ideas tossed about, but in his young hands, they had found new life. It appeared that this young man preferred his father's more unconventional approach to composition rather than that of the old masters. I smiled, unable to hide the pride that swelled my heart. Even though my music would never be heard, his would. One day the world would bow to him, for he would hold its heart in his hands.

I embraced and kissed him on the brow, noting from the corner of my eye Meg watching us. She smiled, turned, and walked back to the kitchen, letting her men fill the small house with their combined harmony. When we finished the piece to his satisfaction, Erik ran off to grab one of his mother's sweets.

Our son might have inherited my musical talent, but I had also given him my temper. It was softened by his mother's serenity and gentleness to be sure, but it was there, none the less. Nowhere was that temper more evident then when he and Erica were in the same room together. It was as if one was oil, the other vinegar. Both were fiercely competitive when it came to music, neither giving way to the other on the piano. The solution to the squabbling, the hair pulling, and the screaming, was to sit them side by side and make them play four hands. Soon, sulkiness gave way to laughter, even harmony. After a time, they grew to enjoy friendly competition, even each other. Erik composed songs for Erica that mysteriously found their way into her recitals at the Conservatoire.

During the long months of recuperation from the attack, Maurice's visits became less frequent, and after a time he came only sporadically. Meg however, kept a wary eye on me. I did not begrudge her the concern. The episode had scared both of us. I had no desire to leave her a widow. I had grown much too fond of her and our son to abandon them now.

The building at St. Hubert's was finished as promised. It more than exceeded my expectation and Eduard's team's competence pleased me. The businesses Étienne and I had carefully nurtured would be in safe hands.

Earlier that year Étienne had been distraught over the death of his wife, but now, with fall encroaching, he seemed to find solace in the unlikeliest of sources. He became a frequent visitor at the practice sessions held in the new wing of the hospital.

"You would find finer entertainment in the salons, my friend, not here," I teased him when he arrived one day with his newspaper, ready to take the chair beside the large, stained glass window.

"The salons are dull and boring, Erik. I rather prefer the chaos here." Where upon he settled himself into the chair, and opened the paper.

"Suit your self," I replied, preparing for the lessons ahead. Throughout the months of recovery, I had not completely abandoned the students at St. Hubert's. I would not have been able to. Music was, and always had been, an all consuming passion. It brought unexpected pleasure to share that passion with the children at the hospital. Under hawk-like supervision from Meg, I resumed teaching the gamins, though I found my talents hardly needed. Two young men had stepped in, in my stead. I had no need to search far for the source of their assignment. This time I accepted Christine's gift with grace, for I was tired, and felt the years more than I would acknowledge.

However there were three students that no matter what, I could never desert. Julie, because she had asked, and little Céline who, despite her blindness, had talent to spare. She had become Julie and Gilbert's ward, and with them, had found a home. Then there was Carlotta. Her I could abandon the least. No matter the years, the Italian dynamo would always be there. She had become my responsibility the night I had picked her up in those odorous rags. An invisible cord bound us in a perverse joke played by the universe.

With the lessons over, Étienne set his paper aside, rose, and offered his hand to the aging diva. Carlotta accepted his offer with a smile. They headed out into the gardens, followed by her dogs. Étienne had recently brought her another one. She had been beside herself with joy.

Somehow these two lost souls found comfort in each other's company, as I found comfort in their friendship and the love of my family.

My family. I watched them with an undeniable mix of pride and joy as they gathered around the table in the garden at the house in Brittany. The children cavorted, their happy, excited voices lifting above the adults' chatter as they pursued Phillippe in a vigorous game of tag.

Phillippe had joined us in a rare visit, and now tumbled in the grass with his children as they engulfed him in arms and legs. He adored his brood, and when he could, spent as much time as possible with them. In the years since Rome, his talents as a singer had come to be in high demand on the European stage. Despite his rigorous schedule, and four years spent in the army, he and Christine had still managed a family. That he and Christine adored each other was clear. It shone in their eyes as they glanced at one another over the children's heads. I smiled, shaking my head at the thought how in my rage at the discovery of his identity, I had nearly brought that love to an end. With the years, he had matured, growing into the handsome features given him by his parents, though when I looked at him, I could really only see her, his mother.

Glancing at him as he tumbled with Gérard and four year old Jean-Paul in the grass, I could not hide a broad smile. With all the years, and all that had happened between us, Christine had still given me a son, and I had truly grown to love the man he had become.

It was one of the last beautiful fall days, and the family had gathered for an impromptu picnic in our garden. These, or the musical evenings at our apartment in Paris, were times I loved best. A deep sigh escaped me.

"What is it?" Hélène's quiet voice said from beside me.

I gave her a lopsided grin. "I was just thinking that none of this, none of them," I gestured toward the crowd on the lawn, "would have been possible without," I paused and glanced at my friend, letting our eyes meet, "without the rose," I finished.

Hélène nodded. "It was for the best, for both of you." She looked out at the family, at her daughter as she held Christine's youngest child. Anne-Marie had been born two years previously. She found the boisterous activities of her brothers and nephew not quite to her liking. Meg's soft tones attempted to soothe the threatening tide of tears.

Hélène slipped an arm around my waist in affection. "The rose may have had her thorns Erik, but I think her grace released something even more beautiful than she." She said, her arm around my waist tightening a bit. With a small nod and a smile, Hélène released me, joining the party gathering at the table.

I smiled to myself, joining them as well. There was no use on dwelling on might have been and ifs. There was the here and now, and right now, my family needed me, as I needed them.

Chapter 64

With affairs tied up in Paris, Meg and I decided to return to the house in Italy. The schools in Rome were a match to the Conservatoire, and they were close to our home. I refused to leave our son to the mercies of boarding schools, not without our supervision, every now and then.

With the passage of years, I had grown tired of Paris and its congested streets. I longed for the peacefulness of the estate and quiet mornings in the country. The years had caught up with me, and I wanted rest.

While Christine and Phillippe accepted the news with resignation, it was with no small amount of trepidation that I broached the subject to Étienne and Carlotta.

We had shared a quiet dinner in a small café, and now sipped wine in the garden of St. Hubert's. It had been a pleasant evening and I was reluctant to break the spell. It would perhaps be the last time I would see my friends.

"Si bene," was all Carlotta said when I finished. She rose from her chair with a bit of flourish, disappearing down the hall leading to the rooms of the more permanent residents.

Étienne shook his head, a smile barely contained under his thick mustache. "She'll be all right Erik. I'll look after her."

"I would not have asked this of you."

He laughed and spread his hands. "She and I are too old to get into trouble, and too comfortable to have it any other way. You and Meg take that boy of yours and teach him to play with the masters." He gripped my shoulder.

Just then, Carlotta returned with a package in her hands. She tossed her head in a shade of her old, imperious self. "Long ago you show me kindness, yes?" Her eyes focused on my face.

In all our years at the Opera, she had known me as a shadow, an invisible antagonist. Yet now her eyes looked on me as if she knew who I truly was.

"You didn't let me die in the streets, and you give me back my music. Why?"

"I had to," I said quietly, for it was the absolute truth.

"Humph." She thrust the package at me. "We are finished. You, I think, will need this now more than me."

I took the bundle. She hooked her arm through Étienne's and directed a slight bow in my direction. "Maestro."

I bowed to her in return. Inside the cab on the way home, I unwrapped what Carlotta had given me. Amongst the layers of paper was my cloak.

Chapter 65

Meg and I sat on the portico, enjoying the coolness of the evening. Lanterns flickered with a warm glow as they swayed from the hooks above the profusion of potted herbs in the faint breeze of the evening. If there was one thing that had not changed with time, it was Meg's love of flowers and herbs. The pots cascaded with blooms, and the sweet scent of lavender filled the space around us.

The laughter of two young voices drifted to us through the open windows, even over the tones of the piano. They were learning a new piece, and having fun with it. Their laughter was easy and full of a camaraderie borne of long companionship. I had to smile when I thought how many times Christine and I had had to pull them apart just to keep the peace. Now they rarely did anything without the other acting as support, or directly participating in whatever activity they happened to pursue.

Meg rested her head against my shoulder, and my arms around her tightened. She was fifty five, and the gold hair had begun to silver, but she was still my golden sea, the one who bound me to this new world around us.

It was late summer of 1909. The turn of the century had come, and with it, a profusion of inventions. Where there had been the quiet hum of conversation, now there was the clunk and thunk of machinery. Entertainments were no longer confined to theaters or concert halls.

One could have an orchestra and even singers at parties, courtesy of the gramophone. Theaters sprang up nearly overnight, specializing in something called the cinematograph. A few brave men conquered the air in flying machines, and trains ran underground, easing congestion in large cities. The automobile replaced horses as a means of transport, and everywhere in the cities was the stink of petrol.

It was no longer my world. It was theirs. It belonged to the young people now practicing at the piano. For the last few years, they had swirled around us, maintaining a controlled, if delightful chaos on the estate.

With her wavy, dark brown hair and bright, blue eyes, Erica had blossomed into a beauty like her mother. She was nineteen, and had half of Rome seeking permission to court her. She shook her head and with a mischievous smile, tossed the cards and notes into the fire. Then in an eerie, but affectionate, imitation of Carlotta, Erica announced, "I too young to marry. Everything for music. Boys, they always be there." She shrugged her shoulders, theatrically batting her eyes. Despite the teasing, the children had both adored the aging diva. A pillow flew at her from the corner of the room where Erik sat, reading. As Erica caught it, the two burst into laughter. They teased each other mercilessly, but supported one another with a loyalty rarely found in families. God help anyone seeking to drag them apart.

As with his relation, Erik had grown into an exceptional student. At fifteen, he was far from the little boy I had taught to play the piano. He excelled at anything revolving around music. His talents had won him many competitions, and though he accepted the accolades, the honors only made him work harder. He continued to devour books with a voracious hunger and pursued physical activity with near single minded devotion. He played tennis, rough housed with his friends on the football field, and rode horses as if he was a part of them. However it had been his choice of a competitive sport that had given me pause. He had taken up fencing in earnest, becoming the captain of his team in school matches.

I shuddered to think of swordplay as a spectator sport. The last time I had held a sword, I had fully intended to kill the man on the other end of it. As Fate would have it, the killing had not come to pass, but blood had been spilled that day.

Of course Erik had known nothing of this as he admired the sword hanging on the wall of my study. At ten, his curiosity had been insatiable, and he would not be put off with vague excuses. So I had taken the thing down and placed it into his eager, young hands. A sigh escaped me as I watched my son admire the weapon, and an involuntary image of the blade striking Raoul's shoulder flashed before my eyes. I had kept the thing polished, and the silver skull face gleamed and grimaced at me in all its hideous glory.

"Yours, papa?" Erik asked, his hands sliding over the hilt. I nodded.

"Will you teach me to use it?" He asked, slashing the air with the blade, testing the heft.

I arched a brow at him. "No." His face grew long with disappointment at that one word. Rarely did I forbid him anything. "It is a weapon, and like me, an antique likely to break." I held out my hand. Reluctantly, he passed the sword back, hilt first. "However, if you wish, we will arrange for lessons." I finished, hanging the thing back in its place.

"Yes papa," he agreed enthusiastically, and with the first lesson, threw himself into the sport with a devotion he showed only to his music. After a time, I realized that this pursuit, as well as the others, helped him channel the somewhat volatile nature he had inherited. With a heavy heart and a grudging reluctance, I supported him in his choice. I found it impossible to acknowledge that I had been his age once, his age and living in a cage.

Now at fifteen, he was a young man who had many hearts in Rome all a flutter. The girls surrounded him whenever he played. Though he was courteous to all, he managed to slip through their eager hands. His get a ways from the theater or concert halls, of necessity, grew more inventive, usually involving friends from school. The boys did not mind, always eager to help as the rewards were pretty girls to escort home later. Erica, more often than not, managed to be close by, and together, they would slip through the congratulatory crowd.

Erica had joined us in Italy when she had turned fifteen, and the years had flown by in her company. She and her father had made one tour of the Americas, and were now preparing for another. This time, Erik would join them. Meg and I would be the poorer for his absence. Phillippe had suggested we accompany them on the trip.

"My dear fellow, I barely wobble as it is. Ships and trains are not for me. I rather enjoy the life of a country squire," I replied, laughing. I was seventy four and much too used to certain comforts, one of which were two young people in the house. With their imminent departure, I sensed a deep melancholy take root in my bones. Even though they would be gone only a few months, I felt as if something was leaving with them, a certain sense of innocence.

I sighed, and drew my wife closer. In the last year, we had buried both Étienne and Carlotta. They had died within months of one another. With my friends, I buried a part of me, and a loneliness I had never expected to feel again dug its claws into me. Friends were lost, and the world I had known was nearly gone.

Chapter 66

Despite the blazing fire, the heat could not dispel the creeping chill in my bones. Every joint in my wretched frame protested to the slightest movement. Please, just let me go, I whispered to the silence of the room, closing eyes against the pain. How much do you want of me? How much more is there to do?

Then I felt gentle hands on my shoulders and soft, tender lips against my cheek. My hand reached to take hers, raising it to my lips. My wife came around to face me, eyes meeting eyes. *For her*, the inner voice whispered, *you stay for her.*

Meg handed me the pills and water. I accepted them with resigned silence, and she kissed me warmly on the cheek. "It is time, my dearest. You would not disappoint them, not today."

"Humph. You are cruel to drag an old man from his fire," I muttered, unwilling to release her hand. Meg laughed a little, bending low to whisper in my ear.

In all our years, the love had grown and deepened, and if possible, I loved her now more than ever before. "You, my dear, are a minx," I said looking into her smiling face.

"No more than you deserve," she answered. "Now, let us go, and not keep them waiting." She drew me to my feet, draped the cloak over my shoulders, and led me out of the apartment.

It was February 1914. It was a bitter winter, and I was grateful for the deep folds of the ancient cloak. Outdated as it was, it still provided a shadow of warmth in the automobile. Meg sat beside me, holding my hand, but despite the love that glowed from her, despite the folds of the cloak, I felt cold. It wasn't even physical cold.

The years had hurtled forward, and I had grown uneasy. With the advent of the new century and all its curious inventions, had also come increased tensions, both domestic and world wide. With all the potential of a fused powder keg, the world was set to explode in crisis. The journalists were only too accommodating in spreading unease and tension with coverage of a war here or there, strikes, and rebellions. Everywhere the cafés were full of hushed conversations concerning the latest discoveries, scandals, and controversies.

Long ago I had ceased to pay heed to the gossip, and yet I could not shut out the world completely. It belonged to my children now, but as I watched its transformation into an unquiet behemoth, I mourned the world they would never know, the one that had spawned me. Even though there had been cruelty, there had been beauty and innocence as well. It had given me Meg, and a family.

While we made our way through the streets, I looked out the window of the automobile at the people going about their daily lives. The routines had not changed, just the means. Electric lights had replaced gas lamps, and automobiles had taken the place of the horses, but young boys still sold newspapers on the corners, and women carried baguettes in their baskets.

I sighed and turned to Meg. She grasped my hand more firmly and smiled. If anyone understood, she did. I had adapted to the changing world as I had had to. At times, that adaptation had been reluctant at best. Now I was a ghost, a shadow of a world that no longer existed, a ghost who went through the motions of living.

We had come from Italy the previous fall, and this time, there would be no going back to the estate nestled in a pleasant corner of Tuscany. This marked our final return to the city that had been our home despite protracted absences. We took up residence in apartments purchased for their privacy. They were on the top floor of three, consisting of an entire floor of the building. There were balconies where Meg could grow herbs, and a room large enough to accommodate a grand piano. The apartment was also close to Eduard's offices, for no matter my age, I could not abandon the work that had given me a new life. The young men in the office tolerated my presence when, every now and then, I appeared on the doorstep.

When the driver stopped and opened the door, and I had a chance to finally look where we had come, I leaned back against the seat, closing eyes in a vain attempt to still the sudden swell of warring emotions within my heart. This was the last place on earth I had ever expected to be.

Meg's hand on mine was gentle but insistent. "Not tonight Erik. We bring it to a close, here, now." I looked at her, at the love shining in her eyes. Her hand touched my masked, right cheek. A gentle smile played across her lips. "No more demons. No more ghosts to fight."

With a nod I acknowledged her request and accepted assistance from the driver, then grasped my wife's arm as she led us up the stairs of the château.

The strains of a waltz drifted through the open windows and doors. Everywhere lights blazed, and men and women swirled in their finest gowns and suits. For once, I felt very much out of place. I had never been comfortable around large groups of people, let alone with society as whole, and certainly not around people with titles. The swirling mass of bodies in the hall in front of me only wanted to make me flee back down the stairs.

The pressure of my wife's fingers against mine, and the sudden appearance of our children beside us, brought any thoughts of escape to an end. They greeted us with affection, helping to steer our way through the assemblage toward the far end of the room. Along the way, introductions were made and polite small talk adhered to. Christine was radiant in an ivory gown, the ruby pendant I had given her ages ago sparkling at her throat. It was matched by a pair of earrings and a ring, gifts from her husband. She held me to her, and once again I was filled with the incredible love I had just for her. Erik escorted his mother, and as we walked, I noted that the women, no matter their age, turned to either openly stare, or give him side long looks. He ignored their gawking, his eyes only on his mother. As we made our way through the throng, I could only wonder at the fortune that had given us these young people as children.

It was Erik's twentieth birthday. How the years had flown by! Was it only yesterday he had been born? How could it be that now he turned every female head in the room? How was it possible? Had I actually made that young man with the woman beside me? For his part, Erik had grown into a handsome man, his blond hair kept longer than fashion called for, but it suited him. His sharp, green eyes missed nothing as he glanced about the room. Somewhere Meg and I had given him height, and he now towered over us, his frame well filled out. I smiled. Perhaps all that exercise had not been wasted.

With a quiet word, Erik dove into the crowd, his blond head soon lost among the milling bodies. Meg turned to me and smiled. Was she thinking what I was? Her eyes clearly said she was, and my hand on hers tightened. He was an echo of the Erik of long ago, of us.

Before anything could be said, Christine's children surrounded us. Their sudden appearance from out of the twirling mass of dark suits and ball gowns gladdened my heart, and brought melancholy ruminations to an end. They fluttered around us as they led us toward the cleared space before the piano. Gérard had successfully completed his architectural studies and had been given a post with one of my smaller firms. So far, my manager proved a hard task master for this young man. She would let nothing slip by her, and probably was harder on him for the simple fact that he was her son. Jean-Paul had elected to become an engineer, working alongside his brother. The two were as inseparable as Erik and Erica. Where one was, the other was not far away. They were boisterous, always ready with a joke, and had become the favorites of the young set. Their sister, Anne-Marie was a complete opposite. Petite, quiet and studious, she had chosen to follow in her grand-mother's footsteps, becoming a nurse. Gilbert had found her a position at St. Hubert's, and it seemed the young woman and the profession were perfectly suited to each other. Erica had elected a completely different path from her siblings, pursuing music with unequaled passion. Her voice made her popular with audiences and musicians alike, and she could be found almost anywhere, whether on a formal stage, or the dimly lit piano clubs.

As we were directed to our seats at the small stage area directly before the piano, another familiar presence joined us. Hélène had lost none of her grace or poise during the years. She smiled warmly at us, her eyes meeting mine. It had been a long time since we had seen each other. She had never come to Italy, never giving a reason why. She had stayed in Paris with both our friends during their last days, unwilling to leave their side, perhaps unwilling to leave her other child.

I acknowledged her greeting with an inclination of my head, and as if that had been a hidden signal, what had been chaos, slowly became still and utterly silent. A roomful of people turned toward the piano.

A cellist appeared, seating himself beside the piano, while Phillippe gazed out over the assembled crowd. With his strong, tenor voice, he began to sing one of my favorite pieces by Donizetti. The haunting beauty and lyrical passion of the piece came through in all the notes. With the years, Phillippe's voice had grown stronger, and I could understand the almost unreasoning popularity that that voice had created. When he finished, another voice joined him, a voice I knew only too well. It was a voice that was still beautiful, though nothing like that of the shy, trembling girl on the stage of the Populaire. This was the voice of a mature woman, a woman who had confidence in her talent. They sang the duet to wild acclaim, and as Phillippe left her, the Comtesse de Chagny lifted her head slightly, her eyes meeting mine. Erica sat at the piano, hands poised for a signal from her singer.

Christine's voice lifted in a plaintive note, and as the song proceeded her eyes never left mine. Each and every word echoed of things said and done long ago, never forgotten, a night when hearts burned with confused misery, passion and fright.

When it was done, the room exploded with spontaneous applause, and all I could do was acknowledge Christine's glance with a slight nod. Tears, and long buried feelings threatened to overwhelm me. I could not let them, not here.

"That's just the warm ups we do. You should hear when we really sing," Phillippe laughed, taking the floor once more before the piano. When the room quieted, he continued. "This night is special indeed. Not only is it a young man's birthday, but our musical betters have at last seen wisdom, and awarded him the Prix de Rome!"

Applause once more filled the room, and shouts of awe came from somewhere. Erik's hands gently grasped my shoulders, and he whispered so only I could hear. "For you, papa. It is for you." Where upon he took his place at the piano and gave the audience a demonstration of just why he had been given the prize.

Between the pride and the tears, I heard some of what he played. The Prix de Rome, the most sought after honor for a musician. It was his, and so was the world.

When Erica joined him for a lively rendition of the Italian Polka, I rose, and with a look at Meg, made my way away from the crowd. The Prix de Rome, most musicians never even came close to it. Erik had done it, and he was only twenty. The world would bow to him.

I smiled as I walked into the shadowed hall. My son, the son of a man ostracized from the world for his face, would now give it beauty.

I chuckled mirthlessly, and glanced about me. Even though the hall was darkened, there was light enough to make out the imposing, family portraits. So this was where she made her home. I supposed it suited her. She had always been fragile, looking for direction. Raoul had given her that.

I shook my head and sighed. How could I have given her anything, when I had lacked it myself? All I had known was music. I had given her that.

"I'm glad you came," her voice spoke from the shadows. "He wished to surprise you."

Slowly, I turned to face her. She was still beautiful, still regal. The gold locket with its rose hung at her throat. Other than the locket and her wedding ring, the Comtesse de Chagny wore no other jewelry.

"Meg left me little choice," I answered, tears openly running down my cheeks. I did not know whether they were tears brought on by her songs, or the pride in my son, and I did not particularly care. "It's his birthday."

Christine smiled. "Never the less, you are here. That is something." She paused for a heartbeat, eyes searching mine. "He is a good son Erik, not at all what I would have expected."

I looked at her and remembered years of bitterness, sorrow, acceptance, and affection, always affection. In the end, we would always have that.

"I stayed away. I would not interfere in your life again." I ventured. Were there unshed tears in her eyes?

"I could not forget, did not wish to forget. The harder I tried, the more I heard you sing in my mind." She approached, closing the distance between us. "The school, I think it saved me. I didn't want it, but Meg persuaded me. It was you, wasn't it?"

I inclined my head. "It was the only thing I had left to give. Meg, she can be persuasive at times." I smiled wanly.

Christine laughed a little. "Indeed she can."

Suddenly her small fingers wrapped around mine. "I'm glad you found each other. You two are a good combination. I see that in Erik _fils_. You gave him the best of both of you."

I looked into her eyes and slowly raised her hand to my lips. "As you and I would not have done."

"No," she answered, "as we would not have." Lightly, ever so lightly, she laid her palm against the masked side of my face.

My arms folded her into a gentle embrace and held her for eternity. The trembling, impressionable girl I once had yearned for was long gone. In her stead was a woman of assurance, a woman who had held vigil with Meg over my miserable frame, a woman for whom my affection would never fade.

On that February night, on the eve of Erik's birthday and triumph, Christine and I reconciled.

Chapter 67

Who would have predicted that everything we had known and cherished would explode in fire that August? All the negotiations, all the comings and goings through palatial halls, had been for naught. An assassin's attack on the German Archduke as he toured the Balkans in June of that year was enough to spark the fire on the world's powder keg. All any of us could do now was watch it burn and explode around us.

The newspaper lay forgotten on the desk as I watched the last of the day fade away. Life in the streets below went on, but with an undercurrent of tension and unease. Even now, youths were running through the neighborhoods, shouting exhortations for men to take up arms and fight for their land. The French had never forgotten the humiliation of the loss of the rich lands of Alsace and Lorraine to the Germans. Revenge for that loss had been deeply rooted in everyone, and now people saw this declaration of war as an opportunity to take those territories back.

I shook my head. Always men would fight over something, whether it be land, religion, even women. I sighed and turned from the window. No, men would never outgrow that particular passion. They would do all that was necessary to protect their women.

The soft rustle of skirts brought a smile to my face. I glanced at Meg, drawing comfort from her presence. Her ashen face spoke what we dared not voice. I drew her into a tight embrace, holding onto her as if that would stave off the fear that consumed us, the fear for our young men.

For while exhortations to arms were being called, we were only too well aware of who would do the fighting. For once, I was glad that Erik was not home. This madness would not touch him, at least for a time. He had left on yet another tour of the Americas, becoming rather fond of jazz, a style of music alien to me, but not altogether unpleasant.

As the weeks drew into months, it slowly became evident that, as in all things, the powers that be had overestimated the gravity of the initial conflict. Like a fire it spread, and what began as a war in Europe, soon engulfed the world.

Though enthusiasm for the troops burned in people's hearts, once the truth of the true cost of the battle to save Paris surfaced, the talk in the streets grew subdued. People realized that victory, should it come, would be hard won indeed.

The battle to save Paris had been a race between the German, French and British troops. As the German army overran the countryside and came ever closer to the city, hundreds fled in panic, but many, like Meg and me, stayed. There was nowhere else to go. At tremendous cost in lives, the Germans were finally halted thirty kilometers outside of Paris, and the flash of guns lit up the evening sky, turning night into day.

I was seventy nine and wished I had never lived to see such fury unleashed. The more I read and heard of the hostilities, the more I found myself walking the streets of the city so once familiar to me. What would become of this, of us? What would befall the children?

No matter where I was, somehow at the end of the walk, I would find myself staring at the colonnaded building with its gold angel on the roof. I stared at it as if by some strange magic it would give me answers. Had it really been my home? Had I truly spent eighteen years in its tunnels?

I shook my head. Its opulence and grandiose magnificence was incongruous among the buildings surrounding it.

I sighed and turned my steps home, the cane beating out a staccato rhythm against the stones of the street. If anything or anyone was incongruous, it was me.

Chapter 68

Christmas that year was a restrained affair. No one seemed in the mood for too much singing or laughter, though Erica's soft playing was a pleasant distraction for the rest of us.

The three young men stood gathered together in the far corner of the salon, talking quietly.

Erik had come home within a month of the war's outbreak, canceling all his performances for one that needed him more. French blood was being spilled everyday, and the summons had gone to every able bodied man of fighting age. France needed men to fill the rapidly dwindling ranks of its army.

Erik and his nephews had received their orders that very morning. There would be much preparation for them in the days ahead, but for tonight, they had time with family. Their subdued voices were full of speculation as to where they would find themselves a month from now.

I glanced around the room, at my family, and wondered what would become of us.

Meg, Hélène and Anne-Marie held a conference of their own on the other side of the room from the boys, while my two Christines stood beside the window, arms linked.

She had come, for I would not leave her alone to her grief and worry. There was nothing she could do. It was in the hands of the doctors, and she would only have been in their way. So I had brought her here, to family.

Raoul had collapsed that morning, the strain of the negotiations of the past months finally breaking him. Meg had received the call from Gilbert earlier in the day, and we had gone to be by her side.

When I saw Christine so pale, so frightened and fragile, my heart screamed out to her. All I could do was hold her. It was all the comfort I could give. It was all I had left.

Raoul remained unconscious through most of the day. By early evening, his condition had been stabilized, though he was not out of danger. He was alive, and for her, it was solace.

We had taken her home, only to confront the prospect of her grandsons leaving for war. With her son already gone, it was not much of a Christmas for the Comtesse de Chagny.

Chapter 69

I glanced at the frost covered window, to the cypresses beyond. Their heavy branches bowed under layers of ice and snow. They would wait patiently for the sun to relieve them of their burden. I had no such luxury. No one would take this last thing from me, no one, except me.

I turned my eyes to the pale face upon the pillow. The years had not been kind to Raoul de Chagny, certainly not the last few weeks. But then, were any of us the same as those who had played out that fateful performance?

Raoul's stroke had aged him ten years, and he looked more my age than his sixty eight years, but he lived. He would have to learn to use his legs again, and his voice, but he lived. He was hers, and she would not be alone.

"I hated you for taking her away," I began, remembering events of years past, events and feelings brought to focus by words, but words that needed to be said, before it was too late, for both of us. "I wanted nothing more than to cut your heart out that day, and to punish her for her betrayal." I shook my head at the emptiness of it all, and laughed sadly. "When it came to it de Chagny, I could not do it. Her love, if love it would have been, would have come at too high a price. I saw the love for you in her eyes, and I did not have the courage to break her. So I let her go," I paused, glancing at the still figure in the bed. "We both used her Raoul, you and I. We both wronged her. We both wanted her, but never gave the child a chance to say what she wanted. You have been good to her. It is more than I would have done, and you gave her a good son. I could not go on hating you, Raoul," I paused, glancing at the man lying helpless in that bed, remembering a snowy day in a cemetery. "Not after your son gave me back my music." I shook my head and sighed. "Christine is now the woman we both wanted." I smiled a little. "It is not a bad thing for a woman to be loved so. She loves you with all her heart Raoul, of that I'm certain. Find your feet, you miserable wretch, and stand by her side. Don't make her a widow yet."

I was about to leave when his ragged struggle for words drew me to his side. His pale eyes locked onto mine. I now only seldom covered my face. I had been right. The years had caught up, and it no longer made a difference. He did not look away as I brought the face he had hated close to his. Raoul's lips trembled as he tried to form the words. Finally, two came out.

"Pity, you."

I nodded in understanding, drawing away. What were we but two old men, well past everything that would have mattered earlier?

"Rest, and do all else for her. If not, I'll become your worst nightmare." I told him, my eyes flashing with what I hoped was some of my old fierceness.

The door opened, and Christine's fragile form appeared. The graceful and confident woman had been shattered by the last weeks. She had once more succumbed to the fragile girl she had once been. She was pale, drawn, and on the point of exhaustion. Despite the nurses we had hired, she refused to leave Raoul's side. Then too, the absence of letters from Phillippe ate away at her last bits of strength.

With a nod to the man in the bed, I escorted Christine through the halls of her château to the music room.

I was too old and tired to do anything more than play simple melodies for her. I played from memory. Even with glasses, it was difficult to see notes on scores properly these days.

She would not sing, but sat beside me, eyes filled with affection. Her hand reached to touch my face. I stopped playing, drawing her close. I let her cry, let her wash out her sorrow on my shoulder.

When Meg came to take me home, she found me at the piano, playing softly to the exhausted woman sleeping on the sofa. We sat with Christine long into the evening when Meg finally put her to bed. It was a sad thing when all of us were watching each other die a little more every day.

Chapter 70

Sheets of rain beat against the windows, the gurgling of the water a music all its own. I lifted the cup of tea to my lips in a vain attempt to dispel the chill of the February day, knowing it was useless to even try to fight the pain of my joints on days like this, but for them I had to. For them I had to make the effort. I had to be here, for certainly Raoul could not.

I looked at the women of my family as they sat together and wondered how it had all come to this. How was it possible that at my age I had suddenly become their protector? In a twist of Fate, how was it that I was responsible for him?

The absence of our sons had drawn us together as all the years had not done. The boys' departure had made us into a family, despite ourselves.

There had been nothing for it. With thousands of other families across France, we sent our sons to war.

I watched in numbed stupefaction as the women embraced the boys, one by one, sending them on their journey. Last minute packages were thrust into eager hands as the young men embraced the mothers and sisters. They were after all, still only boys, the oldest among them twenty three. How much of life can one know at twenty three?

The women were brave, holding back their tears, braver than I. I could not stave off their flow, not with Gérard, not with Jean-Paul, and certainly not with Erik. The child I had made was a child no longer. He was a soldier, needed by his country, and he was leaving for a cauldron of fire. God alone knew if we would ever see him, or any of them, again.

When I let him go, I felt as if a part of my life was slipping from my hands forever, and there was nothing, absolutely nothing I could do to retrieve it. I could only watch as Meg seized him once more for a quick kiss and hug.

The shriek of the train whistle echoed through the cavernous station, puffs of steam enveloping the massive, black engine in billowing clouds. Hundreds of arms pulled apart, hundreds of eyes said silent goodbyes. Girls were pried away from loved ones, their cries and tears drowned in the cacophony of noise from the train. Perhaps it was just as well that the young men would not hear the laments of their dear ones. This was not an easy journey, for anyone.

With a final glance at our group, the three young men boarded the train as it began to roll out of the station.

While our sons journeyed to distant fields of battle, a battle of a different sort was being played out in the château.

It had become a second home to Meg and me. Meg refused to leave her sister to face Raoul's recovery alone, and I could not. In the end, our daughter set up rooms for us and we stayed. It was easier than driving to and from Paris each day. Petrol was in short supply, and the troops needed it more than we. With Erik gone, there was nothing to keep us in the city.

Because of a war, we became united. We lived in the house of a man I had never thought to call friend.

Chapter 71

Christine held my hand, her blue eyes filled with concern.

"Raoul refuses the nurses, he refuses the doctor. He just lays there, papa. He does not know that he's killing her with this refusal. He barely tolerates me."

I held her shoulders. She was a grown woman, and yet she would always be my child, the daughter of my heart.

I kissed her hair as I had been wont to do all her life. "We do what we must when we hurt. He is hurting, but he will not say it." I said quietly, eyes studying her.

The strain of the past months was slowly wearing Christine down. Though she was only forty three, the lines in her face had deepened. There was no news of Phillippe, other than the occasional article in a newspaper of his troupe's triumph on this or that stage, and the two tattered letters that had come a month before. Even Raoul's connections were of no help in this matter. Most requests for news of family members were met with silence. There were too many to deal with effectively. At least in this, the Comtesse de Chagny was sent a polite, if impersonal letter, stating that the matter was being looked into, and would she please have patience.

I raised Christine's chin, looking at her. It was hard to believe that this beautiful woman had come into my life as an abandoned baby. "Do you trust your father?" I asked.

"Of course! What…"

Placing a finger over her lips, I kissed her cheek. "Keep the nurses out of Raoul's room for an hour."

She raised a brow in curiosity, but I would not elaborate further. I directed my steps to Raoul's bedroom, fully prepared to beat him senseless if I had to.

"I did not give her to you so she would have an invalid for a man! Now walk!" I screamed at him.

"Hate you," he rasped, eyes burning with rage, hands trembling with the effort of holding onto the chair for support.

"Oh yes. Hate me, for I will be here night and day, and I will make you walk de Chagny. I will make what is left of your miserable life a living hell if you let her down." I thrust my face in all its disfigured glory within inches of his. "Use it Raoul, use me. I'm past caring, but I will see you walk for her."

He let go of the chair, reaching for me, the anger in his eyes a living thing. His frame trembled with the effort, but eventually, the left foot moved a fraction. With a sob, he crumpled to the floor.

"Good," I said quietly, placing a hand on his shaking shoulder. "That was one. I never said I'd make it easy on you."

"Hate you." He sobbed, tears running down his face.

"You go on hating me, and I'll teach you to walk again."

Chapter 72

While our sons fought a war on the fields of France and Flanders, Raoul and I fought a war of our own within the walls of his house. It was a war of wills, and this time it did not matter who was stronger, but who would win. It was a struggle for his life, his love, one he had lost hope for, one I would make him fight for.

With each day he became stronger though no less willful. It became a process of wearing down his resistance.

I would appear in his room first thing in the morning, taking a seat in the chair, allowing him time to realize that I was not leaving until we had finished. His eyes flashed anger, defiance, and eventually resignation.

"Get it done," his voice was a hoarse whisper as he stared at me in the chair.

We would go through the routine, I pushing, he challenging, until it became a game to us two old, feeble men, a game where the stakes were high.

Though there were no swords or bloodletting this time, still Raoul and I fought a duel, and still it was for a woman named Christine.

I do not know what possessed me to sit by his side, day in and day out, and force his feet to move. I only knew I did it for her. I wanted him on his feet, needed him to walk beside Christine again. I could not stand that grief stricken look in her eyes, the helplessness she fought against when he refused the doctor and nurses. I would not see her suffer through his wasting away, not when she needed him.

So where once I would have gladly left him lying in the snow with a pierced heart, I became his task master. I was not easy on him. I did not budge in my determination, and he finally accepted the challenge. He understood I did not do this for him, or me, but for her, for Christine.

With his acceptance, our morning battles became nearly civilized, and his "I hate you" a customary end to our small war.

He took his first steps outside his bedroom in Mid-March of 1915. I did not help him. He had his canes. Before an audience of family and nurses, Raoul de Chagny took his first, halting steps toward his wife.

Seeing her tear stained face look at him with tenderness and love was enough. It was why all those battles had been fought all those mornings, for that look in her eyes, and the knowledge that she would not be alone.

That evening, as I stood in the library near the window, I saw her reflection in the glass, and turned to face her.

When Christine looked at me, her eyes glistened with tears. Her hands reached to gently frame my face, and slowly, tenderly, she kissed me.

A kiss. Life can turn on a kiss. All my life, a kiss had been all I had wanted, a kiss given freely. I had eventually wrenched one from her, wrenched it by force.

Now, as she held my face in her hands, and her eyes spoke what she would not, Christine gave me the one thing I had so long ago dreamed of. She gave it freely, with no hesitation, only tenderness and affection that so many years ago had been all my desire. A kiss given of her own choice, healed us both.

Our lives had gone in between. All that remained was affection. I took the hands that held my face, kissed the palms, then let them go.

With a small smile, the Comtesse de Chagny left the room as quietly as she had come.

I had given her her Raoul back. That night, as I held my wife in my arms, I was truly whole. There were no more shadows, no more demons. They had all been laid to rest with a kiss.

March 1915

Dear Father,

Please don't you and Mother worry. We are well, and have received as much training as possible. Our officers are good men who have pulled us through the first skirmish already. It is truly frightening how good we have become at our new trade. Those of us who were painters, writers and musicians, have exchanged instruments of our former trades for instruments of a different sort: machine guns, rifles, spades and ladles! They all make music of their own, a music that is ever present.

While it is true that an army will stand and fight, a hungry man is not worth much in the field, so our rations are adequate, if lacking in finesse. However, I would gladly sacrifice a month's worth of these meals for one of Mother's treats.

Yesterday, we had to put down one of our mules which had gone lame. I expect we'll be eating unhappy Navette with the next round of sausages.

Your loving son,
Erik

Late March 1915

My Dear Father,

We have been sent on to Ypres. We expect to be here some time if the equipment trucks are any indication. There is an endless convoy of them, both coming and going, though the roads are nothing more than mud fields. The trucks become stuck in the quagmire that the fields become once it rains, blocking everyone's progress. It is easier to struggle to the front with protesting mules and groaning backs, than with the vehicles. We carry what we can, passing exhausted troops marching back in the endless rotation that has become our routine.

Heavy fighting has taken place here already as evidenced by the charred stumps that once were trees, and the holes that fill the line of vision to the horizon. There is not one patch of land that has been left untouched, and yet, a few flowers manage to poke their heads above the desolation.

The groan of engines and boom of artillery is nearly constant. We have become inured to the noise. It is when it grows deathly silent that we worry. For then we know the enemy is out there, laying wire or mines. Ironic that we should prefer the shriek of artillery shells to the silence of the night, but it is so. At least with the artillery, we know what to expect. With the silence also come the insidious enemies that are more numerous and hundred times more annoying than the Bosches could ever be. With them, the game is understood. With the rats, that is something else altogether. They sneak into our food and we beat them, adding their pitiful bodies to those already piling in the fields. It is the business of this war, and we have become frightfully good at it.

For now we exist in our narrow worlds. The trenches serve as home, though more often than not, we might as well swim in them rather than stand. The rains are incessant and we wonder if we'll ever be dry again.

Love to you and Mother,
Erik

Late March 1915

Dearest Father and Mother,

One of the pesky journalists was here. While we say nothing to these gentlemen, leaving that for our officers, he did offer pictures in exchange for cigarettes. Even though our work is hard, we do find amusement where, and when, we can. The card games are nearly continuous, and as long as someone has something to throw into the pot that will be of use to someone else, they are welcome to sit in. Some of the men have rescued odd bits from the abandoned village, fashioning curious, but necessary items. Their inventiveness would challenge the top designers working in Paris! Edmond found a litter of kittens God only knows where, and immediately auctioned them off, keeping one for us. The thing has made a pet of even the hardest among us. It probably will not be much of a rat catcher, but its presence is solace to some of us, especially the men from the farms.

Thought you would like to know that not all of what we do is fighting, just most of it. We manage to endure that because tomorrow will surely be better.

Yours always,
Erik

April 1915

My Dear Father,

It has been a terrible day and everyone is still reeling. The Germans have unleashed a terrible new weapon-gas. The men in the front lines were caught unaware and unprepared. The devastation amongst the troops is too shocking for words. It is not so much the loss of life, but the suffering of the survivors that makes this weapon so ghastly. Those who died are the lucky ones. The agony and misery of those now lying in and around the first aid station, is not to be believed. There are too many of them to shelter in the hut, so we do what we can, while waiting for the ambulances to evacuate them. Is it possible that men can unleash such suffering on their own kind?

It was the British troops that bore the brunt of this particular attack. However with this weapon now in the field, we have all become its target. Until we are given some protection, we are helpless against it. It is insidious, coming in on a mist that creeps along the ground.

My unit is safe. We were on rotation to the back lines when the attack occurred. We are all accounted for, even Edmond's cat, if somewhat quieter than usual. Even the card game is played out in silence, as each man contemplates what is ahead. Most of us do not look past more than the hour of his relief on watch, but tonight is different.

A man can fight a bullet, a knife, even find his way around the artillery shells, but this is a silent, invisible killer. Its deployment has frightened the hardened men around me as nothing ever could.

I expect that if one side has harnessed this beast, it will not be long before we have our own version. When we finally leave these fields, will anything ever grow here again? Will the grass be green or red for all the blood we pour onto the ground?

We try to stay focused on our necessary duties but occasionally, I find my mind drifting to our days in Brittany, and your lessons on the piano. I have learned to play other music now Father, but I would once again like to play four hands with you.

Yours always,

Erik

Chapter 73

The letters came apace, and we awaited each one with anxious hearts. Meg wrote to our son and the boys nearly every day. Between Erik's letters, and those of Gérard and Jean-Paul, we had a different image of the war than the journalists, or the government, wanted people to believe. On occasion, there would be sketches included with the notes, giving us vivid images of what their lives were like in the field.

I could only shake my head in sorrow at what the young men endured. Though never a religious man, I often found myself in the chapel of the château, silently praying for the children's safe deliverance.

We stayed on the estate. There was nowhere else to go. People abandoned Paris for the country in the forlorn hope that their lives would be easier without struggling in claiming daily rations. Rationing had come to full effect, and no one was exempt. Even those with means found their purses strained, as costs of basic goods rose ever higher.

The streets of the city were emptied of all her able bodied men and what remained were husks barely able to shuffle along, or urchins that clung to their mother's skirts. The women filled the posts left empty by the men. Their faces were grey and ashen with exhaustion as they waited in line for bread, yet they persevered. They still had families to care for, that depended on them for livelihood. There was no choice.

On a rare visit to Eduard's offices one day, I was overwhelmed to see only one or two grey heads at the desks. The rest were women, and among them all stood Christine, directing their work with confidence and firm resolution. The lessons of long ago now found use and I smiled, despite the desolation and anguish that tore at my heart. Watching as she conferred with one of her workers, I realized that everything, absolutely everything I had ever known, was gone. The world was tearing itself inside out with war, men were dying by the thousands, and I, like some sad reminder of days gone by, still remained.

In silence, I left the building, my steps slow, but sure. There was only one place I wanted to be. Only that one place could bring solace.

I sat on the balustrade, glancing at the ornate columns, at the windows I had had so much trouble replacing. I heard the echo of Étienne's hearty laugh as we had shared the first of many bottles of wine. I saw the look of compassion and understanding in his eyes as he had handed me the sword. And Carlotta! Oh that damnable woman! Her and those hateful dogs, gone.

I glanced toward the rooftop. The angel stood there, straining toward the heavens, toward its home, and I heard a voice crying out its defiance, its rage and pain, and a tear dropped onto my hand. For him? Was there a shade of him that still remained? Would anyone remember?

I felt gentle hands wrap around me, and a soft kiss on my cheek. "Let's go home, Father." Christine quietly whispered in my ear as slowly, she drew me to my feet.

I looked at her, at the woman she had become. The concern for her sons and husband was deeply etched into the planes of her face. She would not speak of it. None of us did. We went through the days, one at a time. It was all we could do.

I let her lead me away from the grandiose structure, toward the waiting automobile. As her arm held my waist, my heart filled with the warmth of love I had only for her. My eyes drifted to the angel high on the rooftop and I was glad, so very glad that on that night so long ago I had found her, found my daughter, my angel.

Hélène had been right. It had just taken a lifetime to understand. Just as I had saved her, Christine had saved me. Her love, her innocence had halted my plunge into ever deeper darkness. We had both needed each other, as now, we needed family.

May 1915

Mon chèr grand-père,

Rumor has reached us that the Bosches sank the Lusitania. If so, then the chances of the Americans joining us in this party are good. It's about time. They would not let us do this by ourselves and not enjoy in the fun, would they?

It's a damnable business this standing about in trenches and ducking our heads whenever artillery shells whiz by. The Bosches have dug in, and so have we. No one is going anywhere for a while, except to forage, drag the wounded back to the lines, and exchange goods in the caches. They leave sausages, we leave wine. All this around us, is nonsense. We attack, retreat, and attack again, and nothing changes, except the loss of good men each time we go out.

I am being sent on to yet another post where, apparently, they have more need of engineers, than here. Seems to me that mucking about in mud is not the way to fight this thing, and one place is much like another. However, I go where they send me. I do what I must, and survive. I wish the Americans won't take too long to decide on joining this dance. With them on our side we'll mop up the dance floor, go home, and sit with pretty girls.

My love to you, and ma chère grand-mère,
Jean-Paul

Late May 1915

Mon chèr grand-père,

Rumor persists that the Italians have switched their allegiance. Is this true? We are told little, and what does filter through, is most often gossip than news.

This business is getting worse everyday. One of our couriers was shot yesterday. Two men died trying to drag him to the trenches. The third succeeded, though it cost him a leg. All that for a dog! These beasts are our lifeline out here. They carry messages between the lines, bits of food, even medicine. Mostly, their blind courage inspires the men, though there are times when the fire from artillery is so heavy the handlers refuse to send them on their missions.

Once again we have been given short rations! What there was, was damn near inedible! Will this never end?

Au revoir,
Jean-Paul

Chapter 74

While the months wore on and the fighting continued with no end in sight, enforced rationing and attacks against allied shipping began to take its toll. Shops closed because there was little, if anything left to sell. Lines for what was available grew ever longer and tempers shorter. People drew together, sharing what they could. Some turned their skills toward helping the soldiers, however they were able.

We saw less and less of the two young women of our family. The hospitals in and around Paris were inundated with wounded, and there were not enough nurses or doctors to care for them. When she would visit, Anne-Marie was exhausted. She spent the time sleeping, only to go back to the city, and do her shifts all over again.

Erica traded performing gowns for the uniform of the Croix Rouge, choosing to serve as an ambulance driver, and like her sister, she was seldom seen at the château. They shared our apartment in Paris, but seldom even saw each other.

While no one lacked for anything on the estate, I knew that eventually the resources there too, would become strained. Then also, Raoul was quickly finding his legs and I grew restless sharing the same roof with him. I proposed to Meg we leave, but it was Christine who confronted me.

"And where would you go Erik? Where do you think it would be better?" She demanded, standing just inside the doorway of the parlor, arms crossed over her chest. Her eyes held a stern look as she watched me. The grey of her simple suit only accentuated the regal air around her. With Raoul's recovery, so too, Christine had regained her composure. She was every inch a Comtesse, even to the graying hair. Somehow that only added to her dignity. Yet in this woman who stood before me I still saw the girl I had once sung to.

"I want to go to my house with Meg, to her roses and my piano," I answered, sinking into a chair.

She shook her head, still looking at me. "It will be winter soon. Brittany will be cold. What will you do for heat? There are more restrictions on oil and coal."

"I am tired, Christine. I want to go home." I did not meet her eyes, and looked anywhere but at her.

She released a sigh and came to stand beside the chair, her hand touching my shoulder. "You are home. Stay. He needs you," she paused, taking a breath. "I need you."

I shook my head, refusing to look at her. "He walks. He is yours and I have no desire to____."

"Interfere? Oh my dear, sweet Erik," she came around to face me, bending to my level so our eyes could meet. "You gave us our life back. Our sons are gone and soon, everything we knew will be forgotten. All we have is each other now. Stay, you and Meg." She lightly kissed me, then pulled away. "Stay. I will not let friends want. Besides, I have a piano, if not the roses."

I remained silent to her plea, gazing out the window at the leaves blowing across the garden. Soon that too would be the end of all of us, just dust blowing on the wind.

A light, gentle touch brushed against my cheek, and when she spoke, Christine's voice was soft and gentle. "Stay. If for no other reason, please, stay for me. You have given kindness to many. Allow a friend to return the goodness you once gave her."

Slowly I turned to look at her. Only deep, abiding affection looked back at me. "You made Raoul walk for me. Now I'm asking you to stay, for me."

I looked into her eyes, into eyes I had once endlessly longed for. They were still the same eyes. They still belonged to the girl I had so shamelessly used, but they were the eyes of a friend.

Hesitantly, I touched her cheek. She laid her hand atop mine. All these years, and a part of me was still afraid of her, was still in love with her.

"Whether you admit it or not Erik, you brought us all together. You made us into a family," she paused, and with her other hand, touched my ravaged cheek. A smile lifted her lips. "I won't let you leave. Not now."

I sighed, took her hand in mine, and kissed it. For some reason, mist blurred my sight. "Through the winter then," I murmured.

"Through the winter," she repeated, her warm lips kissing my brow.

The quiet click of the door closing was the loudest noise ever made.

"She's right you know," Meg's gentle voice finally broke the silence. She looked at me across the parlor with a knowing smile. "As strange as it is, you did bring us all together, despite ourselves. We've become stronger and better for it." She rose from the sofa where she had been quietly reading, and came to my side, extending a hand in invitation.

I took it looking into the brown eyes I loved so well, and for the first time realized the truth of her words. In all these years, all our lives had become intertwined to where we now were a family, all of us, even Raoul and I.

As Meg helped me walk to our room, I recognized what had been born in that house, in that fire of long ago. It would endure, even if we did not.

Chapter 75

When November turned into a chill December, a delegation of allied uniforms came to see Raoul one day. With their departure, the peace of the château transformed into organized chaos. Furniture in unused rooms was stowed and replaced with cots, and the extensive lands to the rear of the building sprouted an assemblage of tents almost overnight. With the tents, came an endless procession of ambulances.

Like many of its neighbors, the Château de Chagny became a refuge for broken, agonized men.

The women did not hesitate joining the nurses in caring for the wounded that filled each and every corner of the house. Men of many nationalities found themselves lying beside one another, and I supposed that for them, it was no different than the trench lines. Many of the French units served with Algerian and Moroccan troops. The Canadian and American volunteers had been mostly incorporated into the ranks of the British army, though some served under the French flag as well. A few wounded German prisoners found their way as well to the sanctuary the château had become. The rooms of the house echoed with many languages, and yet there was really only one. What all these men wanted was to finish this bloody business and go home to their families.

To the women of my family, it did not matter what color a particular man was, or what uniform he wore. They moved among the cots like the angels they were, dispensing smiles, warm words, writing letters, or holding bowls of food when the men could not hold their own.

I moved among the sea of white sheets, mind reeling from the carnage lying about. Most of the faces that looked back at me were the faces of boys grown to old men within days. They were haggard and haunted by sights no one should be subjected to. Most of them would live and heal, ready to fight on the lines once more. Some died during the nights. Many never reached the refuge the ambulances drove them to.

My crimes, and there were many, paled to nothing when I saw the cost of this war laid out in the rooms of Raoul's house. I saw it in the faces of my family as they struggled to give comfort to the living, and the dying.

When I could stand the misery no longer, I found the piano, and gave these broken men the only thing I could-music. It was the one thing that was sane in this madness. It was the only thing that made sense, for I could not comprehend the wholesale slaughter of men.

The music room at the château became a refuge within a refuge. It had been left unoccupied so the men, doctors, and nurses would have a place to forget, even for a few, brief minutes, the agony around them.

Often when I played, there would be small groups of soldiers gathered around card tables or talking amongst themselves. It did not matter. I played anyway, the strains of Mozart and Chopin soothing me, if not them.

Somewhere in the fields were our own children. Though we never dared speak it, the concern for their safety ate away at all of us. With the long, winter evenings ahead, and the house filled with leavings of the war, we six drew ever closer to each other. We were all we had. Hélène, Meg, the two Christines, Raoul and I remained of what was sane in a world gone mad.

While there would be no spontaneous Christmas truce for the men in the fields as there had been the previous year, a final truce and peace came between Raoul and me. I saw it in his eyes one day as we sat at dinner. His eyes met mine, and a small smile curved his lips. I gave him a slight smile and nod in return. The swords of long ago were buried. We were both too tired and feeble to continue. There was a war around us and no more reason to continue our own.

Chapter 76

Despite the misery of the wounded, despite the horrendous loss of life and occasional shelling of Paris proper by German guns and airplanes, life continued.

While Meg, Hélène and Christine persevered in their care of the men at the château, my daughter and I resumed work in Paris. Despite a war, demand for building was high. The government found itself in dire need of munitions factories. Where contracts for building new ones were generous, it was cheaper and faster to refit old, existing buildings. The work was demanding, strenuous, and Christine's presence at many negotiations only inflamed tempers already grown short. The situation was made even more precarious because most of the engineers refused to discuss business in her presence, unable to believe a woman would understand the intricacies of engineering. Christine could not carry this burden alone, so once more, I took my place beside her in offices I had not thought to occupy again.

With the commencement of the New Year, a letter from Eduard's lawyer arrived, reverting ownership of the combined firms to the Marchand family. It was how we learned that Eduard, and most of the young men with him, would never return. A cold, impersonal note to say lives were gone. Letters informing families of the fate of loved ones crisscrossed the continent. After a half hearted attempt at the beginning of the war of sending bodies home, the idea was quickly abandoned. With appalling losses everywhere, it became expedient to bury the dead where they lay. All a family could expect was a dispassionate announcement, with a few personal mementos attached, if that.

I was eighty one years old, and it was January1916, when Christine and I walked through the offices that echoed with Étienne's hearty laugh. Now the constrained silence grated against the nerves. I quickly lost myself in piles of documents that had accumulated on the director's desk. For a time, it allowed me to forget what was happening around us, allowed me to forget the ever present ghosts of my friends.

Christine and I worked long into the evening, breaking only for a quick meal at one of the cafés. By silent agreement, we avoided returning to the château and its content of wretchedness, at least for this one night.

We walked arm in arm through the darkened streets. Only minimal lighting broke the night, as everyone adhered to the government's restrictions. It felt good to have my child beside me. I smiled a little as I recalled how we had walked the streets of Rome, when there had been no war, only thoughts of a young man in her head.

By the time we began to steer our steps back toward the offices, our journey had brought us to that infernal building. Even in the shadows of the few street lights that were on, it was an imposing sight. While not all entertainment had been curtailed during the hostilities, the grandiose, extravagant productions had been toned down in respect for the fighting men, and to save materiel. Now my house stood silent, dark, and empty. Like me, it was beginning to show the strain of years.

"It is still your house, isn't it, Father?" Christine's voice broke the heavy silence. I sighed, squeezing her hand.

"It is where I existed," I said in a heavy, melancholy tone, eyes on the behemoth before me. It continued to haunt my sleep, though no longer with nightmares of anguish and fires. It pulled at me, called me to it, called me home. An invisible cord bound us. It would never let me go, and I could never abandon it. "It is where I found music, passion, heartbreak, a man, and a friend." I glanced at my child and smiled weakly. "It allowed me a measure of redemption." I caressed her cheek. "It is not so easy to let go."

She embraced me, kissing me lightly on the cheek. "Do not worry, Christine. I will not become its ghost, at least, not yet." I chuckled, holding her hand more firmly.

She nodded, accepting the words for what they were, a comfort for her and a lie for me. The ghost was not so far away. He bided his time, though he grew restless, and in this world of fire, it would be an easy thing to let him loose, to let him once more have reign, but the opera was not finished. I refused to give in to his wishes. His time would come, but not yet. I glanced at my daughter's gently smiling face. No, not yet. There were still too many things to do.

We walked back to the offices, back to our work, that in the middle of a war, made little sense. But then, what did?

Chapter 77

Even before the automobile came to a stop in the drive, I knew. Raoul and I exchanged glances. He had seen its approach as well, and I did not forget that he had served. If anything, the grim set of his mouth was more telling than the ominous presence of the automobile.

Though many vehicles had come and gone to and from the château in the intervening weeks, none had the distinctive, portentous aura like this one vehicle, and yet it, in itself, would be indistinguishable on the street from any other. It was black, like the rest, and yet its presence brought a very cold chill up my spine.

By mutual accord, Raoul and I sought out our wives. They were gathered in the small sitting room off the kitchen, preparing a light breakfast. More and more, we six found our realm at the château narrowed as more wounded were moved in. Meg and our two Christines had not noticed the approach of the automobile, and only Hélène's eyes indicated that she had seen it pull up. I gave her a slight shake of my head, moving to stand beside the window, eyes drawn to the grey morning, and the activity in the drive.

Two women disembarked, their long, winter coats nearly sweeping the snow covered ground. The small stature of the one and the Croix Rouge brassard on the coat sleeve of the other, immediately set them apart from any number of the Croix Rouge personnel that had come through the château's doors. Two men followed them out of the vehicle, and though I did not know the man in the American olive drab uniform, there was no mistaking the other. If nothing else, I would know his height and blond hair anywhere.

With an excited cry and a sudden stream of tears springing from my eyes, I made my way to the side door of the house, followed by the family, for at my outcry they had left off their activities, finally noticing the arrival of our dearest blood.

When the four reached the threshold, eager arms embraced them. Even the American found himself the recipient of warm embraces.

While not official combatant nations, America and Canada had sent many volunteers, most coming at their own expense, some joining the fight because they thought it the right thing to do. Some did it for adventure, some to break away from family. Whatever their reason, the men served well, and with distinction. They were welcomed wherever they went, and at Château de Chagny no less than anywhere else.

When we repaired to the sitting room and coffee and tea was passed around, I could not help the distinct feeling that something portentous hung in the air, something none of the four was willing to broach. It shone in Erik's eyes whenever he looked at his sister, a shadow of sadness that quickly disappeared when she turned to smile at him. I did not ask, knowing full well that whatever news they had brought would eventually come to light. There was enough sadness in the house for the present, without adding to it. So for now, we enjoyed the unexpected and delightful pleasure of having our children home.

The American, Michael, was a surgeon, working alongside the French units. He had asked for, and been granted a transfer to a hospital in Paris where his skills would be of more use than in the trenches. Instead of Paris, he had found himself posted to this particular place.

"All in due course," he laughed, shrugging it off. "From the look of things, my hands will be needed here as much as in Paris. If you'll excuse me, I'll walk around a bit, and make some friends." He left our small gathering to acquaint himself with the situation.

"The army is only as good as its clerks," Raoul muttered, looking after the disappearing figure of the new doctor. "One stroke of the pen and you find yourself on the other side of the world." He cackled, clapping Erik on the shoulder. Erik only smiled, nodding silent agreement.

When Erik took Christine's hand and led her outside to the drive, it was late afternoon. The day would soon be done, and as I watched them from the window, I was grateful that whatever news had come, that Erik was the one to tell her. She, at least, would be spared the dispassion of the army. They stopped by the ornate fountain that was now filled with leaves and snow. He turned to face her. Whatever and however it was said, was between them. I saw him embrace her in his strong arms, his head bowed over hers.

Hours later, when silence ruled at least in our small portion of the house, I woke from restless slumber to find Meg gone. With effort and heavy steps, I shuffled my way to our daughter's room. Erik's soothing, reassuring voice came through the half opened door in quiet counterpoint to the plaintive weeping from within. He held his sister's shoulders as her cries tore through her. Meg and Christine were already there, and apparently, had been for some time.

Erik's eyes finally saw me and beckoned me to his side. He rose, his place beside Christine taken by her mother and aunt. Meg and the Comtesse comforted the child they had both come to call their own.

With a glance at the women, Erik drew me aside. "Jean-Paul was killed while fortifying a sap. The unit met up with Jerry. A scuffle ensued. It's not an uncommon thing. We often find our trenches right alongside those of the Jerries. This time, someone tripped a mine and blew the whole, with all the men in it."

"No! I will not bury my son! They can't take him from me!" Christine's cries tore my heart to pieces, and there was nothing I could do that would give her comfort.

I sat with her, trading places with Meg, who rose to embrace her son as only a mother could. My old, weak arms held the child I had found so long ago, my eyes meeting those of a woman I had yearned for many years before. Tears streaked her face as her fingers brushed Christine's hair. We sat there, in a silence broken by a daughter's weeping, united by sorrow.

"How is it possible I will bury my son?"

"No one will ever know, and no one will ever have an answer," Raoul said from the doorway. He stood leaning heavily on his canes. "But they will do it all over again when this is done. It is the way of governments everywhere."

There was not much we could say to that, or wanted to, for deep inside, all of us knew he was right. We sat with Christine long into the night, the five of us, for we were a family now, unbreakable in our loyalties.

Morning found us gathering in the kitchen. It was clear that none of us had slept very much at all. When I finally shuffled my way into the room, I found my daughter already there, seated at the table, a woolen shawl draped around her shoulders, Michael sitting next to her. Two cups were set before them, and apparently they had been talking. He too, showed signs of wear. He smiled a little when he saw me enter.

"I am sorry, Madame," he said gently, his hand lightly touching her shoulder. She nodded, but did not speak. Her eyes would not rise from the cup she stared at, as if reading its emptiness would give her the answers no one could.

Michael rose and went to the stove where the kettle was boiling. "Tea?" He asked. I nodded, looking at his drawn face.

"A long night, for all of us," I said quietly, glancing at Christine.

"For none more so than her," he proffered the cup of steaming liquid in my direction. Our eyes met and he shook his head. "It is never an easy thing to tell them of their loss." He nodded toward Christine, and I understood he meant mothers in general, not just this one sitting silently behind us.

"Doctor," a nurse called from the doorway, "they need you."

He acknowledged her call with a nod. "I'll be right there." He set the cup down, giving me a lopsided grin. "So it goes. No rest for any of us_____."

"Until we're in our graves," Raoul finished for him, coming into the room, his wife close behind.

"If even then," I said under my breath, watching Michael disappear down the hall, his tall figure brushing past Meg as she too, joined the gathering.

We held a memorial for Jean-Paul a few days later. It was a small, family affair. There were no drawn out harangues by the priest, only quiet remembrances of a young man who had loved to laugh.

When we walked from the chapel back to the house on that blustery, January day in 1916, I saw Anne-Marie's hand slip into Michael's, their fingers entwining around each other.

Meg's arm slipped around my waist. When I looked at my wife, I knew that as it had been at the Opera house, so it would be here. Love would rise from the ashes, and life would continue.

January 1916

to

February 1919

Chapter 78

With Jean-Paul's death, Christine buried herself in work. Despite efforts to dissuade her, she insisted on staying at the château, helping the nurses.

"I need to stay, Father. I need to do it for him." She hugged me fiercely, her face pressed to my shoulder. I held her for a long time, remembering years long past when I had held a little girl in my arms.

"I'll be all right, Papa. Right now Erik needs you and maman." She lifted her eyes to mine, giving way to a tremulous smile. "Remember the promise we made each other. It still stands. Besides, if nothing else, I have Erica and Anne-Marie to keep an eye on me."

"Very well," I nodded, kissing her lightly. With a final hug, she released me and disappeared into the château.

By his own choice, we stayed with Erik in Paris. It was close to the de Chagny's, and yet distant enough from the front lines to give him rest and the distraction that all young men sought. However if my father's heart knew my son, there was a much more important reason for his decision to stay in the city. Erica too, had arranged time away from her duties, and they stole what time they could in each other's company.

They even treated Meg and me to an impromptu musical evening, their laughter for a time lifting the bittersweet melancholy that gripped me. I knew this would not last, that it was only a fleeting moment of peace from the engulfing horror to which both had to return.

For them I smiled as they gently drew me toward the piano. While I played, their voices filled the apartment with soaring harmony. I glanced at Meg who returned my smile with one of her own before slowly walking away to our bedroom.

When I finished, I joined her, leaving the young people their privacy. They had little enough of that.

"You'll eventually have to tell her," Meg said quietly, helping me out of the jacket. I nodded, eyes drawn to the photograph of a young Christine looking back at me.

"She adores you Erik. She will not walk away." My wife spoke to that dark, secret place in my heart that I did not dare acknowledge existed. She spoke to the fear that some day I would lose Christine altogether.

"For them she needs to know." Meg began to loosen the shirt, but I caught her hands in mine and brought them to my lips. When the tears would not be stopped, Meg drew me into her arms, holding me to her heart. "Je t'adore mon coeur. Je t'aimerais toujours."

"I'm afraid, Meg, afraid for them. What will we leave behind?"

She kissed me, smoothing the sparse hair back from my face. "They'll muddle through, like we did." She smiled, resuming what ultimately had become a nightly custom. Though I had ceased wearing masks and make-up years before, still, the ravaged side of my face needed attention. It had become Meg's habit to rub cream over the ruined cheek to keep the skin supple. It and Maurice's pills had become a ritual for us.

Oh yes, Maurice still kept a wary eye on me, and gave me a thunderous lecture of disapproval when he discovered I had once again resumed work at the offices.

His disapproval aside, I ached to see Meg reduced to a caregiver for an old and weary man. So I did what I needed to do, the consequences be what they would. I had fought for Raoul's recovery and I refused to become a burden to my wife. I would not subject her to the anguish I had seen on Christine's face. I refused to succumb to the aches and pains that now followed me on a daily basis. I worked alongside my daughter when I could, because I refused to give in to the weakness, because I would not be an invalid to Meg.

Yet despite my best efforts, every now and then, age put me in my place.

So it was the following morning as I finished shaving. The pain gripped my chest, and with nauseating vertigo, the world spun from under me. Only a pair of strong, gentle arms prevented my fall. They lowered me to the chair, and after a minute of rummaging, Erik held out the pills to me. His eyes were full of that anxiety I had seen on his three year old face. "Your pride will kill you, Father. I'm going to wake maman."

"No," I whispered through the ebbing pain, gripping his wrist. "No. She must not know."

"But, papa---."

"Please." It was a request from my innermost heart as my wizened, gnarled fingers held his powerful, young hand. Our eyes locked, and it was most strange to look at me as I had been at twenty. Only it wasn't all me. Meg was there in the softer lines of chin and eyes. The combination of us studied me with intense concern.

We sat there in silence, my son and I, and as the pills slowly began to take effect, and the pain diminished, I noticed the bandages swathing his right shoulder. He saw my look, shook his head, and smiled. "A memento from Fritz. A scratch, nothing more. Are you all right now, Father?"

I nodded weakly. "Just need rest."

I watched as he proceeded with his toilette, noting that he favored the right arm. I suspected that there was more to the 'scratch' than he wanted me to know.

"How is it with Fritz?" I ventured for something to say in the silence that had fallen between us.

Erik cleaned off the razor and his chin before turning his eyes on me. For a heartbeat, those eyes aged forty years, and I realized that I would never comprehend what he had to endure on a daily basis.

"A little muddy Papa and the food could be better." While it was kindly said, there was an edge to his voice that precluded any further discussion of that subject.

I nodded in understanding. He had come home to get away from the war, not talk about it. As our eyes met in silent exchange, we realized we both had our secrets to keep. A smile passed between us.

I reached out a hand and he gently pulled me to my feet. I led him to the piano and began a search through the stacks of scores on top of it. "I want you to play something for your mother, something I stashed away years ago. Now, where is it?"

"Papa, she's sleeping."

"Precisely," I said with a smile as my eyes alighted on the sought for music. "Ah," I handed him the pages. "Go on, play," I whispered. As his fingers began to evoke a gentle melody from the instrument, I went to sit by Meg's side. Taking her hand in mine, I watched her wake.

My wife smiled when she saw me, then her eyes widened in surprise as she became aware of the music. It was a piece I had written for her when Erik had been born. I had played it that night as she held him in her arms and we brought our family full circle.

"Thank you for our son," I kissed her softly, tenderly, all my love for her bound in that one touch of our lips.

Chapter 79

The result of my attack was a short, but pleasant visit from Gilbert. We had not seen each other in months, and it was good to spend time in his company, even if that company was forced by circumstances.

By the time he arrived, Meg had already left to meet her mother at the school. Through all the ensuing events, Hélène had still found time to run the school and teach aspiring ballerinas. I could not help a low chuckle. How the girls in the dormitories at the Populaire had screamed when I had chosen to pull some prank. How many years ago had that been!

As with all of us, the war had taken its toll on my friend. Being a doctor, I knew Gilbert had seen his share of mangled bodies, but nothing could have prepared him for the atrocities that now came his way on a daily basis. Though he was half my age, the look in his eyes made him appear thirty years older. I shook my head as we made our way to my study. This damned war would be the end of us all.

He did not lecture or harangue, but quietly proceeded to examine me under the watchful scrutiny of my son. We confined our talk to the gossip of the day, neither willing to venture to another topic with Erik in the room. I knew that like us, Gilbert and Julie worried for their son's safety.

When at last Gilbert set aside his instruments, and his eyes turned to mine, the look he gave me was filled with concern. "I won't give you Maurice's lecture," he rummaged in his bag, at last handing me a bottle of pills. "But don't make me bury a friend. These are stronger, but they'll only stave off the inevitable if you continue this way, Erik."

I pocketed the pills, looking out the window at the snow covered streets. "I need to be here for Meg, for Christine. They cannot do it alone."

Gilbert sighed, laying a hand on my shoulder. His eyes connected with Erik who nodded and quietly left the room.

"They will bury you if you pursue in your stubbornness and not leave off." Gilbert said, taking a seat beside me. "They are strong women Erik, stronger than we give them credit for. Christine will be all right. She takes after her father." His eyes softened a shade and he smiled. "In many ways, she's as stubborn as you, but then this is not about Christine, is it?" He cocked his good brow at me.

I looked at him and had to stifle the impulse to laugh at how strange a pair we made. Between the two of us, we had one decent face.

"I thought not," he said quietly when I looked away from his scrutiny to study the snow outside, as if that would assuage my fears.

"I hate being old. Everything creaks, and not much functions properly." I turned to him, and all my years were in my eyes. "I hate being old for her."

He nodded, smiling a little, understanding my meaning. "It is the vagary of Nature, my friend. It is why we leave the young Eriks and Alains behind."

I sighed, closing eyes against the sudden swell of unbidden tears threatening to spill. "There is so much I still want to do with her."

Gilbert rose and his strong hand grasped my shoulder. "Then do it, while you have time. No matter how you fight it Erik, you are not a man of twenty. That heart of yours will not beat forever and I can only do so much. Leave off. Spend time with Meg." He gathered his bag and I heard him exchange quiet goodbyes with Erik before the door clicked shut.

"Your mother must never know he was here." I turned to my son as he came into the room.

"Why? Why won't you tell her?" His tone bordered almost on anger.

"She would only worry needlessly."

He stared at me. "Don't you think that's part of her job, as your wife? She loves you--no, she adores you, papa. You're only hurting her with your silence." He paused, letting his words ring inside my head, a head that was filled with pain, fear, and longing for the strength I had once had.

"If I know Mother, she suspects." His voice had grown quieter and gentler. Now he stood beside me, his green eyes never wavering from my face. "You can't hide these attacks from her forever. Tell her."

I finally looked at him, truly looked at him, into an echo of my face as it might have been, and sighed. "No, not forever, I no longer have that, but as long as I can, I will."

"I don't understand!" He cried out, running fingers through his hair, a gesture that once had been so familiar. "Surely you love her?"

"More than you could possibly understand," I said quietly, for it was the absolute truth.

"Don't you think she should know?"

"What good would it do? What do you think it would do to her?" I shook my head and took his hand in mine. "I saw what that kind of worry did to her once. Not again." At his questioning glance, I elaborated. "Your mother nearly lost me once already. I will not have her spending her days with a helpless old man!"

There it was, even before I could stop myself. My fear laid out in the open between us.

He didn't move. Only his eyes acknowledged the secret that had been laid bare. Erik gently squeezed my hand, then let it drop.

"All right, Father," he said slowly, tenderly. "You have my word. Maman won't know, not from me." With a light kiss to my forehead, he left the room, left me to ponder the gnawing dread and apprehension of a dark and abysmal future.

I had begun to drift into pleasant, and much needed sleep, when a cherished voice called from the hall.

"Erik! Allez! Vite! Vite!"

I stepped into the hallway in time to see Erica shrug off the attentions of the housemaid. The woman slid quietly into the kitchen, and Erica tapped her foot with impatience.

"Erik! We're late! Allez!"

Then she saw me watching her and the impatience melted, replaced with genuine warmth. I was captivated by the young beauty she had become. When she smiled, there was a definite echo of her mother, and my heart filled to overflowing tenderness for her.

"I am sorry grand-papa. We have to go," she gave me a quick kiss. "I will come tomorrow, I promise. Where is he? Erik!"

"I am coming," his voice drifted from his room. "Has no one told you patience is a virtue, my dear?" He answered, coming into the hall, jacket half on, hair disheveled.

She grasped the dangling half of the jacket, helping him pull it on. "Yes, yes. You have told me many times, but we are late."

He smiled at her. With a few, swift strokes of her fingers, Erica quickly smoothed his hair and handed him his coat. "That's better, but please hurry," she beamed a smile at him, and as I watched their exchange, I could not help the thought that they would be good for each other, despite perhaps, the odd circumstances that had brought them together.

As they were about to leave, Erik turned to me, his eyes willing me to obey his silent wish to rest. I gave him a slight nod in acknowledgement. As the young couple walked out the door, I thought how far the years had come that now the father would obey the son.

Chapter 80

I stared at her in startled amazement.

"Before you ask, no one sent me. I sent myself to visit a friend," the Comtesse de Chagny said, removing her hat, gloves and wrap.

Still in a daze, I closed the door, watching Christine's elegant figure with unmitigated interest.

"When you decided to keep secrets Erik, you forgot one thing," there was unmistakable fire in her eyes as she turned them on me. "Me."

"There are no secrets," I lied, brushing past her. "Everyone seems determined to draw the last breath from me today," I muttered, making my way slowly to the kitchen.

"Where's the maid?" Christine's tone was stern as she followed me.

"I sent her off," I answered as I set about to make her tea. "I could not abide them then, much less now."

"Meg will be furious with you," she said quietly, taking a seat at the table.

"I will not be dictated to."

Christine pursed her lips, the dark eyes studying me as I set down her drink. Her fingers wrapped around the cup. "Stubborn and prideful, as ever."

"Humph." I sat down opposite her. A quiet, uneasy silence fell between us

"How do you do it?" She asked at last, her penetrating gaze fixed on me.

"What?"

"Live with yourself, knowing you're intentionally hurting the woman you vowed to love."

I stared at her. I don't know what I had expected her to say, but it was not this. It was not this knife that sliced into the innermost part of me to find and skewer my fears, my pain.

She shook her head. "I don't understand you. You claim you love Meg, and yet you are blind as to how you are tearing her apart with your silence. How do you do it?"

"Christine, please___," my voice faltered under the fire flashing from her eyes.

"No, tell me. I'd really like to know how you manage to look her in the eye each morning knowing she's worried sick about you. How do you think she carries on, knowing you could die anytime?"

"Enough," I whispered.

"Oh I've barely started."

"Enough!" An old flash of anger burst through my cry, and I had to turn away so she would not see the tears in my eyes.

"Touched a cord, have I? Good." She chuckled sadly, shaking her head. "You and Raoul are a pair. It's a wonder Meg and I have stood by your side. You would both rather die than admit pain or defeat. You forget that there are those around you who care." She paused, reaching across the table to grasp my hands. Her eyes softened when I looked at our entwined fingers, and her tone gentled when she resumed.

"You can't ignore those who love you Erik, anymore than you can ignore the pain in your chest. You are not alone, and you are not under the Opera house. You have friends and a family. Let us help." Christine's hand reached to touch my right cheek, eyes looking into mine. Her fingers wiped the unbidden tears that had begun to fall. "What are you so afraid of?"

I looked into her eyes and saw only deep affection reflected back. "Being old," I whispered, giving voice to the deep abiding fear, baring my soul to the one who, for a fleeting moment, had glimpsed the hell of my other life. "Of leaving Meg. Of truly becoming a ghost."

She smiled then, the smile suffusing her eyes with infinite tenderness. "I might try being one. Maybe I'll like it," she said gently.

"Oh Christine," I said in a whisper, taking her hand, raising it to my lips.

She rose and came to stand beside me. "My angel of music," she whispered kissing my brow, and with tenderness, drew me to her as the cries began to tear through my frame.

"Remember how it was?" Her voice held a tinge of wistfulness as she held my arm and we stared at the columns before us.

It was early afternoon, and it had been Christine who had suggested a short walk. This place had not been my expected destination. I stared at the building, waves of animosity and affection warring within my soul. "I thought I would never leave it."

"I was so scared when Hélène brought me there."

"I'd play out my rage and anger, trying to escape my loneliness."

"I heard your voice and believed my father's angel had come."

"I was beginning to lose reason."

Christine turned to me then, her eyes soft and loving. "A part of me loved you even as I walked away."

I sighed, gently squeezing her fingers. "It was better that way. You would not have stayed."

"No, perhaps not," she replied, acknowledging the truth. "We came out all right, ghosts and demons notwithstanding."

Christine faced me, caressing my face with her gloved hand. "Walk with Meg the last few steps. Let her strength be yours." She raised her face to glance at the angel high above us then looked at me once more. "In the end, we'll all be ghosts, but there's one thing we can take with us." She lightly kissed my cheek. "It's the love of a friend, the love of a partner."

I kissed her hand, raising my eyes to the angel. There was no longer a cry of defiance. His song had gathered harmony and there was acceptance in his voice. Somehow, we had indeed come out all right.

I leaned on Christine's arm as we began to make our way back to the apartment. Deep inside me, the fears and the dread had been quieted by the one I had least expected to ever be a part of my life again.

Chapter 81

Long after the sun had set, I sat in my darkened study, Christine's words ringing in my head. Not even the grumblings of hunger could rouse me to action. Earlier I had dismissed the maid yet again amid a fit of anger brought on by her incessant meddling and prying.

Now I just sat in my chair, recalling our duet before the Opera. Always a duet, Christine and I, even now, in the sunset of our years. She was right. I had just been too consumed with my own anxieties and concerns to pay much heed to anything, let alone the one closest to me. Dear, sweet Meg. How had she stood me all these years?

When at last I stirred to action, night had come. The streets below were lit with the few lights that could be spared. Somehow I would have to tell Meg of my deep, abiding, all consuming fear.

As my slow, hesitant steps brought me into the hall, I caught the strains of light piano music coming from the salon. The notes were familiar, if long forgotten, but never had I heard them played with such obvious feeling. Curious, I shambled closer to the glass doors to see, transfixed by the scene before me.

Erik sat at the piano, fingers unerringly finding the keys as his eyes scanned the score before him. Of course the music was familiar. I had written it, ages ago.

Meg stood beside him, watching him, her elegant figure wrapped in the cashmere shawl I had given her on her birthday.

"These are all brilliant. Why didn't he ever publish them?"

"He's an intensely private man," Meg answered, running her hand over the piano. He smiled at her a little, letting the last of the melody hang in the air. "Yes, yes he is, to a fault."

Meg turned to him, a small smile on her lips, her fingers brushing lightly through his hair. "So are you. You are like him, in so many ways." She leaned forward to kiss Erik's brow, her hand lightly caressing his cheek. "I wish____," her voice broke off in a sigh as her hand dropped to her side. She turned away, walking to the window, eyes focused on the all encompassing darkness.

He rose and came to stand beside her. "What is it?" She shook her head, turning to face him, nestling her hands against his chest. "I'll never forget the look on his face when he saw you for the first time."

He remained silent, hands resting lightly on her shoulders. Meg chuckled. "Such a complete look of adoration. I thought he would never release you from his arms."

Meg's wistful tone wrung me to pieces, yet I smiled at the memory the words elicited. It was true. He had been so small, so helpless, and so loved!

"Of all your father's works, his buildings, his compositions, you are the creation he's proudest of, the one he'll always come back to." Meg dropped her hands, moving back toward the piano.

"I was a surprise then?" Erik laughed softly.

"For your father, yes," Meg smiled, caressing his cheek. "But a much cherished one."

He looked at her, holding her hands in his own. "He adores you. I've never seen anyone so in love like you two. Every glance, every touch, and the love is there. I watch you and wonder where all that love comes from."

Meg sighed, turning away once more, eyes unseeing. It was a long moment before she spoke. "We nearly didn't have each other. It took a long time before____," she wrenched herself away from his scrutiny, her voice breaking on a cry.

His strong, young hands descended onto her shoulders. "He would never willingly hurt you Maman, you know that." His voice was infinitely gentle.

She turned to face him, cheeks glistening with tears.

As I watched their interplay, I ached to be beside her. It should be me giving her comfort, not my son, yet my legs would not move.

"He's fought for Raoul, for Christine, but when he needs me, he won't let me near! I can't do it if he won't let me!" Her cries exploded, and he drew her into the protective circle of his arms.

"He's scared, Maman. Scared of what's coming. He's never had to face his own mortality. It is something we do everyday on the line, something we have learned to accept. He's never had to, and it scares him." He kissed her hair, gently lifting her face to look at him. "Mostly, he's scared of leaving you."

Something, a noise outside, or the creak of a floorboard, made him lift his eyes from her. They fell directly on me. For long, silent moments we were caught in that connection of our eyes alone. Then I understood it had been me, my groan of misery that had alerted Erik to my presence.

He broke the look, drawing his mother to arms' length, looking into her face. "I think Papa has something he'd like to say to you," he said quietly, slowly letting go of her.

With infinite slowness, Meg turned to look at me. I had come into the room, eyes unseeing for the tears that blinded them. I held out my hand to her. When her fingers wrapped around mine, it was as if it had been our wedding day. I lifted the hand that held mine and kissed it.

I only briefly registered the weight of Erik's hand on my shoulder as he gently squeezed it on his way out of the room.

"Forgive me," I whispered to my wife as I folded her into my arms.

"How do you feel?" Meg asked some time later in the privacy of our room.

"Terrified beyond measure," I answered, fingers brushing against her cheek. "Frightened of losing you, of becoming that ghost I sought to leave behind." I smiled weakly at her, running fingers through the strands of silver that fell over her shoulders. All her hair was silver now, not a shade of gold in it, but she was still my golden sea. "But no longer afraid to face it, not with you beside me."

Meg leaned down to kiss me, her lips burning on mine. "I will always be there," she whispered, then smiled. "If Red Death wants you, he'll have to come through me." She drew back a little, hands framing my face, the brown eyes acquiring a serious, smoldering look. "Tonight Erik, let me show you how young we are," my wife kissed me once more, but this time it was not just a light kiss, but one that demanded, and received, response in equal measure.

As our hands explored one another, the anxieties and the fears that had driven us apart were replaced with acceptance of the future, by unfaltering loyalty to one another that surpassed even the union of us in our son. For all our nearness in the past months, we might as well have been strangers. Though we had shared the same bed, the warmth and closeness we had known, had, for a time, disappeared.

As my wife's hands caressed me, I felt the deep, abiding love for her rush back with such intensity that I thought I would burn from it. This time I would let nothing stop it, would not let it falter. I would take her strength and make it mine. We would walk toward the sunset together, she and I. Years ago we had begun our journey when Meg had held out her hand to shattered Erik. Now we would finish it, side by side, as it was meant to be.

Chapter 82

Per Erik's request, we went to Brittany, he and I, to the little house that so long ago Meg and I had made our own. I had never thought to buy a house in or near Paris. This was the place Meg and I knew best, where we were comfortable, the place where eventually we would come back to, this small house where our family had begun.

While I watched Erik trim his mother's roses, I remembered how it had been when he had been small, running and exploring the world that had been opening before him. Echoes of his delighted laughter rang in my ears, and in the mist of years, I saw myself showing him his first butterfly.

A heavy sigh escaped me. Where did nearly twenty two years go? It did not seem possible that the young man now in the garden was my son.

When he shrugged out of the jacket and continued to work only in his shirtsleeves, I turned away with a wistful smile, walked to the piano, and began to play. The sight of him in that garden vividly brought to mind the day Meg and I had made him, a day so deeply etched on both of us.

True to her promise, Erica joined us later that evening. She drove from Paris in one of the new, sought after automobiles. It had been her money, her talent that had purchased it. While she had cancelled all her tours for the duration of the war, she still recorded her music, her talents making her one of the most popular young musicians in Paris, if not the whole of France. Despite shortages of food and fuel, people still needed something decent in their lives, now perhaps more than ever. If Erica could give it to them through her music, who was I to protest the means? I had never been comfortable with the idea of the gramophone, and forbade its use in my house.

We had a quiet dinner in one of the tiny cafés still in existence in the village, then the two of them treated me to the music they had learned in America.

I watched them sing and laugh together, and my only thoughts were for them to grab what happiness they could while they had it. Who knew what tomorrow would bring?

"Ah, d'accord, enough," Erica leaned away from the piano, laughing, throwing me a wicked grin. "I'm sure grand-papa has had enough of our discordant voices. Come, I need to do your shoulder." She rose and took up the bag she had deposited in the parlor earlier that evening.

Erik followed her into the kitchen. Perhaps out of curiosity or a desire to be near them, I followed and prepared tea, while Erica's skilled hands dealt with the bandages swathing his shoulder.

In the last two years, she like many women had overcome inherent squeamishness of blood, becoming accomplished in binding that which other men tore asunder.

When the last of the linen fell away and I saw for the first time what my son confronted and endured every day, I realized how insignificant my own fears became in the face of what went on around me.

As Erica began to clean and disinfect the barely healing wound, Erik gritted his teeth, closed his eyes, and clenched the hand that rested on the table into a fist.

Her fingers were sure, not prolonging his agony anymore than they had to. "It's healing nicely. They did a good job." She said quietly.

"The medics do what they can, with what they have, which is not much." He answered neutrally, looking into her eyes.

Erica tossed all the used linens into the basket she had brought, drawing a new packet of bandages out of her bag. She placed another package wrapped in paper beside his hand.

"From the nurses?" He asked.

"Non, your maman. Now hold still." She began to rewrap the injury that had nearly cost him an arm.

Seeing the raw shrapnel wound on my son, finally made me understand that it was not the dying or leaving of friends that took courage, but the facing of it. These young men, Erik, Alain, Gérard, and thousands like them, did it every day, and they did it well.

I sighed and walked out into the garden, leaving the two young people alone. Glancing toward the stars shining brightly overhead, I gave them a wan smile. Walking with Meg into the sunset would not be such a terrifying thing. I could walk there now, and if I did become a ghost, well, at least I would have a house to haunt.

"Stay. It's a long drive back," Erik said gently as they stood inside the hallway. Erica was dressed in her coat and was pulling on gloves. She glanced in my direction where I sat in the parlor, in the chair beside the window, and shook her head.

"I think not. You and your papa need some time alone." She took up her bag and handed him an envelope. "This is mainly why I came." She came to me, giving my cheek a quick kiss.

"Au revoir, grand-papa, and please, burn everything."

With that, she left the house, Erik following close behind. He held the car door for her, and she gave him a light kiss before sliding in and driving off.

"Will you tell her?"

"Tell her what?"

"That should be obvious. You care for her, she cares for you. How much clearer can that be?"

He turned to me, and never was there a more startled look on anyone's face than on his that moment.

"She's my ___!"

I waved a hand, dismissing the remark. "Your affection is clear."

"You--are you suggesting what I think you are?!" He cried out, half in stupefaction, half in anger.

"I've watched you over the years. The heart does not lie. You love her."

"Of course!"

"No, you love her." I threw my full meaning behind the words.

Nothing but silence greeted my statement. "I thought so." I said gently, approaching him inside the doorway where he leaned against the jamb in misery.

"Tell her, before it's too late."

He shook his head, eyes leveled on me. "You cannot possibly be serious."

"Oh but I am, Erik. I have never been more serious about anything in my life. Grab the one chance for happiness before it's gone, before there will not be any others."

"She's Christine's daughter!" He moaned in wrenching heartbreak.

I wrapped an arm around the strong shoulders suddenly gone weak in his struggle with his conscience. Guiding him to the chair I had so recently occupied, I sat opposite him, studying the thoughts that warred across his face.

"Erica is your relation in the only thing that matters, the love of her family." I said at length, eyes never leaving his face.

He furrowed his brow in a silent question.

I took his strong, young hands into my gnarled, old ones. "Long ago, I found a child on a street in Paris. I gave her a name, a home, what passed for love. She married the son of the Comte de Chagny. They named their first daughter for me, though heavens know why," I chuckled, recalling that day as if it had been yesterday. "Then your mother and I had you, and a second family. While I love Christine as my daughter, and she will always be my daughter, technically, she is not." I chucked him under the chin and rose. "Make of the information what you will. Grab the chance you have. I had to wait twenty years for mine, and now, my time is up. I will go to my grave regretting I did not give your mother more. Tell her Erik. Make her your wife and tell her you will stand by her side. In the end, it's the love that matters."

I began to walk away when his voice stopped me.

"I will not make her a widow. There have been enough made already."

I looked at him, at the sudden weight of the war in his eyes. It was the only reference to the fighting he had made.

I nodded, saddened that that would be his choice. It was his choice, not mine, and I would not push him further. He was a man now, a braver man than me, and he would have to accept the consequences of his choice, as once, so long ago, had I.

Chapter 83

The following morning we went to the beach, and while Erik took his exercise, I watched over the burning basket of bloodied linens.

We had not mentioned our discussion, nor would we ever again. At some point that previous evening, I had ceased to look on him as my son and instead acknowledged him as a man, entitled to his own life, his own choices.

I glanced at the squabbling gulls overhead, and shook my head. When did it become so hard to let go? With Christine, I had not been so reluctant to release her. It was not even a question of their parentage. They were both my children, and yet I found it harder to let go of the one, than the other.

I looked into the distance, seeing Erik's silhouette framed against the grey of the early morning sky. Was it perhaps as Meg had said? Was it my pride in him, and the reluctance to release him to this stupid, bloody war that made me want to hold on to him a little longer? Or was it just the fact that he was truly my son, a son I thought I'd never have?

I roused myself from musings that would only take me down a slippery slope when I heard his clear laugh.

"At least we'll have a hearty breakfast." Erik deposited a basket full of sea creatures at my feet, and struggled back into his shirt and jacket. I helped him, glancing with apprehension at the basket. I had never been fond of fish, let alone the various clams and mussels so famous in this region. Seeing our breakfast at my feet, I inwardly shivered. What was he trying to do? Poison his old father? Punish me for my suggestion last night?

"It will not be as bad as all that," he smiled at my dubious expression, wrapping an arm around me. "I promise."

While he prepared our meal with animated relish, I opened the package Meg had sent. Inside the wrapping were croissants, made by her hands. I smiled and a warm glow of love and tenderness for her spread through me. How she must have saved to make just a few of those!

The meal proved extraordinary. With limited supplies, my son had managed a miracle. He laughed when he saw my face confronting the pile of shells on my plate.

"It's all right, Papa, they won't bite." He teased, his green eyes carefully watching me.

With infinite hesitation, and grudging acquiescence, I placed one of those things in my mouth. To my startled delight they proved rather tasty.

He laughed good humouredly, watching me polish off my share of the bounty. "It is good to know Papa, that life can still surprise you." He gave me a wicked grin and a wink.

Later we sat together at the piano. Where his hands flew over the keys, mine could barely follow. We laughed, falling in step on a slower piece, our music ringing through the house, our heads bent together, one blond and full, the other sparse and gray.

"Good night, Father," he kissed my brow. "I'm glad we came here. This is where you and Maman loved best."

While I continued to read, he went for a walk.

Much later, as sleep began to claim me, music drifted to my room, music that spoke of longing, sorrow, love and home all at once. The haunting melody was unfamiliar, but there was no doubt who had composed it. I smiled, letting my son's music wrap around me. If I had given him anything good of myself, it was that.

Chapter 84

When I opened my eyes, it was barely dawn. I looked out the window to see Erik sitting on the bench under the trellis, under the now trimmed roses. Ambling downstairs, I made tea. It was our last morning here, the last morning of peace and solitude before____. I dared not finish the thought, shrugging it away.

I joined him on the bench a short time later, and while we warmed our hands against the cups, we watched the day break in companionable silence. When there was light enough to see, I finally noticed the papers beside him.

"My orders, and my commission," he answered quietly to my silent question, sipping his tea. He rose, shook his head, and looked out at the rising sun. "We're going to Verdun. It will be a slog all the way. The Germans will not give way easily." There was nothing I could say to ease the desolate, yet resigned tone in his voice. He was the soldier, not I, and my experience did not encompass this.

He looked at me and smiled. "Never fear. I will do my duty when it comes to that. I was just sitting here, thinking about what you said. It will not make me change my mind, but at least now I don't fear what I feel. I thank you for that." He extended a hand to me. "Let's make some breakfast. My stomach is growling."

We arrived in Paris only to find ourselves at the de Changy's a few hours later. They had finally come to their house on the outskirts of the city when the situation at the château had become untenable.

From the moment the door opened, there was nothing but love and goodwill suffusing the walls of the stately home. Christine welcomed me with a warm embrace, and as she let go, glances of understanding and gratitude passed between us. She smiled, her eyes bright with affection as she went on to embrace Meg and Erik.

How was it possible that after all these years, after all that had happened between us, the affection had only deepened? Oh there was nothing of that insane, burning craving of long ago. Oh no! Not that! What remained was the warm love of friends, and as I watched Christine walk arm in arm with Meg, the sight only made my heart grow fonder toward her.

Even Raoul and I had at last achieved a measure of peace between us. He walked with a cane, but he walked, and he had acquired the old spark in his eyes. We shuffled together to the salon where the family had gathered in its entirety, with Michael demurely taking his place beside Anne-Marie.

There were, of course, three notable exceptions, but for now, we were all here, sharing the warmth of our circle. Who knew how long we would have it?

It was a multiple birthday celebration, with the warmth and laughter of the celebrants filling the air.

Only I stood a little apart, watching the gathering with peacefulness and contentment. For so long in my earlier life I had despaired of ever having this. Now, on the threshold of sunset, it had come.

A light touch on my arm drew me from reverie. Hélène stood beside me and with a light touch, drew her fingers across my ruined cheek.

"Happy Birthday. I knew. Even then, I knew there was a good man inside you," she smiled her mysterious smile. "I'm glad I was right." She turned, her elegant figure lost among the crowd.

Not for the first time I wondered what had prompted her to help a miserable wretch out of his cage. I would probably never know, and perhaps it no longer mattered. Her act of kindness had allowed me to live another way than as a slave, and perhaps in these people around me, in my family, I had at last become a decent man.

"Your turn," Meg whispered in my ear as she squeezed my hand.

Yes, it was my turn to hand my children their gifts. In the sudden and expectant stillness of the room, I handed Christine the keys and deeds to my various businesses. It was a symbolic gesture at best, for the businesses had been hers for the last two years. Now they were hers in name as well.

When her fingers took the keys from my hand, I smiled at her, comforted by the knowledge that she would let nothing stand in her way. She would survive, despite the raised eyebrows. She had learned well, and there was nothing more I could ever teach her.

To Erik, I handed a dog-eared book. It had been one of my favorites when I had been his age, one that had helped settle many restless nights. Over many years, I had scribbled comments in its margins, even some sketches. Among the dust of a ruined grotto Meg had found it, rescuing it from the mob. It had been her gift to me that first Christmas we had shared together. Perhaps if nothing else, the old book would allow my son to know me. There was nothing else I could give him that he could take to the field other than the respect I had gained for him, not only as a man, but the soldier he was. When I looked into his eyes and saw him smile, I knew that the only thing he had really wanted had been given already. I patted his shoulder and sighed. What he would do with that gift was up to him.

Mercifully, dinner was called, breaking the solemn moment.

It was after the meal that the family's conspiracy caught me off guard. With a flourish, Erica uncovered the gramophone, but before I had a chance to flee the room, Erik's strong, young hands descended onto my shoulders, keeping me in place.

"Ecoutez, grand-papa," Erica said as she placed a disk on the player. Music swelled, filling the room. I heard her voice issue from the machine, and at first, it was the eeriness of hearing that voice coming from the disk that surprised me. When my ears finally caught the melody, I sank into the nearest chair, overwhelmed by the sudden flood of feeling I could not begin to sort out. My eyes misted, and I felt Meg's fingers gently twine around mine.

The children had taken some of my long forgotten compositions, set words to them, and added a bit of orchestration to a few of the pieces. I had no doubt as to who accompanied Erica's soaring voice. The passion of Erik's playing came through each and every note.

When it was done, and everyone repaired to the music room, only I remained sitting in the salon, in the silence, overcome with emotion, too weak to move, even if I had wanted to.

I had never had a birthday, until Meg started it. Then my daughter had continued it, giving me no choice but to accept gracefully. Now my children's gift to me left me astounded.

"Come, before they start wondering what we're up to," the Comtesse de Chagny's gentle voice broke the silence. She held her hand out to me.

Taking her small fingers in mine, I raised my eyes to hers. "How Christine? How is all this possible?"

She smiled, and helped pull me up. "Love. They love you, Erik. We all do. You should have seen them sneaking the scores so you would not know, stealing time at the studio." Christine's voice wrapped around me like a warm shawl as we made our way to the music room, and I finally understood the reason behind all the rushing of the two young people. Erik's choice of spending his leave in the city made sense now. He and Erica must have planned this for some time. I shook my head, resigning myself to whatever other surprises lay in store.

"Come, Papa. Just this once," my daughter twined her arm around my waist, her tone gentle, yet firm. She would brook no argument.

I threw Raoul a look that begged interference. He smiled and shook his head. "You are on your own in this. I will not help you."

With a sigh, I gave in to Christine's gentle insistence, and took my place. With the explosion of the flash, they finally released me, my family.

As the photographer continued his work, I drew Meg to my side, and we watched the proceedings in quiet companionship.

When it was their turn, Erik and Erica would not stop laughing and teasing each other. The affection between them was evident, but it was no longer my business. I had given him what he needed. The rest was up to him.

Turning, I walked away before Meg could see the sadness in my eyes. She found me later on the balcony, and I folded her to me, resting my cheek against the curve of her neck. "I wish I could have given you more," I whispered.

Her arms around me tightened. "What we have is more than I dreamed, more than I ever wished for." I kissed her then, watching as Raoul and Christine, arms entwined, came to join us. In the quietude of the night, we four shared a balcony, shared closeness that none outside would ever understand. We four had come full circle, and now only waited for sunset to claim us.

While Meg and I were saying goodbye to the Comte and Comtesse at their front door, two voices drifted to us from the shadows of the shrubbery beside the house.

"What's this?" It was Erik's deep baritone.

"I'm sorry. I promised not to, I know, but I can't stop." Erica's voice choked on a sob. A quiet, muffled hush followed, before I heard him speak again. "It will be all right."

"Will it? Oh Erik! I'm so afraid!"

"Hush."

"I've lost a brother, my father's gone, now you. How much more is there to give?"

"Whatever it takes. This will not go on forever." His tone was comforting, trying to give her strength where hers failed her. There was a long pause before he resumed. "I need to know that you will be here."

A sad chuckle rose in answer. "Where would I go?"

"Oh, you might find some dashing Englishman more your fancy, for all I know."

Her sad laughter drifted up. "Hardly. My heart is here. Always was, always will be."

"I will come back. I promise. Besides, you owe me dinner." There was a pause, and then Erik's bright laughter reached my ears. "And a few clumps of hair."

"Was I that mean to you when we were children?"

"On more than one occasion. Don't worry. I'll collect on the debt you owe me." After a moment's hesitation, his soft voice resumed. "I have to go."

"I know." It was a sigh carried on tears and heartbreak.

"Chin up. If anything happens, I know you'll be there to pull me through. You wouldn't let me down now, would you?"

"No. I would go to hell and back for you."

"Let's hope it will not be so far. Now, I really have to go. The train leaves in three hours, and I do need some sleep."

"Oh God is my witness Erik, I love you!" Erica's voice cried out, choking back on her tears. "Is that so wrong?"

" Non, ma chèrie," he said softly. "Je t'aime aussi. I will return. Depend on it. Until then, au revoir mon amour." His dulcet tones were a whisper.

"Au revoir Erik, au revoir, mon coeur," she caught the last on a cry. Her plaintive sob as she fled into the night echoed in the sudden silence.

Erik's tall figure walked slowly past the gate fronting the drive, to quickly disappear in the shadows.

My heart wrenched with sadness for the two young lives that once more felt the war's relentless presence. A few days of peace had brought them together and now, war once more, was tearing them apart.

With a sigh, I walked with Meg toward the waiting automobile.

Erik was away first thing before dawn. He would not let us past the doorway of the apartment. When he looked at me over Meg's shoulder, I understood this was easier for him, for us, for his mother. As he pulled away from her embrace, Meg's fingers clutched his coat, but this time he would not let her pull him back. He stepped back, lightly kissed his mother's brow and gave me a nod, quickly turned on his heel and disappeared down the staircase.

I did not try to soothe away Meg's cries of misery. She needed to release her anguish, as so recently, had I. I wrapped an arm around her and closed the door.

Chapter 85

By March of 1916, it became clear that Verdun would indeed, be a slog. Erik's words rang in my head while I tried to follow accounts of various battles in the journals. Both the French and German troops were bogged down, and despite the slaughter of flesh and bone, little progress was made by either side.

His letters continued to arrive on a regular basis, their narrative telling of the progressive deterioration of the situation.

The trenches of a year ago seem a luxury compared to the bare ditches we call home here. There are no fascines to support our walls, just the will of the earth to stay in one place. The men huddle under machine gun platforms for any relief from the weather. When we do not wish it, we get buckets of rain. In the summer, we will be thankful for the dew on our parched lips.

The rain was so heavy during the past two days that whatever walls we had painstakingly constructed, washed away. We found ourselves standing hip deep in mud, staring at our enemies staring back at us. Some men had been literally caught with their pants down, and as eyes met eyes, the tension and silence of our suddenly small world, was palpable. No one moved, not them, not us, and we all stood there, letting the rain pelt our skins. Then my captain slowly turned, and lit a cigarette. We watched as his counterpart emulated the gesture. All up and down the line, officers turned their backs and pretended not to see the men lifting spades instead of rifles. The collective relief from both sides of the trenches rose above the field, and for one day, we shared a respite from the incessant warring with our enemies. For one day, we were all just men fighting the elements. It would not stop us doing our duty the next morning, but for a moment we could share some civility in this charnel house.

When Dante wrote his works, he could not have possibly imagined this. The fields have become red as armies of both sides continue to feed this beast with mindless and heedless regularity. The men walk the line as if they were ghosts. There is nothing in their eyes, and many will welcome Death when he comes, for he will give them peace from the ceaseless pounding of guns, stink of decay, blood, and mud. I walk among them, and cannot even give them hope that tomorrow will be better.

There are grumblings in the ranks, and they begin to echo through the army. Something must be done for these men who are slaughtered callously, not by the enemies' guns, but by their own generals. They are sent on hopeless, senseless missions that do nothing but give the Boches the ground we took months before.

I sighed, laying the latest letter aside, meeting Raoul's solemn look.

"It will only get harder for them," he said quietly, handing me a glass of wine. "It always does, before the tide turns."

"Surely the generals know they do not have an infinite supply of men."

He chuckled, though there was no mirth in it. "You have never been in the army, Erik. The generals do with their men what they want. They can, and do, throw them away like so many pieces of paper. No," he shook his head and took a seat next to me, steepling his fingers. His pale eyes acquired a far away look to them. "No, the situation cannot continue. Something will happen, but it may not be what the army expects."

We were in the parlor of his house. I had made it a habit to visit once a week, whether Christine was there or not. We had begun to share afternoons, for I refused to sit by myself in a café, and he was someone to talk to. Our swords lay long buried in the sand.

Raoul looked at me and I had a sense that perhaps he knew more of events than he was willing to reveal. He had, after all, served in the army, and for years, as a diplomat, accomplishing both with distinction. This was his field of expertise, not mine.

"Men have been known to rise up, even in the field of battle."

"Mutiny?" I whispered, disbelief shading my voice.

"If there is no change in policy or tactics, it might come to that." He answered, sipping his wine. I stared at him, sudden heaviness squeezing my heart. If the army rebelled, what would happen to France?

Chapter 86

It was a cold day when I decided to visit Raoul. Though the rain held off, the dampness in the air permeated even the thick folds of the old, nearly threadbare cloak. After all these years, I could not part with it. It had become a part of me, a part I could no more shed than I could shed my face.

I smiled at the thought. For all my life, I had wanted to do just that. Now it no longer mattered. I had not too many years left upon the earth, and what I did have, was better spent than in useless concern over my appearance.

Nearing the wide open gate, I saw a military vehicle parked before the house. Probably one of his acquaintances come for a visit. Raoul had, after all, served many years in the diplomatic corps. His connections among the politicians and military men were many, even now, when he was no longer active in the service.

A wan smile lifted my lips. We were a sad pair, he and I. In our younger days, we would have torn each other to pieces. Now, we were old men who found themselves as companions, if not friends, because a war had taken away our sons and ravaged our country. Life could not have presented greater irony.

The door of the house opened, and two uniformed men stepped out, still exchanging quiet words with someone. They finally nodded and the door closed behind them. They descended the three stairs, shook their heads, slipping their caps back on their heads. "As I live and breathe, this does not become any easier." One said, opening the driver's door of the automobile. "At least that one is over." The other replied, sliding into the passenger seat. With an angry growl, the engine started, and the car pulled out of the courtyard.

Their words puzzled me, but I shook it off. It could have been anything, and it was, after all, Raoul's house, and his business.

I found him sitting in the parlor, in his chair beside the window, slumped and unmoving, for the world looking as if the very life had been drained out of him. He did not acknowledge my presence in any way, only continued staring at a spot only he could see.

Tossing the cloak over the back of the other chair, I poured two glasses of wine, holding one out to him. "What is the matter? What did the army want with you? Are they so desperate that they recruit raisins?"

He shook his gray head, and when he raised his eyes to mine, his cheeks glistened with rivers of tears. There was nothing in his eyes but shock and disbelief.

I sank into the chair opposite his, still holding the wine out to him. Almost as if he noticed it for the first time, his trembling fingers took the glass, his pale eyes meeting my green ones.

"He's gone, and I might as well have put the bullet in his head." Raoul whispered in misery. "She will hate me." He cried, his shoulders shaking. Setting the wine glasses down, his as well as mine, I reached to clasp a hand over his, trying to still its uncontrollable trembling.

"They shot him like a dog!" He moaned.

"Who is gone Raoul? Make sense, my friend. Who was shot?"

Finally his eyes focused on my face, and at long last he became aware of my presence. "He had access to so many people, so many places. He spoke five languages, did you know that?" He shook his head. "He thought to put his talents to use when the war broke out. He didn't wait. I supported him in his choice." Raoul looked at me, eyes pleading. "What could I do? They would have made him go anyway. I might as well have pulled the trigger the day I asked him."

"Drink your wine," I proffered the glass again. He was not making sense, but he was in pain. I curbed my impatience, knowing that the story would unfold, in its own way.

"He fought for his country with his voice. The Germans shot him for that. At least it was one bullet. They do worse to spies." The voice was hollow, devoid of any feeling, and yet his eyes spoke of the raw pain in his heart, the pain that was tearing him apart.

When our eyes met, understanding began to dawn and we two sat frozen in our combined sorrow. My heart hammered with pain as great as Raoul's as my mind began to slowly put the pieces together. Then and there, in the parlor of that house, I thought the world would cease altogether. Fate would not be that kind to two, old men.

Hesitantly, through his tears, Raoul revealed the rest. Phillippe had volunteered at the first drum rolls, but unbeknownst to any of us, not in any infantry unit, but for espionage. Through his popularity and peerage, Phillippe had had access to high society and places not open to others, not only in France, but throughout Europe. For him, it had been a perfect choice. Who would suspect a singer who wowed crowds every night? Of course he would not have been able to tell anyone, least of all his wife. The long silence from him, and the army, was now understandable. Any attempted contact with family would have endangered him, his mission, and his family.

He had been deep behind enemy lines when the mission had been compromised and Phillippe found out. The German intelligence corps did not bother with a trial. Phillippe and the entire theater troupe with him, were summarily shot by firing squad.

"Does she know?" I asked quietly when at last I could find my voice. "Is his mother aware of any of this?"

"How could she be?" Raoul shook his head in misery. "She's been at the school all morning." He lifted his eyes to mine. "She will damn me for letting him do it and she will be right." He paused, staring listlessly at his hands, now lying limply in his lap.

I sighed as I looked at his guilt ridden face, the slumped shoulders, and the helplessness of the man I had once hated in the face of his heart wrenching grief. Rising from the chair, I clasped his shoulder. It had been many years since the day we had fought one another in the cemetery. All we had left was the bare comfort we could give each other.

"You did not kill him Raoul, the war did. It was his choice, his alone. Phillippe fought for his country the best way he knew how. He knew the danger. You should be very proud of your son." I said gently, pausing to glance out the windows at the beating rain. Sometime past, it had started, and with it, had come the early afternoon darkness. I glanced back at Raoul and sighed. "Christine could never hate you," I said softly, a vision from years past floating before my eyes. Even as she had walked away into the tunnels under the Opera house, there had not been hate in Christine's eyes, only sadness and perhaps something else, but that had been long ago, and none of us were the same. "It's not in her heart."

For long minutes, there was no reaction, and I wondered if he had heard me at all. Under the cacophony of rain came the growl of an engine, and I glanced out the window to see Raoul's car slowly pulling to before the house.

"She's returned," I said quietly, turning to him. "Do you wish me to stay?"

"No," he shook his head, rising from the chair. "No. That is for me. You go and find your daughter. She will need her father." He swallowed, and drew something from the pocket of his coat. With trembling fingers, he held it out to me. It was a band of gold. "His wedding ring. It was his wish that Christine have it should anything__." He shook the thought away. "He didn't take it with him. They wouldn't let him." Raoul looked at me with haunted eyes as his fingers pressed the ring into my hand. "God only knows I wish I could take away this pain from that child."

I gave him a quick nod as I slipped the ring into my pocket, avoiding looking into his eyes. I had to flee this house before Christine walked in, for surely then I could not hold back the threatening tide of tears, and I would not let her see those, could not. I had to find my daughter, had to bring her what comfort I could, for surely by now, the two army men would have found her, and told her.

Gathering the cloak, I walked out the door as quickly as my old legs would carry me, giving Christine only a brief nod as we passed each other on the steps. What she thought of my brusqueness I could not tell. I had to find my child. What had she ever done that Fate would be so cruel and take away another of her men? Was not one son enough to sacrifice that now she had lost a husband too? How much more would be lost before it all came to an end? Before men would come to their senses?

Chapter 87

Christine sat in the office, facing the window, and I doubt she even knew I was there. I found her silence and utter stillness more frightening than I would have the tears and the weeping. I could have dealt with that, but this total numbness unnerved me. There was not the slightest reaction from her, not a sigh, not a blink of the eyes, nothing.

Rage and anger such as I had not felt in years rose in me against all this madness and senseless slaughter of good men, and all I wanted to do was tear something apart with my bare hands, or at least hear the crash of something, anything to break this dreadful stillness.

Instead, I lifted the telephone and called Meg. Perhaps the two of us could break through our daughter's self made wall.

As I set the ear piece down, I caught the scratchy sound behind me. The gramophone continued to rotate the disk, the needle riding endlessly in the groove. I lifted it, setting it in its cradle. Christine had put one of these machines in the office, claiming it helped her think. As I turned the machine off, a sigh escaped me. The recording that had been playing had been one of Phillippe's first ones.

No more would he laugh with us, or sing for her. No more. Tears stung my eyes as I remembered how we had practiced, how I had raged when I had discovered his name. Now we would have to bury him, as we had buried his son.

When Meg arrived, she carried one of her heavy shawls. There was sadness in her eyes, but no tears. She went to Christine, and wrapped the shawl around our daughter's shoulders. "When this is done, the rivers will be salt and the women will have no more tears. We will all be dry." She said, running her hands over Christine's hair. Not even Meg's gentle touch elicited a response from the woman beside the window.

I shook my head, heart breaking for the silent statue that sat in the chair. "Something has to come of this. It has to. All this," I gestured toward the window, toward the silent woman, "cannot be for nothing."

"Yes, something will come of this," Meg answered quietly. "But at what cost Erik? How much will be asked of us? Of all of us?" She shook her head. "Will whatever comes be worth all the blood, all the sorrow?"

With the assistance of our driver, who carried Christine as if she were a child, we took our daughter to the de Chagny's house. It was where she called home, where she could recover from the shock she had plunged into.

When we brought our daughter to their home, Raoul and Christine were there to meet us. While I fully expected Phillippe's mother to be collapsed in tears, her dignity in the face of her anguish surprised me. She refused to give in to her sorrow before us, before me.

They led us to Christine's room where we laid her on the lace covered bed. As everyone was leaving, and she was closing the door, only then did I see Christine hesitate, her hand tremble on the handle, her lips drawing tightly together. Raoul's hand wrapped over hers, and with visible effort, she drew herself up into the Comtesse she was and slowly, they walked away.

Much later, when only the stars shone in the sky, did I see her sitting by Raoul's side, her head against his shoulder, his arms wrapped around her.

I turned my eyes away and walked back into the house, giving them their privacy. Before all this would be done, we would all do our share of weeping.

May 1916

My Dear Father,

At long last, there is a break in the incessant carnage that is our life. Most of us have forgotten that life exists beyond the ditches we call home.

The news of Phillippe saddens me but this is war, and it is a fact of our lives. Widows are made every day, on either side of the line. When this is done, there will only be the very young or old men to take our place.

I have read your words but I will not change my mind. I love Erica beyond anything I ever thought possible. I want to give her what at present the German army won't let me--a husband, not a soldier who is there for one day and gone the next. If my time at home has shown me anything, it is the love I want to give her, the love you have for Mother.

My decision stands, but perhaps now I can tell her what all these years I had to hide. I thank you for that.

For now, I continue to inform families of their losses. The pile is not getting any shorter.

All my love to you and mother,
Erik

Late May, 1916

Dear Father and Mother,

The grumblings in the army have ceased, for now. We are all too busy to pay attention to how we live, or what we eat. The pounding of guns is a constant drone in our ears, and I think that for all my life, I will hear nothing but the whoosh, bam, crack of field guns, followed by the staccato counterpoint of machine guns.

I note with interest that our government has bowed to the unremitting political pressure of the Germans, and renamed our valiant escadrille. It is just as well. The Americans are brave, giving much needed support on our attacks. The men have taken to giving them short salutes when they fly by. Often they return to base, missing a man or two. It doesn't stop the youngsters from volunteering. Rather, it seems to inspire their enthusiasm. Strange I should call them youngsters. Most are not much younger than me, and yet the replacement troops call me 'old man'. If one is to survive out here a few months, one becomes old and hardened in a hurry.

My love to you always,
Erik

Chapter 88

On the third day of Christine's collapse, when even Gilbert's ministrations could not move her, I cried my rage at the heavens, at the unblinking stars. "No! You will not have her! You will not take her from me!"

Though Raoul and Christine tried weakly to restrain me, Meg held them off with a shake of her head, her eyes watching me with infinite tenderness as I passed by. My steps led to only one place, the place where I needed to be.

She was so pale, so weak. Rivers of tears flowed from my eyes. They were for her, for she would not cry and vent her sorrow, allowing herself to heal.

"Oh my dear, sweet Christine," I barely choked out, sinking down on the bed beside her, gathering her into my arms. "My sweet child," I cried to her, holding her, my old, gnarled fingers stroking her face, her hair.

I sat with her thus, tears unstoppable. Years before, when she had still been only a child, I had sat with her like this, nursing a raging fever. I had thought then how fragile she had been. Her weight now in my lap was no more than it had been then. I brushed fingers across her brow, whispering how much I loved her.

During that bout of fever I had allowed no one near her, had made herbal concoctions and forced broth down her throat, and held her.

As it had been then, so it was now. I would not release her to the darkness she seemed determined to enter. She had pulled me from mine and I would not let her go into hers, not without a fight. I still had that one left in me.

While I sat with her, holding her to my heart, my voice began to drift in the stillness of the room. I kissed her pale brow, and though I could no longer sing, my voice called her, called her through the darkness that was sweeping her away.

I began to tell her a story of the night a baby girl named Christine had saved a wretched man named Erik. I whispered to her how that little girl had brought light into his life, had taught him to live, to love, to perhaps be a decent man.

I would not lose that girl now. The darkness would not have her. It would have to go through me before I would give her up, and even then, I would fight for her.

A half strangled sob startled me from my musings. I looked into blue eyes that looked back at me.

"Papa," she whispered and as her body convulsed with the release of her anguish, I held onto her through the storm, eyes watching the sun rise on another day. I held my child as she poured out her heart against my shoulder.

When she fell asleep from sheer exhaustion, I still sat with her, afraid to let go.

When Meg and Christine finally came into the room, I gave them a slight nod, arms tightening a little more around the woman sleeping in my lap. Their relief was palpable and they quietly withdrew, leaving Christine to recover.

When at last she came out of the dressing room, I was sitting beside the window, looking out into the small garden below.

Her hands settled on my shoulders and her cheek pressed against mine.

"I made a promise to you once. I nearly broke it. I am sorry," she whispered, coming around to kneel beside the chair.

I looked at her, smiling a little as my fingers brushed against her face.

"I would not have let you go so easily."

Christine took my hands in hers, eyes fixing on me. "I heard your voice calling me. You were in so much pain. I couldn't leave you hurting like that, no matter how much I wanted to be with Phillippe." She kissed the hands she held, sighing deeply. I felt a stray tear fall on my skin.

"I heard you tell me a story," she said slowly, her one hand caressing my right cheek as her other continued to hold my hands. "A story about a girl named Christine." Her eyes met mine. "You named me for her, for your Christine, didn't you?" It was not an accusation but a statement of fact, and there was only tenderness in her voice.

My old fingers traced the contours of her still beautiful face. She was 45 years old, but here, in this moment, she was 15, and we were back in Italy on that fateful evening when she had lifted my mask.

"I had no other name that would suit an angel." I tried to smile but failed in the attempt.

She smiled for me, kissing my brow. "I love you, perhaps now more than ever. You have been, and always will be, my father." She rose to embrace me. "You gave me a home, a family, your love. Most of all," she smiled at me, truly smiled, for it reflected in her eyes, "you gave me your music."

I took her hands in mine, kissed them, studying her. The last three days had drained her, but she would recover. She was strong and she had finally let go her despair. Time alone would heal her heart, but at least now she could begin to conquer her sorrow.

"I had to tell you, needed you to know what you always meant to me. I could never find the right way." My fingers brushed against her hair, and this time I gave her a wan, lopsided grin. "You needed to know, for the children, for Erica," I sighed, glancing away from her for a moment before bringing my eyes to hers, "for Erik," I whispered the last.

This time Christine almost chuckled and shook her head. "I have not been blind papa, but I am relieved." She kissed me, and slowly drew me to my feet. Her arm slipped around my waist, and we began to make our way out of the room.

"We'll have to plan their wedding, for surely they will not," Christine said with a trace of humor. I chuckled softly, holding her tightly. It would take time for her to recover fully, but for now, she was here, with us, with family.

Chapter 89

We buried Phillippe among the monumental angels for company. The women were regal, the men stoic. It was always thus as this ritual repeated itself up and down the European continent.

I looked at my two Christines as they stood beside each other, and sighed. We had now buried two of our own. How much more would be asked of us? How much more would we have to endure before this madness of war was over?

Meg let go my hand when she saw her sister approach. A brief glance passed between the two women before Christine gave a slight shake to her head. Meg accepted it with the briefest of nods, took Raoul's arm, and slowly they made their way toward the massive gates bordering the cemetery.

"He would not want to see you cry. Not for him." Christine's voice was quiet as her fingers wiped the stray tears from my cheeks.

"He was a good man."

She smiled a little. "Yes, he was. I wanted you to be proud of him."

I traced the planes of her face, looking into pools of dark brown that so long ago I had wanted to drown in. "I could not have been prouder of him had he been my own."

Christine looked away, toward the angels surrounding us. When at last she spoke, her voice trembled with barely checked anguish.

"But he was! He was the son of your heart Erik, the heart I spurned many years ago. You gave him your music, your love, as once you gave it to me."

She turned to look at me and the pain of long buried feelings suddenly finding voice was in her eyes. "I taught him what you taught me." She shook her head almost as if in shame. "I wanted you to know that your lessons, your heart, had not been wasted."

I took her hand, not quite knowing what to say to her revelations. So I held her in a light, comforting embrace instead. She sighed against my shoulder.

"I was always a fool Erik, a frightened, gullible fool. I threw your love for me at your feet, only to hurt and regret it later."

I closed my eyes, the arms around her tightening a little. Watching Christine struggle against her feelings, I understood that on that night long ago, I had not been the only one to leave in pain.

"Do you regret your choice?" I asked softly, drawing away so I could look into her eyes.

She smiled a little. "Not the choice, but the way it was made."

My hands brushed her hair. "It could not have been made any other way. I was not exactly in my right mind. I wanted you, needed you, but was it love? I think not. An obsession, most definitely, an obsession I was powerless to stop. You enthralled me. Then you freed me. Oh yes. The kiss that Beauty gave the Beast showed him what love should be."

I released her to look where Meg and Raoul waited. "There was pain and heartbreak, but I am glad that it was you who taught me." I gently squeezed Christine's hand, turning my eyes back to her. "Because now I know what it is to love a wife, to love a friend."

She smiled and touched the right side of my face. "You were always in my heart, and always will be," Christine's arm slid through mine as we began to make our way toward the gates, "whether you want to be or not. It is too late for me to let you go."

Recalling her ire at me a few, short weeks ago, I held onto her arm a little more firmly. "I much prefer being your friend," I said quietly. In answer, Christine laid her head against my shoulder as we continued our walk.

Early June 1916

My Dearest Family,

The word has been given, and we shall hold to it: *Ils Ne Passeront Pas*. They Shall Not Pass! Though we are exhausted and stretched on the lines to the breaking point, we cannot give more ground. Like Leonidas and his 300, we will make our stand. The Germans will probably overrun us in any case, but we have to make the effort. We have to stop them. There really is no other choice. The men will give their all, but we will not budge one more centimeter. We cannot.

Love to all,

Erik

June 4, 1916

To My Cherished Family,

We breathe easy tonight. While we stared Death in his face, he withdrew, quietly, stealthily, without fanfare. He will come again, no doubt of that, but for now, we give thanks to the Russians. Their maneuvers on the Eastern Front have forced the Germans to withdraw their troops from this sector, giving us a much needed respite.

We rejoice in being alive for one more day.

Yours always,

Erik

Chapter 90

"Papa! Regardez! Les poilus sont là-bas," the child's voice rang out clearly in the early morning stillness.

Traffic had not yet engulfed the streets, and only a few enterprising souls were about. In another hour the city would come fully awake and the endless lines for food and interminable gossip would begin once again.

For now, in the early morning hush, the child's demands to be heard were unmistakable. A few heads turned at his clear, sharp voice, then turned to glance at the group of soldiers gathered on the corner by a café, but most passed by without giving the men much thought. Fatigued men in uniform had become a frequent sight on the streets of many cities.

I paused in my stroll with Christine to look across the street at the huddled group of men. They were 'hairy ones' indeed. Trench life offered few luxuries, and the men on the corner were exhausted. Their light blue coats carried the stains of the mud that would never wash out, no matter how diligently they scrubbed. They supported one of their own, a man who only stared off into some fixed spot only he could see. They had started to call it shell shock, but I knew from Gilbert it was more, much more.

I gave them a slight nod of acknowledgement before continuing the walk toward the office on my daughter's arm. We had made this early morning outing together, as Meg would be spending the day with her sister, and I would not submit to the mercies of the housekeeper. So I accompanied my daughter, with a strict promise to leave the work to her.

"Hello Maman," the voice came from within the shadows of the doorway of the building. "Grand-papa."

Christine froze, her hand squeezing tightly on my own. "Non," she breathed.

"Ah oui, c'est moi," Gérard whispered.

Christine found her feet at last and nearly ran to where he sat on his pack, watching her with tired eyes.

When I thought she could possibly have no more tears, Christine cried as she gathered her son to her breast, this time crying with unparalleled joy at having one of her own returned to her at last.

I turned away, giving her time with him, time to realize that while he had come home, he would never be the same.

"What's this?" I heard her voice tremble with tears.

"Gone," he answered with a sigh. "I'm tired. I need a bath."

She laughed. "Of course. Papa."

Between the two of us, we helped him rise. With his one arm, he swung the pack over his shoulders.

As we walked back to the apartment, Gérard leaned heavily on his mother, favoring his left leg, the left sleeve of his jacket, where his arm should have been, negligently tucked into a pocket.

So this was how they would come home after being subjected to hell on earth. They would return all used up, with haunted old eyes before they were twenty-four.

I sighed and hugged him to me. He was home, and for now that was all that mattered.

Chapter 91

Though Gérard's homecoming brought the family immeasurable joy, it quickly became apparent he had come home a troubled, young man. First there were the startled, half angry, half terrified reactions to loud noises, whether out in the streets or inside the apartment. Then came the screaming nightmares and more than once, I found him huddled in some corner of the apartment, trembling, his eyes unseeing. I could only wonder what horrors he had had to endure to now suffer another kind of pain.

When neither Gilbert nor Michael could offer us a solution to Gérard's ordeal other than time, patience, and sedatives, I despaired of him ever having a life again, a life with family, a life of peace, and perhaps a measure of happiness.

In his deepest troubles, it was his mother's steadfastness that calmed him, her unflappable nature that gave him comfort. He accepted the sedatives with resignation. They helped to drive away the worst of his torment.

Though Christine tried not to show it, I saw in her eyes how his pain tore her to pieces. This time I could not help her with her sorrow. Even music would not chase these particular demons away.

When we began to wonder what the future held for our young man, it appeared one afternoon at the office, in the form of Céline.

The three of us looked up from the drawings spread on the table at her bright and cheery "Bonjour."

Despite his nightmares, Gérard had begun to help his mother with the work. He had after all, directed one of my firms before he had been called to serve. The work soothed the specters that pursued him.

I had come this day to lend a quick opinion on a current project. Meg and I had made plans to spend the day together. She would be coming soon to collect her fossil.

Now Gérard, Christine and I collectively looked at the pretty young woman standing in the doorway. Neither the dark glasses nor the cane she carried detracted from her charm, or the warm smile she beamed at us.

"I am sorry if I interrupted your work," she hesitated for a moment, turning her head to follow the sound of the shuffling papers on the table.

"No, not at all," Christine answered. "We were finished."

Céline smiled. "Good. I came to ask if you'd like to come to the concert tonight at the tower. My students have been asked to play. They are raising money____."

"We'll be glad to come," Christine answered, eyes covering her son and me with a glance that would bear no refusal. "All of us," she added, drawing herself to full height.

I had to hide the broad smile that I felt creeping to my face. When and how had it happened that my daughter had become the head of the family?

"Very well. I will expect you at six." Céline lifted her head, and it was uncanny how she seemed to look directly at me, even though I knew she could not see. She smiled as if she had read my thoughts.

"It's your breathing, monsieur Erik. My students are all excited to know they will be playing for my teacher."

I took her hand, kissing it lightly. Over the years, as I had watched her grow, I had always had a soft spot in my heart for this young woman. She had continued with her music, even after I had stopped teaching her. She had, in turn, joined Hélène at the school, and was now an accomplished teacher in her own right.

"I would not miss it, my dear, and an invitation was not necessary. You know we would have come," I said gently.

"I'll be going then. Thank you." She gathered her stick, turning to leave, when Gérard came to her side.

"Allow me to walk you out," he said, placing an elbow under her hand. Their quiet voices drifted to us for a few moments as Christine and I exchanged glances.

A fund raising concert for the Croix Rouge or no, Céline's appearance at the office had been a carefully calculated strategy. No one wore a dress designed to impress young men to simply extend an invitation to a musical evening.

I shook my head, trading knowing smiles with my daughter. She sighed, and briefly hugged me. "There was nothing for them to lose, except maybe, an afternoon." She whispered, leaning her head against my shoulder.

Two months later, Gérard and Céline became inseparable. They did everything together, and on occasion, she spent a day at the office with him.

However it had come about, their affection was genuine and her presence calmed him. His horror filled dreams became less frequent, and his adjustment to regular life grew easier with her beside him.

When they came to seek permission to marry, no one was more surprised than they at our ready acceptance. Perhaps at long last there would be happiness for the family.

The wedding took place in October, with only families present, and even we filled the tiny space.

On my first sight of the chapel I stood still, recalling an afternoon when I had showed it to a very young woman, an afternoon when a kiss had been exchanged.

Meg smiled at me, squeezing my hand. "They wanted a special place. I couldn't think of any other more appropriate."

I nodded, wrapping my hand over hers, and let her lead me inside.

For their gift, Raoul gave them land and I the house that once would have been Phillippe's.

They settled in, and it was not long before a certain look appeared on Céline's face, a look I remembered well and with fondness, when it had settled into Meg's eyes.

November 1916

To My Loving Family,

With the rotation of units, we have been given a few days of peace and relative quiet. We find ourselves alongside equally exhausted British troops.

Weak smiles are exchanged, and cigarettes passed around. It is what one does to kill time between relentless anticipation of death, and the boredom of finding oneself a prisoner of Mother Nature. Torrential rains of the past days have turned our 'playground' into quagmire. One cannot take a step without fear of getting stuck in the mud, and never coming out again.

In this, at least, the guns have been silent. No one can move them, neither our enemies nor us. So for a few days, we live as men, huddled in the few tents in the rear camps, awaiting our turn at manning the front lines.

Erik

November 1916

To My Cherished Ones,

We have a new ally in the field. The Brits call it a tank, and its arrival was a complete surprise to all. A terrific noise heralded its appearance, and all of us, Brit, American, Algerian, and French watched in awe as the mechanized beasts tore through the wires of no-man's land, rolled over gutted fields, straight for the German lines. They, in turn, watched in disbelief as these behemoths came straight for them. Then they bolted, and ran.

Perhaps now, with the tanks beside us, the men can have some hope of eventually going home.

My love to all,
Erik

Chapter 92

The turn of another year had come. It was January 1917, and it would be the third year of the war. France was exhausted. She had no more men to send, and for the past two months, the British troops had borne the brunt of major offenses.

We lived, but even our resources were beginning to feel the strain of unremitting shortages, rationing, and the never ending concern for those of the family still in the field.

We had gathered at the de Chagny residence to quietly welcome the New Year, and to celebrate another wedding. Anne-Marie and Michael married at the house. Their romance had been restrained though it surprised no one. They made a good team, whether at the hospital or not. She had begun to work alongside him more and more and their skills blended well. St. Hubert's was lucky to have both of them, and the family acquired a bit of that rebellious blood the Americans were known for.

Once more I found myself bemused by how the family had grown, all because of a night so many lifetimes past.

Hélène smiled at me, and lightly caressed my cheek. She was still a striking woman, despite the years. "It was in your eyes. It always was. They never lie." For the first time in our association, Hélène lightly kissed my cheek before walking away.

So there it was. The answer I had thought would remain elusive to my dying day.

Erica wrapped her arms around me a moment later, whispering "Thank you," in my ear, before moving off to join the gathering inside the music room.

I glanced at her mother as they exchanged a brief word. Christine nodded and came to stand beside me. Though the pain of her losses would never completely go away, Christine had recovered, and an almost regal air now imbued her essence.

As she leaned forward to tenderly kiss and embrace me, I noted the thin gold chain around her neck, Phillippe's ring hanging from it. I had given it to her when she had released her tears. "They have finally come to an understanding," she said, smiling at me as I sat beside the hearth, basking in the heat of the blazing fire.

"But he will not change his mind."

She sighed and shook her head. "No."

"Stubborn young fool," I muttered but she heard me and mussed my hair.

"Give them time. They are just getting used to the idea that they're free. I know someone who did not exactly rush into things." My daughter arched a brow at me, but before I could react, Julie's startled cry of "Christine!" broke the moment.

As the gaiety of the gathering broke into shocked alarm and cacophony of voices, one rose above them all. "Non! Let me." It was Meg's commanding tone, but for all the milling bodies, I could not see.

The next minutes were interminable as questions were asked and no one had answers. I noted the absence of the two doctors and the shaking of heads.

When Michael finally came to tell me that Meg needed to see me, he said it so softly that even Christine could not hear. Across the room I saw Gilbert doing the same with Raoul, and as the two of us were led away, silence fell over the family. Their eyes watched us with undisguised concern.

The doctors brought us into Christine's dressing room, where Meg was rearranging the gown carelessly thrown over a chair.

"You better sit down, both of you." Though the tone was brusque, I knew from long experience that the harshness covered deep pain.

"What is it? Where's Christine?" Raoul began to walk toward the door in search of his wife, but Meg's hand on his arm stopped him. There were only the three of us in the room. The two doctors had discreetly withdrawn.

"Sit down Raoul. You too," Meg turned her eyes on me, and I finally saw something there that she did not want anyone downstairs to know.

"Meg, please, what's wrong? Where is she?" Raoul pleaded. He had now seen that look in her eyes as well. "Where are Gilbert and Michael?"

"They're giving her something for the pain," she said gently, guiding him to a chair. Meg kneeled beside him, taking his hand in hers, though her eyes looked at me, at my unmoving, alert frame. In the sudden stillness of the room, I felt as if my heart would leap out of my throat. The look of devastation I saw in her eyes did nothing to prepare me for what came next.

"She's been hiding it for the past few months. She swore me to secrecy. As her friend and sister, I promised her." Meg now took hold of my hand as well, and while she held the hands of the men who once had been rivals for the affections of a young girl named Christine, Meg's words sent us both to hell.

"She's dying. The cancer will kill her, and there is nothing, absolutely nothing we can do."

I stared at nothing, heart screaming, writhing in agony, a low groan of misery escaping from my throat. It was all I dared give voice to in the face of the anguish I saw on Raoul's face.

"No! She doesn't deserve this!" He cried, struggling against Meg's restraining hands.

"Raoul listen to me," she was firm but gentle as she helped Raoul sit back down. "Please."

Meg sighed, squeezing my hand, her eyes looking at both of us with barely contained heartbreak. "Christine will need you, both of you, to give her strength, not tears. Give her what you both have done all these years, your love."

She rose, and lightly brushed a hand against my cheek. "And you my heart, give her your music."

Chapter 93

Christine's death sentence cast a pall over the family. For her, we dared not let it show. Her wish had been to keep her pain hidden, and to that end, we did what we could. It was to Raoul and me that the hardest task was given, to literally watch the woman we both cherished slowly die before our eyes.

Once Christine's secret was revealed, by some unspoken agreement, Raoul and I traded days spent in her company. Whether a day spent in their library or one of the many gardens of Paris, each minute I could hold her hand was precious. She was my friend. Her kiss, given in a burning theater, had freed me from a prison partially imposed by men, partially of my own making. There was nothing I could do to relieve her from the prison of her pain but be with her and play. I still had that, and I gave it all to her, along with my heart.

Only once did I give voice to the heartbreak, only once did I let the Erik of long ago find voice through my hands as they poured forth the music he had taught her, music long buried but never forgotten.

When Meg came to take me back to our bed, I let her loving fingers wipe away the streams of tears, only to have more pour out of the faucets that were my eyes. My wife held me throughout that long night, her enduring love and steadfastness a calming balm to the sorrow of knowing our friend was dying and we were powerless to stop it.

Over the following months, Christine put up a valiant fight against the disease that ate away at her. She had good days and bad. When her pain was at its worst, only then would she allow Gilbert or Michael to give her medication. She refused everything else, even my suggestion of opium.

Her hands held my face as she smiled at me, a touch of sadness in her brown eyes. "No my dearest, no. The nightmares it would give me would be worse than the pain. You fought your demons. Let me fight mine, my own way."

On a whim one day, and with Meg's approval, I sent Christine a basket of roses from the house in Brittany.

Her delight and surprise when she saw them gave me immeasurable pleasure. Her eyes lit up, and when she lifted them to inhale their scent, a glance passed between us. All I could do was to kiss her brow and squeeze her hand. The Erik that once had sent her roses was long gone. Only a weak shadow of him remained, and he was her friend.

May 1917

My Dear Father,

The rumblings of the previous year have now turned to full blown action.

Men in several regiments have sat down, and none will be moved. Though they man the line, the men refuse to shoot. Their refusal to sacrifice themselves in yet another futile struggle is echoed by many. While I see the total lack of will in their eyes, my men still persevere in their duty, despite their sympathy for their fellows who are refusing to do so.

With the Russians now dealing with domestic problems of their own, and the Boches digging in deeper, I do not foresee a successful end to this matter. Only a miracle can give us the strength to go on. Another disaster on the scale of the Aisne, and we might as well learn another language.

I am tired, father. I want to go home, to Erica, and perhaps that peace we spoke of.

I look at my men, and we are all caked in mud and blood, at times standing hip-deep in water, standing upright by sheer will alone. We get one day of rest in 24, insufficient rations, rifles that are substandard, and yet somehow, even through all that, we manage a joke now and then, even a smile or two. It is enough to not make us forget that we are men, and why we are here.

My Love,
Erik

Early June 1917

My Dearest Family,

Perhaps the miracle we had all been hoping for has arrived. A new man has assumed command of the army, and already, some of his promises have been implemented. It will take time for the general unrest to die down, but for the most part, the mutinies have been halted.

The army on the whole, has paid a high price for its show of rebellion, though in the end, only 20 men were hanged. Some were arrested, the rest punished at regimental level. I suppose even the new commander realized he could not, in good conscience, execute over 30,000 men!

We breathe easier, as there has been a lull in the planning of any major offensives for the next few months. Whether intentional or not, this is a much needed rest for all the men. Our boots could use a bit of polish.

Love to all,
Erik

Chapter 94

In July of 1917, Céline's son was born, to the great joy of us all. Even Christine ventured to the hospital to see him He was a lusty boy, with full lungs and was most definitely his father's pride and great delight.

When I saw Christine hold him, for an unimaginable reason, my mind flashed scenes of another life, another time before my eyes. She and I singing in the grotto, our duet of Don Juan, and how it had all come literally crashing down when her hands had ripped off my mask.

I looked at her as she held a great-grand son, her once lustrous hair pulled into a loose chignon, the grey overtaking the brown, and all I felt in my heart was tenderness for the girl I had once sought to make my own. I gave that girl a light kiss as Meg and I walked out of the room, giving Christine time with the newest member of the ever expanding clan.

In all my visions of Christine, seeing her as a mother had not been one of them. The image only made me smile and spread warmth to my heart. Who would have believed then that I would become a father, and the head of a family? I shook my head at the thought and rejoined Meg in our walk through the hospital's garden.

By October, Christine had grown weaker. It was decided to baptize the child while she was still able to participate. Once more, the family gathered at the chapel I had restored so many lifetimes past. They named him Phillippe Raoul Antoine de Chagny, a fitting name, since he carried a head full of dark hair and those blue eyes my daughter had fallen in love with that one spring in Rome.

By early November, Céline was enciente once more to the great delight of her husband. On occasion, Gérard still had bouts with the demons that would never leave him, but family life and work had settled him. Though I had known my daughter capable of heading the businesses, deep in the recesses of my heart, I was glad that Gérard had thrown himself into the work, and that his mother would not be alone.

In late November, when the first snow barely covered the streets, Meg found me sitting in my study, staring out the window. She did not need to say it. She took my hand and we sat beside each other in silence, watching the occasional snowflake dance in the air.

Chapter 95

With Christine's death, Raoul and I were like lost children, neither able to find direction. We continued to return to the one place that united us.

For the first few weeks, we continued to visit Christine's cold, stone, resting place, to stand in silence, watched by monumental angels. We would depart as we had come, two broken, old men.

We shared wine at the same café, neither of us talking. It was the company we needed, the knowledge that neither one of us was alone in sorrow.

After a time, my legs would no longer hold up to the long walk to the cemetery. Instead, I walked the Opera grounds, eventually settling onto the balustrade, eyes drifting to the golden angel above. He was silent now, and I would get no guidance from him.

As my haunting of the premises continued, even the flower girl came to know me. She would greet me with a shy smile and hand me a red carnation. I accepted it, though my heart twisted in grief. Red, red for her, like the roses I used to leave. No more duets, Christine and I. No more angry, flashing brown eyes in answer to my stubbornness. It was over.

Each afternoon as I rose to make my way home, I laid the flower before the main door of the theater. Let them wonder. Let them point to the shuffling old man who left flowers. Let them whisper insensé and Le Fantôme. They would never understand what had been born in that house.

Even then, Raoul and I would find each other in that same café, at the same time, sharing wine, even if it was in silence. More than anything else, we still felt Christine's shadow between us, holding us together, for whatever purpose, only the angel knew. His silence gave no answers.

When in early January 1918, Raoul succumbed to a second stroke, I sat at his side not really knowing why, while he struggled to recover. There were no exhortations to walk. He would not, not this time.

I read to him from the newspapers, from Erik's letters. Though the family gathered around him, and Meg took over the running of his household, it fell to me to keep him company. The young were busy with families and work of their own to expend time on two, old men.

Because it was easier for us, Meg and I once more found ourselves living under Raoul's roof. This time, I did not chafe or protest. It was the only thing that made sense, and I was tired of fighting.

So we two sat together like stubborn, dried up leaves, refusing to let go the branch that held us.

Then in February, the letters stopped coming.

Chapter 96

"He's dying," Gilbert's voice was a hammer blow in the stillness of his office. We were gathered in the spacious room, yet with those words, the walls began to close in, and my lungs could not get air.

Christine had taken us to the hospital when word had come that Erik had been among the latest influx of casualties.

Now I sat there and endured words a parent should never live to hear. While Gilbert's voice was calm, the stiffness of his shoulders and the steel in his eyes betrayed his own, barely controlled grief. While Erik *fils* lay among the wounded, Alain had been buried on the battlefield, a plain wooden cross marking his resting place.

I glanced at Meg. She refused to look at anyone, choosing instead to stare out the window into the gardens below, her back stiff, refusing even Anne-Marie's gentle hands to bring her back to her chair.

I could only close my eyes against the anguish I felt for her in my heart. How she had struggled to give him life! Would we now have to watch him die?

"Oh not physically," Gilbert ran a hand through his hair and shook his head. "The injuries will heal, in time. It's in his mind. He's losing the will to live and there is nothing I can do to stop it."

"NO!" I screamed, lashing out with all my grief, all my anger, half rising out of the chair. "Make him live!"

"You tell me how Erik!" Gilbert yelled back, eyes full of agony. "You tell me how to fix his mind!"

As we faced each other, no one moved. They watched us with curious interest, and even Meg had broken her vigil to glance at us, at two broken fathers.

"There has to be something," I said in misery. I could not, would not, acknowledge the possibility of Erik dying. Not my son. NOT! MY! SON!

Gilbert sighed, pulling his anger back under control. "I deal with their bodies Erik, not their minds. My hands are buried in their guts, day in, day out, and I think I will never wash the blood away. I sew them up, only to send them back to the butcher."

He shook his head. "Injuries heal, yes, but without that intrinsic will to live, there is only so much we doctors can do." He paused casting a weary glance at all of us. "I don't know if he is aware of the extent of the damage he's suffered, but he's giving up, a little bit at a time. Without his help, without his own desire to survive, there's little I can do. For now, he's stopped fighting."

I sighed, remembering Erik's strong kicks inside his mother. "He's always been a fighter. Even before he was born," I said quietly.

Gilbert's strong hand descended onto my shoulder. "Then maybe he'll find it in himself to fight one last time. If he lives, it will be by his own choice, not my hands. I will do all I can within my power to heal him, you know that, but he has to help me."

He gave us all a final, sad look before heading toward the door. "I am sorry, my friends," he held up his hands. "These are needed." He left the office, a broken man who was needed by those more broken than he.

Over the next weeks, Meg and I did not leave Erik's side, staying well past the allotted visiting time. He lingered in limbo, as did we, and we were far from the only ones holding vigil for a son, father, husband.

Though before him, before the public, Meg would not betray her pain, her eyes when she looked at me, spoke of our combined heartbreak. All I could do was hold and kiss her, for I could no longer give her that which I most wanted to.

We lived in acute uncertainty, grasping for hope that Erik would find and fight for that spark which I knew was inside him. Anything else was out of the question, for I could not bear the shattered look in Meg's eyes.

When I held her, all I could see was her holding our son the day he had been born, and I would accept nothing else than the fact that he would live.

Only in the privacy of the house would Meg allow her tears to fall, and then, not even before me. What could we say that had not been said?

One afternoon as I passed through the hall of Raoul's house, I heard Meg's soft cries. When I looked into the room, I saw her kneeling beside his wheeled chair, her head on his knee, his hand on her shoulder. They did not see me, and I left them in peace.

Not long ago, a friend had listened to my own fears. I sighed, remembering Christine's flash of anger at me as we had sat at the kitchen table.

I made my way toward the library, glancing wistfully at the recently arrived portrait of the Comtesse de Chagny hanging on the wall. Christine's brown eyes looked at me with undisguised tenderness and affection. It had been painted some time before she had become aware of her illness, when both the men she had cared for, reconciled.

I could not help a small smile and the sudden mist in my eyes. "Is this why you hold us together? Did you know?" I asked, tears falling down my cheeks.

Warmth spread through me and I could hear Christine's voice whisper in my head.

"It will be all right. You will see."

Though it had to be imagination, I felt the brush of lips against my cheek. I turned and walked to the library, to find solace among the books.

Chapter 97

In the weeks that followed, Michael subjected Erik to several surgeries. These were in addition to the one that had kept him barely alive before arrival at the hospital.

Through all this, the spark that Gilbert had talked about had taken root, and with the knowledge that our son would live, Meg and I buried our distress.

It was late, and the nurses had had to gently pry me away from Erik's bedside. They had finished changing all his dressings, and it was time for me to leave. Reluctantly, I gave in to their insistence. I began to walk down the quiet hall when the voice of an angel stopped me, drawing me back toward the room I had recently left. The angel was singing, her voice softly drifting through the hall. She was singing a song Erik had written for one of her many, early recitals. There was no mistaking Erica's voice, or the love bound within it.

Through the half open door of the room, I saw her sitting beside him, her hand lightly holding the bandaged one. She was still in her uniform, and her right hand brushed at the few tufts of blond hair poking from beneath the wrappings around his head.

"I told you I'd go to hell and back for you," she whispered, her voice catching on a cry. "Don't even think about leaving me. I will come after you and pull your hair if you do." She bent and gently laid a cheek against his swathed one. "Don't you dare leave me," her whisper broke into a sob she did not hold back, not this time. "Who will write songs for me, if not you? Who will make music with me?" While she continued to cradle his head, her soft voice began to hum a lullaby I had sung to her once, a song to chase away ghosts and frightful dreams. She called to him, as I had called to her mother, pulling him back to life, to her heart.

When one of the nurses started toward the room with blusters of "It's disrupting the patients", Michael's firm voice stopped her. "Let it be. A little music will do them all a bit of good."

The nurse bobbed her head and left.

"She comes when she can and sings to him," Michael said quietly, taking in the scene at Erik's bedside, then studied me with his dark eyes. "She's the one who brought him in."

I nodded in acknowledgement, understanding the anguish of the young woman singing to her soldier.

"I let her sing to them. What harm can it do? It does not hurt that she's pretty to look at. Gives them all a reason to recover," he gave me a lopsided grin and a low chuckle as he indicated the five other men who shared the room with my son, and their rapt expressions. "This much I can tell you, Erik. He's past the danger point. We just need to let him heal. The rest will take care of itself. Come on, I'll take you home."

"My countrymen have taken quite a liking to your wonderful city," Michael ventured as he drove us to the de Chagny's house. It was Mid-May of 1918, and the American troops had begun arriving on French soil in greater numbers. They had made their first appearance in March that year, but it was not until now that their presence had become significantly noticeable. With their arrival, the Americans gave hope to all that perhaps this nightmare of war would have an end.

"It has always been my home, even during some unpleasant times. It is perhaps why I could never leave it for long, even during my years in Rome."

Michael glanced at me, giving me a wan smile. "I wish I could say the same, but the streets of Chicago were my home, if you want to call it that. When I came here, it was only with the thought of repaying a debt to someone who pulled me off the street and showed me kindness. He lived long enough to see me graduate with honors. He was the only father I ever knew, and maybe I came here to make him proud of me, to let him know his skills didn't go to the grave with him. I don't really know. But I found something here I never thought I would, certainly not during a war." He looked at me and a small smile brightened his somber expression. "I found a home and a family, with you. I am grateful for that. Just thought you'd like to know."

He helped me to the door of the house, his firm arms lending much needed support. "Good night Erik," he said, then in a softer tone, added. "He'll be all right."

Chapter 98

It was not until the doctors began to remove the layers of bandages to allow his body some movement that Erik's true struggle began. Though Michael had informed us early on of the extent of our son's injuries, I was not certain whether any of us, Meg or I, much less Erik, were prepared to face and accept the cold, hard reality before us.

On the day the swathing was removed from his face, Meg and I visited our son to find him sitting beside the window, facing the view of the garden, though he would never be able to see it, or anything else, again. Erica stood beside him, and it was clear that they had been talking for some time. He sat silent, unmoving, and if they heard us enter, they gave no sign.

"They should have left me in that hole." The voice was low and hoarse.

Erica's fingers closed over his arm. "That would have been too easy." Her voice was as near a caress as she could make it. She was dressed in her uniform, the luxurious, brown hair pulled back tightly from her face and under her cap. "Living, that's the harder part."

He shook his head, his breath catching on a sigh. "What kind of living? I can't see or walk, and God alone knows what I look like." The voice, once a clear, powerful baritone, was now barely above a whisper, the result of a bullet that had torn through his throat.

"You are alive. That is important to me. We will make music together. You will write it, and I will sing it. Paris will be at our feet."

"In case you've forgotten, I'm a hand short," he held up his still bandaged left arm. It ended where the wrist would have been. "It will be a bit difficult to compose."

Erica lifted her head, and for a moment, there was silence. "Dictate to me, and I will write it."

"Leave me be," he whispered in resignation, in withdrawal, pulling his arm back onto his lap.

"Erik," it was a plea from her deepest heart.

"Go away."

Erica dropped her hands to her sides, drawing herself to full height. "Suit yourself. I have duty in a few minutes, but I will be back, count on it."

"Don't bother."

Erica gave a shake to her head, turned and started to walk out of the room, tears glistening on her cheeks. She did not seem surprised to see us and acknowledged our presence with a small nod.

As Erica's steps echoed in the hall, Meg threw me a look that begged and pleaded with that part of me that I had for so long fought and struggled against. Her fingers on my hand squeezed tightly as her eyes met mine.

It had taken a lifetime for me to finally accept the face I had been born with. For nearly half that time I had hidden it beneath a mask, beneath a theater, away from society that feared ugliness. Now it seemed, I was the only one who could help my son accept the consequences of his injuries. In a twist of Fate, I was the only one who could.

I nodded in silent reply to Meg's plea, and as she left the room, I went to sit beside my son.

We would never really know how Erik had sustained his wounds. When we asked Erica, all she could say for certain was that he had been found by accident, lying next to Alain in a shell crater, barely clinging to life. The stretcher bearers had taken him to the dressing station, where the medics had kept him breathing. Even that had been a tricky business, but he had managed to survive, to join the hundreds of other broken men at the hospital.

Knowing who had driven that particular ambulance, I was not too surprised that Erik had lived through the grueling transport. Erica would not have let him go, not without a fight.

He had been severely burned, the left hand crushed, and it was only Michael's skills that saved his legs. Erik would forever bear the scars that covered the left side of his body and face. He would have to learn to accept them, as he would have to accept the fact that he would never see again.

In this, only his resolve, his determination to live, to breathe, would help him, that, and the love in his heart for a young woman.

When sometime later, the fingers of his right hand wrapped around mine, I finally allowed the tears to fall. He would accept. He would fight.

Chapter 99

At the beginning of June, and under Michael's strict supervision, Erik took his first, tentative steps. By the end of the month, he could negotiate the room without guidance.

Though we shared an occasional joke, and he laughed a little, I began to sense in my son a withdrawal and the building of walls I recognized only too well. In another lifetime, those same walls and withdrawal had kept me in a mask, and living in hell.

To stave off the all too familiar darkness, I sat with Erik, transcribing what he dictated.

Though Michael had warned and admonished us against overly indulging him with assistance, that finding his own way of doing things was something Erik had to learn for himself, in this case, reason failed me. He was my son, and I would never abandon him.

Music had saved me in that pit I had called home, and if it would help stave off Erik's monsters, than I would help him, however I could, for as long as I could. So I did what my heart told me, because the agony of seeing him struggle was too much to bear.

For a time, we sat at the window of the room in companionship, he dictating, I copying, until he stopped, and with frustrated anger, smashed the washbasin against a wall, crying out his rage. I tried to soothe him, only to have that rage fall on me. I turned away, my heart an agonized knot in my chest.

He no longer allowed his mother near him, and barely tolerated me.

When Erica's gentle arms wrapped around me, it seemed I had been crying to that golden angel for hours. This place, with its colonnaded halls and gleaming mirrors had been a prison for so long. Why did it keep bringing me here? There were no answers here, not from the cold, hard stones, and certainly not from him, that golden, winged thing that mocked me with his silence!

"Come home, grand-father," Erica whispered, gathering me to her. Where was home? This had been such, or at least I had called it that, until I had been forced to leave it. Seeing Erik rage against the prison of his injuries brought my life full circle. In him, I had seen myself, raging in the bowels of this house, screaming my hurt and anger at the one who, perhaps, would have helped me, if I had not let the anger control me.

But all that was long ago. I sighed, letting Erica support me as we walked away from the theater. I could not fight this battle. Erik would have to find his own way, as once had I.

By July, Erik would not admit even me into the ward.

I shrugged off the nurse's solicitous but unwanted attention and walked through the halls that were overflowing with injured men, and yet I felt very much alone.

So once more I sat with him, with Raoul. This time, when he looked at me with those pale eyes, there was understanding, one I had thought never to find, not in him. In a moment of unexpected candor, his raspy voice broke the silence that had fallen between us. "He'll find his way. You did."

I only sighed in reply. I no longer knew how I felt. I had become numb, a shadow, and all I could do was accept what Fate threw at my feet. When I informed Meg of Erik's latest disavowal, she kissed me, and in her serene way, gently reminded me that it had taken twenty years and a lifetime for me to accept me. I could not expect a young man to accept his fate within a few, short weeks.

This time we could not help him. It was his struggle, his choice to make.

When my eyes fell on Christine's portrait as I passed by, her secret smile and warm eyes were a soothing balm to the raw wound in my heart.

"What are you so afraid of?" Her voice echoed in my head, and I could not help but reach and touch her painted hand.

"My angel of music."

"My friend," I whispered and began to walk away, when in one of the mirrors hanging on the wall, I spotted a reflection of Christine and Erica.

The two women stood side by side beside the window, Christine's arm draped around her daughter's shoulders. She was saying something to which Erica only shook her head. Christine smoothed the mass of dark brown, wavy hair from her daughter's face and kissed her. Erica turned into her mother's embrace. Christine held her for a time, eyes closed, before Erica wrenched herself away, rushing out of the room. I barely had time to move aside in the face of her mad dash for the stairs.

"Don't ask, Papa," Christine came up beside me, eyes watching her daughter disappear. She drew me to her, and we walked to the library, her presence filling me with the warmth and love it always had.

Chapter 100

As the fighting in the fields intensified, it became clear that a new will and determination had come into the ranks of the Allied armies, along with the new troops. Not a small part of this was due to the growing presence of American soldiers amongst the men. Their rebellious, unshakeable spirit infected the troops around them, and by the end of August of 1918, talk of an eventual German surrender began.

I accepted the gossip as I had accepted everything else since this war had begun, with resignation. What would be would be, and I no longer had a part to play.

I had not stopped visiting my friends at the hospital. If Erik did not wish to see me, so be it, but it would not prevent me from sharing time with Gilbert or Michael. Some of their own, overwhelming distress had been relieved by an influx of doctors attached to the American army.

It was the beginning of September, and I had, as usual, come to ask after Erik. Meg no longer accompanied me on these visits. Despite her words of comfort to me, Erik's refusal of her had hurt her. She chose instead, to spend time with Raoul, who needed the company, and who would not reject her out of hand.

When Gilbert saw me in his office, a happy grin split the stoic mask his face had become in the last few months.

"I hope you've come prepared," he said, almost gleefully.

"If it is as usual, then I will go home," I rose from the chair, prepared to do just that.

"Not so fast my friend." His hand came to rest on my elbow. "Do you know where your grand-daughter has been?"

I looked at him in curiosity. Since the evening I had seen her rush out of the house, Erica had disappeared. No one had seen her, not even Anne-Marie. She had resigned her duties with the Croix Rouge, and her manager had placed several anxious calls to Christine's office.

"What has this to do with her?"

Gilbert arched his good brow. "I hope that heart of yours holds out. I will not be the one to tell Meg."

"My heart is fine, if only you will stop talking in riddles." I made an effort at my old impatience.

He smiled, placing an arm around my shoulders. "Come with me, and you better be right about that heart of yours."

He led me to the old part of the hospital that was now used for storage, cooking, and laundry. I had never torn it down, choosing instead to build the new facility around it, saving as much of the original as I had been able. Eventually someone would tear it down altogether, for even now the facilities strained under ever increasing demands. But it would not be by my hands, or under my name.

As Gilbert led me through once familiar halls, I had the sense that I could hear the voices of long dead friends. It was imagination, it had to be. Carlotta and Étienne were long dead and buried. Yet as we walked, the voices became louder and clearer.

"Leave me alone!"

"Non. Not until it is correct. Encore!"

"Leave!" It was an anger filled explosion of frustration.

"Encore. You are not five. Again," a calm reply, though tinged with rising agitation.

"Go away!" The voice hissed in rage.

"You will play, then we'll see."

There was a choked sob, followed by the sounds of a few notes hesitantly plucked from a piano.

I stared at Gilbert, uncomprehending. All the while, he had drawn me closer to the old sitting room where once I had brought Carlotta in her odorous rags. With a silent tilt of his head, he directed my gaze into the room.

Two people were there, but they did not see us, and it was just as well. I don't know if I would have had the strength left to face them.

Erica stood behind Erik as he sat at the piano, her right hand held lightly over his as it moved cautiously over the keys. The notes plucked from the instrument were hesitant and afraid, as was he. Yet with each movement of his fingers over the keyboard, his confidence grew.

"Good. Again," her voice was calm, soothing, as she pulled a little away from him, hands resting on his shoulders. "This time on your own. I'm here. I'm not going anywhere."

"You won't leave me alone, will you?"

She kissed the mussed, blond hair. "You would not want me to. Play."

"Nagging woman," he muttered but obeyed, placing his fingers over the keys.

"Stubborn man," Erica whispered, hands tightening on his shoulders, her presence the support and comfort it had always been.

Gilbert drew me after him, and we began the walk back toward his office.

"I heard the piano one evening when I came to get some papers. She was guiding his hand, teaching him to play without his eyes. He rages at her, but she does not give in. She comes, day after day. They sit side by side, for hours on end, at that old piano. I have given orders that they are to be left alone and undisturbed." He paused. We stood just inside the entrance of the new wing. "I doubt she would want anyone to know."

I nodded in understanding. Bidding him adieu, I walked toward the waiting automobile with confidence I had not felt in months.

A wan smile lifted to my face as I settled into the seat. Once, I had given music to a young girl. Her son had given it back to me, and now, his daughter gave music back to my son. Life had come full circle.

It was early September when I persuaded Meg to come with me to the hospital. I had not revealed anything to her, and she probably thought me mad as I led her down the old halls.

When she heard the first notes echo in the air, she froze, her action effectively stopping me as well.

"Erik, what's--?" She began, a puzzled look in her eyes.

I smiled, and like an excited schoolboy of fifteen, pulled at her arm. "Just come, my love. Don't ask."

With hesitant steps, she followed where I led.

Once again they were sitting beside each other on the piano bench, only this time, his hand was confident. There were no strident voices, only harmony as they let the music fill the space around them.

When it finished, Erica turned slightly to frame his face in her hands, her left caressing the still healing wounds.

"Why? Why do you spend your time on me?" He whispered.

"Because there's talent in you I will not see wasted." She answered, and as her hand continued to stroke his cheek, he leaned into the touch for a moment, before pulling away.

"Your time would be better spent elsewhere," he whispered.

"I can't imagine how."

"I can't play."

"Then I'll play with you."

"I can't sing, and all I'll ever be is a burdensome monster."

Erica sighed, her fingers brushing lightly across his distorted lips. "No. You'll be the man who completes me."

"You would accept this gargoyle I have become?"

Erica shook her head. "No, but I will accept the Erik I have always loved, even when he pulled my hair." As she said this, she slipped a thin gold chain around his neck. Wrapping her hand around his, she brought their entwined fingers up to grasp the ring hanging from it. "I will always be here," she whispered. "I will make you as many dinners as you want." There were tears streaming from her eyes, but she was oblivious to those. Her hand caressed the face of the man before her.

With a groan borne of renewed confidence and long denied desire, Erik gathered her into his embrace. Her arms locked behind his neck and pulled him down to her questing lips.

Meg looked at me, as if seeking confirmation of what we had just witnessed. I took her hand, kissed it, and wrapped an arm about her waist. Silently, we walked away.

Chapter 101

When the call came the next day that Erik requested our presence, we walked into the room to find him standing beside his bed, facing us, though he could not see us.

Exchanging a glance and a brief pressure of hands, Meg and I stepped inside, letting the door close gently behind us.

No explanations were given, and none expected, as he embraced his mother. He held her tightly, tears falling down his cheeks. He had come home, as once had I, through music, through unbreakable bonds of love. When I felt his arm around my shoulders, I leaned into the brief embrace, closing my eyes in relief, grateful that his plunge into darkness had been so much shorter than mine. There were no tears as the three of us stood side by side. I was done with those.

On the way home that evening, I asked the driver to stop at one particular spot. Taking Meg's hand, I walked with her toward that colonnaded monstrosity that had been mine for so long.

As the last of the sun's rays were setting, my wife and I stood beside each other, facing that house that meant so much to both of us. I lifted tear filled eyes toward the golden angel high above.

"Did I not say it would be all right?" If it was imagination, I did not care. I saw Christine smile down at me from beneath those golden wings, her red cloak flapping in the breeze. *"What you take is love."*

I turned to Meg, kissing her. Her arms wrapped around me as we walked back to the waiting automobile.

Of Erica, there was no sign, and whatever happened between them, was their secret to keep. Her manager would only say that she had cancelled all outstanding engagements, indefinitely. We left it at that. She was her own woman, with her own choices to make.

Erik continued his recovery with newfound determination and purpose, no longer fighting off the nurses or doctors who came to check his healing wounds. They assured us that at the end of the month, he would be able to go home, provided he followed their instructions, and came in for regular check-ups.

When we told him, he laughed a little. "I've been here so long that this feels like home."

I smiled, clapping a hand onto his shoulder. "I know what you mean."

Erik's lips turned up into a half smile. "I can't imagine you living anywhere else but Paris, or our house in Brittany. Even Italy seemed out of place for you."

"Hmmm, indeed," I looked at him, my own lips twitching into a smile. "There was an angel that always drew me here."

"An angel?"

I sighed, squeezing Meg's hand, eyes meeting hers in a long, silent glance. "Yes, an angel," I whispered, eyes misting with remembrance. "Your mother."

Chapter 102

As September gave way to October, and the fighting on the various fronts intensified in one last burst of raw and lashing fury, a new combatant entered the battlefield in the form of a disease.

There had been two previous outbreaks, both quickly controlled and suppressed. This time, Death chose not to be so cooperative. What he had not taken in the charnel house of the battleground, he took now. He struck those weakened with wounds and hunger first, then fed on the rest.

Even the doctors and nurses caring for his victims were not immune to Death's cold hands. Many died alongside their patients.

Gilbert succumbed during the first two weeks of the outbreak. Julie, already inconsolable over Alain's death, repaired to Gérard's house, and I never saw her again.

When Michael came to the de Chagny house, he found the family gathered in the salon, all eyes riveted on him, on the barely controlled anguish stamped on his face. It was all we needed to know.

He had not allowed us near the hospital for fear of exposure. Now his silence, and his crumpled face spoke what words would not. A choked sob of misery came from beside me, and I saw Christine wrap Meg into her embrace and draw her mother from the room.

I sank into the nearest chair, oblivious to everything and everyone. In his last days, we had been denied the light that had been our son. I had no tears. They had all been spent. Where my heart used to be yawned a bottomless pit, and all I wanted was to throw myself in it.

A hesitant touch against my hand drew me back to the room, to eyes that were looking into mine. Raoul's hand wrapped tightly against mine, squeezing with what strength he had left. We sat in silence he and I, mourning the loss of a son, united in grief, united by a woman we both had loved.

When Michael could finally bring himself to speak, and I could bear to listen, he said they had found Erik collapsed over the old piano, in the grips of fever. There had been little they could do as his lungs, weakened from his wounds, could not cope with the disease invading them.

Michael sighed when he finished, looking at me from beneath drawn brows, as if he had something more to say, but was afraid to.

"Uncertainty does not suit you. What is it?" I asked in resignation. What else could possibly happen that had not happened already?

We were alone. Raoul had long since been put to bed, and Meg had not left our room since the afternoon. Christine was with her, but everyone else had gone, even Raoul's nurses.

Michael and I sat in the salon. I had not moved since he had given us the news. Now he studied me with speculation. At last, he reached into the pocket of his jacket and held out his hand toward me. "Erik, what do you know about this?" In his open palm lay a thin gold chain, a gold band hanging from it.

I stared at it for only a moment before recognition came, along with the tears I thought I no longer had. They weren't tears of sorrow or pain but unexpected joy, relief, and abiding love for the miracle that had been my son.

"Give it back to him," I spoke in a voice that was firmer than it had a right to be. "It's his wedding ring." I closed Michael's hand.

When I came to what had become Meg's and mine bedroom, I found Christine sitting beside her mother, fingers lightly brushing against Meg's cheeks.

When she saw me, she rose in all her dignity, and looked at me with nothing but tenderness and love in those wonderful, blue eyes.

387

"I gave her some of your tea. She's resting, and waiting for you." She kissed me lightly on the cheek. "I will miss him so."

I squeezed her hand, caressing her cheek. "I think they finally found what they both wanted."

When she continued to look at me in silence, I kissed her brow. "Once, long ago, a little girl pulled me out of darkness. Her child pulled my son from his. Now go, so I can be with your mother."

Christine gave me a nod and a brief kiss to my cheek before withdrawing.

When I drew Meg into my arms, she laid her head against my heart, her arms twining fast around me. I brushed her hair with my fingers, letting the silence of the night envelope us in its peacefulness.

Chapter 103

We buried him in Brittany near the home he had loved best, the little house where, not so long ago, Meg and I had made him.

Now we covered him with Brittany's dark earth, and he would finally have the peace and rest from the fighting he had wanted.

Michael had respected my wishes, and given him back the ring. It was our secret to keep, and Christine's. It had, after all, been she who had given Erica the chain. Nothing on this earth would have pried that away from her, nothing, save her daughter's love for a wounded, young man.

As we said our final farewells to the brief, shining light that had been Erik, my eyes drifted over the gathering of family and friends. While new lives had joined us, others had been taken, and I felt a shadow of the man I had once been. I was old and tired. I wanted rest.

Christine's eyes met mine, and in that glance, understanding passed. We would keep their secret. Despite her own losses, this one had shaken her, yet my daughter still managed to maintain a regal air about her. As with all of the people over the European continent, the sorrows had been heaped high. All we could do, was accept this last one with what dignity we had left.

The war had shattered countries, thousands upon thousands of lives, it had shattered families, it had shattered us.

When the formality was over, and the gathering began to drift apart, I saw Raoul sitting by a cypress tree, his wheeled chair nearby. Beside him on the bench rested a cloth covered box. I sat down next to him, and our eyes gazed toward the setting sun, and the serenity of the Channel waters.

"It is an appropriate time of day, for I do not think I can go on much longer," I ventured into the stillness that was broken only by the strident cries of gulls.

"Hmmm. The Germans are suing for peace, trying to find a dignified way out of this." Though his voice was hoarse, and the words slurred, I had learned to negotiate through his hesitant speech. The last stroke had left him a broken man.

"Let them pay, and pay dearly." I spat, not realizing the bitterness of my tone until Raoul turned his eyes on me.

"What price is enough Erik? What price did we pay for our arrogance?"

I stared at him. He sighed and indicated the freshly covered grave with its heap of flowers. "What price did we pay for nearly killing each other? Christine, dead. Our sons, dead. What price would be enough for that?" He paused and looked out at the slowly darkening sky. "Let them negotiate with what dignity they have left. It all has to end somehow. Better to let them walk from the field with some nobility." Raoul looked at me, his pale eyes boring into mine. "Otherwise the price for the victor is too high."

The silence between us grew long and tense.

"I wanted to kill you," I whispered, looking into his eyes.

He nodded. "You probably could have, but I'm glad you didn't." He gave me a slight smile. "And you were right. I never thought to ask what she wanted, only expected her to follow." He shook his grey head before resuming. "You and I are sad examples of men, Erik. It's a wonder she loved both of us."

At the stunned expression on my face, he almost laughed. "Oh don't be so shocked. I have known it ever since she kissed you in the grotto. She loved you as her teacher, as her angel, but mostly, as her friend." He looked at me, and for a time, there was total silence, even the gulls subsiding in their squabbles to listen to his words. "I believe she would have stayed."

I shook my head, fighting back the tears that suddenly stung my eyes. "I couldn't do it," my voice cracked with long remembered sorrow. "I looked into those eyes that had trusted me, that had given me a touch of brightness in my dank hell and I didn't have it in me. Whatever else I may have done in my life till then, I would not break her. She gave me trust as no one ever had." I sighed and shook my head in sadness. "With that kiss, she freed me."

He nodded. "You gave her to me not once, but twice." He met my look, and his lips twitched into a small curve. "When you sent the locket to let her know you lived, you gave her back to me a second time. It was not what I would have expected. And that school. I don't think I ever saw her happier than when she was training aspiring divas." He sighed, signaling to his nurse. "She loved me, of that I have no doubt, but there was always a place in her heart for you."

He rose, and with the nurse's aid, eased into the wheelchair. He gestured toward the box that had remained between us. "I promised I would give you that. Adieu, my friend. I think we shall not meet again." With that, he signaled the nurse to take him to the waiting car.

No, we would not see each other again, not in this lifetime.

I glanced at the package. It was Christine's gift to me and yet, it terrified me. I gathered it under my arm and negotiated my way toward that welcoming house. When Meg closed the door behind me, I thrust that box into the farthest recess of the armoire I was able, and closed the door on it.

It was finished, and all that remained was Meg, and the few days we had left.

Chapter 104

On November 11, 1918, in the stillness of an early morning, the combatants sat in a railroad car, and signed an end to the war.

As if it too had reached accord with men, the disease burned itself out and left as quietly as it had come. In its wake, lay devastation.

Meg and I existed in the solitude of our home, taking walks along the beach or to the café where they knew us of old. Often we had gone there for dinner when one of her attempts at cooking had failed. She and I had both been learning then, one hard step at a time. Through it all, we had endured, and we had finally come home.

One afternoon as we returned from our walk, we found a package left by the door. They were Erik's effects from the hospital, and from his unit. The uniform had been disinfected, cleaned, and folded with care inside the box. To the left breast pocket were pinned his medals.

Meg's fingers brushed lovingly over the wool of the jacket, stopping at the pieces of metal staring her in the face. They were all she had left of her son, the son she had so yearned for, the son I had taken so long to give her.

As she pulled the uniform out of the box, a packet of papers fell from within the folds of the coat.

Meg bent to pick it up, and when she looked at me, her beautiful eyes were misty with tears. "These are for you," she said tenderly, kissing my cheek. Gathering the uniform to her breast, she left the parlor.

The pages were worn, most reused, but each and every one brimmed with music, his music, music he had written with shells exploding and guns firing all around. Amidst all the killing and dying, Erik had created beauty.

I propped the tattered score against the rack, and though my fingers ached with their old pain, I played, letting Erik's voice speak to us once again.

The family made their visits, and though it was a joy to see them all, Meg and I found we preferred our solitude. Only Christine's frequent and prolonged stays truly brought contentment, and the happiness we had known when the three of us had first shared this house.

By late December, people had resumed normal lives, though I doubted that anything would be normal ever again. The savagery of the war had shaken many, and emptied countries of their men. Almost daily, ships arrived, bringing men from foreign lands to take the place of those that had fallen. The face of France would forever be changed, and men like Michael would no longer be an exception.

I sighed and turned my attention back to the demands of the child on my knee. I smiled at the eyes looking back at me, and playfully tickled her cheeks. She gurgled contentedly, catching my gnarled fingers in her chubby ones. I wondered what Christine would say if she knew this child looked exactly like her. When I kissed the child's brow, pleasant warmth filled me, and I felt it spread to the very tips of my fingers.

Yes, she would be like her, an angel.

"Is that what you thought me?"

An angel that lit my darkness.

"A friend who showed you the way."

A friend I will miss to my dying day.

"I am never far away."

"I hope she has not been too much of a bother chèr grand-père." Gérard came to my side, ready to scoop his daughter up.

"No. We were just talking." I handed him his daughter, and as he took her up in his one arm, I marveled at the change marriage and children had made in him. There was laughter in his eyes and a contented peacefulness.

Antoinette had been born that July and was, I suspected, far from the last child in that happy union.

It was Christmas, and the clan had gathered in our home, their laughter and happy voices filling the spaces that for weeks, had been hollow.

There were two exceptions to the gathering, though they would have been most welcome. I believe that as with Raoul, I had seen Hélène for the last time the day we had buried my son.

I let the music of their voices surround and fill me, for I would most likely not hear it again, not like this.

Sunset was encroaching, and this time, I could not fight against it.

Chapter 105

A dull and dreary January rolled into a surprisingly mild February. The year was 1919, and on what would have been Erik's 25th birthday, I walked to talk to my son, though my legs had weakened, and often, I had to rest them.

Meg refused to accompany me, though as I was leaving the house, I saw her place spring flowers beside his photograph, her fingers lingering over Erik's smiling face. I kissed her, leaving her with her memories.

As I approached the small cemetery, the sun beat down upon my shoulders and for once, I wished I had left the worn cloak at home. But like so many memories, it still clung to me, refusing to give in to time.

I sighed, seeking out the bench Raoul and I had shared not so long ago. Like fond memories of friends loved and lost, I let the sun and cloak envelope me in their combined warmth.

Looking out toward the blue Channel waters, I thought I could hear Erik laugh as he had done that morning on the beach.

I shook my head and closed my eyes. He was gone. Soon, I would join him. Perhaps then, we would share another basket of mussels and clams.

I let the sun shine down upon my face, a face that no longer stood so much out of place. There were men much younger than me who had to learn to accept what had been done to them by other men. I had had to only learn to accept what I had been born with.

When I finally looked out at the peaceful little place, the sun had begun its descent. I sighed, rising with difficulty. My old bones were not as flexible as they had once been, and everything took greater effort. Time to go home, Meg would have supper waiting, or perhaps, we would go to the café.

With steps that took forever, I began to walk down the path toward the gate when I saw a vision standing beside Erik's marker. I stopped, uncertain whether my eyes had truly failed me this time. I checked to see if the new glasses were in order, then replaced them.

No, she was still there, the mass of dark brown hair spilling down her back, her light coat gently flapping in the freshening breeze off the sea. She stood there, unmoving, and if she heard my approach, she gave no sign other than a lift to her head.

"Bon soir, grand-papa." Erica had continued to call me that, even though now she knew the truth.

I came to stand beside her, and she drew the coat closer. As she did so, I saw the flash of brilliance on the finger of her left hand. In that moment, understanding dawned, and I smiled.

As Christine had given Erica Phillippe's ring, so Meg had given Erik the ring I had given her that Christmas when I had finally married her.

Witnessed by a priest or no, their union had been sealed by love, and the rings given them by their mothers. A soft chuckle escaped me, for suddenly the reason for Erik's acceptance and cooperation was clear. She stood right beside me.

"The women of this family have an infinite capacity for saving their men," I muttered.

"What?"

"Oh nothing, nothing," I looked at her. There was something in her eyes I could not read. "It is good to have you home, my dear." I took her left hand in mine, holding it firmly, feeling the pressure of the ring against my palm.

If she did not want to say it, neither would I. At that moment, an unexpected gust of wind blew, yanking the coat from her hand, blowing it behind her, revealing the secret I suspect, she had been hesitant to disclose.

Erica's eyes dropped, and though her left hand remained in mine, the right protectively touched the swell of her pregnancy.

"He's not really gone. He's here, inside me. Whether a son or daughter, I don't care, but there will be a part of him that will live."

I smiled at her, brushing the hair away from her face, catching her tears on my fingers. "However short your time might have been, you both had it, you did not let your happiness falter. Now come, you will help me walk home."

She kissed my cheek, and as she wrapped her arm around me, I basked in the love that was her, that had been my son, the love that united all of us in her child.

For unlike the bonds of friendship that had been formed and strengthened over the years, the child that Erica carried truly bound Raoul, Christine, Meg and me into a family.

Chapter 106

With her condition revealed, the reason for Erica's disappearance was obvious.

She had continued to visit Erik at the hospital until the outbreak of the disease forced them apart. He would not have risked her, much less the potential life they may have started. Had he known? I had doubts. There would not have been enough time. He sent her away, and I never asked where. It was not my business. I was happy to have her home.

Erica drove us to Paris a few days later. She needed to see her mother, and it was time for my yearly confrontation with Maurice. Ever since the last attack, he had persisted in discreetly dogging my every step.

As I looked out at the rolling countryside we passed, I could not help a low, melancholy sigh. Here, there were no signs of war, no signs of the rage of men that had burned through Europe for four, long years. Only restfulness flitted by the windows, and deep inside me, I felt my own. There would finally be peacefulness for me.

My hand dipped into the pocket of the jacket, and pulled out the small, cloth covered thing. I felt its weight in my hand, and the memories it brought in my head. There was no sadness, only love, the love for a friend.

Meg's hand closed over mine, and she smiled her most charming smile. I put the thing away and drew my wife close to me.

The offices had not changed, except now, they were filled with men. Christine ruled with a firm, capable hand, and if her title as director raised an eyebrow or two, the questions were quickly suppressed. The war had changed many things, and nothing would ever be the same.

When she came to tell me that Hélène had called to say there would be an auction at the Opera house the following day, and would there be anything I wanted her to buy, I laughed.

A spark of the old Erik flamed for one instant as I waved a hand above my head. "Perhaps only the old chandelier, so it can light the way to where I'm going." I shook my head and caressed Christine's cheek. "No, my dear child, no. What could I possibly want from that house that I have not taken already?" I squeezed Meg's hand as we walked toward the door of the office.

Turning once more to Christine, I smiled at my daughter. "No. I believe I have everything I had ever wanted."

She nodded, smiling in understanding as she watched us leave.

During the night, a touch of snow had come. I asked the driver to make one stop before the journey back to Brittany.

He stopped beside the massive iron gates, and on my wife's arm, I walked to where Christine lay. With a kiss, Meg released me and stepped away.

I lifted my eyes to the pale sun overhead as it tried to claw its way through the clouds. With a sigh, I drew the rose from beneath the cloak, and the ring from my pocket. With fingers that shook as much from age as from the early morning chill, I tied the black ribbon.

"Good bye, my friend. I will not come again. This is my point of no return," I whispered, laying the rose beside the marker.

As I straightened, unexpected warmth filled me, and I drew the cloak closer to hold onto that warmth a little longer.

"Don't forget to find me."

"It's time," Meg's gentle voice penetrated the fog in my head.

"Hmm, so it is," I answered, eyes drifting over the monuments. No, I would not come here again.

I took Meg's hand, and side by side, we walked away from the place where, so long ago, Raoul and I had fought like madmen over a child, over a woman that had united us despite ourselves, a woman who, in the end, had loved both of us.

I sat beside Meg in the car, holding her hand, and only that mattered, her love as she smiled at me. I pulled my wife to my heart, feeling young again. I had everything I had ever wanted.

Epilogue

Erik Marchand died six months later. He died peacefully, in Meg's arms, in the house in Brittany, the house he had called home. He lived to know that he had truly become a grand- father, and that the boy would bear his name. He made only one request. "Teach him to play."

We buried him next to his son. There was no marker. He would not have wanted that. Only red roses marked the spot where he lay. Raoul and Hélène came. With tender affection, she smiled, laid a single white rose on his grave, and whispered, "You did well."

Before withdrawing from public life for a time, Erica played a final concert. She played works by unknown composers, and by evening's end, everyone knew she did not play from memorized scores, but from her heart. She played for them, the two men she had loved best.

When the pandemonium finally came to an end, and only we three remained, I walked with Erica and Meg through the galleries of the house that at one time, had been my father's home, our steps echoing in the stillness. As we walked among the glitter and magnificence, I felt we were not alone.

My fingers touched the marble of the balustrade, and I could hear his guiding voice in my head, feel his fingers brush my hair. *So much of this and that, and take care not to be cheated!* I smiled, lifting my hand to my cheek to seek his, but there was nothing there. How could there be?

"Yes, Papa," I whispered to the air, and joined Erica on the bottom step of that sweeping marble staircase.

When I turned to look to see if Meg followed, I saw her halt and turn to look behind, her hand lifting to her cheek. Was he there, her husband, my father? Did she see what we could not? I would never know for Meg clasped my arm in a firm grip and the three of us walked out the door of the theater, into the now, quiet night.

As we took our places in the car, I lifted my eyes to the golden angel high above. Was it my imagination, or had the shadows there become darker? I shook my head. It must have been a trick of the light.

We came back to the apartment, though none of us craved sleep. Erica took up her son, and I sat at the piano and played. Meg came to sit beside me, setting a carved ebony box between us.

With a gentle kiss, she slipped something into my lap. I looked down to see Christine's locket staring back at me. The rose on the cover had been finely etched. I opened it, and for an instant, felt my heart squeeze with longing and a bottomless ache of emptiness. Phillippe's smiling face looked back at me, and all I wanted was one more of his kisses, one more of his songs.

Meg kissed me and pressed the hidden spring. My father looked back at me, the white mask stark against his face, the green eyes nearly flashing in challenge. So in the end, she had loved him too, his Christine.

I gently closed the lid and slipped the chain around my neck. I would carry them both with me, the two men I had loved best, one who had married me, one who had raised me, one I would always call father.

"Good night, Christine. I think I will read a while," Meg said gently, rising.

"Good night, maman," I embraced her. She and Erik had been the only parents I had ever known. It was too late for me to think of them in any other way.

When Meg had gone, I lifted the lid of the box. There, against the folds of black silk, lay the white mask, the mask she had found as the mob ransacked what had been his home. She had kept it, giving it to Christine so she would remember him.

I ran my fingers over its smoothness, remembering Italy, and how it had been, his lessons, my impatience, his tolerance, his fear when I finally saw his face, his wonderful face.

Eyes brimming with tears, I propped the mask against the rack, and began to play once again. He had taught me. The least I could do was keep in practice.

When it came, we buried Meg as we had buried him, next to their son. I did not cry when her hand went limp in mine. I only gave her a smile and a kiss, for now they would have the time they had always wanted.

As the cool breeze from the sea blew across my skin I would have sworn that I felt fingers brush against my cheek, his voice whisper my name one last time. It was only the wind. It had to be. Ghosts were in stories. There were only memories, memories and deep, abiding love.

Hélène died shortly after Erik, and by her request, was buried next to her husband.

Gérard and Céline had eight more children, all healthy, each livelier than the next. The two doted on each other, and he was content.

Michael directed St. Hubert's for a few years. After a time, he and Anne-Marie had a family of their own, founded a new hospital, and moved away from Paris.

Raoul lived on two more years. Upon his death, his title and lands came to Gérard. He laughed and shook his head. "I would rather go back to the Flanders fields than deal with that mess. No, you will not hang that on me. I love Céline too much to do it to her." He refused it for his sons as well, claiming they would have more interesting occupations than lord of lands.

Anne-Marie would not hear of it, and there would be difficulties, as Michael was not French, and was black.

So at three, Erik Raoul Phillippe Marchand became the new Comte de Chagny.

Erica never married again, perhaps fearing acceptance of her son by another man. She would not say, and I never asked.

I look at him now as he waits patiently for me. At fifteen, he is tall, lean, with the hints of the man he'll be. His light brown hair is tossed about in the wind, but he doesn't care. He looks at me with those penetrating green eyes, and I think that if I were young again, how easy it would be to become lost in them.

"Let us go home," I say, twining an arm through his. "You will play for me."

He smiles at me. "If you wish, chère grand-mère."

"Yes, yes I do chèr Erik."

Oh yes, Papa, we taught him to play. He laughs and fights with the best of them, but when he sits at your piano, well, even the angels need to step away.

I hold him close as we walk toward the old, grey house. He doesn't seem to mind. I wonder if he'll ask me to regale him once again with your tale. I smile and kiss his cheek, his right cheek, for like his music, it is his legacy from the passionate man who raised me, whom I'll always call father. I glance at him beside me and see you in his smile, and I know, somehow know that you are there, all there in that house, where, after all, the opera began.

It is finished. There is no more to say.

Afterword

A book is never written alone. Many friends helped Erik, Meg, Christine and Raoul find a way to tell their story. To you one and all, thanks in due course.

When this saga began, I had no idea where the road would take me. I only wanted to tell Erik's story. Though it started simply, Erik soon took over, directing where the tale would go. He was in my head. (After all, the Phantom of the Opera is in your mind!) It has been a wonderful journey, one I am sorry to leave behind.

While the story is strictly fiction, later incidents during the war years, are based on facts.

Germany was the first nation to use poison gas on the battlefield, and Italy switched allegiance from Austria-Hungary to the Allies shortly after the spring of 1915. The French bowed to pressure from Germany and renamed the escadrille Americaine to the Lafayette escadrille. Many of the young men who flew in it were American volunteers. Tanks were introduced into the field by the British in late 1916, and though it would take some time for them to be perfected, their presence brought relief to the infantrymen. In the spring of 1917, the French army mutinied, partly due to poor conditions in the field, and partly for the waste of men's lives in costly offensives. By late 1917, France was exhausted, its medical system broken. Doctors could not cope with the thousands upon thousands of wounded. Châteaux as far as the Loire valley were either lent by their owners, or commandeered by the army to serve as headquarters, or hospitals. On the home front, women took over the running of businesses and factories to fill the gaps left by the men. In France, oil and coal were strictly rationed, but food in general, was readily available. Conscription favored no one, and by the end of 1917, France's army was dangerously close to being on its last legs. There were no more men to send to the field.

On November 11, 1918, the armistice was signed in a railroad car at two o'clock in the morning, and while soldiers were putting away their guns, the doctors were coping with a particularly vicious strain of Spanish flu. An outbreak in August of 1918 tore through the American troops, killing 62,000 soldiers. In the spring of 1919, a third wave of flu broke out, killing between 21-25 million people. The disease left Europe devastated. The borders of many countries opened, and immigration began in earnest.

The soldiers of World War I lived in unspeakable conditions, and what they endured should make one pause. They stood in mud, drenched or freezing for days on end, under constant fire, with tinned beef to look forward to as a meal, and yet they still did their duty, still preserved a sense of humor amidst the destruction they dealt with day in, day out..

Where letters home would have been censored, I have taken liberties for the sake of the story.

For those interested, among the many films, family stories, and books consulted during the research phase of the story, the most influential have been: Intimate Voices from the First World War by Svetlana Palmer and Sarah Wallis, a compilation of diaries and letters from soldiers and civilians alike; World War I by H.P. Willmott, an amazing volume of information and photographs; Joyeux Noel, a film concerning the spontaneous Christmas truce of 1914; and The Lost Battalion, an incredible film about the endurance and survival of the American 308th battalion caught in an ambush by German troops in the Argonne Forrest.

Thank you first and foremost to my dear husband who, over the past two years, has had to listen to me rave, rant, and incessantly talk about events under a certain Opera house! A more supportive and understanding partner I could not have asked for! Big hugs to Carmela,

Amy, and Carla for letting me bounce ideas off of them as the story developed, and for insights into particular situations. You know which ones are yours. To Jeanne, I owe a huge debt of gratitude for allowing me to 'dish' (but not too much) on our walks, and to Pamela, for her unfailing support of a fellow writer.

Thank you to all the administrators and contributors at www. GerardButler.Net for all their hard work at maintainin.g a terrific site, and for providing wonderful inspiration on this writer's journey.

Thank you one and all, and thank you Mr. Webber for unforgettable music; Mr. Schumacher for a beautiful film; all the brilliant and talented actors who, over the years, have given life to these characters, notably Mr. Howard McGillin, who has personified Erik on the Great White Way for several years, and whose CD, Where Time Stands Still, helped make editing less painful; and finally a hearty Thank You to M. Leroux, for starting the whole thing in the first place. Salut!

Glossary

Academia di Bella Arti	Academy of fine Arts (Italian)
Allez	Let's go; hurry up
Aussi	Also; as well
Cagare	Swear word (Italian)
C'est moi	It's me
C'est mon mari	This is my husband
Charmant	Charming
Coeur	Heart
Crise Cardiaque	Heart attack
Croix Rouge	Red Cross
D'accord	O. K.
De rien	Don't mention it
Ecoutez	Listen
Enceinte	Pregnant
Fille	Daughter
Fils	Son; Jr
Ils ne Passeront Pas!	They shall not pass! (General Pétain (1916)

Insensé	Mad
Je t'aimerais toujours	I will always love you
Là-bas	Over there
Le Fantôme	Phantom
Les poilus	Hairy ones'; nickname for French infantrymen during WWI years;
Ma chèrie/chèr	My dear
Regardez	Look
Si Benne	Very well (Italian)
Toujours	Always
Tres	Very
Tu es	You are
Vite	Quickly

About The Author

Lucilla (Lucy) was born in the beautiful city of Prague, in the Czech Republic, and immigrated with her family to the U.S. in October, 1970. She earned a B.A. in Communications from Simmons College in 1982, and her love of writing led to a few short works published in fan magazines. When not traveling and exploring Greek and Roman archeological sites with her husband, Lucilla loves to listen to classical music, lose herself in the works of Alexandre Dumas, père, and walk in the woods. Phantom's Legacy is her first novel.

She would love to hear from readers and you may contact her at either:

erikslegacy@aol.com, or Lucillaepps@aol.com

Printed in the United States
132236LV00003B/118/P